PRIMARY SOURCE

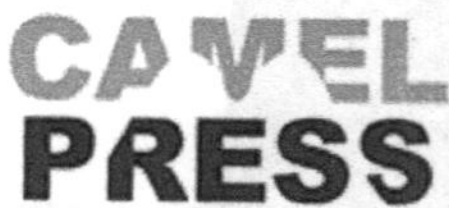

For more information go to: www.Camelpress.com
www.sharonstgeorge.com

This is a work of fiction. Names, characters, places, brands, media, and incidents are either the product of the author's imagination or are used fictitiously.

Cover image photo by Harvey Spector
Cover models: Aimee Santone, Joe Santone and "Gunner"
Series photo of "Aimee Machado" by Lowell Martinson

Sharon St. George author photo by Harvey Spector

Cover design by Aubrey Anderson

Primary Source
Copyright © 2019 by Sharon St. George

ISBN: 978-1-60381-583-3 (Trade Paper)
ISBN: 978-1-60381-584-0 (eBook)

Library of Congress Control Number: 2018958009

Printed in the United States of America

PRIMARY SOURCE

An Aimee Machado Mystery

Sharon St. George

This book is dedicated with love to George and Mary Souza
for their wholehearted support of the Aimee Machado
Mystery series.

ALSO BY THE AUTHOR

Due for Discard
Checked Out
Breach of Ethics
Spine Damage

Acknowledgments

Thanks to Eric and Susan Feamster and to Mary Souza for their medical expertise. To George Souza for his guidance regarding law enforcement and prisons, and to Alex Souza for his explanation of crypto currency. Thanks to Harrison Redden for his computer security expertise and explanations of hacking and cybercrimes. My gratitude to Jennifer Michelle for her eagle-eyed proofreading of early drafts, and to Buckeye Critique Group members Laura Hernandez, Ellen Jellison, and Vickie Linnet for their gentle and thoughtful suggestions. Thanks to fellow members of Sisters in Crime and Guppies for their support and encouragement and to the Crime Scene Writers Group for help with forensic details. Thanks to Jim Ostrich for airplane assistance, and to Kevin Fore for use of his aircraft. Special thanks to Dr. Tom Resk for his advice about autopsies, and to Ann Paschke, Public Relations Manager at UNOS, the United Network for Organ Sharing, for answering my questions with patience and generosity. I want to express my heartfelt gratitude to every organ donor, past, present, and future for offering the gift of life. Any mistakes about organ donation (or any other subject) that may have crept into the story are mine alone. I'm indebted, as always, to Jennifer McCord and Aubrey Anderson at Camel Press for all they do to ensure that my stories are polished and ready to go out into the world.

Chapter 1

———◆———

WHEN DR. HEATH MACALLISTER was pronounced brain dead and placed on life support at age thirty-six, he left behind his beating heart, his liver, his lungs, his skin, both kidneys and his bones. His corneas would have been available for donation as well, but they were severely damaged when a Timbergate Medical Center security guard tripped over MacAllister's comatose body in an unlit and seldom-used stairwell. The guard was rushing to answer a page in the middle of the night when he accidentally stepped on MacAllister's face with a heavy-soled boot.

The ill-fated doctor also left behind his wife, Veronica, and their sons, Thomas and Jeremiah, the two-year-old twins he called Tom and Jerry.

I heard of MacAllister's death as soon as I arrived for work in the TMC Library on a humid Wednesday morning in late September. The sad news came in the form of an email message from Administrator Jared Quinn, addressed to all department heads. I was thrown for a moment, remembering that Dr. MacAllister had asked to meet with me the day before, in what I thought was a lame effort to score points with the medical staff. He had only recently been granted medical staff membership and privileges in general practice at TMC.

Timbergate Medical Center was MacAllister's first medical staff appointment. Eager to make an impression, he had campaigned for chairmanship of the hospital's Ethics Committee. The position usually went to newer members, because that committee met only as needed and required less time and experience than some of the more demanding peer review committees.

Dr. MacAllister had complicated his request by refusing to provide a specific item for the agenda. He had contacted me because, along with my primary duties as Timbergate Medical Center's Health Sciences Librarian, I was coordinator of two medical staff committees. One was Continuing Education; the other was Ethics.

As needed meant rounding up all five members. It could take a week or more to settle on a day and time when they were all available. I had explained that we couldn't call a meeting unless we had an explicit issue that required action. When I'd pressed Dr. MacAllister, he hedged, saying only that he had discovered something about organ donation that was too sensitive to discuss outside of the committee's confidentiality protection. His tragic accident and resulting brain death made it doubtful I would ever know what had been on his mind.

Later in the day, I learned the details surrounding MacAllister's fate from Mary Barton, TMC's Social Worker and Organ Donor Coordinator. During her lunch break, she came to see me in the library. She explained that she had been called in because someone in the Emergency Department was alert enough to notice that Dr. Mac was an organ donor. The Ethics Committee discusses any sort of ethical dilemma that involves the hospital's medical staff, but the topics often relate to organ donation policies and procedures. It's on those occasions that my path crosses with Mary's.

September is usually hot in Timbergate, often reaching

triple digits. The afternoon Mary and I met was no exception. I offered her a bottle of iced tea from the library's break room fridge. We sat at one of the worktables provided for patrons. I didn't know Mary well, having had only minimal professional contact with her. She was around my age, approaching thirty, a Cinderella with honey-blond hair, a flawless nose and soft blue eyes.

My look tends toward Mulan, with black hair and deep brown eyes inherited from my Asian mother and Portuguese father. My name, Aimee Machado, is often confused with *The Mikado* when I'm introduced, so I usually emphasize that it's pronounced *Ma-SHAW-doe*.

Mary sat across the table from me, obviously weary and distracted after the emotional ordeal of counseling and consoling Dr. MacAllister's wife.

"You may not know this, Aimee, most people wouldn't, but a two-fold process could take place when Dr. Mac is taken off life support. His living will was very definite about his desire to be an organ donor, but after his organs are procured, there might be an autopsy."

"Why? Is there something suspicious about his fall down the stairwell?"

"No, nothing like that," Mary said. "It's just that no one witnessed his fall, that's one of the circumstances that can require autopsy. The other is that the accident happened in his workplace."

"Sounds an autopsy would just be a formality. Seems excessive."

"I agree, and not all cases in those categories are autopsied. It may not be necessary, since the circumstances aren't suspicious. Dr. Mac's accident didn't suggest what a coroner would term a 'questionable cause of death.' A death certificate signed by a physician may be all that's needed."

"What were the circumstances?"

"One of his shoelaces was untied. The shoe had apparently

come off as he was descending the stairwell, wrapping around his ankle and causing him to trip and plunge down onto the landing head first."

"You're saying there may be no autopsy?"

"At least not a forensic autopsy, which is what you're thinking, because you're trained in forensic research. Maybe, with the widow's permission, a clinical autopsy will be performed just to determine cause of death for research and study purposes. Probably done in our hospital morgue by a pathologist on the TMC medical staff."

"But you said no one witnessed Dr. Mac's fall."

"That's right, but the people who found him had no reason to think it was anything other than an unfortunate accident. Video confirmation would be nice, but we have no cameras in the stairwells."

"I'm aware," I said. "Jared Quinn is still badgering the home office about springing for funds to install cameras in the stairwells and the elevators. This might be the final push he needs to convince them."

"I hope so, but don't hold your breath. Since the corporate buyout, the new owners have been cutting expenses to the bone. From what I hear, Quinn isn't the only administrator whose budget requests are being ignored."

"Criteria Health Resources took over less than two months ago," I said, "and already every department head I talk to is feeling the pinch. But I've steered you off topic, and I have a question. If Dr. MacAllister's organs are procured, how could there be an autopsy?"

"It's possible, but the effort to do both has to be carefully coordinated. The organs and tissues that are procured for donation won't be present at the time of autopsy, but since his brain death is obviously the result of a head injury, that shouldn't be a problem." Mary squeezed her eyes shut for a moment. Fatigue was obviously catching up with her. Lack of sleep often went hand in hand with her organ donor duties.

"Is that why you came to me?" I asked. "To explain about the autopsy?"

"No. I'm here because I think his death requires a meeting of the Ethics Committee. I wondered if you felt the same." Mary leaned toward me, her hands clasped on her lap. "He approached me recently saying he had concerns about organ procurement and asking what steps to take. I told him to see you about arranging a meeting."

"He did that, and when I asked for an agenda topic, he mentioned organ donation. He wouldn't explain further. Said he'd only address it in committee. Did he say anything more to you about his concerns?"

"No, but he seemed worried, agitated."

"You think we should take this to committee even with nothing specific to be discussed?"

"I think we should," Mary said. "Before he's taken off life support, if possible. Maybe Dr. MacAllister talked to someone else on the committee. He knew all the members. At the least, the committee could order a review of our organ donor protocols and procedures. See if they spot anything that Dr. Mac might have questioned."

"This is going to require some quick action on the part of the Chief of Staff. At this point, we have no one to chair the Ethics Committee. That was Dr. MacAllister's role."

Mary's eyes widened. "Oh, my God. I'd forgotten about that. How horribly ironic," she said. "What do we do?"

"I'll contact Cleo Cominoli. I'm sure she'll see that the Chief of Staff assigns someone as temporary Ethics chair."

"Thank you," Mary said. "How soon can we set up a meeting?"

"First, we need to convince the committee that we have a compelling reason. As soon as I can get it arranged, I'll let you know. You'll attend as ex-officio?"

"Definitely."

After Mary left, I emailed Cleo, a striking, statuesque

woman of Italian heritage. Almost old enough to be my mother, she was both my mentor and my best friend at work.

She replied with a terse message. *CHR liaison officers here. Will call when I break free.*

I'd forgotten that our new parent company had sent two of their people to TMC on what they called a "get acquainted" mission.

It made sense they'd show up in Cleo's office. With a dozen years of experience as Director of Medical Affairs, she oversaw ninety percent of the business of TMC's medical staff organization. She arranged and attended close to twenty medical staff committee meetings each month, most of those involving peer review and patient safety. She also supervised the credentialing process of each doctor who was granted privileges to treat TMC's patients.

When Cleo returned my call, I asked her what she thought of the CHR visitors.

"I'm trying to reserve judgment, but it isn't easy," she said. "They're both in the administration office now. Jared Quinn will be stuck with them until they head back to Transylvania."

"Where? I thought their headquarters was in Southern California."

"Sorry. Bad joke. All they talked about with me was how to cut costs."

"Oh, bloodsuckers, I get it. "

"They seemed astonished that my department could have its own budget when it doesn't directly generate revenue to offset expenses," Cleo said.

"Without doctors on the medical staff, there would be no patients in the house and no health insurance to bill. Surely they could see that connection to revenue."

"It's as if they know almost nothing about hospitals."

"Are either of them doctors?' I asked.

"They claim to be retired GPs who trained and practiced outside the U.S., but they weren't forthcoming about the details."

"Could be they're still learning how things are done in hospitals here in the States."

"Seems that way." Cleo sounded perplexed. "You'd think they'd be up to speed."

"Do you think they've heard about Dr. MacAllister?"

"They know. They arrived in town last night, so they heard about it from some chatterbox employee this morning."

"Did they bring it up to you? Ask for a report or an investigation?"

"Only briefly, wondering if his wife might sue." Cleo laughed softly. "If that happens, they'll probably want to pay the settlement out of my budget."

"Jokes aside, your cash flow situation is safer than mine," I said. "When I bring up my library budget, I get treated like a panhandler."

"Don't worry, your job is secure. Without a health sciences librarian, we'd never pass our accreditation surveys. So, why did you email me?"

I filled her in on my talk with Mary Barton about Dr. Mac's death and the status of Ethics Committee.

"First things first," Cleo said. "We need a temporary chair before we can call the members together, and second, neither you nor Mary has a clue as to a compelling reason for them to meet."

"Except that Dr. MacAllister had some sort of issue about organ donations and procurement."

"And …?" Cleo prompted.

"I'm afraid that's it. And he seemed troubled about it. *Agitated*, was how Mary put it."

"Not much to go on. And now the man is brain dead and on life support. Imagine what his poor wife is going through."

"I can't begin to imagine that," I said. "Maybe fulfilling his last wish will bring her some comfort."

"Which wish? His request for a meeting, or his organ donation?

"I was thinking about the meeting. I'd like to think we could honor his request."

"Even if it's an exercise in futility?" Cleo asked. "We may not get a meeting set right away, but if we do, what's the point if Dr. Mac told no one why he requested it?"

"What if there's someone out there who does know?"

"I'll have to think about that." Cleo's sigh told me she thought I was pushing the envelope. "I will agree we need to appoint an Ethics chair for the rest of this term. That's up to the Chief of Staff. I'll call Dr. Seldon to see if he has someone in mind."

Time to back off. "Let me know how it goes so I can keep Mary in the loop."

With that chore dropped on Cleo's competent shoulders, I turned my attention to my library duties. Lola Rampley, my Monday and Wednesday volunteer, had stayed on past her usual morning hours due to a recent and unexpected windfall of medical texts and journals from an elderly medical staff member who had retired.

He insisted we catalog and shelve every item he donated. Since most modern medical libraries, including ours, leaned heavily toward online collections, cataloging the donated print materials was the sort of chore that delighted Lola. In her eighties, she was capable and quick working with the library's computer programs, but her heart still belonged to the printed page.

I left her to it, but Dr. MacAllister's tragic fall and its consequences played havoc with my efforts to concentrate on routine chores. I found myself delving into previous Ethics Committee minutes, particularly those from before I began working the meetings. I looked for any sort of actions or discussions related to TMC's organ donation program. I found minutes from two years earlier when an updated organ donation protocol had been approved. A copy of the protocol was attached. It had not been revised or reviewed since.

It stipulated that TMC was too small to have its own transplant team, so when an in-house patient at TMC became a potential donor, the physicians who made that medical decision were required to contact the Organ Procurement Organization designated by the Federal Government for our region. At that point, Mary Barton would be called in to coordinate the details with the regional OPO regarding procurement and transplantation of any organs, bones, or other tissues to the appropriate recipients. I was surprised to learn that one donor could potentially save up to eight lives.

Nothing in the minutes of previous meetings, before my appointment as coordinator of the Ethics Committee, indicated potential problems with TMC's organ donor cases. Dr. MacAllister had taken over the chairmanship on short notice just weeks earlier when the former committee chair resigned from the staff and retired with a diagnosis of moderate stage Alzheimer's. A quick check of the symptoms in his stage of the disease told me it was doubtful he would know or remember what had concerned MacAllister.

I put the commitee binder away in a locked file cabinet. Time to check on Lola's work with the donated journals. The tiny woman seemed to have boundless energy, but her level of osteoporosis was evident by dramatic kyphosis, a condition more commonly called dowager's hump. I feared the work she did for me would leave her in pain, but she never complained.

Whenever we crossed paths in the library, I caught a snippet of Glenn Miller or his contemporaries drifting from her ever-present earbuds. Since she began working for me a year ago, her taste in music had moved on from classic country. She'd been a loyal fan of Merle Haggard and his generation of country singers for decades. She confessed to me recently that after Haggard's death, she'd lost her heart for country. Her new passion was the big band sounds of Glenn Miller, Benny Goodman and their contemporaries. She insisted that the music of that genre would relax me on demanding or frustrating days. I'd recently created a big band station on Pandora and discovered she was right.

I watched Lola make her way to the library exit, apparently swaying to "Chattanooga Choo Choo" or some other Miller tune. She was still serving a purpose that fulfilled her and was happily engaged to my other volunteer, Bernie Kluckert, a man in his early nineties.

Then I thought of Dr. Heath MacAllister's dedication to the life-saving gift of organ donation. How many patients, much younger than Lola and Bernie, were about to have their lives cut short because the organ they needed, and had waited for so desperately, would never come?

One donor could save eight lives. Was Dr. MacAllister's concern about organ donation just a ploy to gain attention? Or was there something to it? Mary Barton wanted to know, and so did I.

Chapter 2

———◆———

$\mathbf{D}$R. PERCY SELDON DROPPED by the library at closing time. One of three pathologists on the medical staff, he also specialized in infectious diseases. Seldon was currently serving his term as Chief of Staff, and the privileges of that office allowed him to sit in on all medical staff committee meetings. He and I were acquainted, due to the monthly Continuing Education meetings I managed, but we had not developed a strong rapport. Dr. Seldon approached my desk with a stork-like gait and his head turned to one side. The piercing gaze from that eye made me feel as if I were some morsel to be snapped up from the bottom of a marsh.

I stood and offered him a chair.

"I'll stand, thank you." His clear, modulated voice belied his gangly physical appearance. His tone was confident but lacking in warmth. "You may sit, of course," he added.

It took me a moment to decide, but I lowered myself back into my desk chair. What difference did it make? He was nearly a foot taller than my five feet, four inches.

"Thank you for stopping by," I said. "I understand Cleo

Cominoli filled you in about our need for a new chairperson for the Ethics Committee."

"She did, and she mentioned a degree of urgency, which she said you would explain." He stood in front of my desk, waiting, with no hint of curiosity in his gaze.

"Did Cleo happen to mention that my sense of urgency is shared by Mary Barton?"

"And who is Mary … ah, yes, our social worker. Am I correct?"

"Yes, she's also our organ donor coordinator. We'd like to schedule an Ethics Committee meeting right away, but first we'll need you to appoint a new chairperson."

Dr. Seldon looked at his watch. "This sounds as if it will take a bit of time. I can spare a few minutes." He lowered himself into a guest chair and leaned an elbow on my desk. "What is the urgent matter that necessitates this meeting?"

"That's just it, we're not exactly sure." I explained Dr. MacAllister's visit to my office and his refusal to discuss details of his reason for calling a meeting. "I'm wondering if he had mentioned anything to you about this."

"No, this is the first I've heard of it. That is unorthodox, but he was new, so perhaps he was unaware of the medical staff's meeting protocols." Dr. Seldon sat back in his chair. "In any case, I must say I find it pointless to call a meeting with no stated agenda topics. On the other hand, I agree that the committee chair's position should be filled. I'll give that some thought and get back to you."

Not the response I had hoped for, but I wasn't ready to give up. "We could put Dr. MacAllister's request for a meeting on the agenda. And his mention of organ donation. You could chair the meeting yourself. Our bylaws would permit that." As I spoke, I realized I was grasping at straws. Dr. Seldon confirmed it.

"Call several busy physicians together to chit-chat about a vague reference to organ donation? I repeat, I don't see the point, if there is no specific, compelling issue for the committee to discuss. Nothing that needs official committee action." Seldon blinked twice, rubbed his eyes, and stifled a yawn. "I'm afraid that's my position on the matter. I will begin recruiting someone to fill the chairperson vacancy. In the meantime, if you or Ms. Barton, or Ms. Cominoli, can provide a convincing reason to call the committee together, by all means, let me know." He pulled his phone from his pocket and glanced at the screen. "I must go. A surgeon is waiting in the OR for my interpretation of a lung biopsy." With that, he unfolded himself from his chair, rose to his extraordinary height, and lurched to the exit like a man on stilts.

I reported the dismal results of that conversation to both Mary and Cleo. They were disappointed, and neither had a quick solution. The chief of staff was in a powerful position where the three of us women were concerned. Only our administrator, Jared Quinn, had more authority over us than Dr. Percy Seldon. And going over Seldon's head to Quinn about a medical staff matter was the last thing we wanted to consider. Hospital politics would only condone that if we had proof that Dr. Seldon was a madman along the lines of Hannibal Lector.

After talking to Cleo and to Mary, I walked the interior perimeter of the library trying to shake off my mood and increase blood flow to my brain. I hadn't taken Dr. MacAllister seriously, but circumstances had changed, and I began to believe that he *did* have a credible reason for wanting that meeting. What was that reason? Had he discovered something about organ donation or procurement that was shocking enough to get him killed in that stairwell?

That seemed like a giant leap toward some sort of conspiracy theory, but that's how my mind had begun to work since taking my job at TMC. Dubious circumstances had cropped up a few times before, and in several instances, something that looked like a duck and quacked like a duck turned out to be a duck. It had happened often enough to make me suspect the worst.

I circled the library's interior four more times before landing back at my desk. There, I did what I often do when

I need a sounding board and my boyfriend isn't available. I called my brother, Harry. He was at the construction site of Timbergate's future three-story mega shopping mall. As architect and general contractor of the project, Harry had been entrusted by the city to get the job done on time and within budget. That he won the contract before the age of thirty said a lot about his solid reputation in the business community. He had inherited that reputation and the business from our father a couple of years ago, when our parents decided to retire and live full time in the Azores.

I knew Harry's girlfriend was out of town, so I coaxed him into a brainstorming session by offering to feed him dinner. I'm not a great cook, but he's worse, so he promised to drop by after work. Before I left, I checked out the library's copy of a recently published book on the ethics of procuring and replacing organs in humans. *Homework*.

HARRY DROVE THE EIGHT miles east from Timbergate to Coyote Creek where my boyfriend, Nick Alexander, and I share an apartment on my grandparents' property. Amah and her husband, Jack Highland, own a llama ranch covering several acres. Nick and I live in the converted bunkhouse over their barn.

Harry and I took care of the evening chores, feeding Jack's turkey flock, throwing hay to the llamas, and cleaning all the watering troughs. Then I fed Ginger, Nick's Chesapeake Bay Retriever, who gobbled her food and plopped down on her doggy bed in a corner of the kitchen. She was always a little dejected when Nick was away working for more than a day or two.

Under normal circumstances, I avoid discussing my work outside the hospital. My employment contract has a confidentiality clause, and breaking it could see my job disappear in a heartbeat. But this wasn't an official hospital matter. It was just me, wondering if I was letting my imagination work overtime.

I made a meal of leftover spinach quiche and some green salad mix dumped from a bag. It wasn't ideal, but beer for Harry and green tea for me helped wash it down. Time to talk.

I gave Harry the basics and asked his opinion.

"You're asking me about organ transplants?" he said. "That's way out of my area of expertise."

"I know you're not an expert on the topic, but you do have the cyber skills to dig up information."

"So do you. You're the hotshot librarian."

"But what if this goes beyond my legitimate sources?"

"Really? You're thinking that doctor suspected something illicit?"

"He wouldn't reveal his concern outside committee. Said it was too sensitive. Doesn't that sound like he suspected something fairly extreme?"

"Maybe, but organ transplant schemes pop up in the media and in fiction pretty often. Could be he was overreacting to something and just wanted to get a consensus from his committee."

"That makes sense," I said. "Thanks for listening. I'd have run this by Nick, but he's not due back for a few days."

Harry glanced around my small kitchen. "Where is he?"

"St. Louis. He flew Buck Sawyer there yesterday to meet with some investment managers." Nick worked as a corporate pilot for a billionaire philanthropist with a deep hatred of illegal drug traffickers. Buck's only child, a daughter, had died of an overdose while still in her teens. "I assumed you knew," I said, "since Nick and Rella usually take turns in the cockpit."

Rella Olstad was the other fulltime pilot who worked for Buck. A statuesque blonde and former fighter pilot, she could easily win a Miss Universe contest. She had only recently moved in with Harry. They made a stunning couple. His hunky Eurasian looks and a body toned by years of jujitsu contrasted vividly with her Nordic beauty. I wondered how my brother was adjusting to sharing his luxury condo overlooking the Sacramento River and the city of Timbergate. He was tight-lipped about his personal life, even with me, so I didn't bother to ask.

"Rella might have mentioned it," Harry said, "but I don't always get the details. What's this trip about?"

"Buck is making the rounds of his Midwest and East Coast investment firms. I'm hoping they'll be back home this weekend. How long is Rella going to be in Texas?"

"Not sure. She's teaching at a flight school for another week or so—filling in for a friend who's on maternity leave." Harry pushed his empty plate away and glanced at the wall clock in my kitchen. "I have to go. I'm teaching a seven o'clock black belt class tonight." With a fourth-degree black belt in jujitsu, Harry was a high-ranking sensei who taught as a volunteer at the local dojo.

"Wait. You haven't told me what you think about the timing of Dr. MacAllister's accident. Maybe his reason for calling the meeting was an overreaction to something, but less than twenty-four hours later, he took a tumble down that dark stairwell and ended up brain dead. Doesn't that seem like an odd coincidence?"

"You want to know if I think the doctor's secrecy about the agenda topic could be tied to his accident?"

"Yes. I know it sounds extreme. but does an accidental fall pass your smell test?"

"If we were talking about milk, I'd say it was borderline, but I'd probably give it more time. All you have is a guy who asked you to call a meeting and then tripped over his shoelaces."

"What if I can dig up something more?" Harry loved a mystery. If he wasn't on board, and Nick was unavailable, I didn't have much in the way of help. "What would it take to convince you?"

Harry stood at my door, hand on the knob. "All you have are suspicions. Your newly developed proclivity for crime solving might be at work here. You need at least a scrap or two of solid evidence if you're thinking foul play."

"Okay, then. If I find something solid, are you in?"

"Maybe. Just make sure you aren't tilting at windmills. Do you know if there's going to be an autopsy? It would help to know what the coroner decides as manner of death."

I understood what Harry meant. He was aware that *cause* of death and *manner* of death are not the same. *Cause* refers to the medical reason, as in *extreme blood loss*, but *manner* includes multiple choices. On the death certificate, the coroner or medical examiner picks from half a dozen classifications: *natural, accident, suicide, homicide, undetermined,* and *pending.*

"That might be difficult. Mary Barton thinks if an autopsy is done at all, it will be clinical, done by a TMC pathologist in the hospital's morgue. And only after his organs and tissues are procured."

"So, no forensic exam of the remains?"

"Not likely."

"But the victim's still on life support because he's an organ donor?" Eager to leave, Harry reached in his pocket for his keys, a none-too-subtle hint. "I heard on the news a while back about a patient who was declared brain dead and then woke up. Any chance of that happening?"

"Not likely, but who knows?"

"Any idea how long before the organ procurement takes place?"

"No, but I'm guessing it will happen as soon as possible. Then the autopsy, if one is done, but with an obvious head injury causing brain death and most of the organs gone, it would be little more than a formality, according to Mary Barton."

"Would you accept that and let it go?"

"Maybe. Unless something else turns up looking fishy. Then will you come on board?"

The twinkle in his deep brown eyes answered before he did. "Then we'll do another smell test." He opened my kitchen door and stepped to the deck outside. "In the meantime, have you learned your lesson about playing amateur detective, or do

I have to remind you to stay safe?" Harry was referring to a few times in the past when I'd underestimated the perils involved in snooping out clues to a crime.

I gave him a hug. "I promise I won't put myself in danger over this."

"You'd better not." He squirmed out of my arms. "If you run into trouble while Nick's away, it'll be my butt he'll kick when he gets home."

He dropped down the deck's exterior steps two at a time and headed off to the dojo.

Chapter 3

WHILE I SAT STARING at my door, Ginger got up, walked over and plunked her chin on my lap. She looked at me with what I took for sympathy in her soft brown eyes. Was she lonely and pining for Nick? I knew I was. I stroked her back, admiring her wavy, burnt orange coat.

Nick and I had been living together for several months, and our relationship had developed a comfortable balance after several ups and downs in the two years since we first met. We sometimes spoke of the future in general terms, but we weren't yet bending to the pressure about marriage that our family and friends applied with what they thought was subtlety.

I expected Nick to call in another hour or so. St. Louis was two time zones away from Northern California, so it was almost nine o'clock there. I had time to take Ginger out for a walk and a pit stop. I clipped on her leash and walked up the lane to Amah and Jack's ranch house.

Nick and I liked being close enough for comfort if they should need us. They were healthy and active, and their minds were sharp, but still, with Jack in his late seventies and Amah just entering the same decade, we kept an eye out for any signs of trouble or distress in their lives. They had done me a favor when I was alone by letting me live in their barn-top bunkhouse in exchange for helping with chores and ranch-sitting. Now that Nick lived there too, we insisted on paying rent, though they would only accept half of what anyone else would have paid.

I spotted them waving to me from the veranda behind their house. Jack was sitting at a table tying fishing flies, and Amah was grooming her foul-tempered cat, Fanny. I wondered if Jack used cat fur in some of his flies. My research librarian's compulsive curiosity meant I had to ask. I secured Ginger to a post near the garden and away from the veranda, so Fanny wouldn't go berserk and tear Amah to shreds.

"Come, sit," Amah said. "I'll get you a slice of peach pie. We caught Harry leaving. He took half a pie with him. I'll warm yours and add ice cream." Before I could reply, she put Fanny down, brushed clumps of fur off her cropped cotton slacks and hurried inside. Petite, and even delicate on first impression, she seemed blessed with more energy than most women her age. Maybe a result of her hardy Portuguese genes.

Jack smiled. "You know she won't take no for an answer." He remained bent over his task, a rangy six-foot figure in his ever-present Levi's and plaid work shirt.

"I know." I watched his large, strong hands work gently on the fly. "Are you using cat hair in your flies?"

"Nope. I tried it a couple times, but it's not worth the trouble for what I need."

"Too bad." I glanced down at the clumps of Fanny fur on the deck. "You'd never run out of material."

Amah reappeared with a plate of pie topped with double scoops of vanilla, a fork, and a napkin. She set it all down on a TV tray. "There you go, sweetie."

"What brings you?" Jack asked. "Anything on your mind, or just walking the dog?"

"I'll bet she's lonely," Amah said. "Nick's been away a few

days, hasn't he?" She watched approvingly while I savored a bite of pie. "How much longer will he be gone?"

I swallowed. "Probably until this weekend." She was right, of course. I *was* lonely with Nick gone, but I didn't want to start another conversation about *Aimee and Nick's future*. She had been looking at my ring finger way too often lately, registering disappointment that it was still bare.

"I do have something I'd like to ask both of you," I said. "It's about organ donation. If you're uncomfortable with the subject, say so and I'll let it go."

Jack let out a loud guffaw. "Where in the Sam Hill did that come from? I hope you don't need a kidney, because mine are pretty worn out."

Amah narrowed her eyes at him. "Shush, Jack. This is a serious topic." She turned to me. "Sweetie, are you okay? You're not sick, are you?"

"No, no, I'm sorry, I didn't mean to alarm you. It's something that came up at work and I realized I'd never asked anyone in my family what their wishes are. I don't even know what mine are."

"Well," Amah said, "I have the little symbol on my driver license that says they can take whatever they need." She looked at Jack. "Didn't you opt in, too, honey?"

"Sure, but like I said, my parts must be getting close to their expiration date. I don't know if they'd do anyone much good."

"Do you think I should opt in?" Hearing both had taken that step, I was embarrassed that it had never occurred to me to do it.

"Up to you," Jack said. "Best to do it while you're young, though, don't you think? You know, while your second-hand parts can give someone a long, healthy life."

"Jack, listen to yourself. You do realize you're implying that she might die young?" Amah shook her head. "I can't bear to think about that. Besides, Aimee has to decide for herself about being a donor."

Jack coughed. "You're right, Rosa, this is too close to home." I saw moisture in his eyes. I probably shouldn't have brought it up.

Amah sat down next to me. "Aimee, you said this came up at work. Anything you can talk about?"

"Not until I'm sure it doesn't involve the hospital. And it may be nothing at all."

I finished my last bite of pie and got up to take the plate to the kitchen. Amah took it from me. "You'd better go. Won't Nick be calling?"

It was time for Nick's call, and I didn't have my cell phone with me. Ginger and I headed back to the barn.

Chapter 4

I MADE IT INSIDE just in time to hear my cell ringing. I grabbed it, knowing it would be Nick. But it wasn't. It was Cleo. She almost never called me at home in the evening.

"Hey, what's up?"

"Nothing major," Cleo said. "Mary Barton called me a few minutes ago. She and I have each other's personal cell numbers, and she thought I might have yours. I said I did, but I couldn't give it out without your permission. I told her I'd clear it with you. Said if you wanted her to have it, you'd call her."

"Did Mary say what she wanted?"

"She was vague, but it had to do with the talk you two had about Heath MacAllister and Ethics Committee."

"It's odd she wanted to call me about it tonight."

"I thought so. Ready?"

"Yep." She read off the number. "Got it," I said. "And while we're on the subject, I talked to Dr. Seldon this afternoon and he agreed we need a new chair for Ethics. Have you heard anything from him?"

"Not so far, but I'll keep nudging him to appoint someone

ASAP. I'd better go now, so you can call Mary. Keep me posted if there's something I need to know."

"Of course." I dialed Mary Barton's number.

Her phone rang several times, until finally her voicemail came on. I left a message, giving her my cell number and asking her to call back, hoping she and Nick wouldn't both try to call at the same time.

Eight o'clock in Timbergate was ten o'clock in St. Louis, and I knew Nick would get to sleep early if he was flying in the morning. Instead of waiting for my phone to ring, I called him to say goodnight. After several rings, I expected to leave another voicemail, but he picked up.

"Hey, sweetheart, I was in the shower. Almost missed the phone." *In the shower.* That image shut off my brain for a couple of seconds. Although I loved Nick for his honesty, courage, and humor, I was grateful that he was also gorgeous. Sun-bleached hair, startling blue eyes, a well-muscled body.

"Aimee?" he said. "Are you there?"

"Uh, sorry. Got distracted for a moment." I squirmed in my chair and tried to refocus. "I'm expecting a call from someone at work, but I didn't want to miss your call, so ...."

"I get it. Glad you called. Oops, hold on a minute, my towel is slipping." *Oh, Nick, stop it.* "There, all better. Is the work call important? I can call back. I'll be awake for another half hour."

"It could be. There's been an incident. I don't want to get into it now. I'll tell you about it when you get home."

"*Incident*? I don't like the sound of that. Please don't tell me someone died."

"People die all the time in hospitals, Nick."

"You know what I mean. And the fact that you're being evasive doesn't help."

"Okay, the someone was a doctor on our medical staff. He fell down a stairwell. He's brain dead, but he's an organ donor, so his body is on life support."

"Damn, that's gruesome, but why would anyone be calling you about it after hours?"

"I'm not sure. And if I did know, I probably couldn't talk about it." Harry's warning was running through my mind. *Stay safe. Nick will kick my butt.*

"*Evasive.* Give, Aimee."

Knowing Nick, if I didn't tell him, he'd call Harry, who would rat me out. "He was the chairman of one of the committees I'm responsible for. We're trying to find a replacement. That's really all there is to it."

Nick was not convinced. "Then there's no reason to think his tumble down the stairwell is suspicious?"

"Not really." So far, that was the truth, and I didn't want him to worry when he was so far away, although I couldn't help wondering why Mary Barton wanted to talk to me.

"Knowing how your mind works, I'm going to want your promise before I hang up. If you come across anything that looks fishy about this, tell me you'll stand down until I'm home."

Darn. "Okay. Promise."

"Now tell me you miss me."

"I miss you. A lot. When will you be home?"

"Let's see, this is Wednesday night. I'm hoping we'll be home on Saturday. We're scheduled back here for the next couple days while Buck explores investments in the health industry. Right up your alley, huh?"

"Definitely," I said. "I'd like to know more about the conglomerate that just bought TMC. Maybe it's on his list."

"I'll ask him. What's it called?"

"Criteria Health Resources. They've been pinching pennies like crazy, so they must be pretty devoted to their shareholders."

"That's not how Buck takes the measure of companies he invests in. He's more concerned about how they treat their employees and the environment."

"I know, but he seems to be an exception."

"Hey, enough serious talk, I should let you go so you can wait for your call."

"Wait," I said, "I think Ginger hears your voice. I'm holding the phone to her ear. Say something."

I held the phone for the dog. She wagged her tail, gave a soft *woof*, and danced around in a circle. "Whatever you said, she liked it a lot."

"Same thing I'd say to you if I could get away with it. *Be a good girl.* Only I don't have to tell you not to chase Jack's turkeys. With you, it's a different kind of warning. I don't know what's happening at your work, but please stay out of it." I mumbled something sounding acquiescent, and we said our *good nights*.

Nick and Harry both seemed to think I was a magnet for trouble, and it often came because of my job. I've never denied having a curious mind. That's an essential trait in librarians—imbedded in our genes. We don't like it when a question arises and we can't find the answer. I knew I'd be preoccupied by Dr. MacAllister's guarded concerns about organ donation and his urgent but unexplained request for an Ethics Committee meeting. Doubly so because of his freak accident the next day. The mystery would fester until I got to the bottom of it. My challenge was to uncover the organ donor issue he left undisclosed, and to do that without breaking my promises to Harry and Nick.

My cell rang again a few minutes later. Mary Barton, returning my call.

"Mary, Cleo said you wanted to talk to me."

"I do, but this isn't a good time." I heard strain in her voice.

"Does that mean you're not alone?"

"No, it's not that. It's … complicated. Let's meet for lunch tomorrow if you're free."

"I can be. Cafeteria?"

"Let's do noon at Margie's." Margie's Bean Pot. A diner near the hospital. Great food and a good-natured proprietor who often played impromptu accordion melodies for her patrons.

"Okay, noon tomorrow."

THURSDAY MORNING IN THE library I spent every spare minute preparing for lunch with Mary Barton by researching all the references I could find on organ donation, how the surgical process of procurement works, and the ethics of procuring organs. Dr. MacAllister had wanted the committee to hear him out about organ donation. But why? Online websites led me to articles and news stories about black market organ trafficking. I hoped something in that wealth of material would give me a clue to MacAllister's concerns. I was struck by how much had been written on the subject. By lunchtime, the black-market horror stories were so appalling that I had to stop reading for fear of making myself ill.

Most of it didn't apply to Timbergate Medical Center. I had already reviewed TMC's standard organ donor protocol. Similar protocols were followed by almost all comparable-sized hospitals that did not have their own surgical transplant teams. None of it suggested what might have been on Dr. MacAllister's mind.

MARGIE'S BEAN POT WAS packed when I arrived at noon. Margie was too busy helping patrons to break out her own accordion, so she had compromised with piped-in recordings of sophisticated accordion melodies. The music, combined with colorful framed posters of famous impressionist's paintings, suggested the ambiance of a Paris bistro.

Mary waved from a corner table near the back of the diner. I took a tray and helped myself to my favorite: a bowl of *Pasta e Fagioli* from the soup and salad bar.

I sat across from Mary. "Have you been here long?"

"No, just long enough to get a corner table." She spoke quietly. "More privacy."

I felt my body stiffen, reacting to the tension I sensed in her. "I don't see anyone here from work. We should be able to talk without being overheard, if that's worrying you. What was it you didn't want to talk about on the phone last night?"

She flushed, twisting her lips. "After I called Cleo to get your number, I had second thoughts. I wasn't sure I should involve you."

"Involve me how?"

"It's probably my overactive imagination, but the circumstances of Dr. MacAllister's death have been bothering me."

Me, too, I thought. "In what way?"

"For one thing, I'm concerned about his organ donation."

"But you explained that to me yesterday. The organs would be recovered first, and then there might be a clinical autopsy of the remains, but you said that's not certain."

"Yes, Dr. MacAllister's remains could be autopsied as a clinical, and done in TMC's morgue by a pathologist on our staff, rather than by a medical examiner in the coroner's office."

Mary's tone prompted me. "I'm getting the feeling you'd prefer a forensic autopsy."

"I would. Even after the organ recovery, a coroner's forensic autopsy would be used as evidence in court if there was any question about his manner of death."

"Then you have doubts about his fall being an accident?" A tickle of apprehension traced across my shoulders. "What about the shoe that came off and that shoestring that tripped him?"

"I can't let go of the idea that no one witnessed his fall. The security guard was first on the scene, and he can only describe what he encountered—an unconscious victim lying on the landing."

"You don't think the guard was guilty of harming Dr. MacAllister, do you?"

Mary's eyebrows lifted. "No, absolutely not. He was followed down the stairs by a nurse. She saw the guard stumble over Dr. Mac. She confirmed that his body was already lying on the floor of the landing when they entered the stairwell. She started CPR while the guard called for help."

"Do you know who the nurse was? Is it someone you trust?"

"It was Laurie Littletree, and yes, I'd trust her with my life."

"I know Laurie. If she said the guard wasn't involved, that's good enough for me."

Laurie and I had become good friends a year earlier after a challenging time when we'd been caught up in a mystery surrounding the death of a TMC patient. I waited for Mary to continue, but she hesitated, picking at the three-bean salad on her plate.

"Do you know how soon the organ and tissue recovery will take place?" I prompted.

"There is a window of time, since he's on life support to keep his organs viable, but the sooner, the better. Our regional OPO says procurement teams from at least four transplant hospitals will be involved. There are multiple organs, plus tissue and bone, so it takes time to match all the recipients. Once the procurement teams are finished, Dr. Mac's remains will go to the TMC morgue."

"Then we'll have to wait for now, and hope we can convince our new Ethics chair to review everything each of us knows about Heath MacAllister before the transplant teams arrive."

"Afraid so. In the meantime, I'll work on my mood." A frown crossed Mary's face. "I'm still annoyed by those two liaison officers from Criteria Health Resources. Quinn brought them to my office for what was supposed to be a quick introduction. After he left, they grilled me for almost two hours about my work. It was terrible timing, what with Dr. Mac's brain death and his pending organ procurement on my mind."

"I can imagine. I heard from Cleo about their meeting with her. Did they fuss about your budget, too?"

"Some, but they seemed more interested in our organ donor protocol."

"Did they say why? The protocol must be essentially the same in all of their hospitals that are too small to have an in-house transplant team."

"That's what I told them. but they said they had to review it."

"That makes no sense," I said. "Unless they didn't believe you. Do you know if they were satisfied after they saw the protocol?"

"Who knows? They didn't let on, but they asked me to make a copy. They weren't very forthcoming with their opinions about anything."

"Did Dr. MacAllister's case come up?"

"It didn't. I hadn't heard whether they knew about it, so I figured if anyone brought it up, it should be Quinn."

"I don't blame you, but Cleo told me they do know, so apparently, they didn't feel a need to question you about it." I put my bowl of soup aside. "Seems like they would have, though, because of his organ donor status." I leaned toward Mary. "How strongly do you feel about Dr. MacAllister's death? That it might not have been an accident?"

Twin dots of pink colored Mary's cheeks. "You mean his tripping over a shoelace and plunging down that stairwell so soon after approaching both of us?" Mary glanced around the diner. "You and I agreed his request for an Ethics meeting was peculiar. Telling us the topic was too sensitive to discuss, even with us, outside the committee setting. To me, his accident looks like an uncanny coincidence. Doesn't it bother you?"

"So far, I'm more curious than alarmed. I'm hoping we can find someone who knows what was on his mind. A meeting of the committee should be the best place to start."

"I hope we can make that happen." Mary bit a corner of her lip. "Although when I think of myself trying to explain my suspicions, I'm afraid I'll sound like I've watched too many reruns of *Diagnosis Murder*."

"I want it as much as you do, and I'll be more than happy to back you up." I glanced at my watch. "For now, we need to get back to work."

"Will you let me know when we get a new Ethics chair?" Mary asked. "Maybe by the time we have a meeting arranged, Dr. MacAllister's case will be ready for review, including his autopsy and his organ procurement."

"The new chairperson should see to that. And yes, I'll let you know as soon as I hear."

Chapter 5

LATE THAT AFTERNOON, CLEO Cominoli called with good news. "Dr. Seldon came through. We have a temporary chairperson."

"Who?" I crossed my fingers, hoping it was someone easy to work with.

"Phyllis Poole's stepping in 'til our next regular medical staff election."

"Excellent." Dr. Poole, a skilled urologist, already chaired Continuing Education, which was my other committee responsibility. She and I had a comfortable working relationship, and since Ethics met only as needed, it wouldn't take up much of her time.

Phyllis Poole's pale complexion and whitish-blond hair, along with her brusque demeanor, had earned her the nickname *Dr. Frosty*, but few hospital employees dared speak it, even behind her back. She was the toughest woman doctor on TMC's medical staff, yet she never resorted to bullying or foul language. And no one with good sense swore in her presence for fear of getting on what she called her *shirt* list.

"Have you talked to her?" I asked. "Does she know Mary Barton and I want to schedule a meeting?"

"No, I only just heard from Dr. Seldon. He emailed me that she was willing to serve. That's all I know. You can take it from here. Keep me in the loop if there's anything I need to know."

"Have you heard anything more about Quinn and the visitors from Criteria Health?"

"Just that he's going to be stuck with them for another day. They're in no hurry to leave."

I EMAILED MARY WITH the news about Dr. Poole. The rest of my afternoon was quiet, so I managed to catch up on most of my library chores by quitting time. I had shut down my computer and picked up my purse when my phone rang. *Rats.*

The caller was the last person I would have guessed. Dr. Heath MacAllister's widow, Veronica, introduced herself.

"I'm glad you're still at work," she said. "I've been debating with myself all day about calling you."

"I'm so sorry for your loss, Mrs. MacAllister. What can I do for you?" I couldn't imagine why she would be calling me.

"I asked your hospital's switchboard operator for the person who deals with organ donation. When she mentioned your name, I recognized it. Heath spoke highly of you."

"But I'm not in charge of coordinating organ donation cases. I think the switchboard put you through to the wrong person. Our organ donor coordinator can tell you how your husband's organs will be allocated. Would you like her name and number?"

"Yes, that would be good to have, but that's not why I'm calling. I think you're in charge of the committee my husband was going to chair. Ethics, isn't it? The committee that deals with organ donation issues?"

"That's right, but there's very little I can tell you about that. There are confidentiality rules that apply—"

"Oh, no. It's nothing like that. I just thought someone should notify his committee members and the other places where he had privileges … about his … brain death." I heard her take in a breath. "I didn't know who else to call about this, or how it would be handled. I thought you might know."

"Did your husband belong to an on-call group here in town?"

"Yes, there were three of them who took turns seeing each other's patients for after-hours emergencies, but I've never met the doctors in Heath's group. I'd feel awkward approaching them."

"Did your husband make arrangements for one or more of them to take over his patients permanently in the event of an emergency like this?"

"I suppose so …." Her voice broke, and I realized the timing was bad. I was making matters worse for her.

"I'll make certain our TMC Ethics Committee members are informed, and I'll ask our administrator or our chief of staff to follow up with notifying Sawyer General across town. Would that help you?"

"I'd appreciate that. What about the prison? Could your administrator contact someone there?"

"Excuse me, Mrs. MacAllister, did you say 'prison'?"

"Yes. The private prison in Potterville. Heath worked there part time."

I knew almost nothing about the small town of Potterville, except that it was in a distant, sparsely populated corner of Sawyer County.

"Did you say there's a private prison in Potterville?"

"Yes. The clinic there was Heath's first employer after med school," Veronica said. "It was the only thing available in the Northern California area, and we needed income. Student loans and med school bills were overwhelming, so he took the job."

"I'm sorry, but I've never heard of private prisons. What does that mean, exactly?"

"I'm not sure of the details. All I know is that the private prisons are not owned by states or the federal government."

"How does that work?" I asked.

"Heath said a state, or the federal government, contracts with private prisons to house their inmates." I heard her take in another deep breath and regretted pressing her with irrelevant questions, but she went on explaining. "After we moved to Timbergate, he was still under contract with CHR to treat inmates in the prison clinic every weekend."

"I'm not sure I understand. You said CHR. Do you mean that Criteria Health Resources owns the medical clinic at the prison in Potterville?"

"Yes. Heath said they own clinics in private prisons in several western states. Apparently, a lot of the private prisons contract with the federal government to incarcerate undocumented immigrants convicted of serious crimes."

"Do you know if that's the case with the Potterville prison?"

"It is," Veronica said. "That was most of the inmate population. Heath was relieved to finally open a practice in Timbergate and join the medical staffs of both hospitals here. He had a tender heart, and the prison job was hard on him. He'd planned to quit that job as soon as we made some headway on our loans." She went silent for a moment, obviously overwhelmed at the thought of her bleak future. A grieving widow hobbled by crushing debt.

"I'm so sorry, Mrs. MacAllister. I should stop asking questions and let you go."

"No," she said. "I … it helps to talk to someone. I've been alone with my sons … they don't understand what's happened to their father. Please, ask whatever you like."

"If you're sure?"

"Yes. Please go on."

"I was going to ask how you and your husband decided on Timbergate as a place to locate."

"Oh, that was by chance. Heath met another doctor at the prison, Darwin Iversen, who's been in practice here in Timbergate for a long time. Dr. Iversen convinced Heath that this would be a good place to open a practice. He's one of the members of Heath's call group, but as I said, I've never met him."

Dr. Iversen was a member of TMC's medical staff, so I knew him by sight, but I had no dealings with him, just a general impression of a tall, distinguished-looking man in late middle age. He was not a regular in the library and did not serve on either of the medical staff committees I managed.

"Was your husband still working at the prison?"

"Part time. Dr. Iversen oversees the medical clinic there, and he seemed to like Heath, wanted him to stay on. We needed the extra income, but Heath didn't like driving to that isolated location every weekend … being away from the family."

And now he was away from his family forever. I hardly knew what to say to a woman who had lost so much.

"Mrs. MacAllister, I'll make sure the appropriate people are informed. Please tell me if there's anything else I can do for you."

"You've been an immense help, and I will follow up with Mary Barton. I'd like to know what becomes of Heath's organs. He'd want them to help as many people as possible." She paused, I heard a quiet sob. "He was handsome, you know. He had even joked with me about donating his face for transplant."

With a sense of guilt for wanting to end the grim conversation, I wished the grieving widow luck in contacting Mary and ended the call. I sat for several minutes, gathering my thoughts. How would I feel in Veronica MacAllister's place? Can a soul be bruised by fate? How to accept the loss of a husband, the father of your tiny children? I thought of Nick, and the children who might be waiting in our future. Yes, that would be soul-bruising. I hoped it would lessen Veronica's grief to know her husband's heart would eventually beat for someone else.

CURIOSITY FORCED ME TO boot up my computer and go online, where I quickly discovered that the private prison in Potterville held around a thousand inmates. The site confirmed that the medical clinic at Potterville Prison was owned by Criteria Health Resources, the new parent company of Timbergate Medical Center.

All of it was news to me. Still, if the crime rate in Sawyer County was any indication of the rest of the country, prisons were probably a growth industry. Apparently, privately owned prisons could be a lucrative venture. And each one would need a well-run medical clinic, or depending on the size of the prison, a small, self-contained hospital within its walls. Clever of CHR to tap into that market.

I REACHED HOME JUST in time for Nick's call. Everything was going according to schedule at his end.

"How about you?" he asked. "Any new disasters at your work?"

"No, but I did hear something interesting today. Do you know anything about private prisons? Apparently, there's one in Potterville."

"I've heard of them," he said, "but only recently. Buck mentioned the one in Potterville. He and the warden met about a month ago to discuss drug rehab among inmates. Something they're looking to do in conjunction with the medical clinic that's located in the prison."

"Sounds like a good idea. What kind of impression did Buck come away with?"

"Positive, apparently. Potterville is typical of the sort of area where most of the private prisons are located. Remote, so not a lot of resident complaints, and the prisons do have a positive impact on the local economies."

"You mean during construction of the facility?"

"That, but also the day-to-day operation. Buck says Potterville Prison created hundreds of permanent, full-time jobs. That's huge for an area that far out in the sticks."

"Did Buck visit the facility?"

"No, the warden came to Timbergate for their meeting, but

Buck will want to see the physical layout of both the prison and the clinic before he decides about investing."

I told him about the connection between the prison clinic and TMC. Both owned by Criteria Health Resources. "Other than the proposed rehab program, did Buck mention anything about the medical care of inmates there?"

"Not really. Why the sudden interest in all of this?"

"Not important. You know me. Always thinking about anything medical." I didn't want to bring up the topic of Dr. MacAllister again.

"I'd rather you were always thinking about me, but that sounds so sappy I can't believe I just said it."

"Neither can I, but don't worry, I won't tell anyone. Are you still coming home Saturday?"

"That's the plan, but keep it to yourself if you happen to talk to Delta. Buck told her we wouldn't be home until Sunday. Apparently, he wants to surprise her."

"Why?"

"No idea. I guess he wants to keep some mystery in their marriage. Spice it up a little."

Not a bad idea, I thought, considering Buck was twice Delta's age. Nick and I didn't need any help with the spice in our relationship. He was so often gone for days at a time that we enjoyed a mini-honeymoon every time he came home.

"Any more questions about prisons?" Nick asked. "You've managed to change the subject, but if you're planning on being incarcerated, you do realize it's not like picking a hotel for a weekend."

"We can talk about this when you get home."

"I don't like the sound of that, Aimee." Nick's tone changed abruptly, and not in a good way.

"Okay, I confess. There is something on my mind, but it's not easy to explain. I'm not sure there's anything to it, but I swear it's nothing for you to worry about. I'll fill you in as soon as you're home."

Chapter 6

———◆———

Harry called later Thursday evening just after I finished tossing hay for the llamas, which meant he was missing Rella as much as I missed Nick.

"How about helping me teach tonight? I'm subbing for Mark Takamoto."

"Which class?"

"Nothing complicated. Beginning judo for adults. Seven to nine. Think you can handle it?" I heard the smirk in his voice.

"I can handle dumping you on your butt, bro, so yeah, I think I can. Why are you asking? Is the class larger than usual?"

"Slightly. A couple of newbies who need special attention. I think you know one of them. He says he works at your hospital."

"Really? What's his name?"

"Ramon Silva. Ring a bell?"

"He's the medical interpreter who helped us with a Portuguese-speaking patient a few months ago."

"I remember that. Anyway, he seems like a good guy. Just signed up for classes. I told him you might be helping teach tonight. He was impressed that you're a black belt."

I was one rank below Harry, with a third-degree belt, and he never let me forget it. Nick and I were at the same rank, and neither of us had found time to prepare for the fourth-degree test. By the time we did, Harry would likely be yet another rank ahead of us.

"Hey, I'm waiting here, Sis. How about it?"

I knew I should. I'd been neglecting exercise while Nick was gone. "Okay. See you at seven."

LARGE FANS WERE STIRRING the heavy air in the dojo when I arrived. With a dozen bodies working up a sweat, the space soon became humid. Harry had assigned Ramon Silva as my special first-time pupil. We quickly renewed our acquaintance. Clean-cut and in his early twenties, he was on TMC's list of approved medical interpreters. He attended college part-time, majoring in languages. His primary was Portuguese, and he was also fluent in Spanish, Italian and French.

During a break, we sat in the spectators' bleachers sipping from bottled water. I asked him about his future career plans.

"I'm hoping to work at the U.N. someday," he said. "But I first need to finish my degree."

"Sounds like an ambitious goal. How long will it take to accomplish that?"

"I don't know." He wiped at a rim of perspiration that beaded his hairline. "I'd have to attend school at least half-time to qualify for student loans. I don't know if that's possible with my work schedule, being on call so much of the time. Maybe a career at the U.N. will have to wait until I can finish my education without taking on student loan debt."

I heard that. I was still paying off my own student loans. "I hope you can make that happen," I said, "but it doesn't seem like medical interpreter jobs in our area would provide a steady income."

"That can be the case, but I have contracts with several employers, so I manage to earn enough to get by and even save a little."

"What sort of employers?" There were only two hospitals in Timbergate. I doubted that added up to enough patients without English to keep him busy.

"The police department, rehab hospitals, the jail," Ramon said, "but I also get calls from the medical clinics at nearby prisons."

I set aside the water bottle I'd been holding against my cheek, but the chill persisted. "Which prisons?"

"There's the one in Potterville, here in Sawyer County. The other is a state prison over in Arroyo County."

"Do you visit them often?"

"Only when there's a need. And sometimes I'm able to help online via Skype."

"I remember the case you helped us with at TMC. You used Portuguese then, but I'm guessing you use Spanish most often."

"That's true, but there are some inmates who speak Brazilian Portuguese," Ramon said. "As you assume, Potterville's prison population is mostly undocumented immigrants from Mexico, but there are also inmates from Central and South America and a few other countries."

"I've heard that Potterville is a private prison under contract with the Federal Bureau of Prisons. Do you know if that's true?"

"Yes, that's right. Most of the inmates are serving time for federal crimes. Many of them will probably be deported upon completion of their sentences."

Odd coincidence that I'd never heard of private prisons until Potterville Prison was brought to my attention twice in the same day. I was about to ask if Ramon had ever met Dr. MacAllister there, but Harry interrupted before I had a chance.

"Hey, Aimee, break's over. Let's make sure your student gets his money's worth."

I spent the last hour guiding Ramon through the basics of beginning judo, starting with *ogoshi*, a full hip throw, and one of the first that most students learn. I stayed focused on our work, while planning how to follow up about Dr. Mac and the prison relationship when we were finished. Ramon caught on quickly, making the session rewarding for both of us. After changing out of my gi and into street clothes, I came out of the women's dressing room looking for Ramon, but he had already left.

I hung around with Harry, helping him close after all the students had gone. I knew he'd want my report on Ramon's lesson. He pulled two bottles of pomegranate juice from the fridge in the sensei's office. Handed one to me. We dropped onto opposite ends of the visitor's couch.

"How'd your guy do?" he asked.

"Picked it up quickly. He'll do well if he sticks with it."

"Attitude?" Harry was quick to dismiss aggressive or disrespectful students from his classes.

"Seems appropriate, but I can't really vouch for his temperament. I haven't spent a lot of time around him."

"What I was able to observe looked good so far." Harry chugged the last of his juice. "Are you willing to work with him again if I need you?"

"Sure. It was a good opportunity to spend time on the mat." I drained my drink. "Are you ready to go?"

"Yep. Rella usually waits 'til I'm home before she calls, so we won't get interrupted. Why? Something on your mind?"

"Not really, just … you need to go." No point wasting Harry's time with my curiosity about Dr. Mac's organ donor issues.

"What about you?" Harry stood at the exit door, obviously eager to be on his way. "Won't Nick be checking in?"

"Doubt it. I told him I'd be here until past his bedtime in St. Louis. It's two hours later there."

"Only one hour later in El Paso," Harry said. "Still, we want both our pilots to get good sleep when they're flying the next day."

GOOD SLEEP WASN'T IN my immediate future. I checked my cell when I got home. Nick had texted a brief *good night*, saying he'd give me a wake-up call in the morning. The other two texts were not as welcome.

One was from Cleo, the other was from Mary Barton. Both bore the same news. Dr. Mac had been taken off life support. His remains had been transported to the TMC morgue. His wife was distraught because his request to be an organ donor had not been fulfilled.

It took a few minutes to process that information. What plausible reason could there be for removing him from life support? I glanced at the time. Ten o'clock. Cleo would still be awake. I punched her number. She picked up on the first ring.

"Aimee? You got my message?"

"Yes. What the devil is going on?"

"Good question. Wish I had the answer. I heard it from Mary Barton, who heard it from Veronica MacAllister."

"Did you call Quinn?"

"Tried. He hasn't responded."

"How long ago did this happen?"

"Within the last thirty minutes, Mary said."

"Was she present when he was taken off life support?"

"She was. So was Veronica MacAllister. Dr. Seldon was acting as the primary. He made the decision. He called in Dr. Decker for a second opinion and she concurred."

Dr. Moura Decker was a woman with gray hair and an ample bosom who habitually dressed in muted beige tones. An internist specializing in Critical Care medicine, she sometimes came to the library to pore over medical texts or journals.

"But why would Dr. Seldon terminate life-support?"

"Sepsis resulting in total body organ failure," Cleo said. "That meant Heath MacAllister was no longer eligible to be a donor, so no need to keep him on the machines. Apparently, it was a tough call for Dr. Decker. Mary said she was visibly distressed at the thought of canceling the organ procurements."

"Do they know what caused the sepsis?"

"No, but apparently it could have been any of a number

of things. That'll be addressed when his case is reviewed in committee."

I barely knew Dr. MacAllister, but hearing this horrendous news brought me close to tears.

"Cleo, do you happen to know if Dr. Poole was consulted?"

"Not as far as I know." Cleo paused. "Why would she be? She wasn't on the case."

"No, but she'll be presiding when it's discussed in Ethics Committee."

"You mean *if*. There's no guarantee the case will go to Ethics. It'll be routed first to ICU Committee, most likely."

"But you could use your influence with the ICU chairman. Suggest Ethics should see it because of the donor issue."

Cleo answered after a slight pause. "We'll see. Maybe we'll know more tomorrow."

I tried to reach Mary Barton, hoping to ask her thoughts about Dr. Mac's remains being autopsied in light of this new development. Less than twenty-four hours had passed since we had talked about the options of clinical versus forensic autopsies. She didn't answer, so I left a voicemail asking her to call back.

Despite both Harry and Nick warning me to set aside my concerns about Dr. MacAllister's injury and brain death, this news made that advice impossible to follow. I wondered about Jared Quinn's reaction. He'd had no reason to jump into this situation so far, but the stakes were rising. Now Dr. Mac was dead, and his organs had died with him. A double blow to his widow. What if Veronica MacAllister insisted her husband was the victim of negligence on the part of the hospital? If she hired a lawyer, and if that unlit staircase became an issue, Quinn, as administrator, would have to get involved, if only to protect the hospital's interests.

Chapter 7

CLEO CALLED FOR A huddle in her office Friday morning consisting of herself, Mary Barton and me. She sat at her desk with the two of us in her visitors' chairs. The topic was Dr. Heath MacAllister.

"Here's the thing," Cleo said. "I've asked Phyllis Poole to intervene, since she's the new chair of Ethics Committee."

"Intervene why?" I asked.

"The widow asked my advice about an autopsy of Dr. Mac's remains," Mary said.

"For what reason?"

"Apparently, Dr. Seldon brought it up. He told her he'd like her permission to do a clinical autopsy in TMC's morgue for educational purposes. To see if the origin of the sepsis could be determined."

I looked to Cleo and Mary. "How does this concern us? Or Dr. Poole?"

Mary answered. "Veronica MacAllister reached out to me late last night just after her husband was taken off life support. Said she wanted to talk." Mary lowered her voice and scooted to the edge of her chair. "At first, I thought she needed consolation, but it turned out to be more. She told me she'd sensed an unusual amount of tension in her husband over the past few weeks. He passed it off as ordinary workplace stress. At one point, she answered her husband's cell phone when he was in the shower. A man's voice said, 'No one likes a whistleblower,' then the line went dead. When she questioned her husband about it, he said he'd had to file an incident report about a bungling medical assistant at the prison clinic. Told her not to worry, the incident would blow over."

"Go on, Mary." Cleo's fingers flew across her keyboard. "How long ago was that?"

"A couple of weeks ago, at least. But she mentioned other unsettling calls to their home phone. No messages similar to the one on her husband's cell. When she answered the calls to the home phone, the line went dead. At first, she wondered if Dr. Mac was having an affair." Mary paused, shook her head. "Poor woman, she said that was so unlikely that she decided the calls had to be those annoying robo calls that pester everyone."

"But she didn't let it go at that?" I asked.

"She did at first. Even talked Dr. Mac into shutting down their landline, but since then, she's been getting the same thing on her cell phone. Even after Dr. Mac's accident."

Cleo regarded Mary over her half-moons. "Are the calls what prompted her to ask your opinion about Dr. Seldon doing a clinical autopsy? That seems like a stretch."

"The calls were troublesome," Mary said, "but her main reason was concern about her husband's shoes."

Cleo stopped typing. "His shoes?"

Mary nodded. "Yes. Veronica said the shoes were given to her along with Dr. Mac's clothes and other belongings when he was admitted to ICU and placed on life support."

"There's nothing unusual about that," I said.

"Not ordinarily, but Veronica MacAllister said she'd never seen those shoes before."

"Holy hockey sticks," Cleo said. "The same shoes that were the reason everyone assumed Dr. Mac's fall was an accident?"

The room went very still. I thought I could hear the three of us breathing, air swishing in and out of our lungs.

"And that's why Veronica MacAllister contacted me," Mary said. "Dr. Seldon had told her that it would be a simple matter to do a clinical autopsy in the hospital morgue, but she isn't sure she wants to settle for that option. She wants time to decide whether to request a forensic autopsy."

"Does the widow even know the difference?" I asked.

"She does now," Mary said. "I felt obligated to explain that she should opt for a forensic autopsy if she suspects foul play."

"Then that's what we have to tell Dr. Poole." I looked to Cleo. "What do you think? The phone calls. The shoes. Will that be enough to convince Poole to support Mrs. MacAllister's wishes?"

"Dr. Poole has agreed to hear us out, and if she decides there's reason to question the circumstances of Dr. MacAllister's death, she'll speak to Dr. Seldon."

"The sooner, the better," Mary said. "Where is Dr. Mac's body now?"

"Downstairs in our morgue, and his remains can be kept there until this issue is settled." Cleo glanced at her wall clock. "However, we have no guarantee that Dr. Seldon won't pressure the widow to go ahead with a clinical autopsy. We'll need Dr. Poole to convince him to back off until Mrs. MacAllister makes up her mind."

"Any particular reason why Dr. Seldon wouldn't do that?" I asked.

Cleo clasped her hands on her desk. "He's Chief of Staff here, so he bears a lot of responsibility, but in my experience, he's a bit too keen on being in charge."

"Got that right," Mary said.

I had to agree, remembering my meeting with him in the library. He had balked at the idea of calling for a meeting of Ethics Committee to discuss Dr. Mac's death and particularly his concern about organ procurement at TMC. Seldon had argued that it would be a waste of the committee members' time unless Dr. Mac's agenda topic had been clearly defined before his death.

I asked Cleo if she had arranged a time for Dr. Poole to meet with us.

"She's unavailable until late this afternoon," Cleo said. "Back to back surgeries."

"What can we do in the meantime?" Mary said.

"What about Quinn?" I asked. "Can he pull rank on Dr. Seldon? Say legal counsel wants Dr. Mac's remains sent to the coroner?"

"For what reason?" Cleo asked. "Do you think he'll get involved over a pair of shoes? He'll assume the doctor bought a new pair of shoes that day and his wife hadn't known about them."

I voiced my earlier thought. "He'll get involved if Veronica MacAllister hires a lawyer and sues TMC for negligence."

Cleo nodded. "For sure, but we're not there yet."

The three of us sat silent. I wondered if I was overreacting to the situation and to the widow's grief—imagined the others were wondering the same thing.

Mary spoke first. "Okay then, let's look at this from another angle. Who diagnosed Dr. Mac's sepsis?"

Cleo answered. "Dr. Seldon did. After an ICU nurse brought the signs to his attention."

"But Dr. Mac was only on life support in ICU for two days," I said. "Can septicemia progress that quickly?"

Mary, the only nurse among us, answered. "He had bruising and abrasions from his fall down the stairwell, but nothing that obviously required treatment with antibiotics. He may have had an internal injury that caused the infection. If it was missed, the bacteria in the blood could have resulted in septicemia."

She explained that sepsis, the body's inflammatory reaction, could easily have raged out of control in a matter of hours. We accepted her explanation. The thought that sepsis could strike and kill that quickly was frightening.

"Wouldn't Dr. Seldon have treated the septicemia?" I asked.

"He would have administered antibiotics," Mary said, "but apparently it was too late."

"There's no doubt this case will be flagged for ICU Committee," Cleo said. "Let's hope Dr. Poole can use her clout to also get it submitted to a meeting of Ethics Committee."

"What do we do in the meantime?" I asked.

"That depends on Dr. Poole." Cleo tapped her computer screen. "We'll gather again when she's available. Her last surgery today is a bladder suspension under general anesthesia at three thirty. The procedure takes about an hour. I'd say she'll be free by five. She'll want to hang around the hospital anyway, while her patient's in Recovery."

"I'm going to come back at five with prepared notes," Mary said. "Poole won't tolerate us for long if she thinks we're wasting her time."

Cleo agreed. "You can send them to me ahead of time and I'll compare with mine and put them in order."

"We'll each make notes," I said, "but I'd rather keep them offline. I'll write mine and make extra copies."

Mary and Cleo looked at me with confused expressions, then I watched the light dawn as Cleo spoke.

"You *do* think there's something fishy about Dr. Mac's death, don't you?"

Mary responded before I could reply. "It's possible, Cleo. And Aimee's right. Until we're sure what we're dealing with, we should keep our concerns among ourselves."

"But we're already involving Dr. Poole," Cleo said.

Mary glanced at me. "I trust her. You?"

"Absolutely," I said.

"Then I'll follow up with her," Cleo said. "I think we should meet in the library. Will that work for you, Aimee?"

"Yes. It'll be closed, so we'll have privacy. I'll put on fresh coffee."

With that, we agreed on five o'clock and went our separate ways.

FRIDAYS WERE MY ONLY days in the library without a volunteer, so I had no trouble keeping busy with a variety of routine chores that required only minimal concentration. That left my overactive imagination free to wander. A bizarre sequence of events had taken place in less than three full days. The temptation to sort it all out was too great to ignore.

Helping library patrons and working on the medical staff's continuing education program requests kept me occupied until lunchtime, but I couldn't stop thinking about Dr. Mac's remains. I'd seen the interior of the hospital's morgue before. Located in the TMC basement, it was an utterly lonely place. A wave of claustrophobia washed over me each time I visualized the doctor lying in limbo in one of those pitiless refrigerated drawers.

As the afternoon passed, I concentrated on my list of reasons to seek Dr. Poole's help. There was no point meeting with her unless we came up with a persuasive argument for calling Ethics Committee together. Dr. Mac's insistence on a meeting had topped my list, although without a stated agenda item, how would I convince Dr. Poole that there had been an urgent purpose? I had not been persuaded myself, until Mary Barton and I compared notes after Dr. Mac's fall.

Was it possible he would still be alive if I had taken him more seriously? *No. Do not go there.* Straining my brain to make a case for Dr. Poole had already resulted in a budding headache. I hoped Mary and Cleo were having more success.

With just an hour to go before closing, I had a surprise visitor to the library.

"Aimee, I'm glad you're still here." Ramon Silva approached and stood at my desk. "There's something on my mind. Do you have a minute?"

My first thought was that he had come to ask about our judo session. "Welcome, Ramon. I enjoyed our workout last night."

"I enjoyed it also, but my questions are on a different matter. We touched on it last night, and I thought you would be the person to ask."

"I'm always happy to answer." I shifted into research librarian mode. "That's what I'm trained to do. Tell me how I can help."

"Can you do a search for me on the topic of private prisons?"

Not at all what I expected, but I went ahead, switching into Reference Librarian interview mode.

"Can you tell me more about your topic? It might save time if we narrow it down a bit."

Ramon hesitated, looked down at his feet, then back at me. "Health, I guess. As you know, that's what I do at Potterville Prison—interpret for the undocumented—the illegal immigrant patients in the prison clinic who don't speak English."

I thought we'd already covered this ground, so I was curious to see where he was going.

"Okay, *health*. That's a start. Can you give me a little more information? How about adding *medicine* as another key word in your search? Is there a drug or a disease you want to research?"

I tried to conceal my intense interest in Ramon's topic, but my pulse had kicked up a notch, and I couldn't hide the flush in my cheeks. I hoped he didn't mistake those signs as a reaction to his nearness as he leaned over my shoulder watching the monitor. He was a cute guy with a nice body, but he was no threat to Nick Alexander.

"No, that's not it, exactly," Ramon said. "I wondered what you can find about the medical care of women who are incarcerated at Potterville."

"They have women in that place?" I had not imagined that. "I thought only male prisoners convicted of serious crimes were held there."

"The population of the prison is all male, but there's a special unit now." His grim expression told me his request for information was not a matter of idle curiosity. "They call it a detention center. Asylum-seekers are incarcerated there until their cases are heard, waiting to see if they'll win the right to stay in the States or face deportation."

"Ramon, I could help you further if you were more specific about your work in the prison clinic and about your interest in this detention center you've mentioned." *What is troubling you?* That question was too personal to ask in my role as librarian, but not too personal to ask friend-to-friend at the dojo. While I made a mental note to do that, two more visitors entered the library.

The men approached my desk at a deliberate pace, as if they were keeping to a tight schedule. I had not seen them before, but it took only one guess to know they were the visiting liaison officers from CHR. The larger of the two made the introductions.

"I'm Dr. Gilbert Durham, Criteria Health Resources," he announced in voice that was nearly a shout, "and this is my associate, Dr. Cloyd Coatney." Coatney nodded and flashed a diffident smile under a black pencil moustache.

Durham leaned into the front of my desk, knocking a framed photo of Harry and me onto the floor. He bent down, picked it up, red-faced and breathless, and dropped it on my desk. "You must be the librarian?" I couldn't help thinking he was aptly named: the bull in a china shop. Coatney was his opposite: slender and precise, like his moustache. They both appeared to be nearing retirement age. Durham's hair was thinning and gray; Coatney's was full and dark, but revealed tell-tale signs of a toupee.

Ramon stood aside during this invasion, looking unsure of his role. I was about to introduce him to the CHR duo when he took his phone from his pocket.

"Excuse me, I have to go," he said. "I'm needed in the ER." He hurried toward the exit.

"Wait, do you want me to print the information you wanted and hold it for you? Or would you rather I email it?"

"No, please don't do that." He tossed a quick "Thank you" over his shoulder as he left.

I stared after him, realizing that for the second time, I had not asked him if he'd ever met Dr. MacAllister while they were both working at the prison's medical clinic.

I turned my attention to the unexpected arrival of the CHR visitors, wondering what they could possibly want from me. Coatney enlightened me in a voice as soft as his colleague's was loud.

"Ms. Machado, is it true that you are the person in charge of the Ethics Committee of this hospital's medical staff?"

"Yes, it is. Why do you ask?" *And why is your stare creeping me out?*

"No particular reason," Coatney replied. "We're merely trying to acquaint ourselves with the various department heads." He turned himself full circle, glancing around the library as if it were the most interesting space he had ever seen. "We want to start off on the right foot. Build rapport, so to speak."

Durham bellowed his two cents. "Think of this visit as a *meet and greet.*" He held out a plump, sweaty hand. I shook it, while trying to mask my revulsion. Coatney did not offer his hand. *Probably a germaphobe.*

"I understand that you manage all of this," Coatney said, "Can you tell us more about your duties?"

"Of course, I said. "My main responsibility is the supervision of the hospital's health sciences library. It consumes the bulk of my attention, along with the medical staff's Continuing Medical Education requirements. Although the business of the Ethics Committee is important, it requires very little of my time."

"I see." Coatney stroked his minimalist moustache with a thumb and finger. "Well then, we'll leave you to your work." He nodded and moved toward the exit with a mincing gait, while Durham plodded along behind, as if he were being led by a chain attached to a ring in his nose.

I watched the odd couple until they were out of sight, wondering why they'd come at all for such a short visit, but glad to be rid of them before my five o'clock meeting with Cleo, Mary and Dr. Poole.

Chapter 8

M ary and Cleo arrived together at five o'clock sharp. They had barely cleared the entrance when Dr. Phyllis Poole strode in behind them. She stopped a few steps inside the library and clapped her hands.

"Chop, chop, *amigas*. I can spare five minutes to hear you out."

I suppressed a smile at hearing her use a word common to both the Portuguese and Spanish languages. The woman had pale blond hair and a complexion the color of nonfat milk. No doubt her language was influenced by her Brazilian husband, Dr. Tobias Fausset.

I invited the three women to sit with me at one of the library's small, round work tables. I gave Cleo a meaningful nod, hoping she'd take the lead. She didn't disappoint.

"Dr. Poole, thank you for coming. I'm sure you've met Aimee and Mary, so I'll skip introductions and—"

"Let me save us some time," Dr. Poole said. "Dr. Seldon has already informed me that the three of you are hoping to call a meeting of the Ethics Committee to address Dr. MacAllister's unfortunate fate, but I must ask to what end? Seldon is of a mind that you'd be imposing on several busy physicians without a valid reason." Poole squared her shoulders, though she was already sitting ramrod-stiff. "How quickly can you convince me that he's wrong?"

Cleo took a calming breath, remained unflappable. As I watched the two indomitable women, the phrase *Clash of the Titans* came to mind.

"Our initial reason was the hope that someone on the committee might know why Dr. MacAllister had requested an Ethics meeting just before his accident. He approached both Mary and Aimee with what they perceived as great urgency." Cleo nodded toward Mary, who met Dr. Poole's gaze without flinching.

"Dr. Mac definitely wanted a meeting," Mary said. "He came to me and he went to Aimee, and the next thing we knew, he was brain dead in a TMC stairwell."

"That's a tragic coincidence, I don't see how it warrants taking two hours out of half a dozen doctors' demanding schedules." Poole's nostrils flared. "That's a dozen hours of patient care time lost. Besides that, the poor man gave neither of you a legitimate reason for calling a meeting."

My turn. "Dr. MacAllister told me his reason for calling a meeting was related to organ donation. He insisted the topic was too sensitive to state outside the protection of a medical staff committee. Mary and I both sensed urgency in his request."

"Why would he have mentioned organ donation at all, if he felt the matter required committee protection?" Poole fixed her ice-blue stare on me.

I sighed. "I don't know, but he seemed certain something wasn't right. We don't know if it was an ethical problem, or poor medical practice."

"Or possibly even something illegal," Cleo added. "The three of us believe the least we can do is call the members of the committee together to ask if Dr. Mac had given any of them a hint of what was on his mind."

"The three of you have already tried that argument on Dr. Seldon," Poole said, "and it didn't fly. He has said he'd rather follow up in person with the individual members. If he then feels a meeting is appropriate, he'll notify me, and I, in turn, will inform the three of you. I think that's reasonable. I'm sorry, but what you've described doesn't meet the criteria for an Ethics Committee meeting."

"That's your opinion, and it may be true," Cleo replied, "but something more has come up since we asked you here." She picked up her pen and tapped a sheet of notes on the table. "This new wrinkle is definitely an Ethics Committee matter, and it's time sensitive."

Poole squinted a frown at Cleo. "Well for Pete's sake, give it."

"Dr. MacAllister's widow has raised the question of a forensic autopsy done by the coroner."

"Whatever for?" Poole's usual poker face registered surprise.

Cleo filled her in on all the reasons Veronica MacAllister had given. Her husband's agitation, the troubling phone calls, first to his cell, then to their home phone, and the unsettling matter of the shoes her husband had been wearing at the time of his accident. Shoes Veronica had never seen before.

"This all sounds like the imaginings of someone who watches too many made-for-TV mysteries," Poole said. "None of it is evidence of foul play. All of it could be easily explained away."

"Then let Ethics Committee decide that," I said. "Put Veronica MacAllister's autopsy concerns on the agenda and make sure Dr. Seldon keeps hands off Dr. Mac's remains until this issue is resolved. Ask the members if they will at least agree to respect the wishes of a grieving young widow with two tiny sons who've lost their father." I took the risk of making it personal for her. "You're a wife and the mother of a very young child. I'm sure if you put yourself in Mrs. MacAllister's place, you'll realize that what she wants isn't too much to ask."

Before Poole could respond, and perhaps turn me to stone, Cleo stepped in. "Give us a break, Phyllis. If you're so concerned about time, stop wasting ours and make a decision. When you arrived, you said you'd give us five minutes. Time's up. What do you say? Are you going to call a meeting or not?"

Mary and I exchanged glances. Neither of us would have challenged Dr. Poole that way. Cleo was the warrior goddess we both hoped to be when we grew up.

Poole cleared her throat. "All right, do it. But check my calendar first. And don't even *think* about confirming a date until you have been assured of complete attendance. I want every member of the committee to be there."

"What do you want me to do about the agenda?" I asked. "Dr. Seldon made a point about wanting a topic. Shall we use the widow's autopsy question?"

"No. That's a side issue. If we're going to do this, let's stick to what you really want. The main topic will be organ donation, details TBA," Poole said. "If any of them whine about that, refer them to me."

"Even Dr. Seldon?"

Poole was halfway to the exit before flinging her answer back at me. "Especially Dr. Seldon."

When the door closed behind her, we celebrated with high fives, then sat down again for a brainstorming session. We relied on Mary, since she knew more than Cleo or I did about organ donation.

"I've gone back over every organ donor case at TMC for the past two years," Mary said. "I hate to admit it, but I can't find a single red flag. Whatever Dr. Mac saw or suspected must have been very subtle."

Cleo tilted her head to one side. "Dr. MacAllister was only on the medical staff here for two months. How much would he have known about our donor program?"

"A few weeks ago, I allowed him access to all my files and notes," Mary said. "He wanted what he called a 'crash course' in our donor program, and since he'd just been appointed chair of the Ethics Committee, I thought it would be okay." She glanced at Cleo apprehensively.

"That's fine," Cleo said. "You did nothing wrong."

"How many deceased donor patients have we had at TMC in the last year?" I asked.

Mary studied the ceiling for a moment. "Not as many as we'd like. I can count them on my fingers."

"Cleo, you must have been working Ethics Committee when those happened. And Mary, I know you attend all of the Ethics meetings." I looked from her to Cleo. "Did all of those donor cases go through committee?"

"I doubt it," Cleo said. "It's unlikely there were any red flags. The deceased donors' cases would have been sent for death review in either the Surgery Executive Committee or the Medical Executive Committee if the death had been the result of sub-standard patient care. Otherwise, they wouldn't have met any of our requirements for peer review."

"You mean there's no requirement for our Ethics Committee to review all deceased donor patients?"

Mary began nodding vigorously. "That's right, and that's something I've been pushing for ever since I took this job. The Ethics Committee felt it would be redundant, because the deceased donor cases would have been flagged for review in one of the other standing committees if they met the mandatory criteria used for death review." She slumped back in her chair.

"Then why did you think otherwise?" I asked.

"Because there's so much we can learn. We could create more donors in our community, start a movement—"

"Whoa, Nellie." Cleo stood and raised her hands in the air. "I love your enthusiasm, Mary, but you're getting off track. Let's remember why we're here."

"Maybe she's not that far off," I said. "The part about reviewing all deceased donor cases in Ethics Committee sounds like a promising idea to me. How about adding that to the agenda?"

"Dr. Poole won't go for it. She's already nixed the widow's autopsy inquiry," Cleo said. "Our focus should be on discovering what was behind Dr. MacAllister's mysterious request for a meeting. Unfortunately, we can't go to the source for that information, since he's no longer with us."

"What about that call to his cell?" I asked. "Veronica said it was something about a whistleblower. Dr. Mac told her to forget it, said it was nothing, but maybe he was protecting her. Didn't want her to worry."

"That could be something, but what?" Cleo gathered her notes and purse. "Let's do our damnedest to figure out what was on Dr. Mac's mind before a meeting date is set, or we're going to make ourselves and Dr. Poole look like a quartet of bungling amateurs in front of a lot of pissed-off doctors."

She gave us a farewell nod and headed out the exit doors.

We both stared after her for a moment, then Mary turned to me. "Do you feel as queasy about this as I do?"

"Oh, yeah."

Chapter 9

LONG DAY, LONG WEEK. Home at last. Friday night without Nick. Ginger was missing him, too. She had dragged one of his shirts out of the laundry basket and into her doggy bed, making it clear that I was a poor second fiddle. Restlessness propelled me around the small apartment, looking for a way to bring focus to my overstimulated mind. The week had presented a load of new information. So much that I had to lay it all out in an organized fashion. Might as well do something productive while waiting for Nick's evening call.

I opened the kitchen door and stepped out to my deck, giving Ginger a chance to answer nature's call. While I stood at the railing waiting for her, I searched for the common element among the bits and pieces clamoring in my mind like the moths swirling around my porch light. Was it Dr. Mac's death? No, not by itself. It was his urgent request for an Ethics Committee meeting, followed by his untimely accident almost immediately after. That was the Big Daddy moth, but what about the others?

Back inside, Ginger flopped down and rubbed her face on Nick's shirt. I turned out the porch light, took out pen and notepad, and sat at my dinette table.

Second to Dr. Mac's brain death was his sepsis and his subsequent unacceptability as an organ and tissue donor. Not unheard of in cases like his, but still an unfortunate outcome for any potential organ recipients, and for his widow, who would see her husband's last wish go unfulfilled. From there, the next step was the question of which type of autopsy would be done, if any, and who would decide that?

Mary said Dr. Seldon had recommended a clinical autopsy, using the logic that Veronica MacAllister would have the relief of closure much sooner without the delay of waiting for a coroner's autopsy. Depending on caseload, that could take weeks or longer.

Despite Dr. Seldon's recommendation, Veronica MacAllister had made her wishes clear to Mary. Her husband's remains should be preserved intact until she decides whether to request a forensic autopsy. Her reason went beyond a few troublesome phone calls. It had to do with the unfamiliar shoes found in the stairwell where her husband fell. One of them was unlaced and had slipped off his foot, the lace tangling around his ankle appearing to have caused his headlong tumble. She didn't recognize the shoes as his, but there were a few simple explanations for that. The most likely was that he bought them to keep in his locker at the hospital. Never took them home, and never thought to tell his wife about them. Why would he? They were just work shoes.

I needed a sounding board, but I had no one handy. And because so much of what I was concerned about involved a committee of the TMC medical staff, I had to consider confidentiality. I could talk to Cleo or Mary, or Dr. Poole, but using Harry or Nick could be problematic. With them, there was only so much I could reveal.

My cell rang just as I was adding Laurie Littletree to my list as someone to question. She had been one of the first two arrivals on the scene of Dr. Mac's accident. She might not have anything to tell me, but it wouldn't hurt to ask.

I glanced at my phone. *Yes. Nick.* I answered on the third ring.

"We miss you," I said. "When will you be home?"

"Tomorrow afternoon. Miss you, too. Anything exciting happening since last night?"

"A little, but it's all work stuff."

"Off limits as usual?" Nick was used to my work-related restraints. His job required some discretion too, so we never took it personally when there were topics we couldn't share.

"Pretty much. I'll explain what I can when you get home."

"Speaking of getting home, I have a surprise for you."

Nick's surprises were always thoughtful and usually well-kept secrets until he was ready for the big reveal.

"Can you give hints?" I asked.

"Nope. Not a one. Just be patient. With a curious mind like yours, I know that's asking a lot, but give it your best shot. I don't want you to lie awake all night trying to guess."

"Does anyone else know about it?" He was right. I might not be able to sleep. "Maybe Harry?"

"He's my best friend, but he's also your brother, and you've managed to wheedle things out of him before, so no, I haven't told him about this." I heard Nick chuckling softly. He was enjoying this way too much.

"Rella?" Of course, she was still in El Paso subbing as a flight school instructor, so I wouldn't get anything out of her before Nick got home.

"Give up, Little Lady. Think of this as a chance to practice patience and curiosity control."

With that, we exchanged a few comments of a more intimate nature and ended our call.

Practice patience and curiosity control. *Ha. Fat chance.* I went back to doing the opposite with my list of everything related to Dr. MacAllister that the past week had presented.

Beyond that, I found myself jotting notes about other, less dramatic events. Ramon Silva stood out because he and Dr. Mac were connected by their mutual work at Potterville

"Not sure how an aerial view of the landing strip near Potterville Prison will offer you and your friend Mary any clues as to the doctor's death," Nick said.

"I don't expect that, but I would like to see it. I'd like to see the layout of the prison, too. Morbid curiosity, I guess."

"Do you know how often your interpreter, Ramon, works up there?"

"No. I think it's an on-call arrangement. He says sometimes he helps via Skype. Why?"

"You said you've missed two opportunities to ask him if he knew the deceased doctor. Seems like their paths would have crossed at that clinic."

I nodded. "Or at TMC for that matter. I intend to find out."

NICK AND I HAD used the Cessna 182 a few times before for short trips, so we both felt at home using it for our late-morning flight. In less than half an hour, we approached Potterville, flying east over forested mountains that eventually opened onto high desert and less wooded terrain. Nick and I looked below for signs of a landing strip. He circled the small outpost called Potterville that appeared to be little more than an intersection in two roads with a few buildings on the corners. Hardly one in need of an airport.

Nick widened our circle until the prison came into view below. From our altitude, its appearance was unremarkable. A compound made up of one large building and three adjacent smaller structures.

Nick reached out and touched my arm to get my attention. He pointed toward my window, gesturing for me to look down. I saw a single dirt strip at least a couple of miles from the prison. One large structure stood near the strip. Some sort of generic industrial building, far enough away from the prison that it appeared to be on separate property. Another smaller structure lay on the opposite side of the strip. A long rectangle, broken up by large roll-up doors. I guessed storage units, then realized I was only half right. Not typical storage

Prison. That was something I still wanted to ask Ramon about. Did he and Dr. Mac ever cross paths there? If so, how well did Ramon know Heath MacAllister? Well enough that he could recall seeing the kind of work shoes Dr. Mac usually wore?

Then, thinking of Potterville Prison, I realized there was another connection. The two CHR visitors who had spent the week at TMC were also involved, at least at some corporate level, with the medical clinic at the prison. There didn't seem to be any takeaway from that fact, but I made a note, all the same.

Sleep started to seem like a promising idea, so I got ready for bed, but when I walked into the kitchen to turn off the light, I spotted a huge moth clinging to the wall. Probably sneaked in when I went out to the deck earlier. *Great.* No way could I settle in and read myself to sleep. If I turned on my bedside reading lamp or my e-reader, that creature would surely be hovering around.

The idea of killing a moth didn't appeal to me. The lepidopteran was harmless, so why not turn it out using a trick I'd learned from Jack? I covered the moth with a glass and slid the glass, with the moth inside, onto a piece of stiff card stock. I carried the glass, upside-down on the stiff paper, out to the deck, where I released the moth back into the night. Unfortunately, by that time, I was wide awake again.

That humane gesture cost me two hours of sleep, but I made some good headway into my latest mystery novel.

NICK'S SATURDAY MORNING CALL came at six o'clock, setting the tone for my day. "Hey, Lady, get your sleepy backside up and do your chores ASAP. I'll be home around noon, and I expect your undivided attention."

"What?" I croaked. Still half asleep, I was confused by Nick's cheerful enthusiasm combined with his uncharacteristic demand on my time. Attempting to drag myself into full consciousness, I cleared my throat and blinked a few times. "What's going on? And where are you?"

"I'm in El Paso. Dropped Buck off here so he could catch a ride home with Rella."

"But why?" What he was saying didn't make sense, which made me wonder if this call was real, or if I was still asleep. I pinched my cheek so hard I yelped, "Ouch!"

"What the hell?" Nick said. "Are you okay?"

So, I *was* awake, and this odd call from Nick was real. "I'm okay, just a minor mishap."

"Good. I want you ship-shape when I get home." That sounded promising, and the thought helped clear the last of my cobwebs.

"I'll will be, promise. But Nick, why are you dropping Buck off in El Paso?"

"Business. He'll stay there an extra day while Rella finishes her teaching gig."

I'd made the mistake of saying Nick's name aloud. Ginger appeared at the bedroom door and saw me with the phone to my ear. She padded over and nudged my arm with her nose.

"Your other girlfriend wants to hear your voice," I said.

"Put her on." I listened on speaker while Nick went through the *atta girl* routine. When he finished, I took the phone back and gave Ginger a dog biscuit as consolation.

"You're really going to make it home by noon?" I asked.

"I'll be at the airport at twelve," Nick said. "I'm hoping you can meet me there for a ride."

"Why? Isn't your pickup at the hangar?"

"It is, but I told Buck I'd leave it there for him. Something about Delta using his SUV while her Jaguar is in the shop."

Delta's Jaguar. *Must be nice.* "Okay, then. Noon at the hangar. Shall I bring Ginger?"

"Not this time." Nick chuckled. "Just don't tell her where you're going."

Chapter 10

———◆———

Saturday noon in the Timbergate Municipal Airport parking lot, I stepped out of my aging Buick Regal and into a crisp breeze that brought long-awaited relief after three months of relentless heat. I sprinted over to Nick, who stood outside one of Buck's hangars looking cool and hot at the same time. In his aviator sunglasses, dark cargo pants and khaki shirt, he could have passed for an updated Indiana Jones. Except better-looking, but then I was more than a little biased.

The subtext I read in his smile sent a pleasant rush of warmth through my body. His hug and the lingering kiss that followed added more fuel to the fire. We pulled apart eventually, mindful that we were in a public place.

"Ready to go home?" I asked.

"Not yet." Nick took my hand. " I told you I had a surprise, remember? Time to close your eyes."

"It's here? The surprise?"

"Eyes closed." He touched my lids. "I'll tell you when you can look." I did as he asked, but even so, he took me by the shoulders and turned me in a one-eighty. "No peeking."

I heard the door to the hangar open. It took a heap of self-control to keep from looking, but I managed to stand with my eyes closed until he turned me back around.

"Okay, you can look."

I looked but remained unenlightened. All I saw was one of Buck's airplanes in its hangar—the Cessna 182 we sometimes borrowed for short trips.

"Okay, what's the surprise? Are we going somewhere?"

"Anywhere we want," Nick broke into a beaming smile. "It's ours."

"Our what? I'm not following this, Nick. What does Buck's plane have to do with your surprise?"

He took my hand and led me to the passenger door. "Hop in."

I hoisted myself into the copilot seat. "If we're flying somewhere, I should let Amah and Jack know."

Nick settled himself on my left and closed his door. "That won't be necessary today, but we might do some flying tomorrow." He turned to me with a mega-watt smile, so excited that his eyes seemed to spark with blue lights. "Only right for the new owners of this craft to take it out for a spin."

Finally, I realized what he was telling me. "Oh my gosh, did you buy this from Buck? I know you've always wanted your own plane, but can you afford it?"

"You're close, but I have to correct a couple of your assumptions. First, it's *our* plane, yours and mine. I put it in both of our names. And second, I didn't buy it from Buck. I accepted it as a gift. Buck upgraded to a newer model. He said I'd be doing him a favor if I took this one off his hands. He told me to consider it a bonus."

"Some bonus," I said. "But why did you put my name on it? I'm not a pilot."

"Who knows? You might decide to get your license someday. You'd be a natural."

Flattering as his opinion was, I didn't share it. He had great confidence in Rella, his co-pilot, but she had come to her job with Buck after serving in the Marine Corps as a fighter pilot.

My training and background as a librarian couldn't have been more different from hers.

"We'll see," I said. Nick was so proud of his surprise that I didn't want to burst his bubble.

Back at the apartment we spent a couple of hours catching up on our time apart, but staying away from serious topics, including our work. Time enough for that later. We agreed to devote the rest of the day to whatever activities we found mutually relaxing. By Saturday night, both of us were sufficiently relaxed, snuggled in bed with Ginger at our feet.

"What do you think?" Nick asked. "Take the 182 out for a spin tomorrow?"

"Sure, I guess. Where are you thinking?"

"I hear there's a small airstrip near the prison in Potterville. At some point, Buck is going to want me to fly him up there to have a first-hand look at the place. It wouldn't take long to scout that out, unless you have another idea."

I sat up, grabbed my phone off the nightstand. "Not really. I'm good with whatever." I searched Google Earth, but didn't find an aerial view of the landing strip. "Not finding it online. Want to see if you can spot it?" I handed him my phone.

"I see something, but it's pretty simple, almost makeshift. I'd like to have a first-hand look."

"Me, too." I put my phone back on the night table.

Nick turned on his bedside lamp and narrowed his eyes at me. "Not sure I like the sound of that."

"What?"

"The sound of your 'Me, too.' I hear gears spinning. What's happening in that head of yours?"

"I'm curious about that prison. Don't ask me why, because I don't have a definite reason, just vague curiosity. I'd never heard of it a week ago, then I discovered that I knew two people who worked in the prison's medical clinic. Less than a week later, one of them is dead. I told you about the doctor who fell down the stairwell. He worked there part-time."

All our stirring around had disrupted Ginger, who dropped off our bed and left the room. Probably figured she'd get better sleep in her doggy bed in the kitchen.

"Even the dog knows we've just broken our *no work talk rule*." Nick turned out his lamp. "Sorry I brought it up. How about we put off this topic until tomorrow and get some sleep?"

I plumped my pillow and turned on my side. "I'll try."

Nick leaned in for a quick kiss. "Try hard, because if you're still ruminating about this prison thing and keeping me awake an hour from now, I'll have to go out in the kitchen and curl up with Ginger."

It took a while, but eventually I managed to shut down my thoughts.

I WOKE SUNDAY MORNING to the cooing of doves and the aromas of fresh coffee and toast. I shuffled out to the kitchen and squinted at the wall clock. Seven thirty. Nick stood peering into the open fridge, looking all rumple-haired and adorable in faded jeans and a light blue T-shirt. He pulled back with a shake of his head.

"There's nothing in here but yogurt. Did you eat anything else while I was gone?"

"Of course. Lots of things." Mostly things Amah and Jack had provided. "Look in the freezer compartment."

"Ah," he pulled out a pre-baked frozen quiche, "that's more like it."

I nibbled at a slice of buttered toast. "How long have you been awake?"

"Since the doves started. Could have done without the racket."

"I think their cooing sounds sweet."

"You're in the minority. What you're hearing are nonnative Eurasian doves. Not all bird enthusiasts are happy that they've invaded the States over the past few decades."

"Why? Are they causing environmental problems?"

"There's research going on, but I think the jury is still out."

"How do you know this stuff?"

"Jack. I think he wrote something about them for an outdoor magazine."

"Well, I'm also Eurasian. My great-grandparents were nonnative, so those doves and I have something in common. I'm on their side."

Nick pulled a wicked grin. "Now that you mention it, I have heard you coo a time or two."

Instead of responding, I poured myself a cup of coffee. "Why didn't you wake me?"

I thought about it, but you were talking in your sleep. I didn't want to interrupt, so I killed some time feeding Ginger and all of the barnyard population."

"I don't talk in my sleep."

"Oh, no?" Nick grinned. "Then who is Ramon? And why were you talking gibberish to him about judo and prisons?"

"He's a medical interpreter. I thought I told you about him a few months ago when we had a Portuguese patient at TMC."

"I recall the situation. Something that dicey would be damn hard to forget, but I'm not sure I ever heard the man's name. Any reason he's on your mind now?" Nick unwrapped the quiche and transferred it onto a plate. He put it in the microwave and started the timer.

"It's a work thing. At least I think it is. You must have triggered it last night when you mentioned flying over the airstrip at Potterville."

"When we talked on the phone the other day, didn't you say that medical clinic at Potterville Prison has some connection to TMC?"

"They're owned by the same corporation." I started more toast while Nick served up the quiche.

Over breakfast, I brought Nick up to date with the concerns Mary Barton and I shared about Dr. MacAllister's death. So far, it was all speculation on our part. Nothing was being done about it within the framework of the medical staff organization, so technically, I was not telling tales out of school.

"Not sure how an aerial view of the landing strip near Potterville Prison will offer you and your friend Mary any clues as to the doctor's death," Nick said.

"I don't expect that, but I would like to see it. I'd like to see the layout of the prison, too. Morbid curiosity, I guess."

"Do you know how often your interpreter, Ramon, works up there?"

"No. I think it's an on-call arrangement. He says sometimes he helps via Skype. Why?"

"You said you've missed two opportunities to ask him if he knew the deceased doctor. Seems like their paths would have crossed at that clinic."

I nodded. "Or at TMC for that matter. I intend to find out."

NICK AND I HAD used the Cessna 182 a few times before for short trips, so we both felt at home using it for our late-morning flight. In less than half an hour, we approached Potterville, flying east over forested mountains that eventually opened onto high desert and less wooded terrain. Nick and I looked below for signs of a landing strip. He circled the small outpost called Potterville that appeared to be little more than an intersection in two roads with a few buildings on the corners. Hardly one in need of an airport.

Nick widened our circle until the prison came into view below. From our altitude, its appearance was unremarkable. A compound made up of one large building and three adjacent smaller structures.

Nick reached out and touched my arm to get my attention. He pointed toward my window, gesturing for me to look down. I saw a single dirt strip at least a couple of miles from the prison. One large structure stood near the strip. Some sort of generic industrial building, far enough away from the prison that it appeared to be on separate property. Another smaller structure lay on the opposite side of the strip. A long rectangle, broken up by large roll-up doors. I guessed storage units, then realized I was only half right. Not typical storage units, but airplane hangars.

The flat ribbon of dirt between the hangar building and the warehouse obviously was not qualified to be called an airport. Hardly even a landing strip. It could easily have been a slice of land leveled for some other purpose.

Nick handed me a pair of binoculars. "Look for a windsock." He circled the area, dropping altitude. I spotted a bright orange windsock, nodded to Nick.

"Landing lights?" he said.

He made one last pass, low enough for me to recognize that yes, there were landing lights. I nodded again, and he took us back to cruising altitude, heading toward home. The only reason for a windsock and landing lights was to assist aircraft with take-offs and landings, both day and night.

WE SOON ARRIVED BACK at Timbergate Muni, where Nick taxied the Cessna toward the hangars while I asked his thoughts about what we had seen. "Is that strip near the prison where you and Buck would land?"

He cocked an eyebrow. "Looks like our only option."

Nick opened the hangar door and I helped him pull the plane around and push it into its parking spot.

"I wonder if it's owned by the prison," I said. "It would make sense that a correctional facility that houses a thousand people would need convenient aerial transport. The medical clinic in that prison would be equipped with only the basics. Any one of those inmates could develop a life-threatening problem requiring treatment at a fully functioning acute care hospital."

"We're not sure that strip *is* part of the prison." Nick said. "All we know is what Buck was told. We can use it if we make arrangements in advance. The warden said he'd take care of it when the time came."

"You're thinking that airstrip is owned by some other business?"

"Up there in the boonies, it could be any business that needs to distribute goods beyond the local area."

"It seems like the clinic would use helicopters for transport. Maybe they've worked out an arrangement with the owners of that strip to use it as a landing pad."

"Could be," Nick said. "Whatever the case, it gave us a reason to take a spin today."

"And I have a better picture now of where Dr. MacAllister worked. His wife said he wanted to quit that job." A shudder passed through me. "I can't blame him. What a lonely, desolate-looking place."

THE AFTERNOON HAD GROWN cool by the time we reached our barn-top apartment in Coyote Creek around five o'clock. From our deck, we took a moment to watch the seasonal acorn competition under way in the barnyard. It happened every October, with the llamas and the squirrels competing for the morsels falling from Jack and Amah's blue oak trees. The llamas considered acorns a welcome enhancement to their diet of hay and grass, while the squirrels did their best to snatch and store away what they could in their hidden winter caches.

After checking our phones and finding nothing pressing, we walked up to the main house to fetch Ginger home. Jack stood in the backyard at his outdoor grill with a pair of tongs in his hand and steaks sizzling over the flames. The mouthwatering aroma set off gurgling in my stomach, matched by recognizable growls coming from Nick's direction.

"Better join us," Jack said. "There's way too much here for just your Amah and me."

He didn't have to ask twice. We hadn't eaten since breakfast.

Chapter 11

———•———

GOOD NEWS. CALL ME.

Cleo's early morning email greeted me first thing Monday. I called right away.

"Dr. Mac's autopsy is on the table," Cleo said.

"What? It's happening right now? I don't consider that good news."

"Oh, cripes, Aimee, I didn't mean 'on the table' literally. I meant it's going to be discussed at the Ethics Committee meeting."

"Dr. Poole changed her mind?"

"She sure did. She wants you to put it on the agenda. She would have told you herself, but we happened to be on the same elevator a few minutes ago. She asked me to follow up with you."

"Ah, that's more like it." Cleo was brilliant at handling the business of the medical staff, but sometimes our conversations veered off into misdirection. "Did she say what changed her mind?"

"She reviewed Dr. MacAllister's medical record. That's all she told me. She's already spoken to Dr. Seldon. Told him no autopsy until after the Ethics meeting. He argued that it wasn't necessary to wait. They have some acrimonious history, so that was all it took to raise her hackles."

"She won? He agreed?"

"You bet." Cleo said. "I guess she badgered him until he backed off. She wants Dr. Mac's medical record to be present at the meeting. "

"I'll make sure of that."

"Anything new with you?" she asked.

"Not yet. Just a few loose ends I haven't had time to deal with."

"Let's talk later, then. I know you want to get started on a meeting date."

Galvanized by that news, I called Mary Barton right away to update her and to ask about her schedule.

"You get it set, I'll be there," she said, "even if I'm hit by a bus. I'll show up strapped to a gurney."

"Mary, don't even joke about something like that."

I heard her laugh softly. "Sorry, don't take it literally. You should be accustomed to hospital humor by now."

Literally. Again? Two misinterpretations in one morning. *Loosen up, Machado.*

"I'll have to work on it, but that remark sounded like you were tempting fate."

She laughed again. "Okay, I take it back. If I say I'll be there with bells on, are you going to ask to see my bells?"

I wondered if Mary was overcompensating, trying to lighten her sense of grief about Dr. Mac's death and the loss of his organs. Either that, or maybe she was punchy from being up all night doing grief counseling for some distraught family member. We weren't close enough for me to ask, so I let it go.

My priority was to set a day and time, but there was a catch. Usually, a pre-confirmed quorum would allow me to set a date. Not this time. Cleo, Mary and I had secured Dr. Poole's cooperation, but I had to deal with her ultimatum. A quorum was not good enough. Either every member of Ethics Committee showed up, or there would be no meeting.

It was no simple matter to find a date when Poole and the other five members could work a meeting into their schedules. In addition, I had to factor in ex-officio members like Administrator Jared Quinn, Chief of Staff Percy Seldon, and Mary Barton, Organ Donor Coordinator. By the time we had secured Poole's go-ahead the previous Friday, it had been too late to start making calls.

I began by calling around to the doctors' offices, leaving messages with a few date options for either breakfast or luncheon meetings. I hoped to have something set within a couple of days.

My efforts to schedule the meeting took a sizable chunk out of my morning, but the routine library tasks went smoothly, thanks to Lola Rampley, my octogenarian volunteer. The tiny, white-haired wisp of a woman handled drop-ins, online search requests, and cataloging of new print materials with the expertise she had perfected during a lifetime as a librarian. Heaven help me if she ever decided to hang up her bright orange auxiliary blazer.

By mid-morning I realized that something had been simmering in the back of my mind. It finally came to me. I wanted to talk to Laurie Littletree, the nurse who had been on the scene when Dr. MacAllister's unresponsive body was found in the stairwell. A call to the nursing office confirmed that Laurie was working a day shift on the surgery floor. She would be off duty at three o'clock.

She and I had been through a traumatic incident almost a year ago that built a strong bond of trust between us, although with our busy lives, we didn't often have a chance to get together. I sent her a text asking if she could drop by the library after her shift. She confirmed.

Return calls began coming in from the offices of various members of Ethics Committee, and I spent the next two hours jockeying potential meeting dates and times. The best I could do was a noon meeting on a Monday two weeks away. *Not good.*

Dr. MacAllister's remains would stay in the TMC morgue until then. Unless Dr. Seldon broke his promise to Dr. Poole andcoaxed Veronica MacAllister into agreeing to a clinical autopsy without waiting for the meeting. That thought stirred me to action. I called Dr. Poole's office prepared to leave a message, but a minor miracle occurred, and she took my call right away.

"I know why you're calling, Miss Machado, and I'm a step ahead of you."

"You do? I mean, you are?" This woman made a good case for mental telepathy.

"I've spoken to Dr. Seldon again this morning about the autopsy. That is why you're calling, I presume?"

"Yes. Are you sure Dr. Seldon will comply? He won't pressure Mrs. Macallister?"

"Unfortunate that we couldn't get an earlier date, but nevertheless, he has agreed to wait until after Ethics meets. Let's see how the committee reacts." I caught a hint of hesitation, even doubt, in her reply.

"You're thinking he'll try to sway the committee? But why? What difference would it make to Dr. Seldon?"

"More than you'd think," Dr. Poole said. "Keep in mind that he diagnosed the septicemia that led him to the decision to remove Dr. MacAllister from life-support, and then he called upon Dr. Decker to concur with his decision. Also, Dr. MacAllister's care during his days of brain death on life support was managed by Dr. Seldon. The sepsis began on his watch. That, along with the loss of potential life-saving organs, is doubly tragic. With an outcome like that, Dr. Seldon might be tempted to avoid the more complete autopsy, just to save face."

"But it sounds like doing the clinical autopsy himself would be a conflict of interest," I said.

"That's exactly how I intend to open the discussion at committee." I heard her whisper an aside to someone. "I'm being summoned by my staff, Miss Machado, so if that's all that was on your mind, shall we end this talk?"

There was plenty more on my mind, but I said, "Of course." What else could I do?

The answer came walking through the library entrance shortly after three o'clock: Laurie Littletree, looking as stunning as ever with her delicately chiseled features enhanced by gold hoop earrings and vibrant floral-patterned scrubs. Her hair bounced in a trendy mass of dark ringlets, a style popular with many modern young black women. It suited her energetic personality.

I rose to meet her and guided her to a small table adjacent to the stacks. "Coffee? Tea?"

"Off both for now," she said.

I detected a gleam in her eye that told me there was a reason to avoid caffeine. "Oh, Laurie, tell me, is there news?"

She flashed a brilliant smile. "Yes. In six months, Daniel and I will have our firstborn."

"And ...?"

"We're waiting to see if it's a boy or girl." She ducked her head for a moment, looked a little embarrassed. "At least *trying* to wait. We keep taking turns deciding we want to know, then changing our minds."

My thoughts took a detour for a split second. If it were Nick and me, would we wait to find out? I forced that thought away and focused on Laurie.

"I'm so happy for you, but you're probably wondering why I asked you to drop by."

"Yes, but I'm glad you did. We shouldn't need a special reason to get together. It's just that life gets so busy."

"And now, with your newcomer on the way, it will be even more so, but you're right, we'll have to make the effort." With pleasantries out of the way, I plunged ahead.

"Laurie, there's something on my mind that you might be

able to help with … something I'd like to ask you about … but I don't want to put you in an awkward position, so I'll understand if it makes you uncomfortable."

She smiled, shook her head. "More uncomfortable than what we went through together a year ago? I doubt that." She and I had been involved in solving the murder of a TMC patient back then.

"Nothing as dramatic as that. I'm just curious what you recall about the night Dr. MacAllister was found in the stairwell here at TMC."

"Ah, that. Sure, no problem, but it won't amount to much." A puzzled frown flitted across her forehead. "Just out of curiosity, why are you asking?"

I'd been afraid she'd go there. "I'd rather not get you involved in my reasons, especially now that I know you're expecting."

"Pregnancy hasn't turned me into a sissy, you know." She leaned forward, elbows on the table. "Come on, spill it. I've already talked to Mary Barton, so I know there's something you two are poking at."

I told her the basics, with the emphasis on Veronica MacAllister's concerns about the circumstances of her husband's accident, and the odd bit about his having worn shoes that she did not recognize. I added the part about the disturbing phone calls to her home.

"The woman is distraught," I said. "She's been left suddenly alone with two-year-old twin boys. I suppose it's understandable that she's having trouble accepting her husband's death as an accident."

"I get that. If it were me, and I lost Daniel, I'd want the same thing she's after." Laurie brushed a ringlet off her forehead. "Tell you what, I'll give you my best recollection of that night, but all it amounts to is what I told Mary. I entered the stairwell right behind the security guard. The light was out, so he and I had both turned on flashlights. I heard him let out a yelp, and a couple of your basic four-letter words. When I reached the landing, I saw Dr. Mac on the floor and called for help."

"How long did it take to get him to a trauma room in the ER?"

"The EMT's had him there in minutes, but it was too late. Brain death was confirmed by the ER doc and a neurologist. Someone on duty that night knew he was a donor, so he was rushed to ICU and put on a ventilator. There you have it, Aimee. That's really all I can tell you."

"Did you see anything in that stairwell that seemed off? Anything that stands out?"

"It was dark. It was hectic and everything was happening fast. I wasn't looking for evidence of foul play, I was trying to keep him alive." Laurie met my eyes for a moment. "Aimee, you know it's common for docs to leave an extra pair of shoes in their lockers. And who doesn't get those annoying phone calls where no one is there? Are you sure you and Mary need to go to extremes based on those two implausible details?"

I wasn't sure, but I wasn't ready to let it go either. We still had Dr. Mac's evasive request for an Ethics Committee meeting, and his insistence that he had a critical topic to be discussed. I wasn't comfortable revealing that fact to Laurie. I felt I'd be straying too close to committee confidentiality.

"Maybe all we can achieve is reassuring Dr. Mac's widow that there was no foul play," I said. "To that end, there's going to be a meeting of the Ethics Committee two weeks from now to discuss the incident."

"I'll keep fingers crossed for her." Laurie rose. "I'm sorry there isn't more I can do."

I walked with her toward the exit. "There is one other thing. It occurred to me that you and the security guard who came upon Dr. MacAllister in that stairwell might help by telling the committee what you saw that night. I know you've written an incident report, but there might be additional questions you could answer in person."

Laurie hesitated at the door. "Of course. Whatever you need."

"Thanks. I'll mention it to Dr. Poole, the acting committee

chair. Do you know the name of the guard? I'd like to talk to him, too."

"Buzz Bateson," Laurie said. "He's a good guy. Retiring in a few months."

I remembered Buzz. He helped at TMC's employee safety meetings with things like what to do if a fire breaks out, or if a hostile intruder shows up with a weapon. Those, and other potential disasters we hoped would never happen.

"Thanks," I said. "I'll give him a call. See if he can attend."

"That may not work." Laurie pressed her lips together, gave her head a slight shake. "He's on sick leave. In our ICU right now recovering from surgery."

"I didn't know. I hope it's nothing too serious."

"It's not good. He was crossing the street on his way to Margie's Bean Pot a couple of days ago and got nailed by a hit-and-run driver."

"Oh, no. How is he?"

"He'll live, but he's pretty banged up. Knocked him clear out of his boots."

A chill ran across my shoulders. I flashed back to Mary Barton joking about attending the Ethics Committee meeting. *I'll be there … even if I'm hit by a bus.*

Chapter 12

———◆———

I WAS STILL PROCESSING Laurie's news about Buzz Bateson when Amah called at quitting time, elated with the news that my Uncle Gabe was in town. Gabe had spent a lot of time with Harry and me when we were little kids and he was a teenager. By the time we were teens ourselves, he told us he felt more like a cousin to Harry and me. He said *uncle* made him feel like an old geezer, and insisted we drop the title and call him just Gabe. We kidded him for a while by addressing him as *Just Gabe*, but that soon wore thin.

Gabe was another family success story in the construction trades. His electrical contracting business ranked among the largest in the country. He kept a home base in Hawaii, but his work took him all over the States, and sometimes beyond. I understood Amah's excitement. We rarely got to see him.

Amah's invitation came rapid-fire. "Come to dinner, bring Nick, of course. Harry's coming, Rella's still in El Paso. I'm making all of Gabe's favorites, linguiça rolls, Portuguese green salad, and port wine custard pudding."

That delicious variation on traditional flan got my attention. When Amah stopped to take a breath, I jumped in.

"What time?"

"Oh, yes, six thirty. Will that work for you and Nick?"

"I'll check with him and let you know, but you can count on me for sure."

"Good. Gabe's been asking about the two of you." She didn't elaborate, but I could guess the rest. Were we engaged yet? Any wedding plans? The usual.

I texted Nick right away and got a quick response. He was all in for Amah's cooking and a chance to get reacquainted with Gabe. They'd met only briefly a year earlier. Between Nick's job flying for Buck Sawyer, and Gabe's business taking him in all directions, the two men were rarely in the same place at the same time.

I REACHED HOME BEFORE Nick, so I called Amah to ask if she needed help with dinner. She assured me that she and Jack had it covered, along with Gabe's help. The barnyard chores beckoned, so I quick-changed into jeans and T-shirt, tossed hay to the llamas and replenished the turkeys' poultry feed. I refreshed all the watering troughs and was back in our barn-top apartment in record time. I had just stripped for a shower when Nick walked in and found me standing there in my birthday suit.

"Now this is how every man should be welcomed home." The gleam in his eye telegraphed his intentions.

"Not so fast, mister. I just did chores. I was heading to the shower."

He started unbuttoning his shirt. "Shower sounds good. May I join you?"

WE WALKED UP THE lane to the main house, arriving on time, clean and refreshed. We stepped through the slider into Jack and Amah's combination family room and dining room. Gabe grabbed me in a bear hug, shook Nick's hand, and beamed at us. Amah must have told him Nick and I were on solid ground, probably even hinting that we might make an announcement any day.

Amah and Harry came from the kitchen bearing the linguiça rolls and salad. Jack poured from a bottle of Cabernet Sauvignon, provided by Gabe, with a Portuguese label.

Gabe looked as fit and handsome as he had when I'd last seen him a year earlier. The only member of our clan who turned up with green eyes, he still wore his dark brown hair in a casual surfer style. I saw no sign of the gray that had already appeared in my father's hair, but at age forty-five, Gabe was six years younger than my dad.

His smile remained bright enough to light up a room, and according to Amah, who kept track of these things, it was still lighting up many women's hearts. Despite that, nothing in his conversation hinted at a strong contender for the role of Mrs. Gabriel Machado. I thought the saying about a girl in every port might apply, since his business took him all over the globe.

We finished our meal and were anticipating the rare treat of port wine flan when my cell rang. *Ignore it?* I glanced at the ID. *Cleo.* Had to pick up. I excused myself and went to the living room on the other side of the house.

"What's going on?" I said, hoping I sounded more gracious than I felt.

"Am I interrupting?" She knew me so well.

"Kind of. Sorry. I know you wouldn't be calling unless it was important."

"There's been an incident. I wanted you to be aware, since it's related to Dr. MacAllister's case."

I felt a clunk. *Heart dropping to stomach.* "What is it?"

"A break-in at Veronica MacAllister's home."

"Cripes. Was she at home when it happened?

"No. She and her boys were at their pediatrician's office. It happened in mid-afternoon."

"How did you hear about it?"

"Mrs. MacAllister contacted Mary Barton, who contacted me."

"Why did Veronica call Mary? Surely she called the police

right away." I hesitated, not liking what I was thinking. "Oh, no. She didn't, did she?"

"You got it. She didn't call them, but she wanted the three of us to know about it."

"But she needs this investigated. She's already suspicious about her husband's death."

"I would agree," Cleo said, "except she's too freaked to think straight."

"I'm not surprised. But if there was a lot of theft, she'll need to report it."

"That's why she's freaked. Nothing was stolen. The house wasn't tossed. She only knew her house had been entered because her front door had been forced open."

"That doesn't make sense. Why the break-in?"

"She thinks it was a warning, or a threat," Cleo said. "A toy whistle was left on one of the pillows in her twins' bedroom."

"That's not really unusual. Little boys that age leave their toys scattered around all the time."

"True, but this whistle was one that Mrs. MacAllister had never seen before."

"Like the shoes she'd never seen," I said. "That is creepy."

Cleo continued. "And remember when we met with Mary last Friday? She said Veronica told her about an upsetting call on Dr. Mac's cell phone. Something about a whistleblower?"

"I do, but she said Dr. Mac made light of it and told her it wasn't anything serious." I searched my memory for the details. "Dr. Mac told his wife that he'd had to write up an incident involving an employee at the prison clinic. Nothing to do with Timbergate Medical Center."

"That poor woman. She's convinced someone killed her husband to silence him." Cleo huffed a frustrated breath. "And now she thinks whoever did it will come after her and her children next, assuming she knows whatever it was that had Dr. Mac so troubled. If only he had told her, she could go to the police with some hope of sorting out what happened to Dr. Mac and why."

"Did Mary say what Mrs. MacAllister is planning to do? There aren't many options if she refuses to involve the police." The break-in had to increase the stress the widow was already experiencing. Just hearing about it set my own heart bumping against my ribs.

"She's afraid the police would doubt a connection between her husband's death and this incident, and we can't really blame her. Break-ins happen so frequently these days. A toy whistle isn't going to cut it, especially if she won't tell them about the whistleblower phone call. For now, she won't go to the police, and she's backed off about the forensic autopsy. She doesn't want anyone thinking she's still pursuing anything to do with her husband's death."

"But she did call Mary," I said, "so there must be something she thinks we can do to help."

"Her only priority is finding a way to keep her kids safe, Aimee. That's why I'm calling. You, Mary and I aren't going to tell anyone else at the hospital about the break-in at the MacAllister home."

"I understand. Did you or Mary tell Poole about the break-in?"

"Mary did," Cleo said. "Dr. Poole has made it clear we're to leave Veronica out of it when the committee meets. Poole respects Veronica's wishes to keep her family safe. As far as the committee is concerned, holding Dr. Mac's remains in the TMC morgue pending an autopsy decision is Jared Quinn's idea. Poole consulted with him, and he agreed to tell the committee he wants the option in the event the widow sues the hospital for negligence."

"Good to know, but either way, we still need the widow's permission as next of kin. Unless Quinn asks law enforcement to step in. I doubt he wants to go to that extreme right now."

"Agreed. In the meantime, we have stopped Dr. Seldon from pressing the widow to opt for a clinical autopsy. With luck, Veronica MacAllister will reconsider, and Dr. Mac's remains will be transferred to the coroner for a forensic autopsy. If the results are suspicious, law enforcement will have to be called in to investigate."

"I hope Ethics Committee makes the right call," I said. "We can't let Dr. Mac's remains go to a mortuary until an autopsy decision is made."

"Dr. Poole is chairing that meeting. She'll get the right call."

"There's one other thing we need to do," I said. I told her about Buzz Bateson, who had discovered Dr. Mac in the stairwell, and who was now in ICU, a hit-and-run victim. "If he's conscious, and able to communicate, I think Dr. Poole should interview him before the meeting. Maybe he would recall something, anything that sheds light on what happened."

"You want me to call her?" Cleo asked.

"Please. I'd do it, but you have a gift for getting her cooperation. Just let me know if she agrees."

"No problem. I think I can persuade her." I heard a chuckle. Cleo enjoyed her ability to bend members of the medical staff to her will. "Anything else? Or shall I let you go?"

"One more thing," I said. "About Veronica MacAllister and her little boys. Where are they now? Are they somewhere safe?"

"Good question. I think they're in a motel tonight. Not sure that's an ideal situation long term, but returning to her home with a broken front door isn't an option. Do you have any ideas that don't involve the police?"

"Let me think about it. I'll get back to you later tonight."

Back at the table, everyone else had polished off their dessert. I fiddled with mine while Jack served fresh coffee. No one seemed in a hurry to break the mood by leaving the table.

Amah took a sip from her cup and put it down. "Aimee, was your call important? Are you going to have to leave?"

I glanced toward Harry. "Um, no, I don't have to leave, but it could be important."

"Why are you looking at me?" Harry asked.

"It might involve a conversation you and I had the other day."

"Is this about the doctor who fell down a stairwell and ended up brain dead?"

At this point, Harry had Gabe's full attention. "Damn, that's heavy. What's the whole story here?" He looked back and forth between Harry and me. Nick did the same.

"Why were you being called about this tonight?" Nick asked.

"Because the widow and her two little boys might be in danger."

"She has small children?" Gabe said. "Give, Aimee, what's this got to do with you?"

I pulled in a breath. "Okay, but I'm walking a thin line here. None of this is in the scope of breaking my confidentiality agreement at work, but it's still very much in the range of bad publicity for Timbergate Medical Center. Let's agree that what's said in this room stays in this room."

Nods of agreement all around. Nick and everyone in my family was used to this sort of thing. Gabe narrowed his eyes, pressed his lips together, but agreed. I went ahead with a brief sketch of the situation. I explained that a doctor whose committee was my responsibility had tripped over his shoelaces and fallen down a stairwell. He ended up brain dead and was eventually taken off life support.

The only black eye for the hospital was that the light was out in the stairwell, causing a safety issue. The widow had not threatened to sue the hospital over that, but she was distressed because the shoes her husband had been wearing, the shoes that caused his fall, were unfamiliar to her. In addition, there had been hang-up phone calls to their home phone before the incident. I told them about the one exception being the whistleblower message on Dr. Mac's cell phone. And about the whistle Veronica found on her son's pillow.

"They shut down their landline, and then after her

husband's fall, she began getting the same sort of hang-up calls on her cell phone. The upshot is, she wanted a forensic autopsy, but someone broke into her home, which she took as a threat, and now she's changed her mind."

Gabe leaned in. "You're saying she suspects foul play in her husband's death? That's bigger than a black eye, if someone affiliated with your hospital went after this doctor. A forensic autopsy sounds like a damn good idea. It's what I'd demand in her situation. What's the problem?"

"She's adamant she won't push for the forensic autopsy, and she won't call the police. There was nothing about the break-in that proves she was specifically targeted. Just a whistle on one of the beds in her twin boys' bedroom. She thinks going to the police would do nothing but increase the threat to herself and her kids. All she wants is a place to hide."

Gabe stood up and shook out his shoulders. "This is bull. That woman and her kids should be in a safe house until her husband's remains get a forensic autopsy, whether she wants it or not. If there was foul play, the police have to be brought in."

"Exactly," I said. "But first things first. Get her safely hidden away."

Jack, who had been listening quietly, spoke up. "Nick? Gabe? Harry? Any ideas about a hideout?"

Nick answered first. "Buck might have an idea. I'll ask." He reached for his phone.

Gabe held up a hand. "That might not be necessary. I have something that should be available for a few weeks."

"What is it?" Amah asked. "And can you guarantee she wouldn't be found?"

"It would be very unlikely," Gabe said. "It's a corporate apartment in San Francisco. Used for meetings with global clients who don't want to travel all the way to Hawaii to do business with me."

"And handy for you when you're on the mainland," I said.

"Precisely." Gabe pulled a card from his wallet and handed it to me. "Here's the address."

"But wait, Gabe." Amah reached for the card. "Won't this reveal your name, Machado, and connect the dots back to Aimee?"

"No, Mom, I rent it from a friend as needed. He's paid from one of my corporate accounts set up with a fictitious name. In this case, I'll ask him to keep it off the books until further notice, so there'll be no paper trail. He won't ask why."

"But what about the widow? Won't her name be recorded as a tenant?"

"Not her real name. We'll give her a fake ID. Hell, I'll tell everyone she's my new girlfriend." Gabe shrugged. "Unless someone has a better idea."

"That would work," Nick said, "but she'll have to cut off communication while she's there."

"How will she manage that?" Amah asked.

Harry answered. "She can use a burner phone, but she'll want to stay off email and the Internet just to be on the safe side."

"Aimee? What do you think?" Jack asked. "Will the MacAllister woman agree?"

"I hope so. I'll contact her tomorrow and then let Gabe know."

"The sooner the better," Gabe said.

"If it's happening, I can fly them down right away," Nick said. "You, too, Gabe. You can help her get settled." He looked at me. "Want to come along?"

"You bet. As long as I don't have to miss a full day's work."

"All right, I'll borrow Buck's six-passenger Skywagon. Let's get all of this arranged early tomorrow. We'll take off Wednesday as soon as you can get away from the hospital."

Jack tapped his coffee cup with a spoon. "Hold on a minute, Nick. Who's gonna watch your pooch if both of you are gone all day?"

"I was hoping that would be you."

"More than happy to." Jack gave Nick a thumbs-up.

"Hey, that reminds me." Gabe glanced around the room.

"Where is that wonder dog of yours I keep hearing about? Jack tells me she's quite the educated canine these days."

"We left her at the barn," Nick said. "She's learning that it's okay to be home alone sometimes."

"Tell Gabe about her latest lesson." Jack winked at me. "It's a doozy."

"It's not exactly a dinnertime topic," I said.

"Heck, no one at this table is squeamish." Jack elbowed Gabe. "She can sniff out dead bodies buried pretty deep."

"Cadavers," Nick said, pride showing on his face. "She finally graduated. The training takes longer than any of the other courses. Not every dog makes the grade."

Chapter 13

GABE AND HARRY WALKED back to the barn with Nick and me after dinner. Gabe wanted to see the improvements made to our barn-top apartment since his last visit. As soon as we opened the door, Ginger popped up from her doggy bed to greet us, tail wagging.

"Ah, there she is," Gabe held out his hand for her to sniff. "It's good to meet you, young lady." Ginger sat and offered her paw, which Gabe shook, with a big grin on his face.

Nick nodded his approval. "She doesn't do that for everyone."

With that introduction out of the way, we took Gabe on the full two-minute tour of our modest home. He was duly impressed with the way Harry and his crew had turned a bare-bones bunkhouse into a cozy, efficient apartment.

"Hell, this is nicer than a lot of places I've had to endure when I travel out of the country." Gabe acknowledged Harry with a congratulatory punch on the shoulder. "Excellent work, my man."

Considering the complexity of the three-story shopping

mall that Harry was bringing to near completion in Timbergate, the remodel of our little apartment was hardly a challenge. But Harry beamed anyway, enjoying approval from Gabe, whose respect for quality construction work meant a lot.

Nick pulled cold beers from our fridge, and the four of us gathered on the deck to watch the sunset. At twilight, Jack's turkeys took to the oak trees to roost. The llamas found their favorite spots to drop into their kushed position, legs folded under their bodies in tidy camelid fashion.

The oak-strewn valley beyond Jack and Amah's property gave way to distant layers of mountains to the west, where each sunset lighted the scene differently. Our view that evening was a gentle pink blush. Other times, the setting sun would light a cloud-strewn sky on fire in a blazing biblical fresco. It was an ever-changing panorama I never tired of watching.

The four of us had just begun gazing at the night sky, watching stars wink on, when my cell phone rang. Cleo. Again. *Now what?* I went inside to take the call.

"I know, I know," Cleo said. "You're the last person I wanted to bother with this, but damn, I had to call."

Cleo's use of profanity was a bad sign. The muscles in the back of my neck tightened. "What is it?"

"It's Buzz Bateson, the security guard who discovered Dr. Mac in the stairwell. He's been transferred to a CHR hospital in Southern California."

"Why?"

"All I know is that his condition has deteriorated."

"Do you know if Dr. Poole had a chance to question Buzz?"

"She did not. In fact, she's the one who called me about this. She planned to talk to him this evening, but when she went to the ICU to see him, she was told about his transfer."

"Any idea who his primary physician was? Who signed off on the transfer?"

"Not yet. Buzz's medical record is off limits to Poole, because she wasn't involved in his case."

"Is there any other way to find out?"

"Maybe. I'll investigate tomorrow."

TUESDAY PASSED QUICKLY WHILE I juggled my library work with making arrangements to transport Veronica MacAllister and her sons to San Francisco. It took some persuading, but when I called Veronica with the news about Gabe's business associate's apartment in San Francisco, she eventually agreed with the plan.

I hoped to hear from Cleo about Buzz Bateson's transfer, but when I called her office, I was reminded that she was working back-to-back medical staff committee meetings. She didn't contact me all day, which I took to mean she had no news.

WEDNESDAY MORNING, I CALLED Quinn to let him know I was taking a short day, leaving at noon.

"Anything I need to know about?" he asked.

"No, just a personal day—half day, actually. And I'll ask Cleo to cover for me if anyone has an urgent need for library services."

"All right," he said, "you don't need me to micromanage your time. Just make sure those two CHR visitors aren't planning to show up at the library this afternoon."

"They're still here?"

Quinn muttered something that sounded like a four-letter word. " 'Fraid so. I'm hoping they'll move on after today."

"They've already visited me, so I doubt they'll need to come back to the library."

"There you go, then. I take it you'll be at work the rest of the week?"

"Definitely."

I thanked my lucky stars for the umpteenth time that my boss was one of the good guys—the opposite of how hospital administrators are usually portrayed on TV or in medical thrillers.

"You're sure there isn't something I should know?" Quinn asked. "You're not sick or anything?"

"No. Nothing like that." I thought it was best to keep him out of the Veronica MacAllister situation, at least until Cleo, Mary and I were certain we had things under control for the safety of the widow and her children.

The day before, when Veronica agreed to relocate to Gabe's business associate's apartment in San Francisco, I had let Mary know. She was as relieved as I was.

My attempt to reach Cleo just before leaving for the airport fell flat. Her assistant said she was off the hospital campus to keep a last-minute dental appointment. I asked the assistant if I could refer library patrons to her office for the rest of the day. She offered to take messages. I thanked her and then sent Cleo a text on her private phone explaining what was going on and asking her to text my cell if she came up with any news about Buzz Bateson.

When I reached the airport shortly after noon, everyone else had already arrived. Nick and Gabe stood near Buck's six-passenger Cessna 206. Nick chose it from Buck's fleet, because our Skylane had only four seats.

Veronica and I introduced ourselves, and she pointed out which of her boys was Thomas and which was Jeremiah.

"They're identical, so we usually dress Tommy in blue and Jerry in green," she said. "Otherwise, Heath and I are the only ones who can tell them apart." She spoke of her husband as if he were still alive. I thought how difficult it would be to let go of that last bit of denial.

The little boys looked more like their mother than their father. Fair-skinned and blond. Heath MacAllister had begun balding early, wore glasses, and sported a stubble beard, so any resemblance to him would be hard to detect in two-year-olds.

Veronica and I and got ourselves and her boys buckled in, and once Nick and Gabe were settled in the cockpit, we lifted off for the short flight to San Francisco. The boys seemed to take flying as a grand adventure, peering out the windows, wide-eyed. Their mother was subdued, with good reason. Grief and worry were taking a toll. From her voice on the phone, I had guessed her at my age, but in person, I realized she was in her mid-thirties or beyond. She was an attractive woman, but her beauty was restrained by her mourning clothes and lack of makeup.

We reached the private jet facility adjacent to the San Francisco airport just after one o'clock. It was one in a chain of fixed-base operators specifically built for private jet usage and offered a range of services for private jets. Nick arranged to have the plane tied down, and then escorted us to a car that Buck kept at the FBO in long-term parking. Gabe kept a car of his own parked there, so he led the way to his business associate's apartment in the Russian Hill district of San Francisco. It turned out to be more than a convenient little meeting place. It was spacious, sumptuous, and its many floor-to-ceiling windows offered stunning panoramic views of the city and the bay beyond.

Even Veronica, who had been silent for much of the trip, was wide-eyed as Gabe led us through the vast, three-bedroom expanse. She kept a grip on both of her boys, holding their hands as if terrified that they might cause some sort of damage, although from what I could see, the place was fairly child-proof. There were no priceless antiques or curios sitting around tempting little hands.

Gabe showed Veronica how to operate everything in the place from TV remotes to automatic window blinds, finishing with special emphasis on the security system. He then pointed out a contact list that held every possible number she might need, starting with his own and running the full spectrum from emergencies to public transportation, to grocery stores and nearby restaurants that delivered take-out. Not that she would need much, as the kitchen was already well stocked.

Time was slipping past, and I was getting anxious about returning to Timbergate. I was hoping I'd have time to stop by TMC for a quick update from Cleo about Buzz Bateson when my cell signaled an incoming text. *Cleo.* Finally. It's about time, I thought, but I was wrong. The text was from Ramon Silva, the person I least expected.

When can we talk?

My first thought was that it had something to do with his judo lessons, but we had also talked about his work, both at TMC and at the prison in Potterville. I wanted to talk to him, too. I had never established whether he had encountered Dr. MacAllister at the prison clinic.

I texted back. *This evening?*

Yes, when and where?

I replied. *After seven. You choose where.*

Dojo?

OK

Ramon's message conveyed a feeling of urgency. So much so that my curiosity spiked, along with my apprehension.

I was relieved when Gabe offered to stay in San Francisco for the rest of the evening to make sure Veronica was comfortable in her surroundings, assuring Nick and me that it would be fine for us to go ahead and return to Timbergate without him. He had his own car, and he had further business in the city the following day.

Chapter 14

NICK AND I ARRIVED back in Timbergate a little after five o'clock. I texted Cleo to ask if she was still at work. Her husband, Sig, answered her cell. He explained that she had gone directly home after her visit to the dentist. An emergency root canal had left her a little loopy from the drugs, and she was sleeping it off.

"Can I have her call you later this evening?" he asked.

I remembered my pending meeting with Ramon Silva. "No, it can wait until tomorrow morning."

"I'll let her know, although she might need another day at home."

Sig was a retired dentist who knew all about possible complications of medical and dental procedures. He was also very protective of his wife and her welfare. She and I had been in at least one scrape in the past that resulted in bodily harm to his wife, and I knew he blamed me for that. With that avenue shut down for the night, I switched my thoughts to my meeting with Ramon.

Nick and I stopped at the main house to pick up Ginger, who woofed a welcome. We were relieved to hear that Jack and Amah had done all the evening chores. They even sent us down the lane to our barn-top home with two helpings of Jack's wild turkey burritos.

When Nick was home, we usually went to the dojo on Wednesday nights. If both of us were going that night, I would have to tell him about Ramon's wanting to talk to me. If it wasn't about judo, it had to be about the prison medical clinic at Potterville. Ramon and I had no other topics in common. It was time to admit to Nick that I was being pulled deeper into the mystery of Dr. Mac's concern with organ donation and to own up to my own growing suspicions. Had Dr. Mac come across something that led to his death?

Nick gave me an opening while we were polishing off our burritos.

"Feel like going to the dojo tonight? I know I could use the exercise."

"I do," I said, "but I might have to mix business with pleasure. Ramon Silva is going to meet me there. He just started judo classes last week, and Harry asked me to work with him. That was when you were out of town."

"You're going to be Silva's instructor tonight?" Nick's eyes narrowed just a smidge. "What part is business and what part is pleasure?"

I laughed. "The judo part is pleasure. He texted me earlier while we were in the city. He said he wants to talk, but I'm afraid a talk with Ramon is going to be work-related. You already know there's cause for doubt about Dr. Mac's stairwell accident. Otherwise, we wouldn't have taken the widow and her sons to the safe house in San Francisco."

I went on to explain the coincidence of Ramon Silva and Dr. Heath MacAllister both being employed at TMC *and* at the prison clinic in Potterville, and that I'd never had a chance to ask Ramon if he knew Dr. Mac. I told Nick about Buzz Bateson becoming a hit-and-run victim so soon after he found Dr. Mac in that stairwell.

"Buzz was a first responder. What if that hit-and-run was meant to silence him?"

"Seems like a stretch," Nick said. "but even so, what's the interpreter got to do with that?"

"Maybe nothing, but he seems insistent that we talk. I'm hoping he has some clue to what was on Dr. Mac's mind when he came to me the day before his fall."

"So that's where you're going with this talk tonight?"

"That's it. I've already missed two opportunities."

Nick walked around behind me and gently massaged my trapezius muscles. "Is it too late to ask you to beg off? Stay home?"

"I can't." I reached for his hand. "You're coming too, aren't you?"

"Of course."

SEVERAL STUDENTS WERE ALREADY at the dojo when we arrived. The class was for beginning and intermediate adults. Ramon, already in his gi, greeted Nick and me as we entered. After I made introductions, Ramon walked over to speak to Harry while Nick and I went into the changing rooms.

Out on the mat, Nick worked with a slender, gray-haired woman, a first-time student Harry had assigned to him. Nick would be gentle with her and make sure she didn't hurt herself. Ramon had been paired with me again, and only a few minutes of our workout had passed when he spoke quietly to me.

"Can we talk after class?"

"Yes. I think we should." With that settled, I corrected his stance and grip, and he completed a respectable *ogoshi*, hoisting me over his shoulder and dropping me to the mat.

Ramon offered me a hand up. "Will your boyfriend mind?"

"Not at all. I'd like him to be included, unless you're planning to reveal confidential details about TMC patients. Nick knows I've been wanting to ask you some questions."

TWO HOURS LATER THE dojo was empty except for Harry, Nick, Ramon and me. Harry escorted us out and locked up, in a hurry to get home to Rella, who was back from Texas. She had arrived at their condo just as Harry was leaving for the dojo, so he was eager to get going.

That left the three of us driving to a nearby twenty-four-hour coffee shop. We ordered decaf and razzleberry pie all around. Ramon kept rolling his shoulders to relieve tension, which I attributed to Nick's presence. I nudged Nick's leg under the table. He took the hint by engaging Ramon in a few minutes of small talk, asking him where he was from, about his family, and eventually easing into questions about Ramon's work and career plans.

"Aimee tells me you speak several languages," Nick said. "I admire that. I squeak by in Spanish and French, but I'd like to be fluent in at least one foreign language."

Ramon's shoulders softened. Language was his comfort zone. "You can learn." He took a card from his wallet and handed it to Nick. "It's not so difficult, really. If you want a tutor, call me."

This time it was Nick who nudged me under the table. *My turn.*

"Ramon, there's something I've been meaning to ask you." I moved my empty pie plate and leaned in. "Did you ever meet Dr. MacAllister? Either at TMC or at the prison clinic in Potterville?"

"Sure, both places." Ramon sobered. "Damn shame the poor guy's life was snuffed out by a shoelace."

"You heard about his shoes?"

Ramon nodded. "It's common knowledge all through the hospital. The personnel who transported the doctor back to the ER spread the story because it seemed like such rotten luck. A burned-out light and a loose shoelace. What a grisly warning to the rest of us about safety." He shook his head. "Have you heard how his family is doing?"

I wasn't prepared to go there. Nick knew that, so he left it for me to respond.

"They're coping, from what I hear." Then a thought came. "Did you ever meet his wife or his little boys?"

"No, but he liked to show pictures of them that he kept on his cell phone. We had dinner together sometimes when both of us were working at the prison clinic in Potterville."

Just the opener I needed. "Did that happen very often?"

"Once or twice a month. He was more compassionate with the inmate patients than the other doctors. Really wanted to communicate with them and understand their medical problems."

"Working there must have been depressing for both of you," I said. "Have you been called to interpret at the prison clinic since Dr. MacAllister's death?"

"I'll be going up there tomorrow. Dr. Iversen texted me just before I came to the dojo tonight. He's expecting those two representatives from CHR to be there, and he needs an interpreter on hand in case they want to communicate with any of the undocumented inmates who are clinic patients."

"Makes sense," Nick said. "Are you driving up in the morning?"

Ramon blew a sigh. "Yep. Got to get an early start. There's a long stretch of nothing between here and there."

Neither Nick nor I mentioned our recent flight to Potterville and our bird's-eye view of the prison facility. After half an hour at the coffee shop, I still had no idea why Ramon had asked to talk to me.

"Ramon, I had the impression there was something on your mind. Do you want to tell me about it?"

"I'm not sure I should." He glanced at Nick. "No offense, but it's sensitive, and about work."

"Tell you what," Nick said, "my rig's almost out of gas. Why don't I leave the two of you here while I go fill up? Back in about half an hour?" We both looked at Ramon.

"That sounds good," he said.

With Nick gone, Ramon looked around at the nearly deserted coffee shop. He moved his chair closer to me. "I'm sorry if I insulted your boyfriend."

"Don't give it a thought. He's a big boy."

"Does he know you have to withhold parts of your work from him?"

"Absolutely, and it goes both ways." I reached out, patted the table next to where his hand rested. "Ramon, please tell me what's on your mind."

"I will, but first please promise that you didn't hear this from me." He used a paper napkin to wipe away the sweat that glistened on his forehead and his upper lip.

"Of course. I promise. Are you sure I'm the person you want to tell?"

"Yes. I know you best of anyone at TMC. I don't know who else to trust." He wiped at his brow again. Put the napkin on the table. He hesitated so long before speaking that I thought he'd changed his mind.

"Nick will be back soon." I glanced toward the restaurant entrance. "We don't have a lot of time."

Ramon's words came out in a rush. "There's something wrong big time at the prison. I think Dr. MacAllister figured out what's going on up there." He reached for his water glass with a shaky hand and tipped it out on the table. After we soaked up the spill with our napkins, I reached out to put a calming hand on his arm.

"Ramon, you're obviously very troubled about this. Did Dr. MacAllister confide something in you?"

"No, but I could sense that he was not happy with some of the procedures there." I remembered Veronica MacAllister saying her husband had not liked working at the clinic. Ramon's story certainly matched up with hers.

"But what goes on at that prison clinic has nothing to do with my job at TMC. Why are you telling me about this?"

"Because maybe it *does* have to do with your job at TMC—if Dr. MacAllister's fall down that stairwell was not an accident."

And there it was.

Chapter 15

———◆———

I FELT THE VIBRATION of Ramon's knee bouncing rapidly under the table. *Handle this with care.*

"You have no idea what Dr. MacAllister suspected?"

"No, but he cautioned me to be alert and to let him know if anything I heard while interpreting struck me as odd or suspicious."

"No idea what he meant by that?"

"Just that it involved patients at the prison clinic in Potterville. He said he was going to follow up on it. I thought he might have talked to you."

"Why me?"

"Because he spoke highly of you. More than anyone else at the hospital."

"But if it was a problem at the prison, why would he involve me?"

"I guess you're right. It doesn't make sense." His knee continued its relentless tempo. "You don't have any idea?"

"No. Our only conversations were about TMC's Ethics Committee." Ramon's story didn't jibe with what I knew. Dr. Mac had issues with TMC's organ donor procedure. That had nothing to do with any concern he might have about prison inmates. "Maybe it was something simple," I said. "Did he ever mention feeling that the medical care at the prison was inadequate?"

"Nothing specific. Just what I told you. He asked me to be observant. To tell him if any of the inmates complained to me."

"Because he thought they'd speak to you in their native language? Without fear of being overheard by clinic personnel?"

"Yes, that's what I thought. Dr. MacAllister didn't put it in those terms, but I felt it was implied."

"And did you ever hear complaints—anything that you passed on to him?"

"Nothing too unusual from the convicted prison inmates. I only communicated with those who were ill, and their complaints were mostly related to health. Sometimes things like bad food. But the clinic also treated the undocumented immigrants being held in the adjacent detention center."

"And did you have contact with them as well?"

"Yes. When they had health issues, they were shuttled over to the prison's medical clinic for medical attention."

"Dr. MacAllister treated both?" I asked. "The prison inmates and the population in the detention center?"

"Yes, as did the other doctors under contract with CHR to staff the prison's medical clinic."

"Ramon, is that what's bothering you? Did you hear a complaint from one of the detainees? Something you interpreted for Dr. MacAllister?"

"There was something." I watched Ramon's left eyelid begin twitching rapidly. He rubbed at the lid, then continued. "One of the detainees was being treated for an outbreak of severe allergic dermatitis on his hands and arms. Dr. Mac told me to ask him about exposure to any chemicals or irritants. The patient said he was doing regular janitorial work in the detention housing unit, and that he had to use many harsh cleaning products."

"How did Dr. Mac treat the patient?"

"He prescribed a corticosteroid and told the patient to avoid the causes of the problem. The patient asked about using rubber gloves, but Dr. Mac said that might not be enough protection because the inflammation was so severe. It needed time to heal."

"That makes sense. How did the patient respond?"

"That's the disturbing thing. The patient became anxious and fearful, saying he didn't want to be put in solitary confinement."

"Why would he expect that?" I asked. "It sounds like he was a model detainee if he was being paid to work at the facility."

"That's part of the problem. He wasn't being paid. The detainees were forced to work without pay and were threatened with harsh punishment if they complained. The patient said it had happened to his cousin, who had been swept up with him and incarcerated in the detention center." Ramon pressed his fingers against his eyelid to stop a new bout of twitching. "The patient said his cousin went to the clinic with the same sort of rash and never returned. The word got out that he had been placed in solitary for refusing to work. A month later, he had not been seen again."

What Ramon described sounded as if the prison was using detainees as unpaid labor, but nothing about what he described related to organ donation at TMC.

"You implied that Dr. Mac knew something so extreme about how inmates were treated that it might have gotten him killed," I said. "Is this what you were talking about?"

"I think it's part of the reason. But what if there were other things? Worse things?"

"Ramon, I'll keep everything you've said in mind, but there is another explanation for Dr. Mac's accident. Remember the shoelace? One of his shoes came off in that stairwell. That could have caused his fall. It's the most likely reason."

"But it's not the only one." He leaned in, voice low. "Don't you agree?"

"I'm not convinced either way, but I have another question

for you. Did you ever notice what kind of shoes Dr. Mac wore at work?"

"Why? Oh, I get what you mean. Did they have laces?" He hesitated, thinking. "Damn. I'm sorry, I never noticed."

Before I could respond, I spotted Nick coming through the restaurant door, back from his gas station run. Time had run out.

"Ramon, while you're at the prison tomorrow, please try to think of anything else that might have been on Dr. Mac's mind. Particularly anything that could have involved Criteria Health Resources or Timbergate Medical Center." I wasn't ready to get specific with him about organ donation. That could be a slippery slope into confidential medical staff territory.

"Of course." His response was restrained, as if he felt he had no other choice. He walked from our table to the restaurant's exit with the measured gait of a condemned man.

ON THE WAY HOME, Nick asked if I'd learned anything useful from Ramon.

"Not really. I was hoping for something a lot more specific than what I got."

"Want to talk about it? Do some brainstorming?"

I glanced at the time on his dashboard. Almost eleven o'clock. "Maybe in the morning. I'm exhausted."

THURSDAY MORNING BROUGHT A much-needed shower to Timbergate's parched terrain. Temperatures had dropped to breezy low seventies, and I finally had a reason to wear something other than sandals and sleeveless dresses. In my favorite black slacks, a white knit tunic top and waterproof ankle boots, I was ready for work.

I went to the kitchen for coffee and found Nick standing shoeless at the stove in his washed-out Levis and a white T-shirt. He was flipping pancakes.

"Barefoot in the kitchen, rattling pots and pans. This

picture would be perfect if only you were pregnant," I said, trying to control a snicker.

He pointed with the spatula at the dinette table. "Sit down. You're going to eat breakfast."

"Hotcakes are not going to last me past ten o'clock. I need protein."

"Look in the oven, my dear."

I found scrambled eggs and sausage links. "That's more like it. But what are you going to eat?"

"Don't threaten the cook," he said. "There's plenty there for both of us." I took my share and headed back to the table, where he dropped three golden pancakes on my plate and five on his.

We settled into a few moments of silent eating before I asked about his plans for the day.

"I just heard from Buck. I told you I'd ask him about your hospital's new corporate owners. Turns out his financial advisers say CHR's been showing impressive growth. He's always on the lookout for companies that offer drug counseling and rehab to their employees."

"If CHR is doing that, the word hasn't gotten out around here," I said.

"They just took over TMC, so it's probably still in the works. Anyway, he wants me to fly him down to the corporate head-quarters in SoCal to meet with some of their financial folks."

That made sense, so I let it go. I was more interested in giving Nick a capsule version of what I'd learned from Ramon the night before. He had told me nothing that shed a bad light on the CHR-owned medical clinic at the prison. In particular, nothing to explain Dr. Mac's organ donor concern and why he wanted it discussed in TMC's Ethics Committee. On the other hand, I wanted to hear Nick's reaction to the news that the operators of the private prison were using detained immigrants as free labor. And about the harsh punishment, time in solitary, if they refused.

"Since you and Buck are flying to CHR headquarters in SoCal to meet with their top executives, don't you think that's something they should know about? They're operating a medical clinic in that prison. That sort of thing could taint their reputation. Guilt by association."

"I'll tell Buck about it," Nick said, "but it's not likely the topic will come up in his meetings since it's nothing to do with why we're going there. Your friend Ramon's tale about solitary as punishment for detainees sounds like an unsubstantiated rumor, and not something for Buck to get involved in at this point. What he's interested in is the prison's drug rehab program and how it will be administered by the CHR clinic there. And, of course, CHR's prospectus."

He had a point when I looked at it from his angle, so I let it go and changed the subject.

"This doesn't sound like a day trip." I drizzled syrup on my pancakes.

"No, it'll be at least a couple of days. I'll be back by the weekend for sure." He took the syrup bottle from my hand. "That's why I wanted to have at least one decent meal with you before I go. Even if it's breakfast."

I felt the sting of tears threatening. So many departures on short notice. I was used to it, but it was still disappointing. Even more disappointing was the possibility that the Dr. Mac mystery might put Nick and me at odds. I tried to shake the feeling

"Ginger and I will hold the fort," I said.

Nick and I finished our breakfast, and then went our separate ways. I headed off to work and he prepared for his flight to SoCal with Buck.

I'D BEEN AT WORK for a couple of hours when Cleo called after her morning committee meeting to apologize for not covering with library patrons the day before.

"No problem," I said. "Your assistant sent me a few messages, but the library managed to survive for four hours without either of us. Are you feeling well enough to work?"

"Feeling okay pain-wise, but the pills I'm on make concentrating a challenge. You'd be amazed at the number of typos my word processing program has had to auto-correct this morning. I was typing minutes of an Orthopedic Department meeting just now. I tried to type *below-knee* amputation and it came out *baloney* amputation." Cleo laughed softly. "Now that I think of it, some of our medical staff meetings could be improved by cutting out the baloney."

"Speaking of meetings, do you have to work a lunch meeting today?"

"No. Why? Do you have intel to share?"

"I'd like to run something by you." Even as I said that, I wondered if her head was clear enough to help me process what I'd heard from Ramon about the prison clinic.

"Lunch at Margie's?" Cleo asked.

"Not today. I feel like walking, but only if you're up to it."

"I could use some fresh air."

"Then I'll pick up a couple of vending machine sandwiches from the cafeteria if you think you can stomach tuna."

I heard Cleo's soft groan. "Not for me. I'll bring a protein drink. Meet you at the employee entrance?"

"That works."

"Are you inviting Mary Barton, too?"

"I'd rather you and I talk first. Then we can decide who else needs to know about this new piece of the puzzle." I thought for a moment. "There's a chance it's not even the same puzzle."

"You're sounding very cryptic. Or is it just the Percocet swimming around in my brain?"

"It's probably not your meds." I spotted a patron coming through the library entrance. "Cleo, I've got to go. I promise to make myself clear at lunch."

What I thought was a patron turned out to be Daniel Littletree, Laurie's husband. I had seldom seen him since he began working at TMC as a respiratory therapist, but he was every bit as attractive as I remembered. He still wore his black hair in a long, neat braid. His Native American ancestry had gifted him with strong cheekbones, a firm jaw, and bronzed skin the color of polished maple. With his remarkable looks and Laurie's ebony beauty, I could imagine what a beautiful child they would have.

I quickly learned that Daniel wasn't dropping by for library services. He strode over to my desk with his chin held high and tightness around his eyes.

"Aimee, we have to talk." His rigid jaw muscles made it clear he wasn't happy.

"Daniel, what is it?" I got up and gestured toward a small table where we could sit together.

"No thanks, this won't take long." He clenched his fists, then shook them out. "Laurie told me that you asked her to appear at an Ethics Committee meeting."

"Yes. Buzz Bateson has been transferred to Southern California. Laurie is the only witness we have …." I stopped, realizing I shouldn't divulge committee business to Daniel.

"Don't worry about giving away secrets, Aimee. I know she's been asked to tell your committee what she saw in that stairwell where Dr. MacAllister was found."

"Then why are you here?"

He shook his head. "After that other incident, when you and Laurie were stalked and threatened, do you really have to ask?" He pinned me with a look of disgust. "Think about it, Aimee. She's pregnant. Our first child. I want you to leave her out of this."

"But I've already told the committee chair that Laurie will attend. Has she changed her mind?" *Or had he demanded that she back out?*

"We talked it over. She's already reported everything she saw, everything that happened while she was in that stairwell. It's all in Dr. MacAllister's patient record. She even filled out an incident report. That should be enough to satisfy the committee."

"But the members might have follow-up questions. Something that she hasn't thought of."

"Then you and the chair can decide how to handle that. I don't want Laurie identified with this case until it's clear what really happened to the doctor that night."

What he was saying didn't make sense. "Daniel, the people on duty in the ER that night all know Laurie was in that stairwell, that she administered CPR. It's not a secret."

"That's bad enough, but she's only mentioned in the context of her medical treatment of the doctor. This Ethics meeting is different. She would be testifying before a committee that's investigating the doctor's manner of death. *Manner*, Aimee. You know what that means. They're going to ask her if she thinks he was murdered." He moved toward the library exit. "I don't want that on her. Not now. I'm asking you to tell her she isn't needed at that meeting."

I understood his point. "I'll talk to Dr. Poole about this. Maybe there's another—"

Daniel stopped, turned to face me. "She's already been through hell once." He pointed a trembling finger at me. "You and everyone else might think Buzz Bateson's hit-and-run was random, but I'm not willing to take that chance. I won't let it happen to Laurie and our child." He took a breath, obviously trying to calm himself. "Take care of this, Aimee. You're her friend, for God's sake."

Chapter 16

CLEO AND I WALKED to a pocket park with a small pond a few blocks from the hospital, finishing our lunch along the way. We sat on a bench and watched a mother and her two toddlers throwing popcorn to a flock of eager ducks.

I filled Cleo in on my visit from Daniel Littletree, and when I finished, she stiffened at the news that Laurie had backed out.

"That stinks, Aimee, but I suppose Daniel has a point, even if he does seem to stretch credibility about what happened to Buzz."

"I hope you're right about that," I said, "but that reminds me. You were going to follow up on Buzz's transfer to Southern California. Have you come up with anything about his condition or how long he'll be there?"

"Unfortunately, no. All my corporate contacts are gone since CHR bought TMC. It takes a long time to build those relationships. All I know is that he's in a rehab facility somewhere in the L.A. area."

"Did you find out who signed off on his transfer?"

"Not yet. I've had no excuse to access his medical record,

and I don't want to draw attention by asking around at the hospital."

"Wouldn't it be the primary who was following him in ICU?"

"Probably, but his injuries would have involved any number of specialists. Only one would be the primary." She took in a deep breath. "I'll keep trying to find a way around HIPAA, but don't count on it."

"In the meantime, we promised Dr. Poole we'd have two eye witnesses at the Ethics meeting, and now we have none." I watched a fluffy white duck waddle up to where we sat. It cocked its head at me, looking for a handout. "Sorry, Daisy, or Donald, I got nothin'." The fowl uttered a cheeky "quack" and waddled back to the popcorn-flinging toddlers.

"Sometimes I wish life were that simple for us," Cleo said. "Just figure out where our next meal is coming from."

"That's pretty much what we all do, isn't it?"

"Maybe. Sometimes this job gets to me, though. I feel like we're playing mama duck to a damn large flock of patients, and they have no idea what's going on behind the scenes."

I gave her shoulders a quick hug. "You're not usually so maudlin. Is that your medication talking?"

"Could be. Who knows what they're doing to my mood?"

"How's your pain level? Do you feel okay?"

Cleo wiggled her jaw. "Pain's down to a three, but enough about my dental health. We're almost out of time. Let's get to the rest of what you wanted to tell me. You said it was something about Ramon Silva."

I filled her in on everything Ramon had told me about the prison clinic at Potterville, and the detention facility where inmates were being used for free labor.

"Solitary?" Cleo stood and shook herself. "He said some of the detainees were confined to *solitary*?"

"I know it sounds inconceivable, but that's what he told me."

"As abysmal as it might be, what would that have to do with Dr. Mac and TMC or organ donors?"

"Nothing that I can think of. I hoped if we brainstormed about it, we might think of some possible connection."

"Okay, give me a sec." Cleo took a couple of deep breaths and patted her cheeks with the palms of her hands. "Ah, better. Now I do have one question. Did you happen to ask Ramon if he's ever noticed what kind of shoes Dr. Mac wore at work?"

"I did, and he said he hadn't."

"And you said he was going out to the prison today?"

"That's right. The two CHR officials who've been snooping around the hospital are going to be there at the clinic today. They told Ramon they wanted him on hand in case they needed an interpreter." I got up and brushed some drifting leaves off my slacks. "Ramon implied that he's concerned about something more sinister than what he's already told me."

"I hope not," Cleo said, "but for now, we need to get back to work. I'll keep all this in mind, but I don't know that I can make much sense of it."

"Do you want to give Dr. Poole the bad news about Laurie's backing out of the Ethics meeting, or shall I?"

Cleo worked her jaw for a moment. "I know I volunteered to talk to her about Buzz Bateson the other day, but Ethics is your committee, Aimee. I'm afraid you'll have to *woman up* and deal with Poole directly from now on, or you'll lose her respect." She hooked her arm in mine and we began walking back. "Don't worry, she won't kill the messenger. But let me know how she reacts. She might even cancel the meeting."

"If she threatens that, I'll remind her that Dr. Mac's autopsy is still at stake."

"Good plan," Cleo said. "If she cancels, we don't know how long we can keep Dr. Seldon from pressuring the widow about it."

Back in the library, I put in a call to Dr. Poole's office. Cleo was right, I had to maintain a façade of fearlessness, no matter how intimidating Poole might be—or any of the other doctors on the medical staff, for that matter.

Poole was busy with patients, so I requested a callback. For the rest of the afternoon, I took a slight hit of adrenaline each time my phone rang. At five o'clock, I decided to put Dr. Poole out of my mind and go home. That's when her call came.

"Machado? Dr. Poole here. What's on your mind?"

Here goes. "About the Ethics Committee meeting, I'm afraid we've lost both of the eyewitnesses who discovered Dr. MacAllister in the stairwell." I waited for her response. She stayed silent, so I went on, explaining about Buzz Bateson's transfer to a Southern California hospital and Laurie Littletree's change of heart, brought on by her husband's concerns.

"Bateson's out of commission. That I understand," Poole said, "but Laurie's not one to bow to pressure, even from her own husband. I'm surprised."

I debated with myself whether to tell Poole that Laurie was pregnant. "I'm sure she and Daniel have their reasons."

"Do you know what they are?" Poole asked.

"Um ... I do, but I would be speaking out of turn—"

"She's pregnant, isn't she? I see her at the hospital often enough to know the signs."

"If you know that, you can understand why they're reluctant."

"Of course," Poole said. "And I'm not unsympathetic, or cold-hearted, despite what you may think. However, I am *very* concerned that the committee will not recommend this death be investigated if neither eye witness is available to answer questions about what they observed in that stairwell. Particularly when they're told that the widow refuses to involve law enforcement." I heard her heavy sigh. "This is turning into a fiasco. I have a mind to cancel."

"We still have time," I said. "The meeting is more than a week away. Can't we put off canceling?"

"What will that gain us? This has been going on for nine

days already. The only other significant witness would have been the widow, and we know that's out of the question. She's refused to cooperate."

I hoped Poole wouldn't break her word and try to persuade Veronica MacAllister to attend the meeting. Neither Cleo nor I had told Poole about the MacAllister family's departure to San Francisco.

"Right now, Dr. Mac's widow is experiencing grief over the loss of her husband," I said. "And Laurie Littletree is dealing with her own husband's protective attitude. If we wait a little longer, maybe one or both of those women will have a change of heart and decide to attend."

"You're grasping, Aimee, but you do have a point. I'll hold off for now, but no promises. We're going to need more than what we have."

That was the best I was going to get, so I agreed and we ended our call. Good thing it was quitting time, because my axillary glands had wreaked havoc on my blouse.

Reluctant to go home to an empty apartment, I considered my options. Check in with Harry? Probably not. He and Rella had the same challenges to their time together that Nick and I had. I didn't want to intrude on them. Hang out with Amah and Jack? They'd already been babysitting Ginger all day. Jack usually worked on writing his outdoor articles in the evening, and Thursday was Amah's night to read to patients in a nursing home. I'd gone with her before a few times, but my heart wasn't in it this time, so I collected Ginger and headed down the lane to the empty apartment over the barn.

After evening chores, I treated Ginger to a generous portion of her favorite canned food, and then searched my cupboards and fridge for some sort of dinner for myself.

Soda crackers, peanut butter and Amah's peach jam. Carbs, protein, and fruit. I could convince myself that was a healthy main course. I made half a dozen little cracker sandwiches and settled down in front of the TV with the first three seasons of the BBC version of *Sherlock Holmes*. A loan from Amah.

I had just hit the play button when Nick called to say good night. I paused the disc and we traded a few bits of comfortable conversation, agreeing to stay away from heavy topics. The call made me miss him more.

I was an hour into season one of *Sherlock*, in my pajamas and struggling to stay awake, when my cell phone alerted me to a text. I paused the DVD. The text was from Ramon Silva.

Need to talk

When?

Tonight

Where are you?

Driving. Half hour away

Call me when you get to town?

No. Meet in TMC chapel 30 min

At nine thirty, I didn't look forward to getting dressed and going back to town, but Ramon's urgent message had banished any thought of sleep.

Chapter 17

I REACHED TMC JUST in time and made my way to the chapel, where Ramon was kneeling in the front row of the small, otherwise empty room. At least I thought it was Ramon. The only light source was the flicker of devotional candles. I walked closer, keeping my steps as light as possible, until I was sure.

"Ramon?" I whispered.

His head jerked around. "Aimee. Good, it's you." Even in the dim light, I caught his startled, apprehensive look. He scooted over, making room for me to sit next to him.

"I got here as fast as I could," I said. "What is it? Why did you text me? Is it something about the prison clinic?"

He swiveled his head, taking in the room. "Yes, but we should leave. I only meant for us to meet up here. We need to go somewhere else to talk." His anxiety level was prompting worst-case scenarios.

"Where do you want to go?" I asked.

"I don't know. I hoped you could suggest somewhere private."

Momentarily stumped, I searched my mind for a place

where we wouldn't be observed or interrupted. Only one possibility came to mind. I texted Harry, asking if the dojo was closed. My luck held, and he answered right away, wanting to know why I was asking. I told him to call me, which he did.

"What's up, Sis?"

"I can't explain now, but trust me, I need to use the space for maybe half an hour."

"Is this another one of your covert activities?"

"Sort of."

"Does it involve the situation you and I talked about before?"

"Maybe," I said.

Harry confirmed that the dojo was already locked for the night and explained where to find the spare key, but only after I promised to fill him in the next day.

"Okay, okay," I said. "I promise." I was on safe ground there, because nothing Ramon could tell me about the prison clinic would breach the confidentiality of TMC's patients.

Ramon insisted that we take my car, saying his was not running right and that he had barely made it back to Timbergate.

At the dojo, I locked the doors from the inside, and we kept the lights to the large workout space turned off. We went to the sensei's office, where I lit a crook-neck desk lamp and bent it low to shed minimum light.

I liked Ramon, but after all this intrigue, I was beginning to feel impatient with him. Letting that feeling show would not help. I tried to keep my tone patient.

"Ramon, you have something to tell me. Please, let's do this."

He nodded. "You are the only one I will tell this to. You must decide where to take what I say, and you must promise not to reveal that I was the one who told you." He leaned forward in his chair, elbows on his knees, hands clasped.

My stomach flipped in a full somersault. Whatever Ramon knew had him alarmed, and now he wanted to dump it on my shoulders. I wished I could rewind the evening and simply not have answered Ramon's text. But maybe it wasn't as bad as he thought.

"All right," I said, "I'll keep you out of it. Now please tell me what's on your mind."

"Do you remember when I told you about the detainee at the prison clinic who was treated for a rash?"

"Yes. Did you see him there today?"

"No. But I asked one of the clinic's medical assistants about him." Ramon stopped, gulped in a breath, and then went on. "She said he was not brought back to the clinic for follow-up of his rash."

"But that could be easily explained, maybe—"

Ramon shook his head forcefully. "No, no, let me finish. The CMA and I have become close. Kenzie is like me, trying to earn enough to finish her training. She wants to become a registered nurse."

"Are you saying she's your girlfriend?" I asked.

Ramon's face colored. "I suppose she is," he said, "although we haven't let on to anyone at the prison."

That news was a momentary distraction, but I wanted to keep Ramon's momentum going. I was afraid he might reconsider and shut down.

"Go on, what did your girlfriend say about the patient with the rash?"

"She heard he also had been confined to solitary—just like his cousin—for telling the guards what the doctor ordered ... that he shouldn't work with the cleaning solvents."

Not a pleasant thing to hear, but a prison is a harsh place, and I suspected the detention center was, as well. "Is that why you're so upset? Do you think the detainees are being abused?"

"What do you think? Solitary as punishment for trying to follow the doctor's orders? For wanting a severe skin condition to heal?"

"What about the other man? The cousin? Do you know if

he has been released from solitary?" I wondered how many isolation cells there could be in a facility that size.

Ramon scooted to the edge of his chair. "My friend told me that the first man, that cousin, has never been seen again. Kenzie asked one of the detention center guards about him. She was told that he had been deported."

"Maybe it's a good thing," I said. "Better than being imprisoned."

"We would hope so, but the thing that worries me is that the guard reported Kenzie to her superiors at the clinic for asking about that missing detainee. She was reprimanded and threatened with termination."

"When did this happen?"

"Her hearing was this morning. She told me about it this afternoon, just as I was leaving to come back to Timbergate."

"Did she say what reason she was given for the reprimand? Or which of her superiors issued the termination threat?"

"Something about overstepping the scope of her employment," Ramon said. "It wasn't just one person, there was a panel of three people. One was the nursing director of the clinic, and the two men from CHR home office were there as well."

"The same men who have been visiting here? Dr. Durham and Dr. Coatney?"

"Yes. Kenzie said they were introduced to her as special guests."

"What about Dr. Iversen, the medical director?" I asked. "Seems like he should have been in charge."

Ramon's brow furrowed. "He wasn't present. Kenzie says he shows up at the prison clinic only once or twice a week."

"Is Kenzie all right, Ramon? Are you worried about her?"

"She tells me she's strong, that she'll be okay, but I've encouraged her to look for other work. I don't like leaving her up there in that isolated place." An involuntary spasm shook his shoulders, triggering a shudder of my own.

"Ramon, have you thought of talking to Dr. Iversen about this incident? As the medical director of the clinic, he should have been at that hearing. Or at least have had input."

"No." His eyes widened. "I don't know him well enough. I'm afraid to talk to anyone too closely connected to the prison clinic. That could cause more problems for Kenzie."

"Then what do you expect *me* to do with this information?"

"For now, I just wanted someone to know about it," he said. "I'll be leaving Timbergate for a while, so I gave Kenzie your name and told her she could reach you at the TMC library if she … if she ends up without a job. I hoped that you might help her somehow. Her full name is Mackenzie Eyler. If you meet, you'll recognize her easily. She looks like a red-haired little angel." He gave me her cell phone number and her email address.

"Wait, what do you mean you're leaving? Where are you going?"

"The men from CHR's home office have offered me a full-time position at their flagship hospital in Southern California. It's an offer I can't refuse. In one year's time, I'll earn enough to finish my schooling."

That news took me by surprise. Ramon was leaving town and placing the fate of his girlfriend in my hands.

"Do you realize what you're asking of me? I can't make promises about any of this."

"I know that, but there is one thing I hope you can do." His eyes grew moist and his voice had a ragged edge. "Please find a reason to visit the prison clinic. A reason to meet Kenzie. She needs someone safe to confide in."

"That's an unworkable request. What plausible reason could I have for going there?"

"You're a librarian. Maybe something about taking materials for the detainees to study? To help them learn English words to describe their medical symptoms."

Rats. If the circumstances were different, that would have occurred to me, but I was looking for a way to nix his idea, instead of a way to make it work.

"Won't the clinic hire someone else to interpret for them after you leave?"

"Eventually, but not right away. There aren't nearly enough certified medical interpreters to meet the need, and as the sweeps of undocumented immigrants increase, the need will only grow greater."

I told Ramon I would consider his request, but made no promises. As I drove him back to the TMC parking garage, I heard Nick's voice in my ear. *Stay the hell out of this.*

That reminded me of Nick's trip to SoCal with Buck to investigate the potential drug rehab program that was to be implemented at the prison using the CHR clinic resources. I asked Ramon if he had heard anything about it.

"No. Nothing. But you could ask Kenzie when you contact her. If that was going to happen, she would know." *When you contact her.* His foregone conclusion. I let it drop without responding.

When we reached the space where Ramon had left his car, he hesitated a moment before getting out of mine.

"Aimee, would you mind waiting while I make sure my car will start?"

"Of course not. How long have you been having trouble with it?"

"Not long, but it's not the usual kind of car trouble." He stared out my windshield at his car, shook his head. "On my way back from Potterville, I was driving slowly on a winding stretch, and some tailgater rear-ended me on a curve. I drove off the road into a tree."

"Oh, my gosh. Did the other vehicle stop?"

"No."

"But that's hit-and-run," I said. "Did you call it in? Get CHP to come and take your report?"

"No. I didn't want to wait up there on that lonely stretch in the dark in case the person who hit me came back. I've heard stories about road rage and people being shot. I was able to get the car going and made it this far, but barely." Ramon banged a fist into the palm of his hand. "Damn, I didn't want to tell you about my car, but I don't want to be stranded here in the middle of the night, either."

"Ramon, if you need a ride home, I'm fine with it. If you need to call CHP and a towing service, I can wait."

"That's a problem. I don't have towing coverage." He made a sound that could have been a hiccup or a sob. "I've been driving without insurance, Aimee. I can't call this in. I'm afraid I'll lose my license. As it is, I don't know how I'll be able to take the job in L.A. without a car. I have to get it running."

Hearing that, I remembered that Ramon was over twenty-one, but in some ways, he was still a kid.

"Ramon, don't you have family you can call on for help?"

"My grandparents in Massachusetts raised me. They can't help, they would only worry."

Oh, boy. What to do? Nick was out of town. That left Harry, who had been testing off the charts in mechanical aptitude since the fifth grade. I sent a text. He called. *Peeved.*

"You *do* know it's almost midnight?"

"Yes, and you could at least sound concerned. How do you know I'm not in the Emergency Room—or in jail?"

"Are you?"

"Well no, but you could have asked."

"You're right. Knowing you, either of those is possible." Harry cleared his throat. "What do you want now? Are you still at the dojo?"

"No, and don't worry, I locked up and put the key back where it belongs."

I explained the situation with Ramon's car. Harry agreed to drop by the parking garage the next day to have a look. Of course, he reminded me that I was going to owe him big time, but made it clear that he didn't want my firstborn child.

"What I *do* want, is a report on everything your friend told you tonight. Down to the last infinitesimal detail."

"Deal," I said.

Chapter 18

I DROPPED RAMON OFF at his small apartment in Timbergate after extracting his promise to keep in touch on a regular basis. Home in Coyote Creek, I let Ginger out for a few minutes to take care of business. With her settled back inside, I set my clock for morning but soon realized I wouldn't sleep with all the day's incidents swirling in my mind. Especially since I had promised to relate all of it to Harry.

My dominant left brain insisted that I put those incidents in some sort of order, so I sat at the dinette table in our little kitchen making notes at one o'clock in the morning.

First, Nick had flown Buck to CHR's headquarters in Southern California to talk about investing in the corporate chain. In the two months since CHR bought Timbergate Medical Center, I'd heard nothing that made me think CHR and Buck Sawyer would be a good match. There was the proposed drug rehab arrangement between the Potterville Prison and the CHR clinic, but everything I had heard suggested that had not been implemented.

Moreover, CHR's penny-pinching tactics since taking over Timbergate Medical Center didn't seem to fit with Buck's philanthropic values. He was one of several billionaires who had signed a pledge agreeing to donate more than half his wealth to philanthropy.

Reminding myself that Buck's investments were none of my business, I left that tack and moved on to Daniel Littletree. He had made it clear to me that Laurie would not attend the Ethics Committee meeting to tell what she had observed in the stairwell where Dr. MacAllister was fatally injured. I had relayed that to Cleo, who informed me that Buzz Bateson, the other eyewitness in that stairwell, had been transferred to a rehab facility in SoCal before Dr. Poole could question him.

So, both eyewitnesses who should have appeared at the Ethics meeting were unavailable. Which led to my toe-curling phone call to Dr. Poole to deliver that news, resulting in her threatening to cancel the meeting.

Then came my late-night meet-up with Ramon, who informed me he was leaving Timbergate for a better job. Worse yet, his girlfriend at the prison clinic had dropped a mini-bombshell that made the goings-on at the prison's detention center sound like something out of *Les Miserables*.

Detainees were being put in solitary confinement for requesting time off from work, even when their request was based on a doctor's orders. On top of that, they weren't even being paid for the work they were doing. Was this really happening in modern-day America?

And Ramon had all but begged me to find a reason to visit the prison clinic to meet Kenzie Eyler. I resolved to put that unreasonable request out of my mind before it could take root.

Ramon's tailgater incident was the icing on the cake. Leave it to the only other vehicle driving that isolated stretch at night to be in such a hurry that Ramon was rear-ended and propelled off the road by a hit-and-run driver. I hoped Harry could find a simple fix for Ramon's car.

I took a moment to let a new thought gel in my brain. Buzz Bateson's hit-and-run on the street just outside the hospital, and Ramon Silva's hit-and-run on an isolated mountain road. Was I forcing the two incidents into a pattern because I'd seen that well-worn plot device on so many TV crime shows? Maybe, but then again, it was something to keep in mind.

With all of that off my chest temporarily, I set my alarm and flopped into bed for the few hours of night that remained.

AND THEN IT WAS Friday. The thought that Dr. Poole might pull the plug on the Ethics meeting propelled me from bed with a quickened pulse. If only we had something solid to present as justification for Dr. Heath MacAllister's forensic autopsy.

Over a bowl of Greek yogurt garnished with granola, I scanned my notes from the night before. A lot to process over breakfast, and yet none of it pointed toward foul play in any way related to TMC's organ donor program. Or to Dr. Mac's mystifying intent to act as a whistleblower.

Breakfast finished, I yanked on a pair of gray slacks and a comfy tunic top, hoping its scattering of pink roses would brighten my mood. I left Ginger with Amah and Jack and headed off to work.

AT TEN O'CLOCK, RAMON had already texted me twice about his car, but I had heard nothing from Harry. I felt for Ramon, who had arranged a rental car, something he could ill afford, if he had to drive it all the way to Southern California to start his new job with CHR.

I had just texted him back, following up with a text to Harry, when TMC Administrator Jared Quinn walked into the library unannounced at ten o'clock. Quinn and I got along, and not just because he was a hunk and easy on the eyes, although that didn't hurt. Lola Rampley, my elderly and feisty volunteer, called him *Tyrone* behind his back. She said he was the perfect likeness to a dark and handsome forties film star named Tyrone Power. I looked the actor up online and had to agree.

I was aware of Quinn's habit of dropping in for spontaneous

visits to the various department heads, so I wasn't surprised by his arrival. I offered coffee, which he declined, standing at my desk.

"Are you making rounds," I asked, "or should I brace myself for bad news?"

"Don't worry. You're not in the doghouse … at least not yet." He took a mint from my candy dish. "Phyllis Poole dropped by my office a while ago. We had an interesting talk. I thought I'd run it by you."

"I'm listening."

Quinn dropped into a chair across from my desk. "Do you see any point in going ahead with the Ethics meeting without Laurie Littletree or Buzz Bateson to report what they witnessed in the stairwell?"

My shoulders sagged. "Why are you asking me? Poole's the chair, so it's really up to her."

Quinn smiled. "Cut the crap, Machado. False modesty aside, you know your opinion counts. I want to hear what you think." He fished a quarter out of his pocket and dropped it in my swear jar without being asked. "Expensive morning," he said. "I forked over a buck and a half to Phyllis Poole, and that was in my own office."

I had to laugh. "She's tough."

"Considering how difficult it was to get the meeting date set up in the first place, how do you feel about her canceling?"

"She'd probably be justified if all we were expecting was to hear from Buzz and Laurie. They both prepared incident reports that night, and Dr. Mac's medical record will detail everything that happened once they got him to the Emergency Room. Those can be reviewed when the Emergency Department does its death reviews."

"Then why do we need Ethics to meet?"

"Because Buzz and Laurie are only a part of it."

"What's the rest?"

"Cleo and Mary and I wanted Dr. Poole to ask the remaining

members if Dr. MacAllister talked to any of them about his organ donor concerns."

"Phyllis acknowledged that, but she felt it could all be handled outside committee if she spoke to each of the members privately."

"That wouldn't offer the same legal protection as a medical staff meeting. And did she tell you Dr. Seldon still wants to go ahead with Dr. Mac's clinical autopsy in the TMC morgue?"

"We discussed that, and I've assured her I'll take care of it. There's still the legal question of the hospital's liability in Dr. MacAllister's death, so I have some say about the autopsy. I'll set Seldon straight on that."

"Then why not go ahead with the forensic autopsy right away?"

"There's a problem." Quinn lobbed his wadded mint wrapper into a wastebasket alongside my desk. "Dr. Mac's death is not a criminal case, and the coroner is not involved. Any autopsy done at this point, clinical or forensic, would require the widow's consent. Unfortunately, she's nowhere to be found."

Oops. Quinn was not in the loop about Veronica's departure from Timbergate. I cast a glance around the top of my desk, hoping to avoid Quinn's inquiring gaze. I picked up a pen and reached for a notepad. "I just realized I should be taking notes."

Quinn fished another quarter out of his pocket. "I'm pretty damn sure you're holding out on me, Machado. This quarter had better buy me everything you know that could possibly relate to Dr. MacAllister and TMC." He flipped the coin into my jar, leaned back and crossed his arms. "Spill it. I've got all day."

"You already know all of that," I said.

"Let me make myself even more clear. Do you happen to know the widow MacAllister's whereabouts?"

Trapped like a rat.

"Okay, but you have to understand the need for secrecy about this."

"Give me a break. How long do you think I'd survive in this job if I didn't know how to keep confidences?"

"I do trust your judgment, but this could be life and death."

"What the hell are you saying?" Another quarter hit my jar. "Machado, I'm not playing around here. I want to hear everything that's going on in that calculating mind of yours."

Only for Quinn would I divulge the hodge-podge of facts, suppositions, and wild guesses that I had been chasing after and trying to make sense of. I told him the widow and her children were in hiding because her husband told her he was going to blow the whistle about something, and before he could do that, he ended up dead.

Quinn shot out of his chair and swiveled his head around, ensuring that the library was empty. "He was going to blow the whistle at a TMC Ethics Committee meeting and you didn't think I needed to know about this?"

"Because it wasn't clear what the whistle blowing was about. He mentioned organ donations, but Mary Barton and Cleo and I have gone over and over our donor program and we see nothing out of the ordinary."

"Then why would he mention organ donation and couch it in secrecy?" Quinn asked.

"That's what I've been trying to figure out for more than a week. Mary Barton hasn't a clue, and she's kept meticulous details of all organ donations for the past three years she's been working here. Veronica MacAllister has no idea either."

"Speaking of the widow, I'll ask again. Do you know where she is? How to contact her?"

"Sorry. I can't help. She's left Timbergate and gone incommunicado." Not the whole truth, I thought, but not a total lie.

"Then work on a way to contact her," Quinn said. "If you come up with something, I'll keep it close to my vest. I don't want her in harm's way any more than you do."

"I understand." My lie of omission was probably written all over my face, but I didn't want to reveal what I knew about Veronica just yet.

"Are we done here?" Quinn tapped an impatient beat on my desk with his finger. A busy man with a hospital to run.

"Almost," I said. "There's one more thing on my mind. Not sure how it fits, or if at all, but it has to do with Dr. Mac, at least indirectly."

I told him what Ramon had said about detainees at the Potterville Prison clinic being treated for work-related issues and ending up in solitary.

"And what's that got to do with TMC?" Quinn asked.

"That's what I'd like to know. It's the only scrap of information I've come up with that might have caused Dr. MacAllister some concern, because he worked at that clinic," I said. "But it has nothing to do with this hospital."

"Or with organ donation," Quinn said. "And I have no say about what goes on at the prison clinic, so I'm not able to call for an investigation."

"There is someone who could, if you were to ask. Dr. Iversen is the clinic's medical director, and he's also a member of our medical staff. Ramon said Iversen is there a couple of times a week, and that he leaves the clinic's nursing supervisor in charge the rest of the time. Maybe what's going on up there hasn't been brought to Iversen's attention."

Quinn sat back down, picked up another mint and dropped it back in the bowl. "You're suggesting I talk to Darwin Iversen? I don't know the man very well. Not sure how I'd broach the subject, especially since I have no authority over that clinic."

"You mentioned calling for an investigation. Unless you want to go up the chain of command and contact CHR's corporate legal counsel, Iversen might be the place to start."

"We're veering way off track here. Nothing you're telling me about detainees at Potterville Prison's detention center being placed in solitary confinement will help the Ethics Committee understand why Dr. MacAllister wanted to call a special meeting about organ donors. To 'blow the whistle' no less. About what? None of it adds up."

"Dr. Mac worked at the prison clinic. He was hired by

Iversen. Both men were on our medical staff. Iversen still is. They must have known each other. Maybe Dr. Mac confided in Iversen."

Quinn stared at me, or through me, as he formed a response. "Or maybe MacAllister *didn't* confide in Iversen for a very good reason."

"Ah, I see where you're going. You think Dr. Mac didn't trust him?"

"Like I said, I don't know Iversen that well. I'm not about to let on that there's talk the clinic he's supervising could be endangering its patients."

"But all the clinic docs are doing is recommending patients follow standard treatment protocols. It's the detention center's correctional officers who are meting out extraordinary punishment."

"All the same, I have to give this some thought." Quinn rose and turned to leave, then pivoted and nailed me with his familiar *locked and loaded* glare. "And don't you even *think* about taking this to Iversen yourself."

I hadn't, until he planted the thought in my brain.

Chapter 19

Quinn's visit took a hefty bite out of my morning. I spent what was left of it on busy work: cataloging books, shelving journals and filling requests for copies of online articles. All things Lola Rampley, my retired librarian volunteer, handled on Monday and Wednesday mornings. Bernie Kluckert, my other volunteer and Lola's fiancé, worked Tuesdays and Thursdays, saving me the chore of watering plants and dusting shelves. Fridays, I worked solo and usually enjoyed having the day to myself.

I opted to stay in during lunch hour, raiding my break room fridge for yogurt and a fruit cup. Efforts to put Potterville Prison out of my mind lasted all of five minutes before thoughts of Dr. Mac's death intruded, along with his unexplained qualms about TMC's organ donor program.

Desperate for a distraction, I recalled that Lola had left her iPod behind on Wednesday. I took it from her desk, plugged in the ear buds and turned it on. I wasn't too familiar with what Lola called the "big band sound," but she had assured me that it was from an era of "real music."

She spouted names of band leaders like Glenn Miller,

Artie Shaw and Benny Goodman, and insisted none of today's composers could hold a candle to George Gershwin, Cole Porter or Irving Berlin. Most of Lola's songs were upbeat and apparently written for swing dancing. I took a moment online to find a video and look up some of the moves. The fast tempo involved a lot of twirling and flipping of women over the backs and around the waists of their male partners. If that was how Lola spent her youth, it would explain why a tiny octogenarian with a dowager's hump had so much energy. Enough years of swing dancing would create a resilient heart.

I PROGRESSED THROUGH MOST of the afternoon without obsessing over what I had begun to think of as the *Dr. Mac Mystery*. Around four o'clock, Quinn called to say he'd convinced Poole not to cancel the meeting, stressing that he expected me to provide him with a way to contact Veronica MacAllister well before that date. Eleven days away. I assured him I would do my best, and then called Cleo and Mary with the news.

Not long after Quinn's call, Harry finally checked in about Ramon's car.

It's fixed. You owe me.

Of course.

Payback would probably involve helping him teach at the dojo. I texted my thanks, then shot off a text to let Ramon know. He replied, saying he'd been called to work in the medical clinic at the state prison in Arroyo County. He would be staying the night over there and couldn't retrieve his car from the TMC garage until he got home Saturday morning.

Then Harry came back with a second text.

Have ? about that car call u 2nite

I had questions, too.

CLOSE TO QUITTING TIME, a female vocalist named Doris Day began crooning through Lola's earbuds a song called "It Had to Be You." That got me thinking about Nick and wondering if he would make it home in time for dinner. There was always a chance he would be held over in SoCal with Buck Sawyer. I checked my cell for a text. *No messages.*

I listened to one last song, a haunting instrumental from the fifties titled "La Paloma." When it ended, I turned off the iPod, cleaned the ear buds with an alcohol wipe, and returned the device to where I'd found it in Lola's desk drawer. Mildly curious, I looked up the translation for *La Paloma* and discovered it was Spanish for *The Dove.* The evocative tune replayed in my mind throughout my drive home, reminding me of the cooing nonnative doves Nick had told me were considered an unwelcome species in the U.S.

I pulled into Amah and Jack's driveway, planning to stop and pick up Ginger, when I spotted Nick's pickup parked in his usual spot next to the barn. I drove down the lane while the musical earworm running through my mind switched from "La Paloma" back to "It Had to Be You."

I ran up the stairs to our deck where Nick and Ginger waited. A simple greeting kiss turned into an *I missed you* kiss that would have led to more, except for Ginger, who squeezed herself between our bodies, doing a happy dance and thumping us with her spinning tail.

We went inside, where Nick gave Ginger a couple of her favorite doggy treats and told her to stay on her bed in the kitchen. We had just closed the door to our bedroom when my cell phone rang.

"Don't answer," Nick whispered.

That was my choice, too, but I made the mistake of checking to see who was calling. *Harry.* It had to be about Ramon's car. I answered.

"No." Nick shook his head and flopped on the bed covering his face with his hands.

I turned my back on his antics and muttered into the phone. "Harry, this had better be about Ramon's car."

"Why so cheesed off? You knew I was going to call ... oh, let me guess. Nick's home, right?"

"Never mind. Tell me about the car."

"It took a jolt that loosened a few things. Easy fixes, but I won't bore you with the mechanics. I didn't see any major damage. What I did see was paint transfer on the dent where he was struck by another vehicle. Is Ramon going to report the hit-and-run?"

"No. I asked him about that. He's been driving without insurance. He wants to let this go. Is there anything else?"

"Well, yeah, if you'll give me a minute." Harry's turn to sound cheesed off. "I thought it was important, so I took some photos of the damage. And before you ask, the answer is yes, I used the camera you gave me for my birthday. You said it's the kind crime scene photographers use, so I thought I'd try it out."

"Good for you. I told you it would come in handy someday."

"Have to admit, it's pretty awesome. I took photos of Ramon's car, and close-ups of the paint transfer at the site of the damage. I even scraped off a small sampling of the paint. Do you want all that or not?"

"How would the paint scrapings help? Once you've scraped them off his car, there's no proof that's where they came from."

"Not courtroom proof, but something to offer law enforcement a head start. Help point them in the right direction."

"I suppose you're right. We might as well have the photos and the paint, in case Ramon decides to take his car in for repairs."

"Tell him not to do that," Harry said, "in case he changes his mind about reporting the hit-and-run. I'll email the photos and keep the paint scrapings safe until I see you."

"Thanks, little brother."

"And like I said—"

"I know. I owe you. How many peewee classes am I going to have to teach?"

"We'll see." Harry's chuckle fell just short of evil. "And tell Nick I apologize for interrupting his homecoming."

I ended the call and passed on Harry's apology to Nick,

along with a brief explanation of Ramon's car problem, describing it as a fender bender. I wasn't ready to speculate with Nick about a hit-and-run. That would lead to more misgivings than I was ready to share.

After that, we finished what we'd barely started before Harry's call.

LATER, OVER A DINNER of BLTs, Nick and I shared versions of our days apart. He went first, updating me about Buck's visit with the Criteria Health Resources honchos at their L.A. headquarters.

"Buck was impressed with CHR's financial track record and its prospectus, but the men he met with were vague about the drug rehab programs in several of the private prisons across the country where they have medical clinics."

"Did you sit in on any of those meetings?" I asked.

"Most of them, and I have to say, I wish there had been medical and mental health professionals there to explain how the rehab program works." Nick got up from the table to drop more sourdough slices into the toaster.

"You're saying there were no medical professionals there?"

"None. It was all bean counters. They used a convoluted PowerPoint slideshow loaded with gimmicks to paint a rosy picture of how the CHR Foundation operates its rehab programs." Nick's toast popped up. He spread it with mayo and piled on fried bacon strips. "When Buck started asking pointed questions, he was told the Chief Financial Officer couldn't attend the meetings because he'd taken sick at the last minute. They assured Buck that someone would get back to him with answers in a week or so."

"Did Buck make any kind of commitment to donate to the rehab program or invest in the CHR corporation?"

"No, but that's why I'm flying him to Potterville Prison tomorrow. He wants to meet with the warden and see one of the clinics for himself."

"I thought the rehab program there wasn't up and running yet," I said.

"It isn't," Nick said, "but it's supposed to start up any day. Buck figures the staff that's running that clinic should be completely up to speed by now. He wants to show up on short notice. A surprise visit to see what's going on when no one's looking." Nick added lettuce and tomatoes to his second sandwich and came back to the table. "Your turn. I get the feeling you have plenty on your mind."

"Too much, and all of it leads me to ask if I can ride along with you and Buck tomorrow."

"Maybe, but I'd like to hear your reasons before I talk to Buck."

"Your comment about who's running the prison clinic reminded me that the man in charge is Dr. Darwin Iversen. He's also on our TMC medical staff," I said, "but we've never met, and he's never responded to my invitation to come to the library to discuss our resources."

Around a bite of sandwich, Nick mumbled, "Tell me more."

"I'm thinking I might have better luck if I visit that clinic in person to explain how TMC's forensic library consortium works. The director and staff should know that I can help them access any library resources they might need. Not just forensic topics, but drug rehab information, or even materials to help inmates learn to speak English."

"That's just the kind of thing Buck would appreciate," Nick said. "I'll talk to him tonight."

I felt a stab of guilt for not coming clean to Nick about my original motives: a chance to talk to Kenzie Eyler and to nose around the prison clinic for myself. He knew I was getting deeper into the mystery surrounding Dr. Mac's death, but he didn't know how much deeper.

A second, sharper stab followed when I recalled Quinn's explicit order that I not take it upon myself to talk to Iversen about potential patient care problems at the clinic. But Quinn couldn't object to my talking to Iversen about TMC's library consortium. That was my job, after all.

Nick confirmed my ride-along with Buck later in the evening. In the meantime, I had texted Kenzie to ask if she would be at the prison clinic on Saturday. She responded that she would. She was working an extra shift, trying to earn as much as she could toward the cost of nursing school.

I struggled with whether to try to contact Dr. Iversen after hours to let him know I would be at the prison clinic. Then I recalled Ramon saying that Iversen didn't show up at the clinic more than once or twice a week. It sounded like his role as medical director was limited. Maybe someone else was responsible for executive decisions.

I decided to take my chances. If Dr. Iversen wasn't there on Saturday, I'd introduce myself to the person in charge and offer to explain the benefits of using TMC's library consortium.

A lot of finessing, when what I really wanted was to keep my promise to Ramon. I would meet Kenzie Eyler and hear her out. Maybe then I'd be closer to answering the question that would tie up a lot of loose ends.

What's going on at Potterville Prison?

Chapter 20

BUCK, NICK AND I met at the Timbergate Muni coffee shop for a pre-flight breakfast. We were airborne at nine o'clock in Buck's new Cessna 182 Skylane for the short hop to Potterville. It was the smallest aircraft in his fleet. Nick and I had seen the nearby landing strip, and we knew it wouldn't accommodate anything much larger.

Buck told us at breakfast that he made last minute arrangements to meet with the Potterville Prison warden. He encountered some resistance until he mentioned his intention to donate a significant sum of money toward the drug rehab program being established cooperatively between the prison and the CHR clinic. That was like saying "Open Sesame." Buck was assured we would be allowed entry after presenting our identification at the sally port.

The warden had told Buck that the landing strip Nick and I located was not on prison property. It had been constructed years earlier and sat on a parcel of property two miles from the prison.

The warden said the prison contracted through a property

manager for use of the strip, but he didn't know who owned the property or the adjacent warehouse. He thought the owners and other businesses used the strip occasionally. The smaller building, a row of hangars, was rented out either by day or by month, but he'd heard they didn't get a lot of use. Buck had estimated our arrival time, and the warden said he would send someone to meet us for the short drive to the prison.

The new Skylane took us to our destination in less than half an hour. Nick touched down and taxied to a parking area off to one side of the hangar building, in case another pilot might need the runway.

While he was tying down the plane, a uniformed corrections officer emerged from a burly black vehicle at the frontage road near where we waited next to the Cessna. As muscular as his ride, and a shade less black, the driver approached us with a military gait.

"One of you is Samuel Sawyer?" he asked.

"I am." Buck extended his hand.

"Officer Corbin Lee." He shook hands with Buck, nodded at Nick and me. "I'll be your ride, if you'll follow me."

We climbed aboard the massive vehicle for the three-minute drive to the prison entrance. Officer Lee exited the vehicle and walked to the sally port where he conferred with another officer. He came back to where we waited in his rig.

"Your escort will meet you after your identification is confirmed. Please have it ready."

I had to stop myself from smiling, thinking it seemed harder to get into a prison than it would be to break out.

Eventually, we passed the necessary scrutiny and made our way inside. Buck and Nick were escorted to the warden's office, and I was assigned another escort, a woman officer who led me to the CHR medical clinic. She opened the door, stood aside and nodded. I entered, and she left.

The space was not what I had envisioned. I had expected it to resemble a hospital emergency room. Instead, it was an open space that had a waiting area at one end and half a dozen hospital beds at the other. Only one patient was present, sitting up on one of the beds, but not shielded by a privacy screen.

I recognized Kenzie Eyler right away from Ramon's description. "She looks like a little red-haired angel," he had said. It was true. The petite young woman's mass of curly, strawberry-blond hair seemed to float around her head like a glimmering halo. The angel was taking the blood pressure of the lone patient, a visibly apprehensive Latina who had to be in her third trimester of pregnancy.

A female corrections officer twice Kenzie's size with close-cropped gray hair stood off to one side, observing. The patient's eyes were moist, as if she had been crying. I assumed she was one of the detainees awaiting deportation, since Ramon had said all the Potterville Prison inmates were men. What hell it must be, to anticipate giving birth in a prison clinic. Or would she be deported before her baby was born? If not, would it automatically become a U.S. citizen? Who knew? The rules about those things were changing faster than I could keep up.

I walked toward the only other person in the room, a slender man in his forties with thinning hair and a gray complexion that suggested he wasn't getting enough sun. He wore green scrubs and sat at a desk tapping the keys of a laptop. As I approached him, I felt the eyes of the female corrections officer scrutinizing me with a wary look. It took a moment to understand the reason.

Then it came to me. All my life I've been asked, "What are you?" by people who have a need to identify and classify their fellow human beings by race and ethnicity. They want to put me in the correct box. They know I'm something other than white, but no one guesses that I'm half Portuguese and half Chinese. Most people assume that I'm either Latina or Hawaiian.

In a prison populated almost entirely by undocumented immigrants, mostly from Mexico or Central and South America, that guard was fine-tuned to inspect people by race. It was her job to ensure that the people she dealt with were divided up and put where they belonged, whether it was behind bars, or in another country. Did she see me as a potential terrorist? I suppressed a shudder and kept walking.

The man at the desk looked up when I reached him.

"Help you?" he asked.

"I hope so," I said. "I'm Aimee Machado, from Timbergate Medical Center. I'm here to speak to the clinic administrator about our hospital's library consortium and how it might be of benefit to you and your patients."

"Did you make an appointment?" He didn't stand, offer his hand, or his name. No name tag.

"Sorry, no. I'm afraid this was very short notice. I was able to catch a ride with a friend who is considering donating funds toward your drug rehab program."

His brow furrowed. "I don't know much about that, but there's no one here today except a medical assistant and me. Nursing supervisor. Neither of us can make any binding decisions about administrative stuff."

"No problem," I said. "Maybe when your medical assistant is finished with her patient, she and I can talk. Would that be all right?"

"Sure. Whatever. She gets a fifteen-minute break anyway, unless an emergency patient shows up."

"Thanks. I'll wait at the back of the room, if that's okay."

"Suit yourself." Still no offer of his name. He went back to tapping on his laptop.

I reversed course past the steely-eyed guard on my way to the back of the room. I had an almost irresistible urge to shout, *Boo!* at her as I passed. It would have been satisfying, but childish, so I did it only in my mind.

Kenzie finished with her patient, whose arm was grabbed none too gently by the guard as she ushered the ungainly woman out the door. I waited until Kenzie finished entering her notes into a digital device. The clinic had obviously switched from paper charts to an electronic records system.

I had serious reservations about the switch after reading a

report citing how vulnerable digital patient information is to hackers. Most people wouldn't guess that health records are worth up to ten times more than credit card numbers on the black market.

Kenzie walked to her supervisor's desk, where she handed him her note-taking device. After they exchanged a few words, he nodded in my direction. She walked toward me.

"Mr. Smith said you were here to see me?" At five four, I'm usually one of the shortest people in a room, but next to Ramon's "little angel," I enjoyed the rare experience of feeling tall. She might have reached five feet if she stood up really straight and wore two-inch heels.

We stepped out into the hallway, where I introduced myself and I asked if there was someplace where we could talk privately.

She led me to the clinic's small break room with the usual microwave, mini fridge, and coffee maker. On the room's small table, someone had left a half-eaten apple fritter on a crumpled napkin. Several flies were taking advantage of the bonanza, until Kenzie scooped up the mess, dropped it in a wastebasket and wiped the table with a damp paper towel.

"Ramon told me about you," she said. "He thought we should talk." She pulled a yogurt from the fridge. "Would you like one?"

"No thanks, I'm fine." I wanted to take advantage of having the room to ourselves. "How long is your break?"

"Fifteen minutes, but my supervisor won't care if I go over a little. Half the time I don't even get a break. You wouldn't know it from the quiet day we're having so far, but this place can get pretty chaotic." She popped the lid on her yogurt and dipped in with a plastic spoon.

"Kenzie, I told your supervisor I was here about the joint drug rehab program being arranged by Criteria Health Resource and the prison. I'm the director of the Timbergate Medical Center Library, and I can provide all sorts of supportive materials to the people at the prison who will be managing that program."

"That sounds like a wonderful asset, but truthfully, I don't know anything about a drug rehab program being planned here."

Strange that neither of the employees on weekend duty were up to speed, even if they were lower level employees.

"I'm sure you'll be hearing more about it soon, but I think you know that's not the main reason I asked to talk to you. Your friend Ramon mentioned that there was something bothering you about your work here."

"Yes, but I don't want to cause any trouble if I'm wrong."

"But your concern is not about the rehab program?"

"No, not that." Kenzie went silent. Fidgeted with her plastic spoon. Was I going to lose her?

"Did Ramon tell you where I work?" I asked. "Did he assure you that you could confide in me?"

"Yes, but I'm not sure I really have anything to tell." She kept her voice low. "It could all be my imagination." She glanced toward the open door.

"Do you want to close that?" I asked.

"Better not. It might look like we're telling secrets."

We are, I thought. At least I hoped so, but she was probably right. Her workplace employed a lot of people who were trained to be suspicious about everything.

I kept my voice low, too. "Ramon said something about detainees being put in solitary. Is that what's bothering you?"

"That's part of it, but I think there's more." She put her yogurt carton down and scooted closer to me. "None of the prison inmates who are sent to solitary seem to return."

"But if they're inmates, how would you know that? Wouldn't they just be taken back to their cells?"

"They would," Kenzie said, "but there were some who should have returned to the clinic for follow-up. If their health worsens while in solitary, they should be seen and treated. That never seems to happen."

"Is there a chance they've been released? Or deported?" I asked.

"I suppose it's possible. But somehow the word usually gets out, and I haven't heard anything to confirm that."

"What about the two detainees Ramon told me about? He said they weren't convicted prison inmates. They were just undocumented immigrants being held in the detention center. Have they come back? Have you seen either of them?"

"No, and one is the husband of that pregnant woman I just examined." Kenzie's eyes clouded. "Did you notice she'd been crying?"

"I thought so," I said. "How long has it been since she's seen him?"

"More than a month." Kenzie picked up her yogurt, shook her head and put it back on the table. Too bad. She was thin and needed the nourishment.

"You should try to finish that," I said.

"I'll have more at lunchtime." She glanced at her watch.

"Do you have to go back now?"

"Soon, but there's another thing that bothers me about the patients we see."

"Something besides missing inmates?" I was eager to hear what else was on her mind.

"We seem to have a lot of sick detainees who are being transferred out for surgeries. More than would be expected for the numbers in the facility."

"But they've been living in dire circumstances for quite some time before being sent here, haven't they? Wouldn't it make sense that they'd be less healthy than the general population?"

"I suppose," Kenzie said. "But their diagnoses don't seem to follow that thinking."

"What do you mean?"

"You've heard of cancer clusters? Like in that movie, *Erin Brockovich*?"

"Yes, of course. An unusual number of cancer cases in a geographic area, over a specific time period." Odd she would bring that up.

"I think that might be happening here," Kenzie said.

"Usually clusters indicate exposure to a carcinogen, but I don't know what it might be."

"Why do you even suspect it?" Her bombshell was the last thing I would have imagined.

"We have so many patients who are developing liver and kidney cancer." She clasped her hands on the table and frowned. "We've had to transfer them out to a special surgery center. A lot of my job is to dispense their post-op chemotherapy medicines when they come back."

"IV meds?"

"No, just pills. I'm not trained to do IV chemo."

"Do the patients seem to be responding well to the pills?"

"They do. All of them have had uncomplicated recoveries from the surgeries, and best of all no side effects from their chemo meds, but of course, it will take time to see if any of their cancers return."

"Kenzie, why are you telling me about this? Have you thought of asking your medical director about it?"

"Dr. Iversen? No. The patients are doing okay, so he wouldn't take me seriously. He treats me almost like a child."

"What about Mr. Smith, the nursing supervisor who's here today?"

Kenzie's eyes widened. "No. He's sort of … um, he's been kind of flirting with me. If I tried to talk to him, he might think I'm encouraging him … you know what I mean. It could get worse now that Ramon is leaving."

"I get it," I said. "Then tell me what I can do."

"Ramon said you're a health sciences librarian. I was hoping you could use your resources to see if there's any evidence of a cluster here. You must have some sort of access to the CDC."

"The Center for Disease Control? Of course. I could give that a try."

Kenzie's cell phone chirped. She looked at the message. "I have to get back. We have a patient."

As we walked back to the clinic, I remembered one last thing I wanted to ask her.

"Kenzie, you must have worked with Dr. MacAllister here. Did you get to know him very well?"

She stopped in mid-stride. "Not too well, but I was sad when I heard about his death. He used to talk a lot about his little boys."

"Did you ever talk to him about your cancer cluster question?"

"I did mention it once. He said he was looking into it and told me not to worry, but that was just a few days before he died."

That bit of news registered with a shock. Dr. Mac was going to investigate the possibility of a cancer cluster affecting Potterville Prison's inmates. But it also raised my frustration and confusion level. What did that have to do with organ donors? It didn't add up.

"Kenzie, this might seem like a strange thing to ask, but did you ever notice what kind of shoes Dr. Mac wore?"

"His shoes?" She frowned. "I heard he fell in that stairwell because he tripped, but I don't remember anything about his shoes. Why?"

"Something about employee safety at the hospital." There was no point giving her the honest answer. *His wife suspects foul play because she didn't recognize his shoes.*

Kenzie and I said our goodbyes at the clinic. Nick and Buck met me there, where Buck spent a few minutes in conversation with the nursing director. Then we headed toward the sally port where our escort was waiting to take us back to our plane.

During the quick flight back to Timbergate, I reflected on my conversation with Kenzie. The idea of a cancer cluster was unsettling. I could understand why Kenzie was worried. If it was really happening, she was stuck right in the thick of it. Yet something she had said about chemo pills struck an odd note with me. I'd never done in-depth research on chemo for kidney or liver cancer, but I planned to delve into it when I got back to work.

Chapter 21

NICK AND I ARRIVED back in Coyote Creek early in the afternoon. We stopped at the Four Corners Deli for take-out pastrami sandwiches. Over a late lunch, we compared notes about our trip to Potterville Prison.

"The nursing supervisor in the clinic didn't seem to know anything about the rehab program," I said. "Doesn't that seemed odd, since CHR's people in L.A. told Buck it was almost ready to launch?"

"According to the warden, there's some sort of funding delay."

"Even so, why wouldn't the clinic employees be up to speed? The two I met certainly weren't."

"Aimee, you don't have to protect Buck's financial interests. He has good instincts. Let's let go of work for the rest of the weekend and try to enjoy ourselves."

His message was clear. *Drop it.* I did, but it took effort. Nick and I usually talked over our concerns, helping each other sort things out. This time, he seemed to be guarding his turf. Saying in so many words that Buck's business was none of my business.

I tried to shake off the feeling. It was probably an overreaction on my part. I had hoped to use Nick as a sounding board about the prison clinic, but we seemed to be tilting toward a conflict of interest, so I let it go. Nick had a point. Why waste a perfectly good weekend wrestling with work issues? I could talk to Cleo and Mary on Monday. See if they could make sense of what Kenzie had told me.

My landline phone rang just as we finished our lunch. It had to be Amah or Jack. No one else called me on that phone anymore. I picked up.

Amah lobbed her question at me. "Are you and Nick available for a barbecue tomorrow afternoon?"

"I guess so. Why?"

"Jack and I had a surprise phone call from your Grandpa Machado. He and Tanya are on their way up north to Ashland, where they've both been cast in a production of *Fiddler on the Roof*. They start rehearsals on Monday, but they're going to stop over for a quick visit."

Grandpa Machado and Amah had married young and had their two sons, my father and my Uncle Gabe, before realizing that their own lives were headed in different directions. Their divorce was atypical, in that each wanting the other to be happy led to their decision. Grandpa followed his dream of big city life, and Amah achieved her wish to live a rural life closer to nature.

Grandpa and Tanya lived in New York City, and both were enjoying the second chapter of their lives by following their dream of acting in off-Broadway theatre.

Amah's news was sudden, but welcome. "Then of course we'll be there. What time?"

"Two o'clock?"

"Barbecue two o'clock tomorrow?" I glanced at Nick, who signaled a thumbs-up. "That'll work for us. Have you called Harry?"

"Yes. He and Rella are coming. For once, all four of you are in town at the same time."

Later, Nick took Ginger for a run, and I walked up to the main house to ask Amah for details. She was preparing a batch of homemade raviolis for their dinner, and Jack was busy in his office, probably fine-tuning an article for one of the half-dozen outdoor magazines he wrote for.

"Amah, hold still," I said. "You have flour in your hair." I brushed at it, but only some of what I was seeing was flour. The rest was new strands of gray.

"Thanks, sweetie," she said. "Did you get it all?"

"Sure did."

"Okay, now tell me if you and Nick would like to join us for dinner here tonight, or would you rather I send some of these home with you?"

"Better send them. Nick and I are planning to go to a movie tonight, so we won't be able to eat with you."

Amah gave me a list of things I could do the next morning to help her prepare for the barbecue, including helping her make peach pies and setting out a large glass jar filled with water and tea bags, since only sun tea would do. I promised to show up in her kitchen no later than nine o'clock the next morning.

Back at the apartment, while I still had it to myself, I placed a call to Cleo to ask if she had heard anything new about Buzz Bateson. Nick would not approve, since I'd tacitly agreed to avoid any work-related activities for the rest of the weekend. *Enjoy ourselves*, he had said. Maybe, but I'd enjoy myself a lot more if I knew Buzz's hit-and-run had nothing to do with Dr. Mac's death.

Cleo set my mind at ease, having contacted a colleague in L.A. who assured her that Buzz was doing well at one of CHR's rehab facilities.

"Did you ever find out who ordered his transfer?"

"Sorry, no, but I'm still hoping to think up a legit reason to peek at his medical record."

Cleo had also heard from Laurie Littletree, who had taken time off work to join her husband in Chicago, where he was attending a conference for respiratory therapists. They would be gone for at least another week.

"That means she could be back in time for Ethics Committee," I said. "Did you mention it?"

"No. I figure that's in your ball park. If you do try to pressure her into attending, you'll still have to deal with her husband's objections."

"Laurie's devoted to Daniel, but she also has a mind of her own."

"I wouldn't count on her. She made it clear she doesn't want to be contacted before she's back from Chicago," Cleo said. "Maybe by then, Quinn will try to persuade her."

"Then I'll hold off for now. We still have nine days. But speaking of Quinn, there's something else I've been meaning to tell you. I've had so much on my mind, I almost forgot."

"What's that?" Cleo asked.

"How well do you know Dr. Iversen?"

"Darwin Iversen? As well as I know most of the docs on our staff, I guess. Why?"

"Then you know he's the medical director of the clinic at Potterville Prison."

"Of course. He's held that position almost as long as he's been on our medical staff. What's that got to do with Quinn?"

I told Cleo about my edict from Quinn, saying I wasn't to talk to Iversen about what I'd learned from Ramon and Kenzie about prisoners and detainees being put in solitary at Potterville Prison. I almost brought up Kenzie's question about a cancer cluster, but decided to wait until a more convenient time, since Nick would be home at any minute. He didn't need to hear about that. Not yet.

After talking to Cleo, I texted Uncle Gabe, who responded right away. He was hanging out in San Francisco for at least another week, maybe longer, and had been checking on Veronica MacAllister and her boys regularly.

With a sigh of relief, I told myself that even if I couldn't stop obsessing about the *Dr. Mac Mystery*, at least I knew all the people I worried about were accounted for.

Not quite, said a voice in my head. *What about Ramon and Kenzie?*

Darn voice. But it was too late. The voice was right. How vulnerable was Ramon? Maybe he was better off in L.A., out of the prison environment. But what about Kenzie?

She had suspicions, had been called on the carpet for asking about the detainees in solitary. What's more, she had identified an anomaly in her patient population that led her to suspect a cancer cluster. All of that, and she was still working there, unprotected and in the line of fire.

What could I do to reassure myself? I couldn't talk it out with Nick. He sat on the other side of the issues that were bothering me. He had to show loyalty and support for his boss, at least until there was some concrete reason to take my concerns about Criteria Health Resources, and their purported drug rehab program, more seriously.

I considered calling Mary Barton. She was an exceptionally smart nurse. Most of the questions Kenzie raised would be the sort that Mary could answer. Before I could pick up my phone, Nick and Ginger arrived home. My talk with Mary would have to wait until work on Monday. The same for Ramon. He planned to start his new job in L.A. on Monday, so he would be traveling all day Sunday. No point in trying to reach him. I had Kenzie's contact info. That was almost as good.

Nick and I kept our movie date, but my mind kept wandering to the many after-effects of Dr. MacAllister's death. His widow and sons were in hiding, and two key witnesses to his fatal injury were unavailable. The only good thing was that those people were out of harm's way. Until I met Kenzie Eyler, I tried to convince myself that there was no foul play involved in what happened to Dr. Mac. But her revelations opened at least one new can of maggots—the potential cancer cluster at Potterville Prison. And I had no intention of bringing that up to Quinn until Cleo, Mary and I had ample evidence that either it was real, or Kenzie was imagining a problem that did not exist.

If she was proved right, what if one or more of those prisoners who had been transferred out for surgeries and then returned to the prison was going to need a kidney or liver transplant?

Was that what was on Dr. Mac's mind? What he wanted to bring up for discussion at TMC's Ethics Committee meeting? Cancer clusters? Prisoners as organ recipients? Had Dr. Mac wanted Ethics Committee to propose an investigation of the prison clinic? I made a mental note to ask Mary Barton if prison inmates were eligible to receive organ donations. Come Monday, she and I would have a lot to talk about, but first I had to keep my promise to Nick. I had to get through the rest of the weekend while pretending work was *not* on my mind.

NICK AND I WOKE Sunday morning to a change in the weather. Finally, the morning temperature was chilly enough to call for a second layer while we were outside doing the morning chores. Even the llamas were inspired by early October's crisp morning air. The two youngest treated us to an impromptu bouncing display, crossing the pasture by springing up in gravity-defying leaps, and then dropping down on all fours, repeating the graceful movements in a camelid dance that was joyful to watch.

I SPENT MOST OF the morning helping Amah. I followed her recipe for peach pie filling while she prepared her special barbecue sauce. We teamed up on the potato salad, while Nick and Jack took care of the outdoor chores. Ginger supervised from where she was secured to the trunk of a plum tree.

Barnyard animals were fed and watered, the lawn mowed, and the picnic table cleaned of fallen leaves and acorns. Nick and Jack covered it with a new length of oilcloth patterned with pink and blue hydrangeas, Amah's favorite flower and mine, since it dominates the landscape of most islands in the Azores.

Things were shaping up by noon, so Nick and I went back to the apartment to shower and change. The strain of our "no work talk weekend" kept me on edge. I couldn't seem to think of anything else to talk about. If Nick noticed, he didn't say so, but he was unusually quiet. I was glad that Grandpa and Tanya were going to be at the barbecue. It promised to be a distraction.

Leaving Ginger home with a full bowl of kibble and fresh water, we walked up the lane to the main house to find Harry and Rella already there. Harry and Nick fist-bumped. Rella and I nodded to each other. After the many months that she and Harry had been a couple, we were friendly enough but still had not lapsed into an easy rapport. I was her boyfriend's big sister. She was my boyfriend's co-worker and, to some extent, his ex-girlfriend, although that history was fuzzy. But it was baggage we both still lugged around. At least, I did. *A little bit.*

The four of us hung out in the backyard while Amah and Jack bustled inside, having told us to relax and visit until Grandpa and Tanya arrived.

"Hey, sis," Harry said, "what's the latest on your friend with the car trouble?"

Shoot. I still had not told Nick about Ramon's hit-and-run. All he knew was that Harry had helped Ramon get his car running. "All good," I said. "Thanks for helping."

"Has he headed south?" *Dang, Harry.* Next, he would blab about the hit-and run. Nick and Rella both looked at me.

"He's leaving today," I said, "but we're here to relax. Nick and I agreed not to talk about work this weekend." I fixed Harry with sisterly daggers. He got the message, but a little too late.

"What's up with your friend Ramon?" Nick asked.

"Job offer down south." I squeezed his hand. "Hey, we said no work talk, remember?"

Amah's semi-feral cat, Fanny, chose that moment to snare

an unsuspecting house finch. She immediately hopped up on the picnic table, apparently to show off her catch to her human audience. Everyone leapt into action at once, yelling, waving arms, and startling Fanny into letting her prize go free. The ruckus averted any further questions about Ramon's car. Then, just as things calmed down, a familiar voice spoke out behind us.

"Ah, here they are." The voice of James O'Brien.

"What? How?" I heard myself squeak, sounding like an asthmatic in the throes of an attack.

James walked over to where Nick and I stood, wrapped an arm around my shoulders, and reached across me to offer his hand to Nick. "Mr. Alexander, long time since Boston. How have you been?"

Not that long, I thought. Nick and I had last run into James four months ago when we attended a play in Boston. Grandpa and Tanya had been in the cast, and to our surprise, James had been the director. His appearance at our picnic was like a déjà vu moment on steroids.

Back in my pre-teen years, James had been my girlhood crush. His sister was in my dance class, and because both of our families lived in Coyote Creek, our parents took turns driving us home. A typical high school boy, James liked any excuse to drive, so he often volunteered when it was his stepmother's turn.

When I looked at James back then, my childish imagination transformed him into Dudley Do-Right, my favorite movie hero. He had a strong face, gentle eyes, and a thatch of reddish-brown hair. As an adult nearing forty, he still bore some resemblance to Brendan Fraser. Lola, my octogenarian library volunteer, met him over a year ago in the library. In keeping with her habit of comparing attractive men to bygone matinee idols, she insisted he resembled an actor from the fifties named Burt Lancaster. When I looked Burt up, I disagreed. He was ruggedly handsome, but he had a lot of teeth.

When I was eight and James was eighteen, he was unsure

how to cope with a little girl's infatuation. He humored me by saying when I grew up, we could get engaged. I was eleven when he moved to New York to go to grad school. I promised myself I'd wait for him, but puberty kicked in a couple of years later, and I realized daydreaming about James was not nearly as much fun as flirting with boys my own age.

Nick shook hands with James and made nice. "I'm fine, O'Brien, how about you? What brings you to Highland Ranch?"

"Jack's barbecued ribs. Wouldn't miss them," James said.

His answer was far from enlightening. Eventually, Amah and Jack emerged from their family room, followed by Grandpa Machado and Tanya. All four carried bowls and baskets to the picnic table. Arms unburdened, greetings were exchanged all around.

Grandpa folded me in a warm hug and planted a kiss on top of my head.

"There she is, our baby girl." I'd be his baby girl for as long as we both lived, so no reason to point out that I was nearing the end of my third decade.

Grandpa shook hands with Nick, with a somewhat subdued, "Nice to see you." I interpreted his greeting as *Why haven't you given my granddaughter a ring?*

He tackled Harry next, first with a handshake, then the clap on the shoulder reserved for the males in the family. "Just look at you, boy. All muscles." Right away, he picked up on the fact that Rella was there with Harry. "And who is this lovely lady?"

Harry introduced Rella to Grandpa, Tanya, and James. Finally, with all of that out of the way, Jack followed up on the question Nick had asked earlier.

"I'm guessing you didn't travel all the way from New York for a barbecue. What else brings you here, James?"

James laughed. "I guess it's obvious my work brought me, since I showed up with Tony and Tanya. I think you already know they've both been cast in a dinner theatre production of *Fiddler on the Roof* in Ashland. I've taken the job of directing, so I'll make sure all of you have complimentary tickets when it opens."

"How long is the run?" Amah asked.

"November through January." He took out his wallet and handed one of his cards to each of us. "Get in touch with me about tickets as soon as you decide on dates. I'll be in Ashland until the play opens. After that, I'll be heading back to New York."

THE NEXT TWO HOURS blew any chance for the relaxing afternoon Nick and I had promised ourselves, although it was not the fault of the food. Jack's ribs were grilled to perfection. Amah's potato salad was as good as it gets, and I got credit for the peach pies.

The tension level between Nick and me always spiked when James O'Brien was around. It didn't help that Nick and I were already struggling with where his job and mine seemed about to converge. I did what I could to hide my discomfort, and Nick seemed to be doing the same.

James appeared to be unaware of the pressure front that was building around our picnic table, but he was a trained actor before he became a director. Make-believe was his life's work. After a second helping of pie, he finally announced that he had to get back to his motel room and make some calls. Grandpa and Tanya opted to stay on and visit. Amah and Jack offered to drive them back to the motel later in the evening.

Harry and Rella made apologies for eating and running, but they had another commitment back in Timbergate. Harry was teaching a women's self-defense class at the dojo, and she was assisting. Not with jujitsu, but with some of the gruesome techniques she had learned in the military for putting bad guys out of commission. I never got Harry alone long enough to ask if he brought the paint scrapings he'd taken from Ramon's car. That would have to wait at least another day.

Tanya and I began helping Amah clear the table, taking dishes and utensils into her kitchen. That left Nick, Jack, James and Grandpa outside to do whatever man stuff needed to be done about the grill and the patio furniture.

Tanya and Amah engaged in easy conversation, making me proud of both of them. I could not imagine being married to Nick, divorcing him, and becoming good friends with his second wife. I was still working on warming up to Rella, and she and Nick had never graduated beyond a couple of buddy dates before they both moved on.

I stepped into the laundry room to put some plastic bottles in Amah's recycle bin, and when I turned around, I slammed face-first into James' chest. He had come in behind me with some empty beer bottles.

"Ow," I stepped back, touched my fingers to my lip to see if it was bleeding. "Didn't know you were there."

"My fault. I should have spoken up." He took my head in both hands and brought my face close to his to take a look. "Are you hurt?"

"Stings a little, but I'll be fine."

And before James had time to let go of my face, Nick stepped in, carrying a few more plastic bottles.

"Um ... not sure what's happening in here, but I get the feeling I'm interrupting." He put the bottles in the bin. "I'll give you two some privacy."

Oh crap! I thought.

"Oh, hell," James said.

Chapter 22

"Shall I talk to him?" James asked. "Explain this wasn't what it looked like?"

"No." *Hell, no.* "It'll be fine. I'll make sure he understands." I wasn't sure I'd succeed, but I was certain that letting James defend my honor to Nick would be worse than doing it myself.

"You're sure?"

"Really. It's all right. Nick is reasonable. He isn't the jealous type."

James winced. "Could have fooled me."

"You should probably go. It'll be awkward to talk to Nick while you're still here."

"I do have to leave." He looked at my mouth and frowned. "You're going to have a sore lip for a while."

"Good," I said. "It'll remind me to watch where I'm going."

We both managed a half-hearted laugh.

"Aimee, are you sure you're okay? You and Nick I mean?"

"We're better than okay," I said. "It's just that we've had a difficult week because of a work-related conflict. We've been under more stress than usual, but it'll pass."

"Okay, then. I hope the two of you will come up to Ashland for the opening of *Fiddler*."

"Wouldn't miss it," I said. "Grandpa and Tanya would be disappointed."

Back in the kitchen, James said goodbye to Amah, apologizing for leaving early and thanking her for inviting him.

"Our pleasure," she said. "Jack and I will drive Tony and Tanya back to your motel later this evening. You go ahead and take care of your business calls."

As soon as the door closed behind him, Amah took me by the shoulders. "All right, young lady, are you going to tell me what just happened in the laundry room?"

I explained, pointing to my damaged lip.

Amah's mouth twisted in a sympathetic smile. "Oh, dear. No wonder Nick came out of there looking like he'd been clobbered by a foul ball."

"He isn't usually jealous, but he's always been edgy around James. I need to go explain what happened."

"Well, he should take your word for it. You definitely have a fat lip to prove it."

"Good, do you see any blood?"

Amah laughed. "A little, but maybe you can squeeze out a bit more."

NICK AND I WALKED back to the barn side by side with a cloud of silence between us. I wanted to wait until we were alone before I brought up the laundry room incident. Inside our apartment, I took a stab at it.

"Nick, I think you got the wrong impression when you walked in on James and me."

"Not now, Aimee. Ginger needs to go out." The poor dog was standing at the door whining.

"When you get back, then."

"Soon enough." He and Ginger headed down the steps and out into the llama pasture.

I looked at my lip in the bathroom mirror. It looked puffy to me, but my lips are naturally full, so I took Amah's advice and gave the sore spot a little squeeze, coaxing out a few crimson droplets. There, clear-cut proof that James had been inspecting my injury. There was nothing else on his mind, or on mine.

Back in the kitchen, I watched Nick and Ginger out the window, thinking what a disaster the day had become. We had agreed to enjoy ourselves and set aside the tension already building between us before the barbecue. That was problematic enough without the reappearance of James O'Brien.

Thoughts about the prison clinic reminded me of myriad questions that remained unanswered. All of them seemed to have one thing in common: *Dr. Heath MacAllister*. I was about to jot them down when Nick and Ginger came back inside. Nick gave his devoted canine one of her favorite doggy bone treats. Extra large. She plopped on her bed, held the snack between her front paws and chomped away.

"All better," he said.

"Are you talking about her, or about us?" I asked.

"A little of both," he said. "Ginger and I talked it over." He smiled, and I felt a load of bricks tumble off my shoulders.

"What was her advice?"

"She reminded me that you took a worse hit yourself not so long ago, and you eventually listened when I explained." He sat down at our dinette table. "So, I'm listening."

I relayed the incident just as it happened, pointing out my puffy lip, and the blood I'd purposely left drying there.

"You do look like you took a punch," he said. "But you must admit, what I saw gave a different impression at first glance. And your friend O'Brien does have an annoying way of showing up in our lives. I get the impression he'd swoop in if he thought you were available."

"At least James lives a continent away, Nick. Do you know how much effort it's taken for me to deal with Rella's constant presence in our lives?"

"Rella? Come on, she and Harry are crazy about each other."

"I know. And I'll admit I've been guilty of jumping to conclusions about her in the past."

"About Paris?" he said.

"Of course. We'll always have Paris—and now, today—to remind us things aren't always what they seem."

"So how bad is that lip? Can we kiss and make up?"

"Maybe not on the lips, but there are other places you can kiss."

DRIFTING OFF TO SLEEP later that evening, I wondered what Monday would bring, and whether our job loyalties would continue to put Nick and me at odds with each other.

Chapter 23

"CANCER CLUSTER? IN NORTHEAST Sawyer County?" Mary Barton said. "Have you checked it out at the CDC website?"

Mary had come to the library Monday on her lunch hour. I put up the *closed* sign, and the two of us sat in my break room, sharing the leftover ribs and potato salad I brought from home. Cleo was tied up in a Credentials Committee meeting, so we had promised to fill her in later.

"I did check," I said. "Not just the CDC, but a few other sites as well. According to what Kenzie Eyler told me, liver and kidney cancer incidences in the prison inmate and detainee populations at Potterville are no way within the normal range, yet there's no evidence anything has been reported. No investigation has been requested."

"Bizarre," Mary said. "Either the CMA you talked to at Potterville is dead wrong about it, or her superiors are working to gather documentation. Something like what she suspects would mean wading through a lot of red tape at the CDC. What else did you glean from your time at that clinic?"

"Other random tidbits. I'll throw them out, and you can tell me your thoughts." I wiped barbecue sauce off my hands with damp paper towels and pulled out my notes. "First, the two staff members who were on duty at the clinic seemed uninformed about a joint prison and CHR drug rehab program that was supposed to be launched within less than a week. "

"That's odd, unless they're not going to be involved in implementing the program."

"That was my thought, too, but surely they'd have been informed that it's in the works. It seems like shoddy management to leave them completely out of the loop when they have direct patient contact on a regular basis."

"You said 'supposed to launch.' Has there been a problem?"

"The warden told Nick and his boss there's a funding delay, which is interesting, since Buck Sawyer's sole reason for the visit there was to discuss helping fund the program."

"Good thing he did his due diligence before he committed funds."

"I agree, but I don't think he's backed off for good just yet."

"Then let's move on," Mary said.

I told her Kenzie's story of prison inmates and detainees who are sent to solitary, never to be seen again, including the husband of the pregnant Latina.

"How reliable is this young woman you talked to?"

"I believed her. She is young, but bright and committed to her patients. She went so far as to ask about one of the patients. He had been sent to solitary and hadn't been seen for at least a month. Got herself in trouble with her supervisors."

Mary's head jerked back. "Why, for God's sake?"

" 'Overstepping the scope of her employment.' Sounds ridiculous, doesn't it?"

"They should have thanked her and started an investigation. She needs to get out of that place."

"I know, but she's trying to save up for nursing school, and she doesn't have a lot of other options in Potterville, unless she wants to clean rest stops along the highway."

"I'm not seeing any connection between what you've told

me and Dr. Mac's organ donor concern." She glanced at her watch. "Anything on that angle?"

"I'm not sure, but that's the main reason I wanted to talk to you, even if Cleo can't be here. I have a couple thoughts. I'm counting on you to tell me if they're too far-fetched."

"Okay, this sounds intriguing." She walked over to my fridge and took out a bottle of tea. "May I?"

"Of course. Grab one for me while you're at it." I went on. "Now, about organs, there are two parts to this. First, we know Kenzie said several inmates, and some of the detainees, have been diagnosed with liver or kidney cancer. They've been transferred to some sort of surgery facility, had their cancer surgeries, and then were returned to the prison or the detention center once they were well enough to be back in their regular housing."

"I'm following," Mary said. "They must be receiving their follow-up treatments at the prison clinic. Is Kenzie involved with that?"

"Yes. But here's what's odd. She says she's not trained to do IV chemo. All she's doing is dispensing pills."

"To patients with liver or kidney cancers?"

"Yes. I did some quick online research, and at least for liver cancer, oral meds don't seem to be indicated."

"Chemo for liver cancer is pretty complicated."

"What about kidney?"

"Kidney cancer doesn't respond well to chemo, whether administered IV or as pills." Mary shook her head. "So, who's supervising the treatment for these patients?"

"Dr. Iversen is the medical director, so I suppose it's up to him to set up the regimens that Kenzie follows."

"Do you know how well the patients are responding?"

"According to Kenzie, so far, so good. But it'll take time to know if any of their cancers recur. The best news she had is that none of them are suffering any side effects from the chemo pills."

"I'd like to know what they're taking. Do you suppose you can find out?"

"Probably. I'll text Kenzie this afternoon and let you know."

"Good." Mary narrowed her eyes. "I just had another thought. Do you suppose Dr. Mac was looking into adding some of the Potterville Prison inmates or detainees to an organ donor registry?"

"See? That's why I needed your advice. I don't even know if prisoners are eligible candidates for organ transplant."

"This may surprise you, but yes, they are. At least U.S. citizens are. I'm not so sure about undocumented immigrants in our prisons. I'd have to contact UNOS to get the word on that."

"UNOS?"

"The United Network for Organ Sharing. It's based in Richmond, Virginia. They're my go-to people, and the primary source in the country when it comes to information about organ donation and procurement. It's a fascinating subject, and one reason I love my work." She smiled. "UNOS is even on Facebook and Twitter."

"All right." I glanced at the time. "We both need to get back to work, but what have we accomplished here?"

Mary swallowed a sip of tea, emitted a sigh. "Let's see. 'Cancer cluster' popped out at me. Along with the fact that it hasn't been considered by anyone except the lowliest person on the clinic staff."

"And maybe the smartest," I said.

"It may lead nowhere, but it's worth digging deeper. I'm going to contact a friend at the CDC. He might have some advice about how clusters are identified and verified."

"That would be great!"

"I'll also ask an oncologist friend why the prison clinic's post-op liver patients are getting chemo in pill form. And why kidney patients would be getting chemo pills at all. Targeted drugs or immunotherapy are tried first for kidney cancer." Mary hesitated. "Even more interesting than that is the patients are showing remarkable progress in their recovery with no side effects from the chemo."

"Is that unusual?"

"All of what you've told me is unusual. If it's true, it's remarkable enough to garner considerable attention from the medical world far beyond Potterville, California." She stared through me for a moment, then gave herself a little shake. "What the *hell* is in those pills?"

"All questions for Dr. Iversen," I said, remembering Quinn's edict that I was not to confront Iversen myself.

"I have to go," Mary said. "Are you going to fill Cleo in?"

"As soon as I have a chance."

Mary stood, hesitated for a moment. "How are you feeling about the Ethics meeting?"

"Like there's still a lot to do and we have only one more week. We'd better make the most of it."

"Be sure to ask that CMA at the Potterville clinic to tell you exactly what those chemo pills are," Mary said. "Get the generic name. And find out if the one for the liver patients is the same as what they're giving the kidney patients."

"Are you going to call UNOS?" I asked.

She stopped at the door. "You bet I am. I'll try to find out whether any prisoners or detainees at Potterville are on the organ recipient list."

"Find out whether anyone involved with that clinic has ever contacted UNOS to ask if Potterville's noncitizen inmates or detainees would be eligible to receive an organ here in the States."

"Got it," Mary said. "There's been a lot of debate about whether noncitizens can receive transplants, with valid arguments on both sides, but someone at UNOS might be able to give me the current status."

"I hope so. I'll get back to you with Kenzie's info on the chemo pills, as soon as I hear

BY LATE AFTERNOON, I had texted Kenzie twice asking about identifying the chemo pills she had been dispensing at the Potterville Prison clinic and had not heard back from her. I hoped it would be as simple as comparing the pills she was dispensing with chemo pills listed in the Physicians' Desk Reference. The PDR, a comprehensive resource on FDA-approved prescription drugs, is found in virtually every doctor's office, pharmacy, clinic, and library in the country, and online.

Surely, there would be a copy on hand at the prison clinic with hundreds of full-color pill images. Every medication in the PDR includes information on dosages, side effects, and safety information, such as contraindications, pregnancy ratings, and interactions with other drugs, food, and alcohol.

As medical director, it would be up to Dr. Iversen to prescribe the correct pills for each patient. If he didn't keep a physical copy of the PDR at the clinic, he certainly had access to the online version. Kenzie should know how to look up the information either way. My only concern was that she do it without the knowledge of Dr. Iversen or anyone else on the staff. She had already gotten into trouble for "overstepping."

As I thought about that, I realized there was a safer way to get what Mary and I needed—a clear photo of the pills. I texted Kenzie again, asking if she could sneak a couple of photos with her phone and send them to my personal cell phone. I stressed that no one at the clinic should find out. Especially her supervisor. I didn't want Kenzie to lose her job.

Or worse.

Chapter 24

As quitting time drew near, it occurred to me that two of the people who would be attending the Ethics meeting were involved in the decision to take Dr. MacAllister off life support. That was probably a plus. Dr. Seldon and Dr. Decker could explain to the rest of the committee about Dr. Mac's medical status and why his sepsis made it impossible for his organs to be procured.

Then came another thought. Why not put Buzz Bateson's case on the agenda to demonstrate to the committee the reason he would not be available in person to tell what he'd seen in that stairwell as a first responder?

With Buzz's medical record pulled for the meeting, it would be easy enough to discover who had ordered his transfer to the CHR rehab facility in L.A. Dr. Poole was the only person who would see the agenda in advance, and I knew she would have no objection. With my last few minutes, I began drafting agenda items. Even with the meeting a week away, it was not too soon to start lining up the ducks.

I started with Dr. Mac's request for an Ethics Committee

meeting to discuss a sensitive matter related to organ donation. Did he reveal his concern to any other members of the committee? Does the committee want to call for a retroactive review of organ donor cases at TMC? Did Dr. Mac ever talk to committee members about whether inmates at the prison or in the detention center could be organ recipients?

The next item was Dr. Mac's autopsy. Should it be done as a clinical or forensic? If it's done at all. Dr. Seldon's position was that there should be a clinical autopsy and that he could perform it in TMC's morgue. Administrator Quinn had contacted corporate legal counsel for an opinion, since there was the liability issue of the burned-out light in the stairwell. He was told to hold the body in the TMC morgue until the widow could be consulted about her wishes as next of kin. The dark stairwell was only one issue. Her assertion that the shoes that contributed to Dr. Mac's fatal fall down the stairwell were not his own could still lead her to cry foul play. That would involve a police investigation and a forensic autopsy.

I set the agenda aside with the hope that by meeting day, it would be more complete. There were several unanswered questions on my mind that may or may not be added.

One was Kenzie Eyler's shocking notion that there could be a cancer cluster among the Potterville Prison inmates and the population at the adjacent detention center. Should CHR home office be notified? Would Quinn ask Ethics to offer an opinion?

It bothered me that I had not heard back from Kenzie about the chemo pills. That wisp of a woman was smart and capable, but she seemed extremely vulnerable because of her small size and her youth. Add to that a much older male nursing supervisor who had been hitting on her. Worse yet, her boyfriend had left to start a new job that took him hundreds of miles away.

Quitting time had come and gone, so I texted Kenzie again,

asking her to check in with me when she could. Then I closed the library and headed home.

NICK AND I MANAGED to get through most of the evening without him bringing up the subject of Buck Sawyer's potential investment in Potterville Prison's rehab program. Likewise, I kept my misgivings about the prison clinic to myself.

Amah and Jack gave us something else to think about when they invited us up to the main house for dessert and coffee. We were sitting around the glass-topped dining table in their family room, with Ginger curled up at Nick's feet, when Amah's conversational opener took us by surprise.

"Jack and I are wondering how you two would feel about moving in here."

"We're already here," I said.

"You're in the barn," she said. "We mean here, in the main house."

"What?" My fork slipped out of my hand, bounced on the tabletop and dropped to the floor, flipping my last bite of cherry pie across the carpet. I picked up the fork while Ginger snagged the morsel of pie and looked up at me to see if there was more coming.

Nick reached over, took my hand and turned to Amah. "I think we need to hear you out, Rosa."

"We've been contemplating this for a while," Jack said. "We're thinking of selling off a few of the llamas and getting out of the turkey business."

Amah smiled at Jack. "We want to downsize, simplify our lives. We'd like to have more freedom to travel for longer periods of time without putting an extra burden on you two or on Harry to look after things."

"But we don't mind," I said. "It's never been a burden."

"Honey, we're considering buying a second home on Faial," Amah said. "You know how nice the climate is there. None of the wicked heat we have here."

"Faial, as in the Azores?" Nick said.

"Yep." Jack nodded. "Aimee's mom and dad are there. And her Uncle Gabe keeps a small condo on the island, too. He says we can use it as long as we want while we get the lay of the land and decide whether to make a permanent move."

"How soon would you be going?" I asked.

"We might make a trip over there in the next month or so," Amah said. "We won't do anything final for a year, if at all. We're not even sure if we want to do it, but we thought we should run it by you, because you'll be involved if we decide to go ahead."

"This is strictly preliminary stages." Jack said. "You know, exploring our options."

"Have you talked to Harry about this?" I asked.

"He's next," Amah said. "We wanted to run it by you first, since you'd be more directly involved."

The conversation continued for another half hour, until Amah and Jack told us they had answered all the questions they could.

"Just keep it in mind, and we'll talk again," Amah said.

Back in our apartment, we put on light jackets and took a couple glasses of wine out on the deck to watch the sunset. Ginger came along, content to settle herself at Nick's side.

Jack and Amah's news kept both Nick and me from thinking about anything else for the rest of the evening. I had trouble imagining life in Coyote Creek without Amah and Jack. They had assured us that if their plans worked out, they would still return to the ranch and stay on for a month or so every fall and spring. They insisted that they would be fine using the barn-top apartment instead of staying in the main house.

"Do you think that's realistic?" I asked Nick. "They're agile and in good health, but they'd have to go up and down the outdoor stairway every time they entered or left the apartment."

"Let's not get too far ahead of ourselves, or them," Nick

said. "They're in no hurry, and they're obviously giving this idea plenty of thought and taking their time."

"Even so, if we're not on board with taking over the main house and the management of their property, their desire to relocate will be a lot more complicated."

"I agree," Nick said. "Their only other option would be Harry, and in his line of work, that's not realistic."

"Not with his mall job nearing completion. Who knows where his next project will be? He can't keep his business going if he's tied down to ranch-sitting nearly full-time in Coyote Creek."

"And Rella's in the same boat as me," Nick said.

"Here today, gone tomorrow," I said, hoping Nick didn't sense resentment in my attempt at humor.

"And back the next day." He reached over and patted my knee. "Or the next week. Or the next month." He reached down and scratched behind Ginger's ears. "Not fair to either of my girls, but that's the job I signed on for." He reached out to take my hand. "This decision has to be up to you, Aimee. You're the only one of us whose job keeps you close to home."

"I hadn't thought of it that way, but I suppose you're right." Did that mean he was in no hurry to become a permanent part of my family? Or simply that it wouldn't matter if we were married or not? His job would still frequently take him away from home. "I guess I've been primary backup for them all along. The only difference is, we'd have a bigger house to live in."

"It's a great old farmhouse," Nick said. "Don't you think you'd like living in it?

"I love the house, but I'm not crazy about the idea of cleaning their snake's aquarium and feeding it live mice every few weeks."

Nick laughed. "What if I promise to be the snake wrangler?"

I raised an eyebrow at him. "Promise?"

"Let's put all that aside for now. We could be making better use of our evening." He nodded toward the indigo mountains to the west, silhouetted against a vivid crimson horizon. A view guaranteed to make any sailor, or lover, take warning.

Later, I did my usual check for texts and emails before turning in. I found an email from Harry with the photos of Ramon's car attached. Harry's message said he would get the bits of paint transfer from Ramon's car to me next time he was in Coyote Creek. Or I could drop by his mall jobsite during lunch hour the next day. I answered that's what I would do unless he heard otherwise.

Next, I checked my phone and found a text from Kenzie Eyler sent a couple of hours earlier.

Need to talk.

I didn't like the looks of that. It was nearly eleven o'clock, but I responded, just in case she was still awake.

Want to call me?

Now ok?

Yes.

My phone rang immediately. I told Nick it was a work thing, grabbed my jacket and went out on the deck.

Chapter 25

"Kenzie, what's going on?"

"Are you alone?" I barely heard her breathless question.

"Not exactly. I'm outside. My boyfriend is in our apartment getting ready for bed. What is it? Did you get photos of the chemo pills?"

"No. Not yet. I'm calling about something else. It's the pregnant woman. The one you saw with me at the prison clinic."

"What about her?" I remembered the Latina woman who had looked so apprehensive.

"Her name's Helena Torres. She's a detainee, and she's afraid she'll lose her baby." Kenzie sounded near tears.

"Why? Is she in labor? Is something going wrong?"

"No, not that. I mean, lose her baby after it's born." As she said that, Nick opened the door to the deck to check on me. I shook my head, waved him back inside.

"Kenzie, I'm not making sense of what you're saying. Please, take a deep breath. Try to calm yourself."

I heard her intake of air, then a pause, and finally she spoke more slowly. "Helena speaks just enough English for me to get the basics of what she's saying. From what she told me, she made friends with another woman detainee about her age who recently gave birth at the clinic's offsite surgery facility. The other woman was sure her newborn baby was healthy. She could tell, because it wasn't her first delivery."

"Then what's the problem?"

"Her baby boy was taken away from her," Kenzie said. "She was told he was stillborn."

"But what does this have to do with your current patient?"

"Helena said another pregnant detainee had been told the same thing when she gave birth. She's afraid the babies are being stolen. Afraid hers is next."

That seemed too far-fetched to take seriously. "Kenzie, she's probably overwrought and letting her imagination run wild. Besides, I thought you said she'd be deported before her due date."

"She might. She isn't due for another three weeks, but now she's been told that she'll be kept here until her husband is released from solitary, so they can be together if, or when, they're deported."

"But that's good news about her husband. At least she knows she'll be reunited with him."

"Yes, unless it's a lie," Kenzie said. "She doesn't trust anything she's being told, and she's terribly worried that someone might try to steal her baby if it's born while she's detained here."

At that point, Nick poked his head out the door again, giving me a questioning look. I shrugged, signaling I couldn't end the call just yet, and he ducked back inside.

"Kenzie, have you tried contacting Ramon? Maybe you've misunderstood what this woman is trying to tell you."

"Yes, I've been trying, but I can't get through to him." I heard a sniffle.

"He had to drive all day Sunday to reach L.A. and then report to work this morning," I said. "I'll bet he got in late and just crashed. You'll probably hear from him tonight."

"I know. I thought of that. If he doesn't get back to me by midnight, I'll try him again first thing tomorrow morning."

"Good idea. And if you're working tomorrow, you need your rest, too." *And so do Nick and I,* I thought. "There's nothing any of us can do about your patient right now, but I promise to stay in touch until we figure it out. Please let me know when you hear from Ramon. And I'll do the same for you."

"Thank you, Aimee. I'm sorry, I didn't know who else to call."

"That's all right. And please keep working on getting those photos of the chemo pills. It's important, but make sure no one sees you doing it."

"I will, but you haven't told me why you're asking about the pills. Is there something I should know?"

Yes. She should, but not yet. "Kenzie, we just want to make sure those pills are doing what they're supposed to for the cancer patients."

"Oh my God," Kenzie said. "Do you think I'm dispensing phony pills?"

"We're not sure, but we need to identify that pill. I'm so sorry to lay this on you, but you're our best chance—our only chance—to know one way or the other. Can you tell me who prescribes that medicine?"

"I don't know. They're stored in bulk in our pharmacy cupboard."

"Who gives you instructions about dispensing them?"

"Mr. Smith. My nursing supervisor. He says that's how it's been done since before he started working here."

"Just to be safe, make sure he doesn't notice you taking the photo."

"I will." Her voice caught as she ended the call.

Back inside, I found Nick in the bedroom in his sleep shorts and T-shirt, pulling back the bedcovers. I hedged when he asked about my call.

"Ramon's girlfriend. She's worried because she hasn't heard from him since he left for L.A. this morning."

"She's the medical assistant you met at the prison clinic?" Nick said.

"Yes. Kenzie Eyler." I went into the bathroom and started brushing my teeth, hoping he wouldn't press for more details.

He followed me. "She's calling you about him at this hour? What does she think you can do about it?"

I shrugged, pointed to my mouth, still full of toothpaste. That didn't work. He just waited until I rinsed.

"She's young, and probably feeling vulnerable with him gone. I think she needed someone to reassure her."

"You must have made quite an impression if you're the person she called. She hardly knows you."

"She knows I'm a good friend of Ramon's. That's why she called me, hoping I'd heard from him." Evading the main reason for Kenzie's call was getting tricky, so I told Nick only as much as he needed to know for the time being. "She's not fluent in Spanish, and there's no one at the clinic who is, now that Ramon's gone. She's worried that their patients won't be able to communicate their health symptoms clearly if another interpreter doesn't get hired right away." There, he had at least half the truth, and I hoped he'd drop it, so we wouldn't get into another debate about Buck Sawyer's investment choices.

"She's at the bottom of the pay scale there, isn't she?" Nick pulled back the bedcovers.

"I'm sure she is, but she's on the front lines with patients."

"Then she should be talking to her supervisor about the language barrier."

I didn't want to get into what Kenzie had told me earlier about Mr. Smith, the supervisor who had been hitting on her.

"I appreciate your taking an interest, but after talking to her, I got the feeling she'll be able to sort it out." I gave Nick a hug and a kiss on the cheek. "For now, we should probably get some sleep."

He agreed and was sound asleep in minutes. I lay awake in bed for more than an hour, hoping Kenzie had misunderstood the pregnant Latina's story. *Stolen babies.* Where could Kenzie go with that story? Where could I?

Chapter 26

"You talked to Kenzie last night?" Cleo asked. We were having lunch at Margie's Bean Pot, our favorite diner across the street and down the block from TMC. I had just caught her up on my most recent conversation with Mary Barton and on the Monday night call from Kenzie.

"Yes, but I haven't heard from her today, nor have I heard from Ramon Silva."

"Before we tackle Kenzie's story about missing babies, did you happen to ask if she was able to sneak any photos of the so-called 'chemo' pills that she's supposed to be dispensing to the prison clinic's cancer patients?"

"Yes. Sorry, I was so shocked last night by her story about stolen newborns that I almost forgot to tell you. She hadn't had a chance to do it yet."

Cleo's brows twisted into a scowl. "Well, from what you told me about your talk with Mary Barton yesterday, there's something off-kilter with Kenzie's theory about a cancer cluster."

"That's why we need to identify those pills." I pushed my half-eaten bowl of Hoppin' John aside. "I'll text Kenzie later this afternoon to see if she can give us an estimate about when she might get her hands on them."

"Could be a few days, depending on how often the cancer patients are supposed to take them." She spooned the last bite of minestrone from her bowl. "What do you and Mary plan to do once you have the photos?"

"That's up to Mary," I said. "We all three know how to use the Physician's Desk Reference, either in print or online, but Mary's the only one of us with nursing credentials. She might be able to dig a little deeper if none of us sees anything in the PDR that matches Kenzie's photos."

"Then let's talk about this new bombshell. 'Stolen babies.' Do you think this girl who works in the clinic has gone off the deep end with this? It sounds incredibly far-fetched."

"I honestly don't know what to think. She seems smart and level-headed. If she's wrong, it's more about the language barrier that about Kenzie leaping to a fantastic conclusion."

"What does she expect you to do about it?" Cleo asked.

"For now, she and I are both waiting to hear from Ramon. She thinks he might be able to tell her if she understood the pregnant woman correctly."

"If she did, then someone needs to order a full-scale investigation of that prison clinic and the off-site surgery center that's affiliated with it."

"At the least, they need a reliable medical interpreter. Maybe it's time to talk to Quinn," I said.

"Let's give it a little more time. Wait until Kenzie hears from Ramon."

"We can't wait too long. That detainee's due date is less than three weeks from now. I've never been pregnant, but I know that due dates are only guesses. The baby could come sooner."

"Of course, but there's nothing we can do about that right now. Let's switch gears for a moment. Have you confirmed the hundred percent attendance that Dr. Poole demanded for the Ethics Committee meeting next Monday?"

"So far, so good, but I nearly lost one this morning."

"Which one?" Cleo said.

"Dr. Decker. She wanted to recuse herself because she was involved in Dr. Mac's case."

"Shoot, that's the reason she *should* attend. What about Dr. Seldon? He's ex-officio as Chief of Staff, and he was primary in Dr. Mac's case, up to and including pulling the plug after he diagnosed sepsis." The pitch of Cleo's voice rose a couple of notches. "Did he want to be recused as well?"

"He mentioned it. Said he'd be biased, because he didn't think Dr. Mac needed a forensic autopsy."

"How did you handle that?"

"I handed it off to Dr. Poole," I said, "and she convinced both to attend. Don't ask me how. You know her tactics better than I do."

Cleo smiled. "She's good at convincing, that's for sure. Right now, we'd better get back to work."

"Wait, one last thing. Quinn is still after me to find out where Veronica MacAllister is hiding out."

"How long has it been since he asked you about that?"

"Last Friday. I don't know how much longer I can keep stalling."

Cleo dropped a few dollars on our table and stood. "This is only Tuesday, we still have almost a week before the meeting. He doesn't know you were involved in getting her out of town, so just play dumb. That's what Mary Barton and I are doing. None of us is supposed to know where she went."

"You mean Quinn's asked you, too?"

"Sure. Mary and me." Cleo grinned. "We're just as mystified as you are."

That news brought a surge of relief. If Cleo and Mary could hold out on Quinn, so could I, but for how long?

I made a quick swing by Harry's jobsite before going back to the library. The mall was in its final stages, with only some minor finishing touches remaining. Harry invited me into his work trailer.

"Haven't heard much from you since I got Ramon's car

running." He scooped a few rolls of blueprints off the settee. "Have a seat. Any new developments you'd like to share?"

"A lot, but I don't have time right now. I'm supposed to be back at work."

"Then help me teach peewee class tonight. You still owe me, you know. We can talk after."

"What time?" I was hoping he'd forgotten my debt, but I should have known better. "Do you want Nick to come?"

"Up to you. Or him." Harry's cell chirped. "Hold on." He read his text. "Gotta scoot. Here's what you came for." He handed me a small paper bag with the paint samples he'd taken from the area where Ramon's car had been hit. "I saved the photos to a flash drive for you, in case you need them for backup. See you at the dojo? Seven?"

"Sure, and after class, I'd like to get your take on a couple of things."

"You going to show those to Nick?" Harry asked.

"Not yet. I haven't even told him about the photos of Ramon's car. I'd rather not involve him any more than necessary right now."

There were several troubling details I wanted to discuss with Harry that I had not told Nick. One was that the damage to Ramon's car was caused by a hit-and-run, which led me to wonder if Buzz Bateson's pedestrian hit-and-run was not a coincidence. So far, Nick had only heard about Buzz Bateson's incident. I had never revealed to Nick that Ramon had been forced off the road by a hit-and run driver. All he knew was that Ramon's car took a dent in a fender bender.

Nick knew about Veronica MacAllister's fears for herself and her sons and the "whistleblower" threats, of course, because he had flown her to her safe ho use in San Francisco, but neither that nor Buzz Bateson's fate could be tied directly to all the deplorable things I'd heard since about Potterville Prison. The small amount Nick did know was beginning to look like the tip of the iceberg.

He had not heard Kenzie Eyler's new revelations about

Potterville Prison's inmates and detainees. Almost a week ago, I had told him only about detainees being put in solitary for minor infractions, thinking Buck should know. It was at that point when Nick made it clear he wouldn't go to Buck with any unsubstantiated rumor about his boss's potential investment prospects.

Nick had made his feelings on the subject even more clear a few days later, after our visit to Potterville. When I told him the medical clinic staff seemed uninformed about the drug rehab program, he declared a moratorium on any work talk related to Buck Sawyer's business. It hurt to lose Nick as a confidant, but until I could give him more than suppositions and suspicions, I decided to keep him out of the loop.

The piece I had already told Nick, about detainees in solitary, seemed harsh at first, but not as alarming as Kenzie's more recent fears. I thought her theory about a cancer cluster at the prison seemed far-fetched, but she had topped that with the even more sensational story about detainees' newborn babies being stolen.

All of it was too speculative to spring on Nick, who was still touchy about anything related to Buck Sawyer's potential investment in CHR's drug rehab program.

Go to the dojo alone. I needed to unload on Harry, and I might even need his help, but first, I'd have to secure his promise to keep Nick in the dark until we were more certain about what was going on at Potterville Prison.

When I returned to work, the parking lot near the library was full, so I had to park across the TMC complex in the hospital's two-story parking garage. In an abundance of caution, I tucked the paper bag with the flash drive and paint evidence in my purse and took it back to the library with me.

AT CLOSING TIME, I took the paper bag out of my purse and peeked inside it, reassuring myself that the flash drive and paint scrapings were still there. I hiked back across campus to the hospital's parking garage.

On my way, I spotted Dr. Decker and Dr. Seldon headed the same direction. Awkward, since both had resisted attending the Ethics Committee meeting and had to be coerced into it. I knew they would recognize me, and maybe even want to vent their feelings about the issue.

I didn't want to get into a discussion with them, so I hung back a bit, thinking they'd reach their cars first, in the closer spaces reserved for medical staff.

My plan failed when they stopped short a few feet in front of me, in what appeared to be a heated conversation. I had nowhere to go to avoid them without looking obvious. I slowed my pace, hoping they'd continue walking, but no luck.

Dr. Seldon spotted me first. His eyebrows lifted slightly. "You're the librarian, aren't you?"

I nodded, kept walking their way, hoping to hurry past them as if I were on my way to some pressing appointment.

Dr. Decker eyed me as I reached them in the reserved doctors' parking section where they were standing.

"You have some sort of clerical function related to Ethics Committee, don't you?" She spoke pleasantly, with no hint that she was ticked off about being required to attend the meeting.

"Yes, I assist Dr. Poole by preparing the agenda and taking minutes." *Damn, why did I mention the agenda?*

"I see," she said. "Then I suppose we'll see you there on Monday."

"Yes." I waited for it, but got lucky when neither of them said anything further. I added "Have a nice evening," and started toward my car, parked several yards away, when my heel caught in a small crack in the garage floor and sent me sprawling. My purse went one way, and the little bag Harry had given me flew out and went the other direction.

Dr. Seldon hurried over and took my arm, helping me up. "Are you all right?"

"I'm fine. Thank you."

Dr. Decker had retrieved my purse and the paper bag. "I have your things, dear. Are you sure you're okay?" She gave my purse and the bag to Dr. Seldon. "Hold these for a moment, please." She then took my hands, turning them palms up. "You have some minor abrasions. When you get home, cleanse them and apply an antibiotic ointment."

"I will." I took my purse and the bag from Dr. Seldon. "Thank you—both of you—for your help."

They seemed satisfied enough about my condition that they got into their respective vehicles and drove away, while I wondered if that could possibly have been more embarrassing. I decided falling flat in front of them was still better than getting into an awkward conversation about the upcoming committee meeting.

I tucked the paper bag into my glove compartment, figuring it would be safer there than in my purse, and headed for home, working my steering wheel with stinging palms.

Chapter 27

———•———

"No Nick tonight?" Harry said. We sat in the dojo's viewing bleachers at seven o'clock, waiting for the peewees to change into their gis.

"Nope. Jack roped him into a plumbing project. Something about a new showerhead in the master bathroom."

Harry frowned. "I'm surprised Jack didn't ask me to do that."

"He was going to, but I volunteered Nick, 'cause he could get it done sooner and Amah was excited to try it out. Besides, I wanted to come alone tonight."

"Sounds serious, if you're leaving him in the dark."

"It could be, but I'll explain after class." I nodded toward the edge of the mat, where the peewees were poised to bow on and get to work.

An hour and a half later, the kids were gone, and Harry and I had changed into our street clothes. We sat in the sensei's office sipping bottled water from the mini fridge.

"Okay, Sis, you have thirty minutes to spill whatever's on

your mind. Rella's home, and I'm supposed to be showing up with Mexican take-out from Casa Loco."

He knew about Ramon's hit-and-run, and about Dr. Mac's suspicious fall down the hospital stairwell, but I couldn't recall ever telling him about Buzz Bateson's hit-and-run, so I started with that. I ran through everything Ramon and Kenzie had told me about the prison clinic, even the notion that Kenzie was uncomfortable around her immediate supervisor, the bland-appearing "Mr. Smith," who seemed smitten with her and not too subtle about it.

"She hasn't gone to anyone at her workplace with her concerns. Not Dr. Iversen, the medical director, and not the clinic administrator."

"Who's the administrator?" Harry asked.

"I don't know. Neither she nor Ramon had met the person or even heard a name. All they know is that it isn't Dr. Iversen. He's medical director, but he takes orders from someone. I assume it's an executive at Criteria Health Resources."

"Okay, so we have missing detainees who are sent to solitary after being treated at the clinic and are never seen again, stolen newborn babies, and a cluster of liver and kidney cancers." Harry had ticked off three fingers. "Does that about cover it?"

"That covers the prison clinic," I said and ticked off my own list. "Then we have Dr. MacAllister's death, a break-in and apparent threat at his wife's home, and two hit-and-runs, all related in one way or another to Dr. Mac and/or to that clinic."

"Anything else?"

"Yes, a prison drug rehab program that Buck Sawyer is planning to invest in that will be run by the clinic." I took a breath. "And both the staff people I spoke to at the clinic seemed uninformed and unprepared to put it into operation."

"Hence your reluctance to dump all of this on Nick."

"Obviously. And I'm hoping you'll hold off talking to Rella about any of this. At least until I've come clean with Nick."

"I can do that, but don't wait too long or get in too deep." I saw the depth of concern in Harry's eyes. "You have a boatload of potential crap to sort out."

"And I haven't even let myself think about what it means to TMC. If our new parent company is complicit in whatever is going on at that prison, it's going to taint our medical center and affect everyone I work with."

"How much have you told your boss?"

"Very little. Just the part about detainees in solitary. And he's of the mind that what happens at the Potterville Prison is not in his bailiwick, so he's opting to stay out of it. The only piece of this that affects TMC is Dr. Mac's original request that the committee meet to discuss organ donations."

"Your boss is not even curious about patients at the prison clinic ending up in solitary for trying to follow doctor's orders?"

"I wouldn't say that," I said. "But he has no authority over the clinic, and he doesn't know Dr. Iversen very well. He said he'd rather not broach the subject with him in a one-on-one."

"How, then?"

"We've called an Ethics Committee meeting for next Monday. Quinn has been supportive about questioning the members to see if Dr. Mac told any of them what was on his mind when he asked me to schedule a meeting."

"And you're hoping in the next six days you'll figure out how, or if, what you've been told by this medical assistant at the prison can be connected to the now-deceased doctor's concern about organ donations?"

I felt my shoulders sag. "You make it sound impossible."

Harry laughed. "Hey, Sis, your instincts are good. I know it, and you've proved it to your boss and your two cohorts at work a few times already." He held up his pinky. "Here, I swear I'll keep Nick and Rella out of it for now, but as soon as you have anything solid, you'd be smart to get Nick on board."

I hooked pinkies with Harry. "I will. I promise."

"Then let me think on all of this for a day or so. I'll let you know if anything jumps out at me." He picked up his gi bag.

"Right now, I have a hungry ex-fighter pilot at home waiting for dinner."

WEDNESDAY MORNING IN THE library passed uneventfully, with Lola Rampley fielding most of the requests for resources. I worked on the Ethics Committee agenda with Dr. Poole on my mind. She had not dictated the items she wanted to address, so I pulled up the draft I had created earlier, including the topics Mary, Cleo and I had in mind. Poole would look it over at her convenience and make whatever changes she wanted.

I hoped I could persuade her to approve what I had drafted, but that would mean a lot of explaining, and knowing Poole, it would be a hard sell. All she really expected to do was to ask the other members if Dr. MacAllister had spoken to them about any sort of organ donor problem at TMC. That, and a vote on how much longer to hold on to Dr. Mac's remains while waiting for a decision about autopsy.

I put those two topics under New Business. The first was straightforward. The other doctors on the committee would answer yes or no. If yes, Dr. Poole would ask them to explain. If no, the committee would move on to the second topic.

Quinn would be attending as ex-officio, and he could present his case, with or without Veronica MacAllister present. Basically, Quinn's job as administrator, whether he liked it or not, was to get TMC and CHR off the hook for any liability in Dr. Mac's death. The burned-out light in the stairwell could be a liability problem, but was it the kind of circumstance that would call for an autopsy?

I added a sub-heading under the autopsy question. I listed the two eye-witness first responders to Dr. MacAllister's fall in the stairwell, and why they were not attending the meeting.

First, Buzz Bateson's hospitalization at TMC for his hit-and-run, followed by his abrupt transfer to a facility in SoCal.

Next, either an explanation as to why Laurie Littletree was

not attending, or, if she had reconsidered, perhaps she *would* be present to give her account and to answer questions.

How much could I expect Dr. Poole to allow? Not much, unless I could come up with a lot more evidence than I had at the moment.

I set aside what I had drafted and started an alternative version of the agenda. One that would be seen only if all the pieces of the puzzle fell into place before noon on Monday.

My questions came in no precise order, but I hoped once they were in front of me, I might see a common thread. Something Harry had always been good at. Better than anyone I knew. I started at the beginning, when Dr. Mac had requested the Ethics meeting, and ran through everything that had happened since, both at TMC and at the prison clinic, entering just the facts.

When I finished that list, I started a different list. One of questions based on conjectures, and with no solid facts to back them up.

- Why was Veronica MacAllister so certain the shoes found in the TMC stairwell were not Dr. Mac's?
- Who broke into the MacAllisters' house and left a whistle in the twins' bedroom?
- What to do with the hit-and-run evidence Harry had obtained from Ramon's car?
- Are two hit-and-runs, Buzz and Ramon, a coincidence?
- Are Ramon's job offer in L.A. and Buzz's transfer to an L.A. rehab center, coming within a week after Dr. Mac's death, a coincidence?
- Why is Dr. Seldon insisting on a clinical autopsy?
- Why did Dr. Mac develop septicemia while pronounced brain dead and on life-support?

Those were only the questions that pertained to Timbergate Medical Center. I had even more unanswered questions when I added CHR's medical clinic patients at Potterville Prison to my imaginary agenda.

- Why the harsh treatment of detainees who were put in solitary?
- Why reprimand Kenzie for asking about them?
- Why the mixed messages about a drug rehab program at the prison? Was it a scam to swindle wealthy donors like Buck Sawyer?
- Why didn't Kenzie or her supervisor know more about the program?
- What about about Kenzie's cancer cluster theory and the mysterious chemo pills?

Which of those questions seemed related to Dr. Mac blowing the whistle about organ donors at TMC, or at the prison clinic, for that matter? Like Kenzie, had Dr. Mac suspected a cancer cluster and gone down the same road that I had traveled with Mary Barton? Had he contacted the CDC to ask about a cluster in the Potterville area? Had he contacted UNOS about the status of undocumented prisoners and/or detainees as organ recipients?

Were those issues what Dr. Mac had found too sensitive to mention outside the protection of the Ethics Committee? Why? They didn't rise to the level of whistleblowing. Blowing the whistle almost always involved covering up a crime. So where was the crime? The only thing on my list that came close to crime was that donors like Buck Sawyer might be scammed into funding a drug rehab program that had come to nothing.

I traveled back full circle to the question of detainees being placed in solitary confinement for attempting to follow doctor's orders about their severe dermatitis. No doubt Dr. Mac had been one of the clinic physicians who had counseled his patients to avoid harsh cleaning products. If he was aware that his treatment regimen was putting patients at risk of solitary, he might have felt compelled to report it somewhere. But why at TMC?

More important, how would the use of solitary as punishment have anything to do with his concerns about organ donation?

As THE AFTERNOON WOUND down in the library, I struggled with doubt. No one had gotten back to me with any useful information. It was as if every question I asked had been sucked into a black hole somewhere in the universe.

Then, as I was preparing to close and go home, my cell phone chirped, my office phone rang, and before I could decide which one to answer first, Mary Barton rushed into the library.

Chapter 28

———•———

MY CELL SHOWED A text from Kenzie. I set it aside and waved to Mary as I answered my desk phone.

"Glad I caught you," Quinn said. "Am I right that we're a go for Ethics Committee at noon on Monday?"

"Yes. Everyone's confirmed." *Please don't ask about the agenda.*

"Any chance you have the agenda ready?" *Rats.*

"No, but I'm sure Dr. Poole will get together with me tomorrow or Friday." Technically, as an ex-officio member, Quinn wasn't authorized to approve the Ethics agenda, but it would be darned uncomfortable for me to refuse to let him have a look before the meeting.

"All right, then. Let me know when it's ready." He paused. "And I'm still waiting for word on how to contact MacAllister's widow. Have you made any progress there?"

"Sorry, I still don't have that information for you." I glanced at Mary, who stood watching me with her head tilted to one side.

"Then keep trying." Curt, not at all like Quinn's usually easygoing manner. He hung up before I could reply.

"Quinn?" Mary asked.

"How'd you know?"

She laughed. "Your cheeks are flushed. Who else would make you look so guilty?"

"He asked about Monday's agenda. And whether I had contact info on Veronica MacAllister."

"You lied to him, didn't you?"

"Define 'lie.' "

"Never mind." She pointed at my cell phone. "Looks like you were about to check for messages."

"Oh, right. A text from Kenzie." I opened the message and saw that she had attached photos of the chemo pills. "Look, Mary, she sent photos."

"Great. Send those to my phone, and I'll get busy trying to identify them."

I forwarded the message and photos. "That was good timing, but I'm guessing it's not why you're here. Do you have news?"

"A couple of things. First, negative results from the CDC about any sort of cancer cluster in the Potterville area." Mary brushed a stray lock of hair off her cheek. "Second, I put in a call to UNOS, but the person I usually talk to wasn't available. From what I've found online, even for prisoners who are U.S. citizens, the likelihood of an organ transplant is rare."

"But not unheard of?"

"I found a couple cases, one a liver, the other a heart, and each was considered controversial. Particularly, who's going to foot the bill? Each transplant came with a million-dollar price tag and was partially funded by Medicare and Medicaid. One politician called it a 'lose-lose for U.S. taxpayers.' "

"Nothing about transplants for undocumented immigrants who are incarcerated, either as prison inmates or detainees?" I asked.

"Not that specifically, but I should be hearing back from UNOS soon."

"Maybe that's what Dr. MacAllister was trying to run down."

"Could be," Mary said, "but how would that involve whistleblowing?"

"Yeah, there's that doggone whistle."

"Let's keep looking for it. I'll let you know when I hear from UNOS."

"And whatever you discover about the pills," I said. "Maybe they'll give us something useful if we can identify them, but we only have tomorrow and Friday to sort this out."

"And Monday morning." Mary smiled. "I'm keeping my glass half-full."

"I'd feel better about my half-empty glass if we had a way to communicate with Buzz Bateson," I said. "There must be some way to get in touch with him."

Mary's posture stiffened. "There is something we might try. I should have thought of this sooner."

"What are you thinking?"

"You know I wear two hats here at work. Organ Donor Coordinator and Social Worker."

"Social Worker, of course! Your job gives you access to Buzz's next of kin."

She shook her head. "I should have thought of it sooner."

"Hey, we've had a million other things—other people—on our minds. And he was transferred out with essentially no warning."

"That's why it got away from me. I wasn't called in to coordinate his transfer. That's a break in protocol that shouldn't have happened." Mary bounced up from her chair. "Still, all I need to do is get with Human Resources and say I want to follow up with his wife, family, whomever. A Social Services courtesy call."

I reached out and grabbed her hands. "Yes, of course. They can tell you where he is, how he's doing, whether they've been communicating with him. Want to call HR now? From here?"

"Too late now. Everyone will be gone for the day. I'll do it first thing tomorrow morning."

"And let me know right away?"

"Count on it," Mary said.

I left work with that brushstroke of hope painting rosy edges around my gloomy mood.

AT HOME I SPOTTED Nick and Ginger in the llama pasture playing catch with a Frisbee. The llamas watched from a far corner of the field, wanting no part of it. Nick waved, trotted over to greet me with a kiss, looking all flushed and adorable.

"How was your day?"

"Just the usual," I said. "Clearly not as much fun as yours. Must be nice to have time off."

"Don't be too sure." He nodded toward the far end of the pasture. "Jack put me to work. Guess what we were doing."

"Shoveling?"

"Correct. Those animals create a lot of fertilizer."

"Something to think about if we end up responsible for this place." I headed up the stairs to the deck. "I need to get inside and change."

Nick and Ginger followed me inside, where I spotted a vase with a single red rose on our dinette table.

"What's this?" I asked. "My birthday's next summer, and Valentine's Day is four months from now."

"I spotted Rosa in her garden. I told her I was surprised to see that beauty blooming in October, so she gave me a lesson in Roses 101."

"About how they bloom in summer and again in the fall?"

"That, and she insisted I take it for you." Nick ducked his head, looking sheepish. "I think your grandmother is psychic. Either that, or you must have mentioned that we've been out of sync lately."

"I haven't," I said, "but she's very observant. Is this a peace offering?"

"At least a truce." He picked up the cut-glass vase and held it out to me. "Amah says you used to help her tend her rose garden when you were little."

"Because I'm her namesake. She's Rosa, and Rose is my

middle name." I inhaled the fragrance, bringing a flood of childhood memories of special times with my grandmother.

"What do you say?" Nick eyed me speculatively. "Truce?"

"You mean we can start communicating again? About CHR and Buck?"

"Maybe we can take a stab at it." Nick took the vase from me and set it back on the table.

I smiled. "Is that some sort of pun about roses and thorns?"

"Wish I could say I thought of that."

"I'm willing to risk a thorn now and then. The truth is, I have a lot of concerns about CHR that go beyond Buck's potential investment plans."

"Concerns you've avoided sharing with me?"

"Because Buck's a gazillionaire investor. Why would he want advice from a lowly librarian with a negative net worth of several thousand dollars?"

"And because when you did try to talk to me, I shut you out?"

"More or less." I sat at the table, leaned toward the rose, and touched a velvety, blood-red petal.

Nick sat across from me. "I won't promise to go to Buck with anything you tell me, nor will I promise *not* to, but I'm ready to listen if you're willing to read me in on what's going on."

My tension level dropped, and my shoulders softened. "I'd like that, because if there *is* a relationship between CHR and Dr. MacAllister's death, I could really use your help."

Nick slid his chair closer to mine. "Let's talk."

I signaled a time out. "Wait. First some job-related ground rules. You have to keep in mind that I can't reveal any information about the health or treatment of a TMC patient."

"Know that already. Anything else?"

"I can't reveal anything that takes place in a TMC committee meeting."

"Got it. Pretty sure you've mentioned that before." Nick smiled. "That's it?"

"Those are the biggies. Firing offenses. Everything else would be nothing more than speculation, rumor or gossip, and where I work, there's plenty of that going on all the time. As long as it doesn't rise to the level of slander, no problem."

"Sounds like most of what you're poking into now falls under the heading of speculation or suspicion. Nothing you can't run by me for an opinion."

"So far. And I'll reserve the right to hold back if I'm veering to close to my comfort zone."

Nick leaned back, crossed his arms. "Now my turn. Until this potential conflict with Buck's interests came up, I hadn't felt we needed ground rules. I just told you what I thought was necessary."

"I already know he's connected with agencies that investigate illicit drug activity. I've never asked you for specifics, and I never would. What else is off limits?"

"Ordinarily, I'd say let's avoid his business investments, but we'll make an exception this time, since the horse is out of the barn. The other area that's off limits is his personal life."

"Business, I get. But why mention his personal life? I already know his daughter died of a drug overdose, his first wife is deceased, and Delta is his second wife."

"I tossed that in because Buck is fierce about his privacy," Nick said. "He confides in me, and a few times, I've been tempted to run something by you."

"But you thought better of it?"

"Not because I don't trust you to keep confidences. More a matter of keeping my own."

"Okay then, we've agreed on ground rules."

Chapter 29

———◆———

OVER A DINNER OF grilled cheese sandwiches and tomato soup, I unloaded on Nick with every scrap of information I had gathered since the day more than two weeks ago when Dr. Mac had come to me in the library requesting a meeting of Ethics Committee.

"How much of this does Harry know?" Nick asked.

"Most of it."

"Rella?"

"No, he said he wouldn't get her involved."

"You were worried she'd talk to Buck? Or that I would?"

"No, but you and Rella work for him. I thought if you knew the extent of the digging we're doing behind Buck Sawyer's back, it would be awkward for you. I wanted to be sure there was something—"

"You wanted evidence." Nick went to the stove to refill his soup bowl. Something concrete I could take to my boss." He gave Ginger a pat on the head and returned to the table. "The unanswered question is, evidence of what?"

"Exactly. Dr. MacAllister said it involved organs. Mary and I assumed at first that it had to do with organ donors who were

TMC patients, but nothing we've pieced together so far points in that direction."

Nick's eyes narrowed. "All of what you've told me goes way beyond, or even around, Buck and the potential drug rehab program."

"The only common thread I see between that and everything else I've told you is the connection to CHR's clinic at Potterville Prison."

"There's another connection," Nick said. "Your deceased doctor."

"But we might be forcing that connection. There are other doctors who work at that clinic."

"But the doctor who fell down the stairwell is the one who died, and the only one whose wife is in hiding because her husband was going to 'blow the whistle.' "

I nodded. "And he's the one who came to me for help. That's why I can't let this go."

"Then keep me updated and let me know what I can do to help. I won't speak to Buck unless we find out it's necessary."

"Do you think it's safe to wait? He might decide to go ahead with his donation before we can prove there's something illegal going on at the prison."

"You're afraid if there's an investigation, he'll be charged as an accomplice?"

"Aren't you?"

"Buck's been taking care of business for half a century, but I do see your point. I'll look for an opportunity to talk to him."

"Soon?"

"Soon, but it's not without risk. He won't take it well if he senses his airborne chauffer is offering investment advice."

"It might be worth the risk, if you save him from getting caught up in a high-profile scandal. Besides what's the worst he can do? He isn't going to fire you."

"No, but he might take back his airplane." Nick smiled, took the rose out of the vase and reached toward me, caressing my cheek with its petals. "Meanwhile, enjoy your perfect rose."

I inhaled the fragrance, but couldn't suppress thoughts of dark red blood and merciless thorns lying in wait.

THURSDAY NOON. *COUNTDOWN.* MONDAY's Ethics Committee meeting was four days away to the minute, and nothing was coming together. I closed the library and sat at my desk, contemplating my boiled eggs and apple slices.

Even Nick's offer of help the night before couldn't jar me from my funk. Help with what? I had tried all morning to reach Mary Barton, but only got her voicemail. I wanted her expertise about undocumented prisoners as organ recipients, and I needed her updates about the chemo pills and about Buzz Bateson's situation in L.A. I still hoped to have at least a second-hand report from one of the first responders who found Dr. Mac in that stairwell, and so far, Laurie Littletree had not returned from Chicago.

Another missing piece was Veronica MacAllister's certainty that the shoes Laurie and Buzz found in the stairwell were not Dr. Mac's. Why was she so sure? Uncle Gabe had not responded to any of my texts, and it was unclear whether he was still in San Francisco keeping an eye on Veronica. She was off the grid, so I couldn't contact her directly.

I also wanted to know how many detainees were being held in solitary at Potterville Prison for unjustifiable reasons. And for how long? My only sources at the prison were Ramon, who, thanks to a job offer from CHR, had relocated to L.A., and Kenzie Eyler, who was still working at the prison clinic and most vulnerable, if crimes there and a coverup had led to Dr. Mac's death.

What if Kenzie's Latina patient was right about newborns stolen at birth from women incarcerated at the detention center? How many people would be involved in that coverup? Clinic staff? Prison staff? That prospect made me catch my breath. *Too horrific to be true.*

That thought led to another. It struck with such force that I had to leave my desk and walk the floor to shake off the numbness spreading across the back of my neck and shoulders.

Suppose the story about the babies *was* true. If so, what else might be? What if Dr. MacAllister's concern was not whether prisoners or detainees could *receive* organ transplants, but instead, whether their organs were being *taken* from them?

I ran back to my desk and called Mary Barton again. Finally, she answered. I dropped into my chair. "Mary, how soon can we talk? There's something I need to run by you."

"Same here," she said. "I would have called you back earlier about Buzz, and about those so-called *chemo* pills, but I was double-checking. I wanted to be sure—"

"How about now? It's twelve thirty. We still have half a lunch hour."

"Your place or mine?"

"I'll come to you."

I raced across the hospital complex to the main building, where Mary's small, neat office was located on the first floor near the Emergency Room. She ushered me in and closed her door.

"Who goes first?" She cleared some files off a chair, so I could sit.

"You." I needed to hear her out before offering my mind-boggling theory.

"Then I'll start with Buzz Bateson. I spoke to the head of Human Resources this morning. I used the fact that Buzz was whisked away from TMC to L.A. with so little notice that I had never had a chance to offer my assistance as Social Services Coordinator. I wanted to contact his family even if it was just a formality. Good P.R. for the hospital, that sort of thing."

"Did she go for it?"

"She did. Turns out he was divorced, living alone, no kids, and had used his ex-wife's name as his next of kin."

"Did you reach her?"

"No. She's remarried, and the phone number on Buzz's file is in the new husband's name. When I called, the husband answered. Hadn't heard about Buzz's injuries but wasn't too sympathetic about the whole thing. Said the former Mrs. Bateson was out. He'd relay the message."

"Doesn't sound too promising."

"No, but you never know. They have my phone number. Maybe she'll call if she knows anything."

"If her new husband really gives her the message."

Mary's lips twisted. "Yeah, there's that."

"Any news about the chemo pills?"

"Yes, but first let me tell you about prisoners and transplants." She picked up a sheet of paper on her desk. "I spoke to my friend at UNOS. She found nothing to confirm whether Dr. Mac had asked about transplants for inmates. She said it's very doubtful that a prison inmate, whether a U.S. citizen or undocumented, would be listed as a potential transplant recipient. First, the prison would have to approve. And then there's the question of who pays for the transplant. Remember, we're talking up to a million dollars." Mary looked down at her notes. "And the patient would have to be capable of taking care of the organ, and that involves very expensive pills for life."

"Taking care of the organ? What does that mean?"

"Organs are in such great demand, that it's only fair to offer them to patients who will follow all necessary protocols to keep the organ healthy, including a lifetime of expensive meds to prevent rejection of the organ. If the patient has no medical insurance, it would likely be impossible. Particularly for an undocumented inmate, who would not be eligible for Medicare or Medicaid."

"What if the patient received a good organ, kept it healthy, and then died some sort of accidental death? Can the organ be used again?"

"Good question, and the answer is maybe. There are cases where a secondary transplant has been done successfully, but it's still very rare. Most transplants are from a primary source."

"It sounds like pursuing organ transplants for prisoners is not what Dr. Mac had in mind when he asked for the Ethics meeting. No coverup there, so no need for a whistleblower."

"I think it was something else," Mary said, "and I'll get to that. It goes along with what I found out about the pills."

"If you're going to say what I think you are, it should reinforce what I'm thinking."

She held up one of Kenzie's photos of the pills so I could see. "There is no chemo pill in the national pharmacy formulary that looks like the photos Kenzie sent us."

"Explain."

"It means whatever those pills are, they're not used in the States as chemo drugs."

"Then the prison clinic has a source from some other country? They're doing something illegal?"

Mary sat back. "I guess that's one possibility, but I doubt it."

"I'm listening."

"Try to keep an open mind, because what I'm going to suggest will be a lot harder to swallow than those pills."

"No harder than what you'll hear when it's my turn." I leaned forward, waiting.

"My best guess is those are not chemo pills at all," Mary said. "Not from the national formulary here in the States, and not from a formulary in any other country I'm aware of."

"What, then?"

"Some sort of placebo would be my bet."

"Sugar pills?" I scooted closer. "Then why are the patients getting better?"

"Remember, I said to keep an open mind." Mary shifted in her chair. "It's possible those patients were never sick in the first place."

Yes! Mary and I had walked two different paths, but we had arrived at the same place.

"If you mean what I think you do, I've already come to a similar conclusion. I think it's possible—"

Mary put her finger to her lips. "Say it softly."

I lowered my voice. "Somehow, someone is harvesting organs from patients at the Potterville Prison medical clinic and selling them on the black market."

"And making big bucks off those prisoners and detainees." Mary said. "The idea isn't original. It was done openly in China for years. They took kidneys and livers from their executed prisoners. They claim to have stopped that now. Insisting they only take organs from volunteers."

"Taking organs from executed prisoners is one thing, taking them from living prisoners, without their knowledge, is going to an abominable new level."

Mary nodded, whispered. "What about taking newborn babies? If we're going to pursue this possible black-market scheme, we have to be cautious. Dr. Mac might have suspected the same thing. I doubt it's a coincidence that he died before he could bring it up in committee."

"Before he could blow the whistle," I said. "His widow doesn't think it's coincidence."

"Neither do I."

"You're saying someone working here at TMC might be involved?"

"Maybe more than one person." Mary pointed at the photo of the bogus pills. "I'll keep trying to identify these, but I have to tell you, I'm not feeling good about asking anyone around here for help. Besides, a photo isn't what we need. If I could get even one of the actual pills, I know where I could get it analyzed without anyone knowing about it."

"On such short notice?"

"Not a complete analysis, but at least we'd know if it was really a chemo drug."

"The only way to get our hands on those pills would be to ask Kenzie to sneak them to us. If we're on the right track, she'd be at risk if anyone found out."

"Great risk," Mary said.

"So, what do we do from here? Do you want to talk to Quinn?"

Mary's eyes widened. "Do you?"

"Not really. He's already made it clear that the prison clinic is none of our business, but I do think we should tell Cleo what we're thinking."

Mary sighed, looked at me through the weary eyes of someone who hasn't slept well. "Other than Quinn, she's the only one at TMC that I trust right now."

"I can't think of anything we can do to bear out our suspicions. Except maybe the pills. If we had one ... but no, it wouldn't be fair to ask Kenzie to risk it."

"There must be something we can do. What about Veronica MacAllister? She's already convinced that her husband was a victim of foul play. Is there any way to talk to her again? Get a feeling for why she's so sure her husband was targeted? If we promise not to put her in danger?"

"I've been trying to reach my uncle," I said. "He's been in San Francisco keeping an eye on her and her boys, but I have haven't heard from him for several days now."

"Keep trying."

I USED MY AFTERNOON break to meet with Cleo in the cafeteria, filling her in over pumpkin pie and coffee.

"I'd say illegal organ harvesting is a giant leap, if it were anyone but you and Mary," Cleo said. "Are you thinking about taking your theory to Quinn?"

"Not yet." I glanced around, as if he might materialize. "We don't have anything he would consider proof, and he's already told me not to interfere by talking to Dr. Iversen."

Cleo arched a brow. "Nevertheless, if it turns out to be true, and CHR is involved, it could result in a major scandal that would affect TMC. Quinn should be warned at some point."

"I know. But if it's true, it's already more than a scandal, it's a matter of life and death."

"You mean for the prison patients and detainees?" she said.

"Possibly for them, if their surgeries went wrong, but I was thinking of Dr. Mac, and of anyone else who might be willing to blow the whistle."

Chapter 30

---·---

ON THE WAY HOME Thursday, I mulled over my conversation with Mary. My old hand-me-down Buick was running like a top, but my brain was in neutral and I couldn't seem to shift back into any forward gear. I needed ideas. I needed Harry and Nick and a brainstorming session.

As I dropped off the freeway at the Coyote Creek exit, a piano version of "Misty" began to play on my car radio. I had switched to an *oldies* station a few days earlier, after listening to Lola Rampley's iPod and realizing the old-fashioned music and lyrics helped relieve anxiety and let me think more clearly. I already recognized the voices of long-departed vocalists like Sinatra and Ella Fitzgerald, and appreciated arrangements that allowed their lyrics to be heard over the background music.

The instrumentals seemed to work best when I had to ready my mind for problem-solving. I needed all the help I could get, so I decided to stay tuned to that station, at least until the pieces of the *Dr. Mac Mystery* came together.

I pulled into the Highland Ranch driveway and spotted Amah decorating her front porch in symbols of the fall season. Every year, half-way into October, a scarecrow dressed in a pair of Jack's old jeans and a flannel shirt appeared there, perched on a hay bale. That job was done, but Amah was still struggling with a huge fall wreath, so I pulled over and offered to help her hang it on her front door. Between us, we got the job done. Amah opened the door to test our work. The wreath stayed attached. No wobbling to indicate it might come loose.

Satisfied, Amah gave me a thumbs-up. "Thanks, sweetie, I needed an extra pair of hands, and Jack isn't home."

I glanced down the lane toward the barn. "Looks like Nick isn't either. I don't see his truck."

"They're together. Nick offered to take Jack to pick up some things at the lumber yard. They have a project going. Some sort of upgrade to the turkey cages." She opened her front door again. "Come on in. We'll have pumpkin spice tea. It's brewed and ready."

"Sounds good. And there's something I want to ask you."

Amah and I sat in her open-beamed family room with our tea. Her temperamental cat, Fanny, was curled up near the wood stove, snoring softly.

"You wanted to ask me something?" Amah said.

"I've been trying to reach Uncle Gabe for a few days, and he hasn't returned my texts or my calls. Any idea why?"

"Oh, is this about the woman and her little boys? You want to check on how they're doing?"

"Well, yes. Not a big deal. Just that I can't contact her directly. Gabe's my only way to keep in touch."

Amah wrapped her hands around her cup. "Gabe had to fly to Horta. Something about his work. He hoped it would be for just a day or two, but apparently he's still taking care of whatever the business was."

"I wonder why he didn't tell me." My stomach knotted at the thought that he had left Veronica and her boys alone in the city.

"I suppose he thought I'd pass along his plans." Amah reached out, patting my arm. "Don't worry about the doctor's widow and her sons. They're fine."

"How do you know?"

"Because Gabe flew them to Horta with him."

"He took Veronica and her kids to the *Azores*?" I thought I'd heard her wrong.

Amah smiled. "Your uncle takes his responsibilities very seriously. He didn't want to take any chances leaving them alone in San Francisco, but he had to make the trip, so he talked the widow into going along. Said it might be good for her. Help take her mind off her grief and worry for a few days."

"And she went? Just like that?"

"Well, I don't know how much persuading it took, but she did go."

"Are they staying with Mom and Dad?"

"No. The widow and her sons are staying in Gabe's condo in Horta, where security personnel keep them safe while he's working. He said she feels safe, as long as no one from the hospital pressures her to talk about her husband."

"Meaning me?"

"He wasn't specific, but if the shoe fits … ."

If the shoe fits. Ironic. So much for my chance to talk to Dr. Mac's wife about her husband's shoes. No wonder Gabe didn't answer my texts and calls. I couldn't count on Veronica answering my questions, even if I got through to her on Gabe's phone.

"When will they be back?"

" 'Any day now,' is what Gabe said when he texted this morning."

She read my face. "What is it? You look upset."

"No. Just surprised." I did not want to say too much. She was better off not knowing I was trying to gather proof of heinous crimes committed by coldblooded predators. "Do let me know if you hear again about when they'll be back."

"Of course."

"LET'S SEE IF I have this straight," Harry said. "You've dropped your theory about a cancer cluster? Your best guess now is black market organ trafficking?" He shook his head. "I don't know, Sis. That's quite a stretch. Maybe you've seen that topic in the media once too often."

"Because it's happening too often," I said. "Nick, what do you think?"

"I'm reserving judgement until I hear more."

Nick had come home from his errand with Jack just before Harry showed up at six o'clock asking if I had any food. Knowing the two of them, I had made a run down the road to the Coyote Creek Deli where I picked up three giant sub sandwiches and a couple bags of chips.

Harry had asked another sensei to teach his class at the dojo so he could spend as much time as it took for the three of us to brainstorm the black-market organ theory.

"What more do you need to hear?" I asked Nick.

"Those suspicious chemo pills. What are they? And what doctor signed off on the stillbirth of the detainee's newborn baby? Was it a doctor who has privileges at TMC? Can you find out? Can your gal Kenzie get access to that?"

"I'm afraid to ask her to do anything more for us. If something terrible is happening at that prison, or in that clinic, she's a sitting duck if she's caught snooping."

"Then set those aside for a moment," Harry said. "It would help to know why the doctor's wife has doubts about the shoes that supposedly caused her husband's fall."

"I know that. And I just told you what Amah said. She and her kids are in the Azores with Gabe, and it's unclear when they'll get back."

"They'll fly into SFO when they return, won't they?" Nick asked.

"I'm sure they will, but we won't know what flight, or even when, until we hear from Gabe."

Harry swallowed a bite, cleared his throat. "Did you tell Amah to have Gabe get in touch with you if she hears from him again?"

"She knows I want to hear from him. I didn't go into any

details. Just told her I wanted to be sure Veronica and her kids are okay."

"What is it you want us to do?" Nick asked. "We can't endanger the young woman at the clinic, and we can't get immediate access to the widow. How can Harry or I help as things stand now?"

"Just believe in me, and in Mary Barton. Take our word that we're on the right track. My next plan is to follow up with Ramon Silva. He's down in L.A., and so is Buzz Bateson, the man who was injured in the first hit-and-run. I'm hoping Ramon can find what rehab facility Buzz is in, and maybe talk to him. Compare notes on the vehicle involved."

"What did you do with the flash drive with the photos of Ramon's car?" Harry asked. "And those paint scrapings?"

"They're in my car. I'll go get them." I went out to the deck, ran down the stairs and opened my glove compartment. Where was the paper bag? I groped, pushed aside my operator's manual, my insurance and registration papers, turned on the flashlight I kept there. *No bag.* I blinked, looked again. Not there. Heart pounding, I ran back up the stairs and burst into the kitchen.

"It's gone."

Chapter 31

"WHAT DO YOU MEAN?" Harry said.

"I put that paper bag in my glove compartment the day you gave it to me. It's not there."

"You must have moved it. Brought it inside." Nick glanced around, as if he might spot it lying innocently on one of our countertops.

"I didn't bring it in. I'm sure of it." I said.

"How long ago did you get it from Harry?" Nick asked.

"Tuesday."

"It's been in your car for two days?" Nick said. "Why?"

"I guess I forgot about it."

Harry shook his head. I knew what he was thinking. *Lying, she hid it from Nick.*

"Do you lock your car when you're at work?" Nick asked.

"Always," I said. "I lock it everywhere I go."

"Where else have you parked it since Tuesday?"

"Just work and home—except I went down to the deli a while ago. I might have left it unlocked there. I was in a hurry to get back before you two got here."

"It only takes once," Harry said. "I'll bet that's what happened. I hear it all the time from the cops in my jujitsu classes. An unlocked car is like a welcome mat. Maybe you're lucky it wasn't locked. Smash and grabs from cars are almost a daily occurrence with the way drug problems around here have escalated."

"Not just here. I see it everywhere Buck and I go," Nick said. "If someone looked in your glove compartment and found even a thing as simple as a flash drive, it would be gone."

"But we needed the paint. It's evidence." My chest tightened. "I can't believe I let it slip away."

"It happens," Nick said. "You still have the photos Harry emailed to you, and you can contact Ramon tomorrow and have him collect more paint."

"Good point," Harry said. "Let's move on. What else is on your mind?"

I took a breath and pushed ahead. "The Ethics Committee meets Monday at noon. It's now nine o'clock Thursday night. I need feedback from five people if we're going to put this thing together and make it stick in time for that meeting. Can either of you think how to help me out?"

Nick and Harry exchanged looks. Nick went first. "I'm off work all weekend and next week. If you need a pilot and a plane, I'm your guy."

Harry raised a hand. "Told you the other day that I'd give this some thought. Here's the thing. If there's shady business going on at that prison, or at the clinic there, someone has to be covering it up. Since recordkeeping these days is all done on computers, any coverups are being done on the dark web and/or by hackers."

"I'm listening," I said.

"It takes one to know one." Harry grinned. "If you need any dark web diving or hacking, let me know. I'll work it into my schedule."

"Thanks, both of you. So glad flying and hacking are your

favorite pastimes. I might take you up on those offers but let me sleep on this. There are some things I need to sort out first."

SLEEP PROVED TO BE elusive. I spent a lot of the night struggling with a guilty conscience, because my best chance to discover what was going on at the prison kept leading me back to Kenzie Eyler, which meant putting her at risk. I argued with myself that she *wanted* to be involved. After all, it was she who had told Ramon her concerns about detainees in solitary. And she told me her suspicions about a cancer cluster and about the missing newborns.

As I drifted off, I realized that without Kenzie's input, Mary Barton and I would never have reached the conclusion we had about organs being taken from the prison clinic's patients. Kenzie was an adult, admittedly a young one, but she had a mind of her own. I put myself in her place and realized that even at her age, I would have wanted to make my own decisions. I could at least ask her if there was a way to get me one of those pills without putting herself at risk. Worst case, she would say no, and I would have to accept that.

I TEXTED KENZIE EARLY Friday morning, hoping to reach her before she left for work. I asked her to call me. My cell rang a few minutes later. Nick shot an inquiring glance my way.

"Kenzie's calling," I said.

Nick nodded, opened the kitchen door and took Ginger for her morning outing.

Our conversation was brief. I asked Kenzie about the pills, and without hesitating, she replied that she had already pocketed one of them. She made up a story for her supervisor about a patient who had gagged trying to swallow it. She claimed when he coughed it up, it landed on the floor at her feet, where she accidentally stepped on it. She didn't think she should make him ingest it, so she had asked for a fresh pill.

"You're sure he didn't suspect anything?" I asked.

"I doubt it. Those things do happen," Kenzie said. "It's not like it's that unusual. Besides, he barely listened. Too busy looking at my chest."

"We need to get that pill analyzed right away. Any chance you'll be coming to Timbergate this weekend?"

She hesitated. "Afraid not. I have to work my second job at the Potterville mini-mart this weekend."

Two jobs. This girl was a doer. "What hours do you work there?"

"Night shift."

At that point, Nick and Ginger came back inside. I told Kenzie to hold for a moment.

"Nick, can we fly to Potterville tomorrow?"

"Don't see why not." So eager to fly his very own plane, he didn't ask why.

Kenzie agreed to meet us at the landing strip Saturday at noon.

I was about to end the call so she could get to work, but I had another question. "Have you heard from Ramon since he left for L.A.?"

"He texted me last night. Said he likes the job down there."

"Good to know. He's been gone almost five days. I was a little worried. I've tried calling and texting him a few times, but I didn't hear back."

"Probably because his phone was stolen. He had to have it deactivated. He just got a new one yesterday."

"Is he using the same number?"

"Yes. Do you have it?" I confirmed the number with Kenzie and let her get on with her day.

"Have time to tell me more?" Nick asked.

"Only if you follow me around while I get ready for work."

I filled him in about Kenzie and the pill, and about her having heard from Ramon.

"That's progress, right?"

"It's two steps in the right direction," I said. "We need to get that pill to Mary Barton, so she can ask her contact to identify it. I'll alert her today."

"Think she can get it analyzed before your meeting on Monday?"

"She said she had a source. Apparently, it's someone local. I'll get the pill to her as soon as we get back tomorrow."

"What about your friend, Ramon? How does he fit?" Nick leaned against our bedroom doorjamb watching me flip through the clothes in my closet.

"I'll ask him to email me a few extra photos of the damage. With luck, he can scrape a little more of the transferred paint off his car and send it to me by overnight mail. Even better, since he's down in L.A., he might be able to locate the rehab facility where Buzz Bateson is a patient." I pulled out a blue and white pin-striped shirt dress and began buttoning. "If Ramon finds Buzz, and Buzz is clear-headed, they can compare descriptions of their hit-and-run vehicles."

"You're hoping for a match, of course." Nick followed me into the bathroom, where I dabbed on some lip gloss and ran a brush through my hair.

"Looking good." Nick stood behind me and wrapped his arms around my waist.

I extricated myself. "Thanks, but don't lead me into temptation. I'm almost late already."

He took a step back. "Okay, but we need to talk about our flight tomorrow. I'm not sure going back to that landing strip so soon is a good idea."

"Why not?"

"Call it a gut check. That little strip is damn close to the prison. Showing up there twice in such a short timespan might draw unwanted attention. Maybe we'd be better off driving. We can go straight to your gal Kenzie's home, pick up the pill, and then hightail it back to Timbergate."

"Almost two hours each way, plus meeting with Kenzie, would take up most of the day." I grabbed my purse and headed for the door. "Do we have to decide right now?"

"Tonight's soon enough. Let me think about it. Maybe I'm being overly cautious."

"No." I shook my head. "You have a point. If we're right about the kind of crimes going on up there, the people involved are capable of anything. I don't want to give them any reason to be suspicious of Kenzie. We should stay away from anyplace close to the prison."

WHEN I GOT TO work Friday, I shot off a text to Ramon, asking him to give me a call. He responded with a text an hour later.

What's up?

Will explain when you call.

OK noonish, he replied.

Knowing his phone had been stolen once, I wasn't taking any chances that it had happened again. Anyone could answer my text with a text. Kenzie said he'd texted her. She didn't say she'd *spoken* with him. I wanted to hear Ramon's voice before I revealed more.

Four hours to wait, but that would have to do. In the meantime, I told Mary and Cleo about the pill Kenzie had pinched. Mary assured me that if I got it to her by Saturday afternoon, she could have it identified in time for Monday's noon meeting. I told Mary I was expecting a call from Ramon and asked if she had heard from Buzz Bateson's ex-wife. Negative. She said she'd try calling again.

RAMON, PLEASE CALL. THE morning dragged while I waited, becoming more convinced that Ramon had been ambushed and left for dead by whoever was in possession of his new phone.

Chapter 32

M Y CELL RANG AT twelve o'clock sharp. I picked up, and with a burst of relief, heard Ramon's voice. Just then, Dr. Darwin Iversen entered the library and strode toward me in a case of impeccably bad timing. I managed to mutter "I'll call you back" before Iversen reached my desk.

The medical director of the Potterville Prison Medical Clinic stood before me. The man my boss had forbidden me to speak to about the questionable incidents there. What did Iversen want with me? Any chance he was dropping by to borrow a book or a journal?

The doctor wore his six decades solemnly, his patrician features marred by a furrowed brow. "You're the staffer who works the Ethics Committee meeting, is that right?"

Oh, boy.

"That's right. My name is Aimee Machado." In case he cared to call me by something other than *staffer*. "What can I do for you?"

"There's word about a meeting taking place on Monday. I'd like to be invited."

"That would be up to the committee chair. Would you like Dr. Poole's contact information?"

"I tried that. She hasn't returned my calls. I thought you might have better luck reaching her."

"I'll try, but it's a little late at this point."

Truth was, I hoped Dr. Poole would drop by later in the day to review the agenda, but that was not something I would tell Iversen. Not until I knew where he was going with his request to attend. For all I knew, he was the mastermind behind the suspected organ snatching, the alleged stolen newborns, and any other callous crimes that might be taking place at the prison.

Iversen took a step back. Nodded. "Please do your best."

That's it? Not so fast. "It might help to know your reason for wanting to attend."

The man frowned and bit his bottom lip. I noticed his head quiver from a tremor so faint that I wondered if I'd imagined it. He quickly recovered his composure.

"I'm sorry, what did you say?"

"I said it would help to know why you want to attend the Ethics meeting."

"Fair enough," Iversen said. "Dr. MacAllister was the chair of that committee until his untimely and tragic death. He had expressed to me that I should be present when he called a meeting. Obviously, he died without passing that information along to you."

Huh? Just what I needed, another new wrinkle to iron out. *If* Dr. Iversen was telling the truth.

"Do you know why he wanted you to be present?"

"Unfortunately, no. And I learned only today that Dr. Poole had called a meeting. I was hoping, if I could be there, I might gain some insight from the other members as to why Heath MacAllister asked me to attend. He was quite resolute." Iversen's tremor struck again, for a split second.

"Dr. Iversen, are you feeling all right?" I asked. "Would you like to sit for a minute?"

"No, thank you. I'm fine." He smiled. "I suspect you've noticed my essential tremor. Not to worry, it's benign, and common, especially as we age. Affects around ten million people in the U.S."

"Sorry, I didn't mean to be rude by mentioning it."

"Think nothing of it." He handed me a card. "I'll let you get back to your chores." He walked straight-shouldered to the exit, hesitated there, and then turned back. "Please let me know if you work something out with Dr. Poole. If not today, over the weekend. I'll be working the clinic at Potterville Prison tomorrow and Sunday. I understand from Mr. Smith that you've been there to discuss your library consortium." That caught me off guard. Was it an innocent remark or a veiled threat?

"Yes, I was hoping to talk to you about that when it's convenient." I flashed on Quinn's earlier decree. *Don't talk to Iversen about the prison clinic patients in solitary confinement.* Still, I could justify my presence at the prison clinic as an attempt to offer library services.

"Another time, perhaps." He pointed toward my desk. "About the Ethics meeting, you can always reach me at the cellphone number on my card."

After he left, I sent a text to Dr. Poole, but postponed thinking further about Iversen's visit in favor of returning Ramon's call, praying that he would answer. When he did, the breath I was holding rushed out, making me woozy.

"Aimee? Are you there?"

Breathe. "Yes, thank heaven I finally reached you."

"Why? Is Kenzie okay?"

"She's fine. I spoke to her this morning. And I'll see her tomorrow in Potterville."

I heard him sigh. "Good. I'm going nuts down here where I can't be sure ... I mean, she's right *there*, you know?"

"I know. But we're going to get all this sorted out. That's why I called. Since you *are* down there, you might be able to help with something."

"Anything." I heard the urgency in his voice.

"Did you ever meet Buzz Bateson when you were working as an interpreter at TMC?"

"The name's familiar, but I'm not sure."

"He's the security guard who found Dr. MacAllister in the stairwell. Just after that, he was injured in a pedestrian hit-and-run."

"I don't see what I can do about that."

I explained that Buzz had been transferred to a rehab facility in L.A. and that Ramon was our best chance to interview him before Monday's Ethics Committee meeting.

"If you find him, and he's able to communicate, the two of you can compare the vehicle in his case with the one that struck your car last week on your way home from Potterville."

"Proof that both incidents were deliberate, caused by the same driver." Ramon paused for a moment. "Aimee, there must be dozens, or hundreds of rehab hospitals down here. Doesn't Bateson's medical record document where he was taken?"

"It might, but HIPAA's blocking our way there. Even as hospital employees, we can't have access to his record without a legitimate reason, and that might not happen."

I explained my hope that Dr. Poole would put Buzz's case on the Ethics agenda. If she came to me before closing, I could pull his medical record; if she put off our meeting to finalize the agenda until Monday, we'd be impossibly short on time to get Buzz's whereabouts to Ramon.

"I'll work on it from this end," Ramon said. "Let me know if you come up with any ideas."

"There is one thing. I'm almost positive you'll find him in a facility owned by CHR. That should narrow it down."

"Good idea. I'll start there."

"Oh, and I just thought of something else. This may not be possible, but it would be a big help to know which doctor at TMC signed off on Buzz's transfer to L.A."

"I'll see what I can do. If I find him, I'll ask about that, too."

Knowing Ramon was alive and well lifted my spirits, but I

couldn't help thinking he was still a potential target. He'd been run off a winding mountain road just over a week ago.

"Ramon. One last thing."

"Yes?"

"Have you done anything about the damage to your car?"

"No, haven't had time, and anyway, I can't afford to get it repaired."

"That's good. See if you can spot any paint transfer on your car from the vehicle that hit you. Try to scrape off just a few little samples of the paint and send them to me by overnight mail. That could be important evidence linking your incidents, so be sure the rest of that transferred paint stays in place."

"I can do that after I get off work tonight. You really think it could help?"

"You never know, maybe when Buzz was hit, some paint transferred to something he was wearing. A watch, belt buckle, steel-toed boot."

"I'll check, if I find him."

"Thanks. Don't let anyone see you scraping paint from your car. And please don't tell anyone down there that you're trying to locate Buzz."

"For sure, that."

My lunch hour was only half over, but I had better use for the other half than eating. Time was becoming a more precious commodity with each moment that passed. I called Cleo, filling her in about Ramon's search for Buzz Bateson and about Dr. Iversen's request to attend the Monday meeting.

"Mary and I have nothing concrete on the pills or on the hit-and-runs. No evidence Dr. Mac was murdered, and absolutely nothing but far-fetched speculation about illegal organ harvesting and baby stealing involving the prison clinic."

"Aimee, that committee is your responsibility. There's not a lot I can do without stepping on your turf. I couldn't even get *my* hands or eyes on Buzz Bateson's medical record. Tell me how you think I can help."

"With advice."

"Ask away."

"Should I ask Dr. Poole for a postponement of Monday's meeting?"

"Hell, no." Cleo said. "You know Poole. Ask her to postpone and at best, she'll simply say no and lose respect for you. At worst, she'll call the meeting off altogether and relieve you of your Ethics Committee duties."

"And what then, put another committee on your shoulders?"

"Lordy, I hope not. But let's not travel any farther down that road. As of now, you have seventy-two hours, give or take a few minutes, to pull a litter of rabbits out of your hat."

"And most of those hours are the weekend, when people are off work, harder to reach."

"Then I'll let you get to it." I heard her sigh. "Hey, just so you know, I'll back you and Mary Barton every way I can. If I hear anything, think of anything between now and Monday noon, I'll text or call."

Seventy-two hours to dig into my top hat and pull out an assortment of rabbits. *Clever, Cleo.* My cottontails included Kenzie, Ramon, Buzz, Veronica MacAllister, and Laurie Littletree. They each held a puzzle piece. If the pieces fit together, they might illustrate a coverup of something heinous enough to trigger at least one murder.

The only person on that list who was available was Kenzie. More than any other puzzle piece, we needed an analysis of that questionable chemo pill. Driving all the way to Potterville and back on Saturday seemed like a terrible waste of time, but Nick had his "gut-check" reasons for choosing not to fly back to that landing strip near Potterville Prison. I trusted his instincts.

Adding to Nick's concern, and mine, was the knowledge that Dr. Darwin Iversen would be working at the prison clinic all weekend. I had no idea how he fit with what went on there. Reason enough to sneak in and out of Potterville without his knowledge.

As I sat staring at my phone, my thoughts drifted back to

Buzz Bateson's ex-wife. Would Mary hear from her in time for Ramon to locate Buzz? Did her current husband even give her the message? Maybe not, if he was the jealous type. Without her help, would Ramon find Buzz on his own? Even if Ramon did find him, we didn't know if he was lucid enough to describe the vehicle that hit him. Maybe Buzz Bateson was a dead end. *Maybe he was just dead.*

Chapter 33

———◆———

S*TOP THE NEGATIVE THINKING.* In less than twenty-four hours, we would have the pill Kenzie had filched. Mary seemed sure that before Monday's meeting, she could get a *yes* or *no* as to whether it was a legit chemo drug.

What else was working in our favor? I drew a blank. What was working against us? Easy one. *Time.* And not just the scant hours left before Monday's meeting. The longer it took to discover the truth about the prison clinic, the more victims might be robbed of their organs. Or their newborns.

Kenzie said the pregnant Latina was within three weeks of her due date. That was four days ago. But due dates were just educated guesses. What if that baby came early? Before Monday?

THREE O'CLOCK CAME AROUND as I sat staring at my monitor, seeing nothing but the face of Kenzie's pregnant patient and hearing nothing but the ticking of the library's wall clock. Louder with each beat. No calls or texts from Mary or Ramon. No word when Gabe might be back from the Azores with Veronica MacAllister and her boys. Nothing from Laurie

Littletree to indicate she had changed her mind about attending the meeting.

I'd heard people describe a sinking sensation, but I had never experienced it as strongly as when I admitted to myself that Mary and I could be wrong about the Potterville Prison medical clinic. Or worse, that we were right but could not put together enough evidence to prompt an investigation.

In the past, when I needed backup from someone in law enforcement, it was always Detective Walter Kass of the TPD who came on board. Unfortunately, nothing in this case, if there *was* a case, would be in his jurisdiction.

So what? There was no jurisdictional reason why I couldn't ask Kass for *advice*. But not yet. Not until the pill was analyzed. We needed at least one piece of concrete evidence that something criminal was happening at the prison clinic.

MY MOOD TURNED GRIM again when Jared Quinn burst into the library an hour later and stalked toward my desk. *Boss not happy*.

I knew why he was fuming even before he reached my desk and made a display of looking at his watch.

"Still no contact info for the MacAllister widow? What the hell is the problem, Aimee? Surely there are other people who need to get in touch with her." By force of habit, he fished a quarter from his pocket and dropped it in my swear jar.

I decided the truth was my best defense. "I've been trying all week. Turns out she's out of the country. Someplace where communication by Internet or cell phone is sketchy at best."

"If you know that, you must be in touch with someone close to her. Give me that much, and I'll work on it myself. Legal counsel is all over my ass about avoiding a lawsuit because of the damn burned out light in that stairwell." Two more quarters clinked into the jar.

Think fast. "I can't give you that. The person who told me used a method you wouldn't approve of."

Quinn's head jerked back. "Jesus. What are we talking about? A hacker?" *Clink.*

"Not exactly, but you'd rather not know the details. You'll have to trust me, I'm still working on it."

"If we don't have her, what are we going to accomplish at the Ethics meeting on Monday?"

How little he knew. Maybe we would accomplish shutting down a black-market organ-harvesting and baby-stealing ring. A glance toward the library entrance told me Dr. Poole had arrived to discuss the agenda. She joined Quinn at my desk, nodding to him.

"Jared."

Quinn returned the nod. "Dr. Poole." *Bobbleheads.*

Then an awkward silence. They seemed to be waiting for me to kickstart a dialogue.

"Mr. Quinn, if we're finished, Dr. Poole and I have business to discuss."

"The Ethics agenda, right?"

"That's right," Poole said.

"Mind if I join you?" he said.

"That would not be appropriate, would it Jared? You're ex-officio." Poole's chin raised a centimeter. "You'll see it at Monday's meeting, along with the rest of the committee members."

I felt heat radiate off Quinn's face from across my desk. He was stuck. Poole had refused, so his only option was to back off, and he didn't like doing that.

Quinn made his exit with some portion of his dignity intact. Poole and I got to work. She reviewed the draft I'd put together, asked a few questions, and even agreed that we should give Quinn the opportunity to address the hospital's potential liability exposure due to Dr. Mac's fall in the dark stairwell. I revealed nothing to Poole about what I suspected was going on at Potterville Prison's medical clinic. That had to wait until there was irrefutable proof. All she knew was that Veronica MacAllister had doubts about her husband's fall in the stairwell being accidental and that she had raised the question of a forensic autopsy. A notion she subsequently vetoed.

I had limited Dr. Poole's draft to three topics, all under the heading of New Business.

First, did Dr. Mac discuss his concern about organ donation with any other members of the Ethics Committee? Considering Dr. Mac's concerns, does the committee want to call for a retroactive review of organ donor cases at TMC? *Pointless, but the committee didn't know that.*

Second, a decision regarding whether Dr. Mac's remains should be autopsied. If so, should the autopsy be clinical or forensic? Administrator Quinn favors a forensic autopsy in an abundance of caution, since no one witnessed the doctor's fall. Dr. Seldon favors a simpler clinical autopsy, asserting that although the patient had been considered brain dead, his life actually ceased while under a doctor's care, making forensic autopsy unnecessary.

The third topic was the issue of a possible liability problem for the hospital due to the burned-out light in the stairwell. Has the physical plant maintenance crew investigated the cause?

"So we have neither of the first responders." Poole's snow-white complexion took on a slight tinge of pink. "Unfortunate, but we'll go ahead with what we do have, although it's looking like an exercise in futility."

Perfect opening. "There is one thing we can do."

I explained that if we could locate Buzz Bateson, there was a chance we could use a contact in L.A. to interview him and get a recorded statement in time for Monday's meeting.

"How would that help, if he's already submitted an incident report?"

"There's always a chance he could recall some helpful detail that wasn't in his report. You might want to put together a list of questions."

"Worth a try," Poole said. "Let's do it."

"I'd like to, but there's a problem. "I have no way of contacting

Buzz without knowing which facility he was transferred to, and I'm not allowed access to his medical record unless there's a reason related to my committee work."

Poole was silent for a moment. I waited to see if Cleo's prediction would come true. Was I going to be relieved of my Ethics Committee duties?

Poole stood and dropped the agenda draft on my desk. "Then I'm making it your business. Use my position as Ethics chair to get access to Bateson's medical record. Put his case on the agenda. I'll work on a list of questions in the event you find him."

She rushed out the exit before I could remind her that even if we found Buzz, we were not sure of his mental state. Was he lucid enough to give us what we needed? I considered running after her but held back. First, get access to that medical record, find out where Buzz was hospitalized, and contact Ramon.

I called the Health Information office to say I was on my way. I locked the library and sprinted toward the main tower. TMC was still in the process of switching from paper charts to electronic medical records, so I wasn't sure which method had been used for Buzz's brief admission.

When I arrived, still attempting to catch my breath, the Health Information clerk handed me a paper chart with very few pages, saying she needed it back as soon as possible so she could finish scanning it into a digital file format.

EMRs, electronic medical records, were the wave of the future, although the clerk mentioned that several doctors on the medical staff were unhappy with the switch from paper to digital. Some, who balked at using computers, insisted on writing up their chart notes by hand and having them scanned into the electronic records.

"Supposed to be more efficient," she said. "Kinda makes extra work for us in Health Information."

"Sorry to hear that." I tried to sound sympathetic, while in a desperate hurry to get my hands on that slender folder.

The clerk asked me to sign for the chart before she would

let me have it. I scribbled my name, adding that it had been requested by Dr. Poole for committee business. I promised to return it Monday, immediately after the noon meeting of Ethics Committee.

Back in the library, it didn't take me long to find the page where the transfer to L.A. was documented. The signature line for the transfer order was zero help. Nothing there except a loopy scrawl and the initials *MD*. There were no nurses' notes included in the folder to point me to someone who might have witnessed the doctor's signature. I had better luck with the destination. The receiving rehab facility in L.A. was listed as Criteria Wellness Center. *Bingo!*

Surely, Ramon would have come across that facility early in his search. I grabbed my cell and started punching in his number. My phone signaled a text before I finished. There he was.

Found Buzz.
Have you seen him?
Sorry. No visitors per next of kin
My hopes evaporated. *Call me.*

Chapter 34

RAMON'S CALL CAME IN seconds. "You were right. He's in a CHR facility."

"I know. I just found it myself. If visitors are being screened, how can you confirm that it's Buzz?"

"I spoke to someone on the phone. She wouldn't confirm he was a patient until I used my credentials as one of CHR's medical interpreters. I said I'd been asked to consult on Buzz's case to determine whether his injuries had left him with any speech defects."

"That worked?"

"Only partially. They confirmed he was a patient, but said they'd need a treatment order from CHR before I'd be given any information about his condition or be allowed to evaluate him."

"Oh, were they going to contact CHR?"

A sudden stab of fear for Ramon's safety left me dry-mouthed. The two CHR liaison officials who were visiting TMC at the time of Dr. Mac's accident had also visited the Potterville Prison clinic during the same trip. They had offered Ramon a lucrative job in L.A. too tempting to refuse. Was that a ploy to get him out of the way? Permanently, if necessary?

"No, the rehab nurse left it to me," Ramon said. "Told me to bring her the necessary documentation ordering the evaluation."

"Shoot. You can't do that without alerting people at home office."

"Don't worry, I'm not doing that. Any luck contacting next of kin? Getting me on a visitor's list?"

"We've struck out on that, so far. Still trying."

"Now what?" I heard Ramon's intake of breath. "We need to do *something*. Kenzie's still working at that prison. Rotten stuff is going on there, and I'm scared for her."

"So am I. I'm doing all I can, and so are a few other people I trust. I'll see Kenzie tomorrow morning. I'll make sure she's okay and I'll get back to you. Try not to worry."

"Tell her ... " he broke off for a moment, "... tell her to be careful."

"I will. You do the same. And be sure to stay in touch over the weekend."

AFTER UPDATING CLEO AND Mary with Ramon's information, I considered making a copy of the page of Buzz's chart showing the transfer information. I had already turned off my copier, so I took a photo of the page with my cell phone, then locked the chart away in my file cabinet and closed the library for the weekend.

Driving home, my thoughts shifted from Buzz to Laurie Littletree, the other first responder. I wondered if she and Daniel were home from his conference in Chicago. Could I change Laurie's mind about attending Monday's meeting? She was a woman pregnant with her first child. Surely, she would identify with any mother whose newborn might be stolen.

The idea of using Laurie's own pregnancy as leverage scored a *thumbs down* from my conscience, but without Buzz, and without Veronica MacAllister, I was running out of options. All Laurie had to do was tell what she had observed in the stairwell where Dr. Mac was found and answer the committee's questions. Even one *in-the-flesh* witness would help counter the complaints I expected on Monday that the Ethics meeting would be a waste of time.

NICK WAS SMILING ALL over himself when I got home. I stepped from the chill October air on our deck into our snug little kitchen, where the aroma wafting from a large soup pot brought to mind a favorite childhood meal.

"Fisherman's stew?" I said.

"Your grandmother's recipe, but I put it together all by myself."

"No help from Amah?"

"Nope. Just me and a bottle of Sauvignon Blanc. Most of it went in the stew, but I saved enough for us to drink with dinner."

"I like this new side of you." I gave him a quick kiss and went to change out of my work clothes.

Back in the kitchen in comfy sweats, I asked how Nick spent his day.

"Alone, mostly. Everyone's working but me. I went to the gym. Then to the hangar to take the 182 up for a quick spin. She's purring like a kitten. After that, I gassed the pickup for our trip to Potterville tomorrow, then came home and made the stew." He wrapped me in a hug. "Your turn."

"I like your day better." I dropped into my chair at the dinette table. "Mine was mostly disappointments and dead ends." I recapped what I'd learned from Ramon. "Buzz is so near to Ramon, yet not within his grasp because of that *no visitors* order."

"Who decided that?" Nick asked.

"It must have been the ex-wife, if she's his only designated next of kin."

"No luck there?"

"Mary Barton has tried calling a few times since she first spoke to the woman's second husband. All she's getting is voicemail."

Ginger got up from her doggy bed in the corner of the kitchen and padded over to where I sat. She rested her chin on my lap and looked up at me with sympathetic brown eyes.

"What brought this on, girl?"

"You sounded sad," Nick said. "She picked up on it."

"You really think so?"

"No doubt in my mind." He handed me a glass of chilled white wine. "Here, sip this while I serve her dinner." He poured kibble into Ginger's bowl and ladled fisherman's stew into ours. He joined me at the table with a plate of warm biscuits. "You're thinking it's hopeless, aren't you? Proving that doctor was murdered to cover up organ theft and maybe even missing babies."

"Don't you?" I asked.

"No, unless you give up, and that's never been your style."

"I've never had so many roadblocks. Everything we need is out of reach."

"What about that pill we're going after tomorrow? You'll have it in time for your friend to get it analyzed. If it turns out to be what she thinks, you can go to the authorities with concrete evidence that the prison medical clinic is up to no good."

Nick's attempt to encourage me helped, but I still had to weigh the danger to Kenzie against any proof the pill might provide.

"I feel so guilty involving her," I said.

"Think back. From what you've told me, she's the one who set this thing in motion. She told Ramon about the prisoners and detainees in solitary, then her suspicion about a cancer cluster. Even the possibility of stolen newborns came from Kenzie."

"All true, but she's up there without anyone to look out for her, and she's not armed with any way to protect herself. You should see her. *Tiny*. She'd have to stretch to reach five feet, and I'd be surprised if she weighs a hundred pounds."

"Do you know if she grew up in Potterville?"

"I guess so. Why?"

"It's rural, remote, nothing there but cattle ranches, sagebrush, and the prison. I'll bet she's tougher than you think."

"I hope so. I assured Ramon I'd look out for her, but it felt like a hollow promise."

"You'll feel better after we meet with her tomorrow," Nick said. "Anything else you want to tackle with the rest of this evening?"

"I'm dealing with so many loose ends, I don't know where to start."

"Just say whatever comes into your mind. Sometimes that helps."

"Harry."

"What about him?"

I shook my head. "I don't even know why that popped out. I guess because he said he could help if I needed him to hack something. If I knew how far he could go without getting caught and arrested, or worse, I might ask him to do some digging."

"Such as?" Nick poured the last of the wine into our glasses.

"Let's consider the woman Kenzie told me about. She got it second-hand from her Latina patient, who's pregnant now and close to her due date. If that story is true and the baby was stolen, whoever took it had to have covered it up. There would be a medical record on file at the prison clinic. There should be a fetal death certificate signed by either the doctor who pronounced the baby's death, or by the county coroner. A scanned copy of that should be part of the stillborn's medical record, or at least the mother's."

"You think the death certificate was faked?"

"First I'd like to know if it even exists."

"Then call your brother. Tell him to get his fanny over here. He might have even more ideas about how you can dig."

Harry's footsteps sounded on the steps leading up to our deck twenty minutes later. I opened the door before he could knock.

"Thanks for coming. Did you bring Rella?"

"She's working. Flew Buck down to L.A. They're due back tomorrow." Harry nodded to Nick. "Hope you're enjoying your time off, buddy."

"Every minute," Nick said. "Your sister's latest investigation is keeping me occupied."

"Any idea why Buck's in L.A.?" I asked Harry. "Is he still negotiating with CHR about the prison drug rehab program?"

"Rella didn't say, and I didn't ask, since we haven't brought her in on your prison clinic puzzler." Harry rubbed his palms together. "Now, let's talk about what I can do for you."

I filled him in. "I need to know whether the newborn's death was documented. Whether a death certificate is on file, either at the prison clinic or with the county coroner. I know there's a procedure in place for getting an informational copy of a death certificate from the county," I said, "but we don't have time to jump through those hoops. If a death certificate for that baby exists, I want the name of the doctor who pronounced the death."

Harry pulled his laptop from its case and put it on our table. "Let me see what I can do. I'll need both parents' names and the baby's, if it was named. And date of death, of course."

I glanced at the time. Only eight o'clock. I called Kenzie's cell. She answered on the second ring. I asked if she knew the name of the woman who suspected her baby had been stolen. The one who told her story to Helena.

"Yes. It's Magdalena Paz. She came to the clinic for prenatal checkups during her pregnancy."

"Do you know her husband's name?"

"I might have seen it in her medical record, but I don't remember."

"Do you remember seeing a copy of the baby's death certificate in the mother's medical record?"

"No. The mother never came back to the clinic. Helena Torres told me Magdalena and her husband were deported two weeks after the birth."

"Thanks, Kenzie. I'll see you tomorrow morning. You can let me know then, if you happen to recall the father's first name. And please don't mention this call to anyone."

"Of course not."

For a woman who appeared fragile and in need of protection, her voice was firm with resolve. She was as eager to solve the mystery surrounding the Potterville Prison clinic as I was.

I wanted to add, "Please stay safe," but Kenzie had already ended the call.

Chapter 35

SATURDAY MORNING NICK AND I were in his pickup and on the road before sunrise. The day was dry, good for traveling the winding mountain highway leading to Potterville. Traffic was light, so Nick was able to keep his high beams on during the first half of the trip to help us spot for deer in the dark road ahead. Dawn broke an hour into our drive, transforming the dense timberland from a palette of black and gray to shades of sepia before the sun finally cleared the eastern mountain peaks. We traveled the remaining miles through a forest of green streaked with shafts of golden morning light.

We reached Potterville fifteen minutes early and found our way to Kenzie's house. Easy, since the town was so small, and she had given us good directions. I wondered if she lived alone. If not, had she found a way to explain our early morning visit to her housemates or family?

The front door of her log home opened as Nick pulled into her driveway and parked next to an aging SUV. Kenzie stepped outside and hurried to where we sat in the pickup.

"Hi, my mom and dad are inside. Just getting up. I told them I was going to breakfast with friends."

"Hop in," Nick said. "Tell us where."

"Nick, wait." I scooted toward him, so Kenzie could fasten her seatbelt. "I don't think Kenzie should be seen with us at a restaurant."

"I thought of that, too," Kenzie said. "I brought donuts and bear claws home from the mini-mart last night." She patted her tote bag. "I even have a thermos of coffee and some paper cups."

She gave Nick directions to a rest area a few miles east of Potterville. He pulled in and parked after we assured ourselves it was deserted. Kenzie took her mini-mart feast from her tote, handing the pastries to Nick and me.

"Before we eat, let me give you the chemo pill, Aimee." She handed me a small plastic pill bottle like the kind used by most pharmacies. It was unlabeled and wrapped with surgical tape to keep the lid secure.

"Which patients are taking this pill?" I asked. "The liver or the kidney cancers?"

"Both. It's the only chemo pill we dispense."

I put it in a zipper pocket of my purse to keep the little container safe until I could hand it off to Mary Barton.

Kenzie remained silent for several minutes while we ate our makeshift breakfast and sipped coffee. We finished quickly, all of us aware of the need to get the pill back to Timbergate and in Mary's hands as soon as possible. Kenzie spoke up just as Nick reached for the ignition.

"Aimee, I'm afraid Helena Torres is going to deliver her baby sooner than her due date." She turned to look me full in the eye. "I saw her just yesterday. It could be any day now, and her husband's still in solitary. I don't know what to do. If it happens this weekend, I won't be there for her."

A jolt of apprehension shot through me. *Worst case scenario.*

I didn't know what to say, so I lied. "Try not to worry. We're going to figure out what's going on at that clinic and make sure nothing happens to your patient."

Just then a four-wheel-drive rig pulled into the rest area and parked next to us. Two men got out, young and muscular in jeans, plaid shirts and boots. They glanced at us and nodded greetings, then hurried off toward the men's restroom. Too much morning coffee, I hoped.

They came out, got back in their rig and left without paying us any further attention, but if they were any good at surveillance, that's probably how they would play it. I caught myself envisioning thugs and hit men behind every tree in the forest and worked to get a grip on my imagination.

I had one last question for Kenzie when Nick stopped to let her out at her house.

"Did you happen to recall the name of the missing Paz baby's father?"

She shook her head. "I've tried, but no. I could sneak a peek at the mother's chart on Monday. Would that help?"

"No, don't do that. I don't want you doing anything that could get you in trouble." *Or put you in harm's way.*

AFTER PROMISING TO STAY in touch with Kenzie, I texted Mary Barton on the way back to Timbergate. She gave us directions to her condo and met us at her door with her purse and car keys in hand. I passed her the tape-wrapped pill bottle.

"I'll text you as soon as I know anything," she said, hurrying to her car.

BACK HOME JUST AFTER eleven o'clock, Nick and I were edgy, neither of us able to concentrate on our usual Saturday routine. Ginger had been closed in our barn-top apartment all morning, so Nick took her out while I sorted through the swarm of unfinished business floundering in the deep end of my mind.

I glanced at my wall clock, a gift from Amah and Jack. The black-and-white art deco cat stared at me from its vantage point above the fridge. Its tail switched away the seconds, daring me to do the math. Forty-nine hours left before the Monday noon

Ethics meeting, if we didn't sleep. Thirty-three hours if we did. *Darn cat.* I started a pot of coffee and began making notes.

Nick and Ginger returned from their outing just as I added a fifth item to my list. Noon already. Another hour gone. Pretty sure the cat smirked.

"Ah, fresh coffee," Nick said. "What are the chances there's food?"

"I think we have bread and peanut butter." I put down my pen. "Want me to make PBJs?"

"I see you have notes." Nick opened the fridge and pulled out a jar of Amah's peach jam. "I'll fix lunch. You talk."

"You call them notes. I call it a wish list."

"In any particular order?"

"I'm still working on that." I scanned my notes. "The one that pops out is Detective Kass. I keep thinking he might be willing to hear us out. Originally, I thought nothing about this case was in his jurisdiction, but maybe I'm wrong. Dr. Mac's death occurred after he fell in the hospital. That's in the city limits. And his home, where the break-in happened, is also in Timbergate's city limits."

Nick brought our sandwiches to the table. "Didn't you tell me the widow refused to call the police?"

"Yes, but I'm pretty sure the police department doesn't need her permission to investigate if they have reason to believe there's a crime."

"And you'd like to ask Kass about that?"

"That, and more."

"What about the hospital? How's your boss going to react if you pull the police into investigating the doctor's death?"

"CHR's legal counsel in L.A. is breathing down Quinn's neck. They want TMC cleared of liability. I think they'd rather believe the fall down that stairwell was foul play than to have it deemed negligence on the part of the hospital."

"Sounds like a private talk with Kass is worth a shot," Nick said. "What else is on your list?"

"I'd love to have another chance to talk to Laurie Littletree."

"Didn't you tell me she was out of town with her husband? After that trouble you and Laurie were involved in a while back, Daniel Littletree is not your biggest fan."

"Still not, but Laurie has a mind of her own. If she doesn't want to upset Daniel by attending the Ethics meeting, maybe she'll at least talk to Dr. Poole, report anything she observed."

"Wouldn't she and Bateson have filled out incident reports back when it happened?"

"They did, but no one ever had a chance to question either of them afterward. Maybe being interviewed would have helped them recall more details."

"Do you know if Laurie and her husband are back in town?" Nick asked. "Have you tried to contact her?"

"I've texted her several times with no reply, but I keep trying. That's on my list."

"What's next?"

"Buzz Bateson. I'm still waiting to hear from Ramon Silva. He's trying to get permission to interview Buzz in that L.A. rehab center."

"What's the holdup there?"

"Next of kin is Buzz's ex-wife. She can't be reached, and apparently, she's the one who requested Buzz's 'no visitors' status."

"She's his ex. Why the hell would she care?"

"Who knows? People are strange. And they can be incredibly vindictive. Have you ever watched one of those TV shows where the two sides air their dirty laundry in front of a judge?"

"Sadly, yes, but only once. Amazing that they never run out of people willing to do that for the world to see."

"I know. I don't get it either, but maybe Buzz's ex is that type, dragging around an everlasting grudge."

Nick shrugged. "Either that, or she thinks she's doing the right thing for some reason. What else have you got?"

"Waiting on Mary to report the chemo pill analysis. If we're right, and the pills the clinic is dispensing are fake, we have even more reason to talk to Kass. He can advise us where to go with that incriminating evidence."

"What about Harry? I thought he was going to do some cyber snooping?"

"He was going to try to get a copy of the missing baby's death certificate."

"Wasn't that just yesterday?" Nick asked.

"It was. I told him I'd ask Kenzie for the father's name this morning, which she didn't have. I texted him with that news while we were on our way home."

"Have you heard from Harry since we got back?"

"Not so far. I'll check again." I pulled out my cell and discovered my battery was low. I plugged it into my charger.

"He sent a text an hour ago." I read it to Nick.

Certificate says stillbirth

"What good will that do?" Nick said. "It won't show evidence of a crime."

"I'm not so sure. It's a contradiction to what the mother told Kenzie's other pregnant patient, Helena Torres. Magdalena Paz was certain her newborn was alive and appeared healthy."

Nick reached out to touch my shoulder. "Sweetheart, I hate to dim your hopes, but it's the word of an undocumented immigrant against the doctor who delivered that baby. You know how that will go."

"Not if we can pile on more evidence of a coverup."

I called Harry for details. "How did you do it? Do you think you'll be found out?"

He laughed. "A third-grader could have done it. And no, I won't be."

"Did you get a copy of the certificate?"

"I'm sending it as we speak. Let me know if you need anything else."

I looked at the document on my phone, unsure whether I was seeing what I thought was there. I sent the certificate to my printer. As it fed out on paper, I stared at the signature line.

The familiar scrawl was illegible, except for the initials *MD*. A match to what I'd seen on the form authorizing Buzz Bateson's transfer from TMC to the Criteria Health Resources facility in L.A.

"Nick, look at this." I pointed to the signature.

"What? There's no name. Just a corkscrew scribble and the initials *MD*. How's that going to help you? They're all *MD*s."

"The point is, this matches what's on the order for Buzz Bateson's medical transfer." I blew a breath. Took in another. "This is the link we've been looking for. It connects the doctor involved with Buzz Bateson's transfer to the missing baby at the Potterville detention center."

Nick grimaced. "Aimee, I hate to say it, but you still don't have a name—"

"I know. It's thin. But I'm positive it's a match. The writing can be confirmed by forensics. Now we have two bits of evidence on our side." I got up and paced our small kitchen floor in circles, prompting Ginger to perk up her ears and tilt her head, watching me.

"You're confusing the dog," Nick said.

I dropped back in my chair, phone in hand. "Nick, it's time to contact Detective Kass."

Chapter 36

THE CAT ON THE wall switched its tail with each second as I waited for Kass to answer my text. One o'clock. Forty-seven hours 'til the Ethics meeting if we didn't sleep. Thirty-one if we did. Kass had given me his personal cell number several months ago, during a time when Nick and I needed his help with another criminal situation.

Nick sat across from me, drumming his fingers on the tabletop. "While you're waiting, there's one thing you forgot to put on your list."

"What's that?"

"Buck and Rella are still down in L.A. today. He's still negotiating with your hospital's parent company about the drug rehab program at Potterville Prison."

"Oh shoot, you're right. I *had* almost forgotten. We can't let him go ahead with investing if there's something terrible going at the prison and CHR's clinic there." I touched my phone, willing it to ring. "Have you tried to warn Buck? Ask him to back off until we're sure?"

"On what grounds?" Nick asked. "Buck's been pretty patient with us in the past when we needed him, but we've never interfered with his business affairs. I've had no concrete reason to read him in on this."

"Will he and Rella be in L.A. all weekend?"

"Unclear. Why?"

"I'm still worried about Ramon. About his efforts to contact Buzz Bateson being noticed by the wrong people."

"How can Buck help with that?" Nick said.

"Maybe bring Ramon home. Fly him out of L.A. in case someone down there is in on what's going on at Potterville Prison."

Nick shook his head. "It seems premature to involve Buck and Rella at this point." He nodded toward my phone. "Let's wait and see what Kass thinks about the detainee's stillborn baby and the matching signature on the Bateson transfer."

Minutes ticked by with nothing from Kass, while Nick and I sat at the table in silence, each of us lost in our own thoughts while the cat's tail continued its incessant switching.

The sudden, jarring ring of my landline phone propelled me out of my chair. Not Kass. He never used my landline number. Amah was calling.

"Sweetie, I thought you'd want to know your Uncle Gabe is back in town."

I took a moment to process her unexpected news. "He's here at the ranch? I need to talk to him right away. I'll come up now."

"Slow down, honey, he isn't here at the house. He's with the MacAllister woman and her sons. Making arrangements of some kind. He said to let you know he'll be in touch later today."

"Thank you, thank you. I'll call him."

Ginger jumped up from her bed, reacting to my excitement with a soft *woof* and a spinning tail. Nick signaled her to sit at his side, but she kept her focus on me as I relayed Amah's message.

"What do you want to do?" Nick said.

"Gabe wanted me to know Veronica's back in town. That's

a good sign. I want to talk to her about Dr. Mac's shoes. Maybe she's changed her mind about getting the police involved. Maybe she'll even talk to Kass."

I called Gabe's cell. He answered on the first ring.

"Aimee. I was expecting your call."

"Is Veronica with you? Is she back in the States?"

"No and yes. She's not with me now, but she's back from the Azores, tucked away where she and her boys are safe. I'll be out at the ranch in an hour. Let's talk then."

"Is she coming with you?"

"No. All three of them are jet-lagged. They're going to rest."

We ended the call and I filled Nick in.

"Knowing you, the next hour is going to feel a lot longer than sixty minutes." He massaged my shoulders. "Want to take a quick run to relieve some tension?"

"Good idea." We changed into our running shoes and headed out to the road in front of Jack and Amah's house. Nick let me set the pace, keeping Ginger close at his left side. We turned off onto our favorite side road, one populated by ranches with lots of acreage, where we could run in the crisp afternoon air with minimal traffic.

Nick allowed Ginger to leave his side to do some doggy sniffing and exploring, knowing she wouldn't stray far from her master. When we reached a massive oak tree that marked two miles, we did a one-eighty and headed back, slowing to a walk for the last half mile. Nick patted his left thigh. Ginger immediately heeled.

He took my hand. "Feel better?"

"Physically, yes, but still feeling the weight of questions and doubts."

"Maybe Gabe will be able to help with that."

"Hope so." I picked up my pace, trotting toward home.

"Mrs. MacAllister is coping better than she was when you saw her in San Francisco," Gabe said. "I left her with Lucas and

Wendi on Faial while I took an inter-island plane over to San Miguel to take care of some business."

We were all gathered over coffee in the family room of the main house, where Amah had put out a plate of persimmon cookies.

"Veronica and her sons were at Mom and Dad's house in Horta?" I shook my head. "Then why didn't you let me know? Why didn't they?"

"It was Mrs. MacAllister's request. She wanted time without pressure to think through what to do. Your parents and I agreed to let her have that." Gabe smiled. "I think they were able to guide her in the right direction."

"If anyone could, they would be the ones," I said.

"What did she decide?" Nick asked.

"She's willing to sit down and tell her story to Aimee and whoever chairs the hospital's Ethics Committee."

"When?" Finally, something was going our way.

"That's up to you. Whenever you want to arrange it."

"It'll have to be today or tomorrow. The Ethics Committee meets at noon on Monday."

Gabe handed me one of his cards. "Call the number written on the back. It's secure."

"I'd like to arrange for Detective Kass to be with us. Do you think Veronica would agree to that?"

Gabe nodded. "She might. Can't hurt to ask."

I called Veronica. She okayed Kass. I called him again. He answered and agreed to a meeting. And finally, I called Dr. Poole. She listened to my story as I filled her in on everything I knew and suspected about Potterville Prison and the clinic and how they were tied to Heath MacAllister's death. With no questions asked, she agreed to meet with Veronica, Kass and me.

TWO HOURS LATER, WE three women sat in a TPD interview room. Veronica's sons were being looked after in a separate room by a female officer. Kass had agreed to the interview based on his involvement with me in a previous case. He knew he could trust my instincts.

I had briefed Kass on the phone beforehand with the facts about Dr. Heath MacAllister as we knew them. I asked that he hear us out and decide whether to open a case file investigating Dr. Mac's death. And to advise us where we should go to request an investigation into the prison clinic's suspicious treatment of an alarming number of alleged liver and kidney cancer cases.

Kass arrived just as I finished introducing Dr. Poole to Veronica. I explained that Poole was asked to attend because she had been appointed to chair the Ethics Committee. Fit and in his early forties, Kass wore khakis and a deep blue polo shirt. As always, he looked less like a policeman and more like a golf pro. Only his buzz cut gave him away. I made the remaining introductions, and Kass ran through the formalities, stating that he would be recording the interview.

He then pulled out his pen and notebook and started the recorder. "Mrs. MacAllister, please tell me about your husband, his work, and why you suspect his death was not an accident."

Veronica's flushed cheeks and the blotches of red on the pale skin of her neck hinted at an acute stress reaction. Her hands were shaky as she brushed them through her limp, straw-colored hair. She cleared her throat and began telling Kass of the troubling phone calls to her home, and of the threat about whistleblowers. She said her home had been invaded after Dr. Mac's death. That a toy whistle was left on one of her twin sons' beds.

"Anything else?" Kass asked. "Anything concrete besides the whistle you found?"

"Yes. I have proof Heath's accident was staged." Veronica leaned down and pulled a pair of athletic shoes from her large tote bag. "They said he tripped over a shoelace. Blamed these shoes for Heath's accident, but that's impossible. I'm certain they do not belong to him and that he's never worn them."

"Shoes?" Kass's brow creased and his lips formed a thin line. My breath caught. Were we striking out?

"Mrs. MacAllister," he said, "how can you be certain the shoes aren't his? Could he have bought them without your knowledge? Worn them only at his work?"

"No." Veronica placed her palm on the table. "First, he never wore work shoes with laces. But more importantly, Heath has … had … a special situation with shoes. One of his feet was two sizes smaller than the other. It's known as split sizes, and more common than you might imagine." She stopped for a breath. "Common enough that there are major department store chains that specialize in accommodating people with this condition. Heath ordered all of his shoes from the same place, and always bought at least three pairs at a time." She took another pair of shoes out of her tote, pointing at the strips of material that secured the shoes by adhering to each other. "They're known as *hook and loop* fasteners. This is what he wore. Never laces." Her voice faltered, she swallowed, blinked moisture from her eyes and continued. "I brought this new pair from our home. They've never been worn."

"Split sizes," Kass said. "Never heard of it." I watched him scribbling notes on his little pad. I glanced at Dr. Poole. Her eyebrows lifted.

"Can you help me?" Veronica asked.

"I'll see what I can do," he said. "Can you leave both pairs of shoes with me for the time being?"

"Yes, of course," she said.

He glanced up at her from his notes. "Do you happen to have the whistle you found in your home?"

She pulled a small paper bag from her tote. "Here it is. I thought of fingerprints, so I picked it up by the little chain attached to it." She passed the bag to Kass. "I hope you can find something."

Kass took the bag from her. "Mrs. MacAllister, there's one essential question we haven't covered." He glanced at me, then turned back to Veronica. "Did your husband ever tell you what he was going to reveal at the hospital's Ethics Committee meeting?"

"No, only that if he was right, the impact would reach far beyond Timbergate Medical Center."

With that, I had to speak up. "Mrs. MacAllister, did your husband ever mention that an unusual number of prisoners and detainees were being transported to a facility off the prison property for cancer surgeries?"

"You mean the possible cancer cluster?"

"Is that what he thought was happening?" Kass asked.

She frowned. "At first. Then he seemed to change his mind. He stopped talking about it."

"Is there anything else?" Kass asked her.

"No, that's all I can think of," she said.

"Now," Kass glanced at his notes, looked up at Veronica. "What about witnesses to your husband's fall down that stairwell?"

Veronica turned to me. "Aimee tells me neither of the first responders who found him are available."

I filled Kass in on both Laurie and Buzz Bateson. "We're still working on getting either or both to consent to Ethics Committee interviews, but it doesn't look good."

He flipped through the pages of his notes. "You told me Bateson was in a rehab facility in L.A. with a 'no visitors' order. Let's first see if something can be done about that."

"Then you're going to investigate Dr. MacAllister's death?" I asked. "Will you request a forensic autopsy?"

"I'm afraid that would be premature. We can investigate the suspected intruder in Mrs. MacAllister's home, but before opening a homicide case, I'd like to have more to go on than a toy whistle and the irregular shoe sizes. Those kinds of things can be explained away. I'd prefer to question the witnesses who found the injured doctor before I decide how to proceed."

"If Buzz Bateson's in shape to appear before the committee, there's a chance we can expedite his return to Timbergate," I said. "Nick's boss is in L.A. this weekend and due to return tomorrow on his business jet. I guarantee he'd transport Mr. Bateson back to Timbergate."

"That's good to know. Please ask Nick to alert his boss."

"I will, but there's a hitch." I explained about the 'no visitors' problem and the next of kin situation.

"Kass's eyes narrowed. "Let me look into that. And see if you can arrange for me to interview the other first responder. Mrs. Littletree, is it?"

"Yes. I'll try, but I'm not optimistic," I said. "She's already refused to be interviewed by the Ethics meeting on Monday. I'm still hoping to persuade her to attend."

Kass looked at Dr. Poole. "What are the chances if my attending that meeting?"

"If that will help you decide whether we have a case, I'll see to it," Poole said.

As we were leaving the interview room, my cell chirped. When we reached the lobby, I checked the sender. Mary Barton's text was brief, but clear. *Pill is phony.*

To avoid troubling Dr. Mac's widow with what we suspected about the prison clinic, I signaled to Dr. Poole to wait until Veronica had exited the building. I then told Poole what Mary Barton's message confirmed, and we went to Kass with the new information.

The three of us trooped back into the room we had just left, and I explained in meticulous detail why I suspected that inmates and detainees at Potterville were being robbed of their organs under the guise of having been diagnosed with liver or kidney cancer. I cited the newly confirmed evidence that those patients were being treated post-surgery with phony chemo pills. I emphasized the contradiction about detainee Magdalena Paz's newborn, documented as a stillbirth, when she swore it had been born alive and healthy. I pointed out the matching signatures on Buzz Bateson's transfer order and on the Paz baby's death certificate. I repeated Kenzie's worry that another Latina detainee would be going into labor any day.

"Bloody hell," Dr. Poole uttered a rare profanity. "We can't let another child be born there. Aimee, I want to look at those two documents. There's a chance the signature is familiar to me if it's a colleague I've consulted with on a case."

I scooted to the edge of my chair. "Shall we go directly to the hospital from here?"

"Unfortunately, I can't. Tobias is speaking at a urology conference in San Francisco this Saturday. We're leaving town as soon as I'm finished here, and we might have to stay in the city for the rest of the weekend." She took out her cell and tapped. "I've made a note to stop by the library first thing Monday morning. Is seven too early?"

"No. I'll be there." If Poole did recognize the matching signatures, we would know several hours before the Ethics meeting started at noon.

With that settled, Kass took charge again by asking me to write up a detailed description of everything I knew or suspected about the possibly bogus cancer cases and the disputed stillbirth involving the prison clinic. He spent a few minutes explaining that his jurisdiction did not include crimes outside the city limits. He did agree to contact the county sheriff with our concerns about Potterville Prison and the clinic there.

"Email your notes to me before the day's over," Kass said. "I want to get the ball rolling on this right way, but I can't take it to Henry Preston until I have enough for him to work with."

Sheriff Preston was popular in Sawyer County. Crime stats had dropped throughout the county in the year since he had taken office. I wondered how he'd react to the idea of investigating a private prison filled with federal inmates, most of whom were undocumented immigrants. Sounded daunting to me, but maybe he liked a challenge.

Chapter 37

Six o'clock back at the ranch, Nick had dinner waiting. Barbecued ribs and baked beans from the Coyote Creek Deli. Between bites, I filled him in on the meet-up with Kass.

"Sounds like the widow's explanation about the shoes tipped the scales in your favor," Nick said. "How many killers would have anticipated the thing about split sizes?"

I held up a finger while I swallowed. "Probably none. Although you bring up a point when you say 'killers.' If murder was the goal, why not make sure Dr. Mac was dead? Why leave him alive in that stairwell?"

"Timing?" Nick said. "They might have heard someone coming before they could finish the job. Had to get away without being spotted."

"That's the only answer that makes sense to me."

"So, do you go into *wait-and-see* mode until you hear back from Kass?" Nick must have seen an incredulous expression on my face, because he burst out laughing. "That's what I thought." He wiped his hands on a paper napkin. "Out with it, woman. What's next?"

"He's not convinced about a homicide case yet, but now we

have at least some law enforcement leverage on our side, and Kass agreed to contact Sheriff Preston about the prison clinic. I'm trying to think of every connection, every possible piece of evidence or information he could use when I write up my notes."

"Didn't you already cover all of that with Kass?"

I explained that Kass wanted it documented in writing.

"What about the doctor? What's it going to take to make a homicide case?"

"The problem is there are things we still don't know." I cleared the table and sat back down with a notepad. "Buzz Bateson, for starters. Is he in any shape to be interviewed by the committee? And if he is, can we get him out of that facility in L.A. and back to Timbergate by Monday?"

"Isn't Kass working on that?"

"Yes, but who knows if he'll succeed? I glanced at the cat clock. *Six forty-five.* "And I need to contact Ramon down in L.A. Let him know what's going on about Buzz." I pointed my pen at Nick. "And you need to contact Buck and Rella. If Kass manages to get Buzz discharged from that place, we need them to fly him home. And maybe Ramon, too."

Nick pulled out his cell. "On it."

He made his call while I dashed off notes, trying to establish some sort of order. Contact Laurie Littletree. Surely, she and Daniel were back from Chicago, or at least on their way. If they *were* back in town, I was hoping to use Dr. Poole's influence to bring Laurie around. If Poole was willing. Her reaction to the story of a stolen baby told me she would do whatever it took to unearth the crimes at Potterville Prison. In spite of her own pregnancy, or maybe because of it, Laurie might feel the same.

My mind raced in a new direction, realizing Laurie might have another piece of the puzzle. As a hospital nurse, she worked with all sorts of patients and the doctors who followed their care. She might recognize the matching signatures on Buzz's transfer order and on the death certificate for the disputed 'stillbirth' of the Latina detainee's baby.

I had just texted Kass my notes when my cell rang, still in my hand. Kenzie Eyler was calling.

"Aimee? Can you hear me?" she whispered.

"Barely. What is it? Where are you?"

"I'm at the prison clinic."

"Why tonight?"

"The clinic's night shift CMA didn't show up for work, so I was called in. Helena Torres is in labor."

I couldn't imagine worse news. I choked out a response. "But it's too soon. Are you sure?"

"I'm afraid so."

"Why were you called? Do they expect you to deliver her baby?"

"I probably could, but no. The OB physician has been notified, but Helena's only just started the first stage of labor. It could be up to twelve hours before she's in active labor, and another three to five before she delivers. Mr. Smith wants me to stay with the patient at the clinic to monitor her progress and let the OB know when it's time to show up for the delivery."

"What do you want me to do?" I said.

Kenzie murmured her answer. "We have to get her away from here before she goes into active labor. She's afraid they'll take her baby like—I have to go."

"Kenzie? Kenzie?" She was gone.

I ran out to the deck where Nick was reading a book by the light of his headlamp. Ginger, resting at her master's feet, acknowledged my presence with a flop of her tail.

"We have an emergency."

Nick closed his book and turned off his lamp with annoying calm. "Okay, shoot."

I told him about Kenzie's call, repeating the short conversation *verbatim*.

"Get her out of there?" he said. "That's not much to go on. Any ideas?"

"None that make good sense." I hugged myself against the chilly night air. "All I can think to do is call Detective Kass."

"What would that do? No jurisdiction, no grounds to justify the Sheriff or any other law enforcement agency interfering."

"What's left?" I said. "Unless we can find out where that patient is being taken to give birth. Maybe—"

My cell rang. Kenzie again, her voice muffled.

"Sorry, I have to sneak. I can't get caught talking to you."

"Then hurry."

"When you flew up here before, did you notice a building next to the landing strip that looks like a warehouse?"

"Yes. I remember."

"Helena told me that's where Magdalena Paz was taken to deliver her baby. I think that's where all of the so-called cancer patients have been taken for their surgeries."

"In a warehouse? That's impossible."

"No, it isn't," Kenzie said. "I'm pretty sure there's a secret surgery suite hidden in that building."

"Why do you think that? Do other people you work with know about it? Do your patients?"

"No other employees that I know of. And every patient I've worked with except one was sedated during transport before and after their procedures. Prisoners and detainees are supposed to be transported to a full-service hospital somewhere in the area for complicated medical procedures or childbirth."

"Then how did Magdalena Paz know the truth about the warehouse building?"

"She'd seen her newborn when it was delivered, so she was positive her baby was not a stillbirth. She was convinced she'd been lied to, so while she was still at the secret facility in the warehouse, she turned off the drip line feeding into her IV tube, pulled out the IV needle, then re-taped it to look like it was still connected. When the attendant came to push a sedative into her IV, she pretended it had put her out, but she was conscious and figured out where she was."

"So, she faked being under, but was awake when they took her out of the warehouse and back to the prison clinic?"

"Yes."

"Why didn't she say something then?"

"Who could she tell? Who could she trust? She was afraid to make any accusations, but she did tell Helena Torres about the surgery facility in the warehouse. She warned her it would be dangerous to say anything but wanted her to know that it wasn't safe to deliver her baby there."

"So, you and Helena are the only people up there who know about the warehouse?"

"We're the only *innocent* people who know. But we both have to pretend we don't. Unless you can get Magdalena's story to the police or the sheriff. Someone who can help us."

"This could be damning evidence, but Magdalena's been deported, so we might never find her to tell her story."

"But we've got to save Helena and her baby," Kenzie said. "There must be some way."

"We're trying to think of something. If we fly up there, we can't land at that strip without drawing attention."

"There's no reason for anyone to be there late at night until Helena's in her second stage of labor. That's when I'm supposed to arrange transport and text the OB, and it could be as much as eight hours from now. If we're going to get her away from here, we can't wait that long, or she'll be too close to delivery."

"It's eight o'clock now. What do you suggest?"

"If you fly up right away, no one will be around at the landing strip or the warehouse. It's way too early. When you get there, text me, and I'll find a way to bring Helena to you."

"What about you? If you do this, you'll have to come with us. You'd be in terrible danger if anyone found out what you'd done."

"I can't think of any other way to keep Helena safe."

"Kenzie, there's a chance Nick and I will be spotted and confronted if we land at that strip."

"If that happens, can you pretend it's an emergency? Engine trouble?"

"I'll talk to Nick and get back to you."

"And I'll keep you posted on Helena's progress," Kenzie said, "but from now on, we need to text. I can't risk another call."

"Who else is there with you?"

"It's just me in the clinic. Mr. Smith left. He said he had a migraine and wanted to go home and sleep it off. I think he was just bored. He told me to contact him if anything came up that I couldn't handle on my own. The only other person here is a correctional officer. She's hanging out in the break room, playing games on her phone. She pokes her head in once in a while to ask if it's time."

"Is she the one who's supposed to take Helena to the warehouse?"

"The cover story is that she's taking the patient to the landing strip, so she can be airlifted to a hospital."

"But you're sure she's really going to the warehouse?"

"I'd bet my life on it," Kenzie said.

I was afraid Kenzie might be right about that, but I kept the thought to myself.

"Is that the same CO who was there the day I visited you?"

"Yes." Kenzie chuckled. "She's been chugging diet sodas to make sure she stays awake no matter how late it is when the time comes."

"Then how can you get Helena out of the clinic under her nose?"

"I have an idea about that."

"Kenzie, you said you're supposed to be in contact with the OB. Is it someone from Timbergate? Is there a chance Dr. Iversen is going to deliver that baby?"

"I don't know. He isn't an OB, but he's the medical director here, and he could probably handle the delivery if it's uncomplicated. Mr. Smith said I'm supposed to tell the guard when it's time, and she'll contact the physician."

"Did he say why all the secrecy?"

"No idea, but it sounded suspicious. I didn't want to seem too curious."

Something about Dr. Iversen had bothered me. He appeared to take very little interest in his duties as medical director of the clinic. Either that, or he was up to his eyebrows in the worst kind of corruption. No wonder Dr. Mac had been ready to blow the whistle.

"Kenzie, can you send me a copy of Dr. Iversen's signature? He must have signed lots of the documents filed in that clinic."

"Sure. Why?"

"Just a hunch. I'll explain later."

"Okay, but right now, we have to keep Helena and her baby safe. There must be something—" And she was gone again.

I told Nick Kenzie's idea. "What do you think?"

"I think it's a hell of a risk and could end up getting a pregnant woman killed," Nick said. "Not to mention Kenzie and ourselves. What's she going to do about the CO who's hanging around waiting to transport the patient?"

"She said she had an idea about that, but she didn't explain."

We moved back inside where the lingering aroma of barbecue in our warm, cozy kitchen drew a sharp contrast to the bleak chill washing over me.

Chapter 38

I PACED OUR SMALL living room trying to calm my breathing. Nick stepped in front of me and put his hands on my shoulders. "Whoa, you're making me dizzy."

"I can't help it. The timing is terrible. Most of what we need to put in place to expose that prison is still up in the air."

"Maybe that's where *we* need to be. If you want to go, we can take the Cessna."

"And land at that same private strip where we went before? So close to the building where the detainee's baby will be born?"

"It's either fly, or we spend an hour and a half driving up there," Nick said. "If this plan works, the plane will make for a better getaway."

"What about landing there at night?"

"If that strip is being used for what I think it is, there'll be landing lights on tonight."

"You think that's how the black-market operation works? Buyers and sellers fly in under the radar and out again?"

"Has to be something like that. If that baby is already sold, it could be on its way to anywhere in the world within hours of its birth."

"Then there must be a lot of coordination going on.

Newborns and viable organs are both fragile cargo. If anything went wrong, who knows how much money the sellers would lose?"

"Hundreds of thousands," Nick said. "Or why risk running a criminal setup that complicated?"

My cell chirped. A text from Kenzie.

Can you help?

I showed it to Nick. "What do you think? Can you fake engine trouble if we're spotted landing up there?"

He blew a long breath. "That's the easy part. Getting Kenzie and the pregnant woman on our plane and out of there is another matter."

"Not if Kenzie's idea works," I said.

"Then text Kenzie. If she's been told the patient is being flown to a full-service hospital for the birth, how long does she stay with the guard and the patient?"

I texted Nick's question to Kenzie. She responded in minutes. I gave Nick her answer.

"The phony plan that was fed to Kenzie is that she's supposed to accompany the patient as far as the landing strip where a helicopter or an airplane will be waiting. From there, the CO will release Kenzie to take the vehicle back to the prison. When Kenzie is back at the clinic, she's supposed to call Mr. Smith. When he gets back to the clinic, she can go home."

"Phony is right," Nick said. "If a 'copter or a plane is there, it's real purpose will be to fly the newborn to some unknown destination."

"That's what Kenzie thinks. The guard told her an OB nurse would be on board to accompany the patient to the hospital where she's supposed to give birth." I scrolled through the rest of her text. "She said we should wait at the landing strip. When there's still plenty of time in Helena's early stage of labor, Kenzie will lie to the CO, saying it's time for Helena to be taken there to meet the flight."

"And that's when we're supposed to confiscate the patient and fly her and Kenzie out of there?"

"That's the plan."

"Then we need to stay out of sight until the CO transporting the patient reaches the landing strip."

"If Kenzie's idea works, the CO won't be doing the transporting. Kenzie will be driving Helena to the landing strip by herself."

"So, we just load both of them in the plane and take off before anyone's the wiser?"

"Kenzie said no one will be arriving there until she alerts them that Helena is in active labor."

"I hope she's right. We can hide ourselves, but we sure as hell can't hide an airplane."

I texted Kenzie. And waited, staring at the cat's tail on the wall, sweeping the minutes forward. Almost nine o'clock. While we waited, I grasped for ideas. Whatever might increase our chances of saving that baby.

"Nick, remember that hangar building on the side of the strip opposite the warehouse? If we land and hide the plane in there, we'll be in place when Kenzie shows up with Helena Torres."

"But there's no guarantee we'd find an unlocked hangar. Or if we did, that there'd be an empty space inside."

"I'll ask Kenzie if she knows anything about the hangar."

Kenzie replied, texting that the building had been there for decades and was seldom used. Only a couple of the hangars were rented and locked, the rest were empty.

"Her uncle stows his plane there," I said. "Rents from a property manager in Potterville."

"She's sure about that? The others are empty?"

"I guess she can't be positive." My shoulders twitched. I shook it off. "Nick, I know it's risky, but Kenzie and that pregnant woman could be in terrible danger. And think about that baby. What kind of future will it have?"

"I'll take bolt cutters along in case those empty hangars are locked." Nick glanced at the clock on the wall. "Too bad we can't alert Detective Kass, tell him what's going on, but we're not on solid legal ground here."

"I know. We can't implicate him by telling him what we intend to do, even though he knows what we suspect is going on up in Potterville."

"If we can tie the prison and its clinic to Dr. MacAllister's case, it'll be a whole new ball game."

"Let's aim for that," I said. "When do we leave?"

"The sooner, the better."

"I'll let Kenzie know."

"And I'll gather what we need. Where's your weapon?"

"Nightstand. Top drawer." I looked up from my phone. "What about Ginger? Do we leave her here? Drop her off with Harry? We can't ask Amah and Jack to watch her. I don't want them to know what we're doing."

"We'll take her with us," Nick said.

"You're sure?"

He smiled. "She's a weapon, too."

"So is Harry. We need him to coordinate with Buck and Rella and everyone else we have to be in touch with."

OUR COCKPIT CLOCK READ nine twenty-five as we taxied down the Timbergate Muni runway. Ginger was snug in her kennel, which was strapped down in the cargo area to keep its position steady, maintaining the balance so critical in flying a small aircraft. I was struck for a moment by that thought. Nick and I had chosen to balance the risk to our own lives against those of Kenzie and Helena. I had to believe it was worth the gamble.

The flight passed quickly, without messages from Kenzie or Harry. Either no one had tried to reach us, or we were in a dead zone. There had to be cell service near the prison. We could text reliably once we were in range.

Nick reached over to touch my arm. He pointed out the cockpit window where two faint strips of lights marked our destination. My heartbeat lurched into high gear. *No turning back.*

Chapter 39

Touching down was as smooth as could be expected on a dirt strip. Nick and I sat silent in the cockpit for a few moments. The clock on the instrument panel read ten fifteen. We held our weapons in our hands in case we were approached by someone who was expecting a different arrival. Ginger finally broke the silence with a muffled whine. Nick gave her a verbal command to stay quiet.

"Do you have a cell signal?" he asked.

"Yes, I'll text Kenzie. Let her know we're here."

"Looks like she was right," he said. "No one's around."

"If her plan works, we'll be gone before anyone knows we came."

"Go ahead with your text." Nick reached behind his seat and pulled out his bolt cutters. "I'll check those hangars. Once we get the plane stowed, I'll see if I can douse those landing lights. A set-up this small, there's probably a manual switch." He nodded toward an electrical junction box mounted on the building that housed the hangars. "Looks like all the wiring that runs this operation feeds into that box. It's plenty big enough."

While Nick checked the hangar doors, I texted Kenzie.

At landing strip. Come ASAP

Nick rolled up the door to an empty hangar and trotted back to the plane. "We're good. Let's get this flying machine out of sight."

We pulled the plane around until we had it in position, then pushed it into the hangar, tail first. Nick rolled the door back down with us inside. Ginger was still aboard, locked inside her kennel and staying quiet, except for the sounds of vigorous sniffing. The cold, dark space smelled of oily rags doused in aviation fuel, combined with the sickly-sweet stench of some decomposing animal. Her cadaver dog nose was being put to the test.

Nick turned on his flashlight, setting it to its lowest beam. He swept its dim light across the floor of the hangar until it rested on a raccoon carcass.

"Any word from Kenzie?" he asked.

"Not yet. How about you? Has Harry checked in?"

Nick pulled out his phone. "Nope." He pulled in a breath and let it out. "Now we do the hard part."

"Waiting?"

"Yep."

My cell phone chirped. A text from Kenzie.

Sedative in guard's diet soda. Takes effect 20-40 min

I showed Nick, then replied.

How is patient?

Early first stage plenty of time

As we waited, frigid air seeped into the hangar, numbing my fingers and ears. I had no hat or gloves, only a barn coat grabbed at the last minute. I had forgotten about altitude and the bitter temperatures in the mountains. I checked my watch over and over. Its hands seemed as frozen as my own. Each time Nick and I spoke, our breath escaped in visible gusts. It would get colder the longer we waited.

"It's been more than twenty minutes," Nick said. "Want to text her? Ask how it's going?"

"Not sure we should. She expected to be alone there with Helena and the drugged guard, but we don't know what's happening. I'd hate to interfere with her plan."

"Then we'll wait. She said up to forty minutes, but it's damn cold in here. Are you okay?"

"I can't feel my hands or feet or face, but other than that, I'm fine."

"Same here." Nick's soft laugh emitted a cloud of steam. "We could try that hypothermia trick. Take our clothes off and wrap our bodies around each other for warmth."

"Let's do that when we get home."

My phone chirped.

All clear on our way 5 min

"Nick, she's coming. She says five minutes. Shall we open the hangar now? Get the plane on the runway?"

"Yes. And Ginger's acting like she needs to pee. In the rush to leave, we loaded her in her kennel without letting her empty her bladder first. No idea how long she's been holding it." He opened the kennel door and handed me her leash. "You take her while I handle the plane."

Ginger had other ideas. Before I could attach the leash, she launched herself from the plane, raced over to the raccoon carcass and sniffed it, then streaked from the hangar and across the landing strip. She darted toward the far north corner of the warehouse building. I ran after her but didn't shout out her name on the chance there was someone in that building who might hear.

I turned back to Nick, who was struggling with the plane. He nodded to me to go after her. I vowed to buy a silent dog whistle when we got home. Who knew one of those would come in handy?

As I rounded the corner of the warehouse, I spotted the dog several yards away, sniffing around a section of ground that looked as if it had been worked with a rototiller. Maybe some sort of vegetable garden, but why would anyone plant a garden in such an isolated place?

I ran over to where she kept at her agitated sniffing. I fumbled with my stiff fingers until I managed to attach the leash to her harness. I gave it a tug and whispered, "Come," but she was fixated on that patch of ground. She sat there rigidly alert and refused to move. I knew she was a pro and shouldn't start barking, but I worried she might. If anyone was in the vicinity, they'd be alerted before we could escape with Kenzie and her patient. It might be someone from the prison who had found the drugged guard.

I debated whether to leave Ginger where she sat and go get Nick. I couldn't see him or the plane from where I stood. My view of the landing strip was blocked by the warehouse. I didn't even know whether Kenzie had arrived.

"Who's there?" A man's voice.

That shouted question was followed by the glare of a flashlight shining in my face. I held back a scream, along with the urge to wet myself. I hoped Nick had heard the shout too, but I couldn't be sure.

Play dumb. I had no other choice as the dark form walked slowly toward me.

"I'm sorry. My dog ran off, and I've been trying to find her for hours. I'll get off your property right away."

"Liar. I know who you are. I've seen you before." He came closer. No gun in either hand. Only the flashlight. A big, heavy one. A weapon. *But not a gun.*

"Impossible, I've never been near here before."

I've been told I have a memorable face, but in this case, it was not a plus. I couldn't make out his features with his flashlight shining in my eyes. I had no idea who I was talking to. All I could do was stall and hope Nick would hear us talking. If not, he should at least be wondering why I hadn't gone back to the plane with Ginger. He should have come looking for us, unless he was distracted with loading Helena and Kenzie into the plane.

"You're that damn nosey librarian, aren't you? Just what the hell am I going to do with you?"

He did know me. The man with the weaponized flashlight had to be Mr. Smith, Kenzie's nursing supervisor, who was supposed to be at home sleeping off a migraine. His cover story, I guessed, while instead, he was prepping the secret medical facility in the warehouse for delivery of Helena's baby.

So far, Mr. Smith seemed unaware that on the other side of the warehouse, the patient he was expecting to have transported to him by a female guard was about to be whisked away into the night. But only if I managed to put Smith down before he decided what to do with me.

"I'm not who you think I am," I insisted. "You have me confused with someone else. Look, there's my dog, just like I told you. She ran away. You can check her name tags. My name is on there. It's Alexander. That's me Nicki Alexander." *Come closer, Mr. Smith.*

Although I was not Ginger's primary handler, Nick had told me enough about her training that I knew she would obey if I gave the "Attack" command. Between the two of us, I figured we could neutralize this guy.

"Still don't believe you." Smith held the beam of his flashlight on my face, but his words conveyed a trace of doubt. I counted on it. He would rather chase off a nuisance intruder than engage in a physical confrontation with an irresponsible woman and her unruly dog. He had more pressing priorities. Smith took a couple of steps toward me, staying just out of reach. *Come on, man, just a little closer.*

Kenzie and Helena must have arrived at the plane. Nick would have them loaded and would be coming to find Ginger and me any minute. So, where was he?

Smith waved the flashlight in Ginger's direction. "All right, I guess you're not who I thought you were. Take your freakin' dog and get lost. And don't show up here again."

"Got it." I walked over to Ginger, who was pawing at the patch of ground where she had been sitting.

"Hey, make her stop that," Smith yelled. He leapt toward her, swinging his flashlight. She jumped to avoid him, but his second swipe caught her with a glancing blow to the head that resulted in a high-pitched yelp of pain.

Infuriated, I gripped the jerk from behind in a choke hold, cutting off blood flow to his brain. After a few seconds, the flashlight dropped from his hand and he sank to the ground. I took his flashlight. Knowing he would regain consciousness in a matter of minutes, I checked him for other weapons and found none.

Ginger had returned to her sitting position at the same spot as before. A small gash behind her right ear dripped blood. The sight of it and the coppery smell made me want to go back to where Smith lay and cause him pain. Instead, I tugged Ginger's leash and said, "Come" with as much authority as I could muster. She obeyed but glanced back toward that worked patch of ground. I urged her into a trot, hoping we would reach the plane before Smith woke up.

I almost slammed into Nick as Ginger and I cleared the corner of the warehouse. "There you are," he said. "The women are loaded and ready to take off. What took you so long?"

"Load the dog and let's go. I'll explain on the way."

The wailing of a big-ass siren suddenly pierced the air, coming from the direction of the prison.

I scrambled into the copilot seat and looked back at Kenzie. "What did you do with the guard?"

"I took her uniform and locked her in the custodian's closet. Sounds like someone found her." With a nervous giggle she added, "Too bad I had to leave her in her underwear."

An exhausted Helena Torres, writhing with each new bout of contractions, looked from Kenzie to me. She placed a shielding hand on her protruding belly, and in halting English, said, "*Gracias* for save my baby."

As we lifted off, Kenzie concentrated on Helena's blood pressure, and I kept busy spotting for Nick. We noticed the lights of another plane approaching in the distance, and Nick guided us safely out of its flight path.

"That plane must be the broker, coming for the baby." I

looked back at the darkness below as we gained altitude. "Did you turn the landing lights back on?"

"Nope, I didn't need them for our takeoff."

"Then how will that pilot know where to land?"

"I spotted the twist of Nick's lips. "Good question."

Chapter 40

HELENA'S WATER BROKE JUST as Nick touched down at Timbergate Municipal Airport. Her contractions became longer, stronger, and more frequent. We dropped her off at TMC just after midnight, where an OB/Gyn had been called in to manage the delivery.

Detective Kass had been contacted and was waiting for us at the hospital, along with Jared Quinn. Kass took our statements about what had led to the decision to transport Helena to TMC, and what happened at the warehouse in Potterville. He even took photos of the wound on Ginger's head. We agreed to meet again on Sunday afternoon to discuss the potential consequences of our actions.

From there, we took Kenzie to Harry's condo for safekeeping. Harry brought us up to date. After Detective Kass intervened with the rehab facility in L.A., Buzz Bateson was released into Buck Sawyer's care. Buzz was on crutches and in decent shape, except for a cast on one leg. Both he and Ramon were being flown home by Rella and Buck. Ramon had submitted his resignation to the Human Resources Department of Criteria Health Resources.

Back at our apartment, Nick and I agreed we had achieved our first goal, that of keeping the mother and her newborn together, but the large-scale problem remained. We had no proof of our suspicions about the prison and the CHR clinic, and we were in potential legal jeopardy for our actions. Though it was past midnight, Nick arranged an emergency visit to Ginger's vet. Minutes after he left, Detective Kass called.

He reported that Sheriff Preston remained unconvinced about possible criminal activity at the prison in Potterville.

"You have to understand, Aimee. Preston's not going to take any action involving federal inmates, much less the FBI, without solid evidence. And be prepared. You and your cohorts are going to be in deep shit when the abduction of a pregnant, undocumented detainee is reported."

"You mean it hasn't been? Sheriff Preston doesn't know?"

"Not yet." Kass cleared his throat. "I'm in no hurry to enlighten him, and for good reason. Maybe it won't *be* reported."

My fatigued brain took a moment to work out his meaning. "You're waiting to see if anyone from the prison or the CHR clinic contacts law enforcement?"

"That's right. If I tell all to Preston now, he'll contact the warden up there. If you're right about a black-market operation, that's enough to tip off whoever's involved."

"Ah, I'm with you," I said. "And whoever's involved knows that reporting Helena Torres and Kenzie missing would trigger an investigation. That's the last thing the folks at the prison clinic would want."

Kass cleared his throat. "I have to warn you, though, if they *are* going to cover this up, they'll be hell-bent on silencing you as soon as possible, so watch your back. You said that man you tangled with thought he recognized you."

"He did, and I know who he is, so I'll spot him if he comes

anywhere near me, but I have to warn Kenzie—and Helena Torres."

"Don't forget about that newborn," Kass said.

A shiver ran through me. "You think they'll still try to take that baby? Steal it from the hospital?"

"Depends what kind of financial deal they made with the buyers. There's probably a substantial sum involved. If the sellers collected in advance, things could get very nasty when they don't deliver the goods."

I called Kenzie, running Kass's warning by her and asking if she had been able to get a sample of Dr. Iversen's signature. In the confusion, she hadn't had a chance.

When Nick got home from Ginger's vet visit, I filled him in on my talk with Kass, then we collapsed into bed for the few hours of night that remained. We took a pass on the hypothermia cure. The chill in our veins wasn't from lack of heat. It was the thought of what might happen to even more inmates at Potterville Prison if our efforts failed.

Ginger woke us before six on Sunday morning, needing to go outside. Nick took her, while I started coffee. There were myriad details to pin down before the Ethics Committee meeting at noon on Monday. If I subtracted one more night's sleep, we had twenty-four waking hours until showtime.

While Nick was out, I took to my phone and found a call from Jared Quinn, who reported the birth of Helena's baby. A seven-pound, eighteen-inch girl named Maria Mackenzie Torres. Mother and daughter doing fine. He was arranging safe post-hospital lodging for them, with the help of Kass. I asked how Helena's admittance had been handled.

"Did they know she was undocumented?"

"I took care of it," Quinn said, "but only temporarily. They realize she's an immigrant, of course, because she doesn't speak English well, but they aren't aware that she's undocumented. They assume she's an abuse victim who fled her home wearing nothing but a nightgown."

"But she was in prison garb," I said.

"Not after she and Dr. Poole made a detour into the women's room before heading to Admissions."

"Dr. Poole was there? I thought she was out of town."

"Change of plans, I guess. Here, I'll give her the phone, she can fill you in."

"Dr. Poole, how did you—?"

"Our babysitter came down with a bug, so Tobias and I came home Saturday after his talk. Jared knew I was in house last night when Helena arrived, so he asked me to make a few adjustments to her wardrobe."

"You got rid of her prison uniform? Lied for her?"

"Not outright lies, Aimee. I simply tossed the uniform and replaced it with a hospital gown and then played dumb. But when the truth about this woman's ordeal and that of other inmates is revealed, I'm betting my sins of omission, and yours, will be forgiven."

I had to smile as we ended the call. Over time, my opinion of Dr. Phyllis Poole had steadily grown from arch enemy to trusted collaborator. Her help with this latest circumstance put her right up there with Diana Prince. A real-life Wonder Woman.

Next, I called Harry, who confirmed that Rella and Buck had arrived in Timbergate within the hour, bringing Buzz Bateson and Ramon Silva with them. Ramon had convinced Kenzie to stay in Timbergate, but she was worried about her parents—afraid someone from the prison clinic might show up at their home looking for her. Ramon had convinced them to come to Timbergate to be with their daughter until the threat passed.

Nick and I made a breakfast of scrambled eggs and toast. And plenty of coffee.

"What's your plan for the day," Nick asked. "I'm sure you have one."

"I'm hoping to line up all the witnesses who are willing to attend the Ethics meeting. The only party we haven't heard from is Laurie Littletree."

"You have her number?"

"Yes. I've been calling and texting her for a week with no response."

"Have you tried this morning?"

"Not yet, but I will. In the meantime, I've started a witness list for Dr. Poole."

"Maybe you should start a suspect list. Who's most likely to be behind what's been going on at Potterville."

"That, too. The most obvious is Kenzie's boss, Mr. Smith. But he's got to be taking orders from someone with a lot more seniority."

"That reminds me, we need to talk about what happened when the two of you tangled. You said you were having trouble getting Ginger to obey. That doesn't sound like her."

"I know, but she seemed fixated on a spot several yards from the warehouse. She sniffed at it, then sat there, rigid, as if she was determined not to leave."

"Oh, hell," Nick said, "she was signaling. She caught a scent."

"I didn't see anything except a tilled patch of ground."

"If it's what I think it is, you wouldn't see what caught her attention."

"Why not?" And then I realized what he was saying. "Cadavers? You think she found a makeshift graveyard?"

"She's just finished her cadaver training. It's fresh in her mind. It must have been frustrating for her to be yanked away without being acknowledged and rewarded for her find."

"If we're right, Sheriff Preston will definitely have solid evidence of foul play. Especially when he enters that warehouse and finds a surgery suite."

"If he finds it," Nick said. "How long would it take to dismantle that place?"

"Oh, crap. That can't happen before we convince Sheriff Preston to get a search warrant."

"Maybe it won't. They might not want to give up on such a lucrative enterprise."

"But the woman guard was drugged. Kenzie and Helena are gone. The ringleaders must know they've been exposed."

"Don't forget about Smith. He thought he recognized you." Nick took our empty plates to the sink and came back to the table. "You're the one person who can connect him with what's going on in that warehouse."

"But Smith wasn't sure of my identity. He would have let me go if Ginger hadn't started digging."

"You put him down with a choke hold, Aimee. I think that did away with any doubt."

I rubbed at the chill tracing down my forearms. "It doesn't comfort me to know I'm in his crosshairs."

Nick pulled me into a hug. "Sorry, but I'm trying to keep you safe."

"You're not alone. Kass has already warned me to watch my back."

Chapter 41

⸺◆⸺

I SPENT THE BETTER part of Sunday morning at home preparing for Monday's meeting. With everyone else on my witness list accounted for, I continued my efforts to contact Laurie Littletree. I paused mid-morning for a quick one-mile run, and again to eat lunch with Nick. He brought take-out subs from the Coyote Creek Deli on his way home from a meet-up with Buck Sawyer and Rella. I asked about Buck.

"Has he decided about donating funds to Potterville Prison's drug rehab program?"

"The CHR officials down in L.A. came up with acceptable answers to his questions. Almost had him convinced to go ahead."

"But?"

"Thanks to your suspicions, and what we went through last night in Potterville with the pregnant woman, he's going to pull out unless formal inspections of the prison and that medical clinic come up clean."

"He said that to the CHR people he met with?" Not good news. If the word was out, a cover-up would be under way.

"He did, but not until this morning." Nick shook his head. "And don't worry, he didn't spill the beans about our rescue mission last night. He's smarter than that."

"That's a relief, but his call for inspections still creates a problem."

"I know, and I'm sorry he didn't talk to me first. I'd have asked him to play along until we could find a smoking gun."

"Is it too late? He could contact them, say he's reconsidered."

"Whoever's behind the crimes at the prison is shrewd enough to smell a rat," Nick said. "If anyone at CHR's home office is involved, Buck changing his mind that quickly would only reinforce the idea that the Potterville operation is jeopardized."

"Then we have to move quickly. I don't know if tomorrow's meeting is going to give us what we need." I gathered our take-out wrappers and stuffed them in the trash.

"You do have at least two of the key witnesses." Nick took our empty soda cans to the recycle bin on our deck. I followed, standing next to him at the railing.

"I am grateful for that. Which reminds me, do you know where Buzz and Ramon are staying? Have they gone back to their own homes?"

"No. They're secured in Buck's pool house, at least until after the meeting."

"Did you hear whether they've compared notes about their hit-and-run incidents?"

"They have, and they expect to provide details. Maybe that's enough to set an investigation in motion."

"The TMC Ethics Committee doesn't have the kind of clout to request that, Nick. A hospital committee can only reach out so far. We need the sheriff, and the FBI."

"Then you need irrefutable evidence."

"I know, but a photo of Ramon's car isn't enough. Neither is the gash on Ginger's head."

THAT AFTERNOON, NICK SAID he wanted to work with Ginger to reinforce her cadaver training. He worried that I had confused her by not doing my part when she alerted to the possibility of a cadaver near the warehouse in Potterville.

"Her earlier training was for drugs," Nick said, "and dogs used by law enforcement aren't usually cross-trained for both drug and cadavers."

"But she's not being trained for official police work," I said. "You're a private owner."

"Still, there's chance I expected too much of her by asking her to do both."

"How are you going to do cadaver training here?" I asked. "We don't have any human remains buried in the llama pasture."

"I have a supply of pseudo corpse scent that mimics human death." He saw my revolted expression and laughed. "Don't worry, I don't keep it in our fridge."

"Good thing." I hoped he wouldn't get any of the icky potion on himself.

"Shall I keep her inside until you treat a spot of ground with that stuff?"

"Please. I'll be back to get her in a few minutes."

After Nick came back for the dog, I returned to my prep work, trying again to contact Laurie Littletree. This time with a text. My phone rang after a few minutes. I answered it with a rush of relief.

"Laurie? Is that you?"

"I'm sorry," an unfamiliar voice said. "Apparently I'm not the caller you expected. This is Moura Decker. Have I reached Aimee Machado?"

Dr. Decker was the last person I'd have guessed. "Yes, you have. What can I do for you?"

"It's rather sensitive, and work-related. Something we should discuss one-on-one, but without delay. Is there a chance we could meet this afternoon?"

Work-related? Without delay? I felt a tingling sensation, like spiders crawling up the back of my neck. The only work-related issue we had in common that couldn't wait was the Ethics Committee meeting Monday at noon.

"Of course, Dr. Decker. Where would you like to meet?"

"Let's see, you're in Coyote Creek, or so I've been told."

"I am, but I can meet you wherever it's convenient. The hospital? The library?" I was babbling in my eagerness.

"Oh, no, that wouldn't do. It should be someplace more private."

This kept sounding better. She obviously had some sort of crucial information relating to Dr. Mac's death. She and Dr. Seldon were the two doctors who had confirmed his brain death and agreed to terminate his life support after he developed sepsis. Seldon was the only one who insisted there was no need for a forensic autopsy.

"Dr. Decker, is this about tomorrow's meeting?"

"I'd rather we wait and talk in person," she said. "I'm sure you understand."

"Yes. I'll meet you whenever and wherever you say."

I knew Seldon would be attending the Monday meeting. Decker obviously did not want to meet me at the hospital where we might be spotted. If she had something to tell me about the man, I wanted that information.

"Very good," Decker said. "There's a quaint little church out your way. I understand it's left unlocked on Sunday afternoons for parishioners who like to drop in for private worship. Do you know it?"

"The Coyote Creek Chapel?"

"Yes, I believe that's it."

"It's a couple of miles from my home. What time?"

"I'm afraid it'll have to be late this afternoon. I have hospital patients to look in on first. Shall we say six o'clock?"

I FILLED THE HOURS of waiting by alerting Mary Barton and Cleo Cominoli about Decker's invitation. I asked them for advice about how to relate to Decker. They had both known her much longer than I had.

"She's devoted to the idea of organ donation," Cleo said.

"Hence, her membership on Ethics Committee. I'd say just go with whatever is on her mind."

Mary's suggestion was similar. "She's been a staunch ally of TMC's organ donor program ever since I've been Donor Coordinator," Mary said. "If she's troubled enough to want an urgent, private meeting with you, it could be the kind of credible information we need."

WHEN IT WAS TIME, I kissed Nick goodbye and drove the short distance to the little chapel, setting my wipers on low to clear a light evening mist from my windshield. I arrived fifteen minutes early, relieved to find the building empty and no cars in the parking lot. If Dr. Decker and I were going to have the talk I expected, we would not want to be overheard.

The chill, dimly-lit interior smelled of candle wax and wood smoke. The sound of my boots on the painted concrete floor broke the silence, echoing off the bare stucco walls as I walked up the aisle to the front of the room. An unlit wood stove in the right-hand corner felt cool to my touch. I pulled my jacket closer. Checked the time. Five fifty-five. Decker would arrive any minute. At last, something was going our way. I took a seat in the front pew and waited. To still my rapid pulse and calm myself, I tried a few yoga breaths.

I had begun to relax when a stinging sensation on the back of my neck took me by surprise. I swatted at it, thinking it must be a bee or wasp. My hand contacted something much different. A syringe.

"What? What's that?" I jumped up, spun around and found myself face to face with Dr. Moura Decker, who was shoving the syringe into her pocket.

"What did you do?" I stammered. "When did you arrive? I didn't hear you come in."

"That's because I was already here, Miss Machado. Waiting in the women's room for your arrival. How else to take you by surprise?"

"But I didn't see your car."

"I simply parked it behind the building." She smiled. "You're quite gullible, aren't you?"

The room spun. I groped for the back of the pew and lowered myself down.

"I don't understand," I said. "What are you doing?"

She reached out, took my purse and opened it. I made a feeble attempt to grab it from her, but my hand and arm would not cooperate.

"I'm looking at your driver license." She pulled it out of my wallet. "Ah, there it is." She made a *tsk, tsk*, sound. Her voice came at me from far away. "Oh, dear. You are not a registered organ donor, are you?"

My tongue went slack as I tried to answer. "I was going to next …."

"You were going to? Really, Miss Machado? That's what they all say."

I WOKE UP ALONE in a cell, dressed in the same detainee garb I had seen on Helena Torres. I had been disguised as an undocumented immigrant. My face, my Chinese and Portuguese genes, would make it easy to believe, as long as no one heard me speak.

The artificial lighting and lack of windows made it impossible to determine the time of day or night. My hands were bound in front of me with nylon restraints. My feet were bare. My clothes, boots, purse and phone were nowhere to be seen.

A buzzer sounded outside my cell. The door opened, and Dr. Decker stepped in, her upper torso in a drab beige sweater. A gray wool skirt hit mid-calf, exposing spindly lower legs that looked barely capable of carrying the disproportionate weight of her upper body.

"Well, well," Decker said. "I'm glad you're awake. We haven't had our little talk, have we?"

"Why are you doing this?" I choked out the words.

"Isn't it obvious? I'm silencing you, with the added benefit of procuring all sorts of healthy organs and tissues to give life to any number of patients in need. Killing two birds with one stone, as they say."

Chapter 42

--------◆--------

Dr. Moura Decker, the mastermind behind the organ- and baby-selling conspiracy, checked the watch on her wrist. "I must be going. I can't be late to the Ethics Committee meeting, and it's a rather long drive to Timbergate."

A long drive. That confirmed my location. I was in solitary at Potterville Prison. I still didn't know what day it was. Or what time. Sunday night? Monday morning?

"What time is it?" I asked.

Decker laughed. "Never mind that. We have other things to talk about."

"Like what?" She would get no information from me.

"Since you're not long for this world, I want you to know that what I am doing is a service to all mankind, and not the heinous crime you likely imagine."

"If that's the case, why am I locked in this cell?"

"You brought it upon yourself when you failed to register as a donor."

"That's your excuse? You've appointed yourself organ donation czar of the entire world?"

"Well, someone needed to step up. There is a simpler

solution, you know. It's called the 'presumed consent' system. Many countries have already adopted it. In those countries, organs may be removed after death unless individuals positively indicate during their lifetime that they do not wish this to be done."

"Then why didn't you campaign for a change in the law here in the States?"

Decker sneered. "Try to imagine the uproar in today's political environment. It could take years for a proposal like that to make its way through our legislature, and then, I'm sorely afraid it would fail to pass."

"So, you're making your own laws?"

"I call it my version of 'A Modest Proposal.' Are you familiar?"

"Jonathan Swift's satirical essay, of course. During the famine in eighteenth-century Ireland, he proposed that poor citizens sell their small children as food for the rich. One solution to two problems: starvation and overpopulation."

"There you have it," Decker said. "Like Swift, I have the solution to two problems: the shortage of available organs, and what to do with undocumented immigrants. My solution is elegant. Take the organs the illegals can manage without and distribute them as I see fit. When the donors have recovered sufficiently, they're no worse off. Livers regenerate when a lobe goes missing, and one good kidney is all anyone really needs. The illegals deserve to make small sacrifices so that terminally ill patients all over the world have a new lease on life."

There was more to the story than what Decker was telling, but I didn't want to let on about suspected cadavers.

"So you've taken your concept to a whole new level," I said. "You've outdone Swift."

Decker huffed an impatient breath. "Yes. And you're right, Swift's was satire. He used his pen to prod Ireland's population into taking action to remedy their circumstances." My solution is not satirical. It is workable. It *is* working."

"I suppose you decide who gets the illegal organs."

"Of course. They can't go through the existing donor system. Even though China has been procuring organs from prisoners for years, our country is too squeamish to see the practicality of it. I had to set up my own distribution method."

"A lucrative one, I imagine."

"Enough to fund the mission. I am not in this for personal gain, but my work force must be well compensated for the risks involved."

"You're using undocumented immigrants to solve the country's shortage of organ donors?"

She broke out in a satisfied smile. Not just our country. You might say I'm saving lives all over the world. Elegant, don't you agree?"

Crazy as a loon, I thought, but what concerned me more was the frightening number of fringe fanatics who might agree with her. The Internet seemed to spawn more of them every day.

"Why?" Even facing the prospect of my own death, I had to know what motivated her.

"Why what?" she asked.

"Why are you doing this? What made organ procurement your particular quest?"

Her eyes clouded. "My baby sister died at the age of fifteen for lack of donors." Decker dabbed at her nose with a tissue. "She was mowed down by a drunken Mexican. An illegal. He drove on, nearly getting away with it, while she lay mortally injured in the crosswalk."

"I'm so sorry," I said. "Which of her organs was damaged?" The longer I kept her talking, the more chance I had of putting her out of commission. She had no gun, no other obvious weapon. And from the careless way I was restrained, she obviously did not know about my training in jujitsu—the only weapon I had available.

"Her liver and both kidneys." Decker shook herself, looked at her watch. "Never mind about that. I must get back to Timbergate, where I will persuade Dr. Poole to cancel the Ethics Committee meeting, or at least postpone it until the unexplained absence of Aimee Machado, Ethics Committee Coordinator, is addressed. Where could she be? I suppose I might be asked, if you've told anyone we were meeting last night."

"I did. Several people know, so you won't get away with this."

"Of course I will. I'll have a cover story ready. I suspect they'll never know the real one."

"Speaking of real stories. You might as well tell me about Dr. Mac. Did you arrange his accident?"

Decker looked down at the floor, shaking her head. "A terrible sacrifice. If only he had seen the beauty of my project."

"Then you did stage his accident?"

"Not the hands-on part, but as I said, the members of my workforce are well compensated for the risks they take."

"Yet you see his death as a loss. How do you justify it?"

"Another case of two birds with one stone. Similar to your impending fate, he had to be silenced. In his case, the sepsis that resulted in the loss of his organs was an unexpected and devastating blow. I'll see to it that doesn't happen when your time comes." She tilted her head to the side, scrutinizing me. "That reminds me, a guard will be bringing your breakfast soon. Try to enjoy it. It may be your last meal."

Decker let herself out before I could get close enough to take her down. I heard the buzzer again as she locked the cell door behind her.

Breakfast. It was already Monday morning. I had to get myself freed and find a way back to Timbergate before noon. The drive would take almost two hours. I figured I had four at most.

I considered Decker's parting comments. Three people knew I was meeting Dr. Decker Sunday evening. Cleo Cominoli, Mary Barton. and Nick. But had I told any of them *where* I was meeting Decker? Not Cleo or Mary. Nick? I couldn't remember. Would he drive around Coyote Creek looking for my car? Not likely. He would probably assume I'd driven to Timbergate to meet Decker at TMC.

Nick, call Detective Kass. Call Sheriff Preston. Call the CHP. *Find me.*

Chapter 43

Decker had been gone only minutes when I heard someone approaching outside my cell door. My only chance was to overpower the guard who brought my breakfast. There was no slot in the door to slide a food tray through, so the door would have to be unlocked. I stepped over to the wall, where I would be hidden behind the door when it opened. I clasped my hands together to make one oversized fist.

The buzzer sounded. The door opened.

I heard the guard's "Huh?" as she stepped inside. The cell door closed with a heavy *clunk*. "What the … where?" She placed the tray on a table next to the cot and looked around, spotting me just as my fists came down on top of her head. She dropped to her knees, and before she could make a sound, I applied the same sleeper hold I had used on Mr. Smith when we rescued Helena Torres. I applied pressure to the guard's carotid for as long as I dared. Too long could cause brain damage or death.

No time to spare, I rifled her pockets and vest for anything that might help me escape. I found heavy duty scissors and a set of car keys. And attached to the keychain was the remote trigger that opened and closed the cell door. I used the scissors to cut off my wrist restraints. There were more nylon restraints in her vest pocket. I used one set to bind her wrists behind her back. Her shoes looked somewhere near my size, so I pulled them off her feet and tried them on. They were loose and gritty and gross on my bare feet, but better than nothing. Next, I shrugged out of the upper half of my prison uniform and yanked the top half of the guard's uniform off her slack torso. It smelled of body odor and stale cigarette smoke, but in the circumstances, it was a fine perfume. She began to stir, so I put her back to sleep, then raced my mind through the obstacles still to come.

How the hell would I escape from the prison proper? I had no idea of the layout, or how I would avoid running into other guards. *Fake it.* No other choice. I took a deep breath and stepped outside the cell, using the guard's remote to lock the door behind me.

I turned from the door, looked around to assess my situation, and discovered that I was standing in an unlit and empty operating room. It took a moment for the location to make sense. I was not in the prison. I was in the warehouse. Perhaps alone, except for the guard snoozing in what had to be a holding cell used for patients awaiting surgery.

The guard's keys in my hand spurred me on. Get outside. Find the car that fits the keys. There was only one exit door from the surgery suite. It was on the opposite side of the room from where I stood. Some forty feet away. The door was wide enough to accommodate gurneys and other large equipment, but it was not the double door arrangement typical in hospitals. Instead of a push bar, it had a heavy-duty handle.

My bare feet in the guard's loose-fitting shoes made my steps clumsy as I lurched toward the exit door. There, I listened for sounds on the other side. Heard nothing. Until a muffled voice came from the cell behind me. The guard was calling for help. Time to make a run for it.

I pressed down on the latch, pulled the surgery suite's door open wide enough to peek out. Early morning light filtered through stained and cobwebbed windows into the dusty, unused warehouse space. The perfect cover for Dr. Decker's deception. I stepped out into that space, closing the door to the operating room. On the warehouse side, the door was camouflaged to match the aged and neglected look of the warehouse interior.

Windows faced north, east and south. I peered out all of them, starting with the one facing north. From that one, I spotted the location where Ginger had alerted to cadaver scent. From the east window, I saw that the sun had crowned the dense forest of trees, reminding me of the urgency of reaching Timbergate in time for the Ethics meeting. I estimated the time from the sun's position. Early enough for me to drive to Timbergate by noon if I got my hands on a car.

The window to the south revealed one lone vehicle in a small parking lot. I sucked in a huge breath, filling my mouth with air that tasted of rust, dust, and danger. My chest swelled. My heart thundered. My brain screamed. *Go, go, go!*

As soon as I opened the outside door, an alarm shrieked out an urgent wail.

Oh, hell!

I ran around the corner of the warehouse to the parking lot, clicking the car's remote button to unlock it. A couple of yards from the car, one of the guard's floppy shoes slipped off my foot, tripping me and sending me sprawling on the asphalt. *Freaking shoes! Are you kidding me?* The thought of Dr. Mac falling down the stairwell tripped by his shoes was like a stab of irony to my heart. His shoe mishap was staged. Mine was real.

I scrambled to my feet. A glance told me the car had seen better days. Bald tires, a broken headlight, grimy windows. I wasn't picky. If the aging two-door sedan would run, it was good enough. For a crazy moment, I channeled Richard III.

My kingdom for a horse!

Didn't work out for Richard, but he deserved his fate. I

didn't deserve what Decker had in mind for me, and I wasn't about to give up. The missing shoe was nowhere in sight, and I didn't stop to look for it. I yanked the stubborn driver's-side door open and slipped in, giving thanks to any deity who was listening when the key fit and the engine turned over.

The interior reeked of take-out wrappers and stale food scraps. And apparently, from any number of canine passengers that had never been bathed. Added to the smell of the guard's uniform, the air quality in the car's interior was ghastly. My physical exertions had heated up the fabric, amplifying the woman's body odor to a stomach-turning degree. She apparently suffered from a severe case of *hyperhidrosis,* causing excessive perspiration.

But noxious smells were the least of my worries. I had a meeting to attend.

The clock in the guard's car was no help. It was stuck on twelve o'clock sharp. Every gauge on the dashboard was frozen. I had no idea of fuel level, speed or number of miles driven. No radio. The guard who owned this vehicle had to be one of Decker's minions. If the scheme was raking in big bucks, the people Decker relied on to carry it out should have been well paid. This woman certainly should be able to afford a better ride. Probably used the junker as a cover. Kept her luxury car and other high-dollar possessions under wraps so she wouldn't have to explain how she could afford them.

Traffic was light on the winding mountain highway back to Timbergate, tempting me to press my bare right foot down harder on the gas pedal. I tried to calculate the time with any clues available. The sky had darkened since sunrise, and the overcast made the sun's climb difficult to track. The brightest glow projecting through the cloud cover came from a southeast position. My internal clock told me that nearly an hour had passed since Decker left me locked in the cell inside the warehouse.

After what I guessed was another half hour of driving, the

car developed a cough. I wasn't familiar with every bend in the road I was traveling, but I figured there should be some sort of pit stop between Potterville and Timbergate. Every mountain road in Sawyer County had combination gas stations and mini-marts strategically located to sell fuel and snacks at astonishingly elevated prices. The car coughed again, shuddered, but kept going.

A glance in my rearview mirror revealed a large vehicle, dark in color, cresting the long, curved downward grade I had just traveled. I jammed my bare foot on the gas pedal, pushing it to the floor. The rig in my rear-view mirror gained on me. It would either pass and go on its way, or the driver would follow me until I became an easy target in a stalled junker with an empty tank.

Around the next bend, I spotted a mini-mart and gas station nestled in a curve in the road. I rolled into the parking lot, counting on fumes to keep me going until I could coax the gasping car around to the back of the building where it would not be seen from the road.

I jumped out and headed for the back door of the little market. It was unlocked. I slipped inside, finding myself in a short corridor with restrooms on both sides. Edging closer to the market's public area, I strained to hear if there were sounds of conversation. Nothing. I risked edging further in, and spotted a front window with a view of the road. There it was, the vehicle that had been following me. It ripped past the mini-mart, continuing on its way.

My knees sagged with relief. At last, a chance to get help. A sturdy, dark-haired woman I guessed to be in her forties sat behind the counter on a high stool, her attention focused on the screen of her phone as she tapped with her thumbs. No one else was there. I walked to the counter.

"Please, I need help."

She jerked her head up, her deep brown eyes widening in alarm. "Where did you come from?" Her name tag read: *Jaya*.

I recognized her accent as East Indian. She reached under her side of the counter for something. Mace? Bear spray? A shotgun?

I raised my hands toward her, palms out. "I came in the back way. I'm being chased by a bad man. Please, I need to use a phone."

Jaya's nose twitched. Her eyes watered. "What's that smell?" she said.

It took a moment to realize I had gone nose blind to the smell of the guard's body odor and stale cigarette smoke on the uniform I was wearing, no doubt made worse by my own body heat and the other rancid smells clinging to me from the car I had been driving.

"Please, my life is in danger. Let me use your phone to call the sheriff."

The woman pulled her arm back from below the counter. Empty. Score one for my side. She had decided not to spray me or shoot me.

"Who is after you?" she asked.

I had no time to explain my situation in detail, and if I did, she would not believe it, so I took the easy option.

"My boyfriend. He's angry because I want to leave him. I have to get away before he finds me."

She nodded. "Yes, I see. Do you work at the prison?"

Oh, hell, the uniform. "Yes, I work at Potterville, but I didn't make it to work today. My boyfriend and I argued." I clasped my hands together, beseeching her. "Please, please may I borrow your phone? He wants to kill me. I had to run away. I have no money, no phone."

The sound of brakes screeching drew our attention to the parking area outside the store. *There it was.* The rig that had been following me circled back. For a dizzy moment, I thought my pounding pulse would make my head explode.

I watched as Mr. Smith opened the cab of the oversized pickup truck, jumped out while it was still rolling to a stop, and headed my way. The nursing director of the Potterville Prison medical clinic would have no mercy if he caught me. He might even harm the innocent woman I had asked for help.

"That's him," I said to Jaya, "I have to hide. Don't tell him I'm here."

She nodded. Tipped her head toward the back exit. "I will stall him, but I must keep my phone in case I need it. You understand?"

"Yes, of course."

"You go. Don't worry for me. My husband is on his way. Almost here."

I sneaked out the back, praying that I had not put her in danger.

Chapter 44

---◆---

Outside, I pulled the guard's keys from her car and dropped them in a pocket of the ghastly-smelling uniform top I still wore. She had to be involved in the scheme. There might still be some trace of her fingerprints on the remote that would help to identify her.

I made my way around the building until I caught sight of Mr. Smith's empty pickup still idling in the parking lot. *Sprint for it, one shoe on, one off.* I was almost there when my bare foot came down hard on the knife-sharp edge of a broken beer bottle concealed in a bed of pine needles. It opened a bloody gash on the tender underside of my arch, shooting a lightning bolt of pain up my leg.

Limping, hopping and swearing, I covered the last few feet to the truck and climbed inside, punching the lock button. Smith came running out of the market yelling curses and waving his arms as I gunned his rig and hit the road. In the rearview mirror, I saw another car pull into the mini-mart. *Good.* Jaya would not be there alone with Mr. Smith. I hoped it was her husband.

Blood from my foot pooled on the floor of the pickup,

making me wonder if I would bleed out before I reached my destination. Smith's dashboard clock read ten fifty. After another five minutes, I passed a road sign that told me I was sixty miles from Timbergate. I would have to drive the remaining distance at sixty to make it to the meeting. Impossible on mountain roads.

Smith's cellphone lay in the passenger seat, tempting me to try to make a call or shoot off a text to someone, but the twisting road and the unfamiliar vehicle demanded all my attention. When I finally came to a straight stretch, I broke one of my most sacred driving rules. I picked up Smith's cell and dialed Jared Quinn at TMC. Varsha Singh answered, saying Quinn was in meetings and out of the office until two o'clock.

"Varsha, please listen carefully. This is Aimee Machado. You might know already that I was abducted. I got away, and I'm heading back to Timbergate. Tell Quinn it is imperative that today's Ethics Committee meeting not be canceled. I might be a little late, but I *will* be there."

"Aimee? Where on earth are you?"

"I'll explain later." I swerved to avoid a doe and two fawns bounding across the road. "Please, just do what I asked. And tell Quinn not to tell anyone at that meeting what I've told you."

"Not even the committee members?"

"Especially not the members. But please tell Mary Barton and Cleo Cominoli. Either of them can work the meeting in my place until I get there."

"I'll get hold of Quinn right away," Varsha said. "Be safe."

Chapter 45

------◆------

THE BLOOD TRICKLING FROM the gash eventually slowed and finally stopped, but the puddle on the floor and the slime smeared on the gas pedal made driving complicated. My bare, painfully injured foot slid off the pedal repeatedly. The coppery scent blended with all the other foul odors seeping into my clothes, hair and skin.

I checked my rearview mirrors constantly the rest of the way back to Timbergate, but no one pursued me during the remaining miles. Mr. Smith knew I had his vehicle, which meant I had his fingerprints. No way he could ask the law for help. He might have decided to skip out while the getting was good.

The clock on Smith's dashboard clicked over to ten minutes past noon as I pulled into the TMC parking lot. I spotted an empty space close to the entrance in a row designated for doctor's parking only. I pulled in. Not my rig, and I didn't have time to dilly around in the hospital's parking garage across the street. Let Smith take heat for the ticket, if he hadn't already bolted for parts unknown.

It occurred to me that my appearance would be a startling

sight: a reeking prison guard's uniform, a bare and bloody foot, and wild, disheveled hair. Rather than enter the main lobby, I slipped around to an employee's entrance and made my way to the conference room using stairwells rather than elevators.

I opened the door slowly, praying that Quinn had heeded my request. The room was full, and Dr. Moura Decker had the floor. Her back was to me as she spoke.

"… furthermore, I see no reason to continue this meeting. I'm sorry for Mrs. MacAllister's loss, as we all are, but this idea that his death be investigated for foul play seems—"

"Hold that thought, Dr. Decker, we have a late arrival." Quinn came to the door where I stood. "Come in, Aimee." He coughed, took a handkerchief from his pocket and held it to his nose as he whispered, "Mother of God, you look like hell and you smell revolting. Try to make this quick." Then he walked back to his place next to Detective Kass at the far end of the conference table.

Decker turned, spotted me and the blood drained from her face. "How?" She looked around the room, dropped into her chair, and refused to say another word.

Dr. Poole spoke from the head of the table. "I will now call on Aimee Machado to take the floor.

I scanned the room and saw not only Poole, Quinn, and the committee members, but Cleo, Mary Barton, and all of the other people we had persuaded to attend.

I explained my appearance by telling how I had been abducted and held captive by Dr. Decker and how I escaped. I then asked each of the others involved in the quest for the truth about Dr. Mac's death to speak. Veronica MacAllister told about Dr. Mac's shoes. How he wore different sizes on each foot, explaining why she suspected his fall had been staged.

Kenzie Eyler told of her suspicions about a cancer cluster at CHR's Potterville Prison medical clinic based on the high number of kidney and liver cancer diagnoses followed by surgeries. Mary Barton and I testified that there was no record or evidence of a cluster, and that the post-surgery medications being dispensed to those patients were a placebo and not oral chemotherapy pills as Kenzie had been told.

Ramon told of his hit-and-run incident on the highway from Potterville to Timbergate. He recounted how he and Buzz Bateson compared their descriptions of the vehicle that was involved in each incident. The descriptions matched, and paint samples from Ramon's car and Buzz Bateson's wristwatch had been turned over to authorities for forensic analysis and found to match. I stressed that Mr. Smith's vehicle, currently in danger of being towed from the doctor's parking area, might be involved and should be impounded immediately. Detective Kass pulled out his phone and thumbed a text.

Next, I told my story of Dr. Decker's plan to harvest my organs for her black-market buyers, and then bury my body in the makeshift graveyard on the warehouse grounds in Potterville. I relayed what Dr. Decker had told me about her "elegant solution" to the need for more organ donors.

Balancing on my good foot and leaning against the edge of the table for support, I described the holding cell and the operating suite hidden in the warehouse and went on to relate the story of how Helena Torres had been rescued before she could give birth in that warehouse and have her newborn taken away and sold. When I reached that point in my story, Jared Quinn got up, opened the conference room door and escorted Helena Torres into the room with her newborn daughter, who was swaddled in a pink receiving blanket and sleeping in her arms.

Helena spoke softly, her eyes moist with tears. *"Gracias por mi hermosa niña."* Thank you for my beautiful daughter. Ramon interpreted as she told the committee what Magdalena Paz had seen in the warehouse and recounted to her. That her own child had been born alive but documented as a stillbirth. Dr. Poole added that she and Laurie Littletree both recognized the signatures on the Paz baby's death certificate and on Buzz Bateson's transfer as belonging to Dr. Decker.

By that time, the group was noticeably edgy. Some were

coughing, others were dabbing their noses with tissues or handkerchiefs. Dr. Poole tapped her gavel and entertained a motion to recommend Dr. Mac's death be investigated and his remains be turned over to the county coroner for a forensic autopsy. The motion passed unanimously, except for Dr. Decker, who was not allowed to cast a vote. The committee's action was obviously a formality, since Detective Kass was already on top of the situation.

Dr. Iversen and Dr. Seldon had remained silent throughout the proceedings, seeming stunned and in disbelief. Kass informed both that they would be interviewed by city police, the sheriff's department and the FBI with regard to Dr. MacAllister's death and the organ harvesting and baby-selling scheme involving CHR's medical clinic at Potterville Prison. He then escorted Dr. Decker from the room under arrest and in handcuffs. The meeting was adjourned, and the room began to empty.

Quinn came to me, with his handkerchief again held to his nose. "Have you had a chance to contact Nick Alexander yet?"

"No, I was hoping you or Cleo might have let him know I'm okay."

"We did, but 'okay' is a stretch, Aimee. You look like a zombie and smell like a Dumpster. You'll want toget that foot patched up and hit the shower before Nick catches up with you."

The doctor who drew the short straw in the Emergency Department went to work on my foot with anesthetizing, cleaning, and stitching. He wore a surgical mask the whole time, which I guessed was not about keeping his germs away from my wound, but about protecting his olfactory receptors from the stench that still clung to me. When he finished, with his mask still on, he gave me a sample batch of pain pills and a set of crutches, telling me to use them until I made a follow-up visit with my family doctor to have the stitches removed.

Cleo had told me to call her when I was finished in the ED. She agreed with Quinn that it might be best to get myself decontaminated before falling into Nick's arms. She had told him I was safe but urged him to wait and let her take me home. Her plan was to take me to her house for a shower and a change of clothes and then drive me home to Coyote Creek.

I hobbled out to the ED waiting room to ask a clerk to call Cleo, but before I reached the reception desk, Nick got up from a waiting room chair and came toward me smiling, arms outstretched.

"Aimee, thank God. I've been—" He halted two feet away, huffed a cough, took another step toward me and coughed again. "What the devil happened to you?"

"Nick, please don't come any closer. Wait for me at the apartment. Cleo will bring me home later after I've cleaned up."

Nick stopped, his face revealing conflicting emotions. He stood there contemplating me, his eyes narrowed. "Screw that." He took a deep breath and closed the gap between us. "I thought I'd lost you for good this time. You're coming home with me now."

"But I'm disgusting, I don't want you to—"

"Shhh," he took me in his arms. "If I can't take it, we'll swing through a car wash on the way home and I'll roll the windows down."

Chapter 46

TWO WEEKS LATER, JACK and Amah hosted a gathering that included all the people who had played a part in uncovering the crimes at CHR's Potterville Prison medical clinic. Even Detective Kass was there. Most of the story had already been covered by local and national media. Updates continued to emerge as the extent of the black-market scheme became known.

Drs. Seldon and Iversen had been cleared. Dr. Decker and Mr. Smith were indicted, along with their cohorts, some of whom were prison employees and others, including hackers and money-launderers who had facilitated the criminal transactions from the outside. I asked Kass if either of the two officials who had visited TMC from the CHR home office were involved. The timing of their visit had always seemed suspicious. I even wondered if they had been responsible for staging Dr. Mac's accident.

"One no and one likely," Kass said. "The FBI has Dr. Cloyd Coatney in custody. A forensic inspection of his computers turned up some suspicious activity, and some transactions involving cryptocurrency that don't pass the smell test." I remembered Coatney as the smaller of the two men. The one with the pencil moustache and the toupee.

"Cryptocurrency? Is that like Bitcoin?"

"That's right," Kass said. "There's also Ethereum and a few others. They're favored in criminal transactions because of the difficulty of tracing them."

"Harry spoke up at that point. "Any idea how long the organ thefts had been going on at the prison?"

"It's looking like the operation began about three years ago, not long after Criteria Health Resources bought out the former owners of the prison clinic."

"How were they able to get away with it for so long?"

Kass shook his head. "The lack of oversight up there was one reason. The inspections that were done were cursory, at best. Dr. Decker and her partners in crime started small, but the flood of detainees being funneled into private prisons and their affiliated detention centers all over the country in recent years made the temptation to expand their operation irresistible."

"According to what she told me, she wasn't doing it for money," I said. "She had the irrational notion that she was doing it to honor the memory of her younger sister."

"That may be true, but you can bet that Dr. Cloyd Coatney and everyone else involved was raking in more money than they'd ever have seen doing their day jobs."

"Has Dr. Decker indicated how she knew Dr. MacAllister suspected the organ thefts?" Mary Barton asked.

"No," Kass said. "She's already lawyered up and clammed up, but Mr. Smith, the clinic's nursing director, is singing for his supper. He confirmed Decker was the brains behind the whole scheme, saying she purposely made a point of keeping her distance from the prison clinic. She slipped up when she signed the fake death certificate for Magdalena Paz's baby. Figured no one would ever notice, but that might have caught Dr. MacAllister's attention. When Smith told Decker that

MacAllister had been asking some pointed questions, Decker said not to worry. She'd take care of it."

"The staged accident in the stairwell?" Nick asked.

"No doubt about it. A forensic autopsy proved it. Also confirmed the sepsis was an unfortunate complication of his injuries. By the way, it turns out the hospital was not at fault for the burned out light. According to Smith, Decker's homicidal thugs had substituted a bad bulb for one that was working."

I looked over at Veronica MacAllister. She had her arms around her little boys and her head down. *Time to change the subject.*

"What about Helena's husband?" I asked. "Is he still in solitary at the prison?"

"No, he's back in regular housing, and there's an ongoing investigation of that entire operation."

"That's good news, right?"

"Let's hope so," Kass said.

Amah asked another question that had been on everyone's mind.

"Detective Kass, what about Magdalena Paz? Is there any chance her infant can be found and returned to her?"

Kass smiled. "There is good news there. Coatney has already provided the information that will bring that child back, along with any others who were taken. He's been cooperating with the FBI in hopes of reducing his sentence, but until it's clear how those cadavers ended up buried on the warehouse grounds, no deals are on the table."

I glanced at Nick. He smiled and patted Ginger's head. The day after Decker's arrest, Sheriff Preston had invited Nick to return to that warehouse parcel in Potterville, giving Ginger another chance to demonstrate her new cadaver skills. She got to it right away, and a crude gravesite containing a dozen bodies was unearthed.

Autopsies revealed all had been robbed of vital organs: they were missing their livers, both lungs, both kidneys, and from some, even the hearts had been taken. If things had worked out differently, Nick's dog might have eventually led him to my plundered body, buried in that same tragic patch of ground.

Veronica MacAllister wore black and was obviously still in mourning, but she seemed in better spirits since her husband's death had been explained and the people responsible were in custody. Uncle Gabe's protective measures toward her and her sons had been vital to making her feel safe while they were in hiding. He sat near her, and the two of them seemed to have formed a bond, judging from the relaxed way they related to each other.

After Kass answered our questions as best he could, we all trouped outdoors into the sunlight of a mild end-of-October afternoon. Jack had prepared apple slices for Dr. Mac's sons to feed to the llamas. That experience sent Tom and Jerry into excited giggles as the llamas' soft upper lips tickled the boys' tiny fingers. Veronica MacAllister broke into a laugh at the sight. When she turned to me and whispered, "Thank you," she brought tears to my eyes.

A moment later, Amah called to me from the family room slider. Leaving the others, I went inside to see if she needed help with something.

"What is it?"

"It's the phone," she said. "James O'Brien. Calling from Ashland."

Puzzled, I took the receiver from her.

"Hello, James."

"Aimee? Thank God. I've been going out of my mind up here. Your grandmother didn't want me to say anything to worry Tony and Tanya, but keeping your disappearance from them for even one night was the hardest thing I've ever had to do."

"James, I'm sorry. How did you even know about it?"

"Your Amah called me." He cleared his throat. "In case things turned out badly. She wanted me to be here for your grandfather and his wife."

"Oh, of course. So much was happening so fast, I hadn't

thought about how it would be worrying the family." Amah had told me how difficult it was to hold off calling my parents in the Azores, even for one night, but she was relieved that she had waited.

"Tony and Tanya are fine, by the way. They missed out on the long hours of worry, but I didn't. Your grandmother called me right away to let me know you'd been found, but she asked me to wait until you'd had time to recoup before talking to you."

I looked out the slider and saw Nick walking toward the house. "James, I'm fine, and there's no reason to worry Grandpa Machado and Tanya, or even to tell them about it after the fact."

"Of course." He hesitated. "Aimee, I'm calling now because I'll be returning to New York in a few days. I'll be taking a flight out of Timbergate, but first, I'm dropping by to see my father and sister in Coyote Creek. Is there a chance we might have coffee while I'm in your neighborhood?"

"I don't think so, James, but thank you for being there for my family. For shielding Grandpa and Tanya. I'm sure it wasn't easy for you."

"We go back a long way, Aimee. I feel like they're my family, too."

Nick reached out to open the slider.

"Goodbye, James. Give my best to your dad and Keely."

"I will. Goodbye, Aimee. Please stay safe."

"I'll do my best." We ended the call.

I saw concern in Nick's eyes. "Everything all right?" he asked.

I put my arms around his waist and leaned into his warmth. "Everything's fine."

AFTER ALL THE COMPANY had gone, Jack and Amah asked Nick and me to stay a bit longer.

"We need to talk, but we wanted to wait until the others left," Amah said. "Come, sit."

Uh, oh. I glanced at Nick. His eyebrows lifted. We gathered around the family room table.

Jack took the lead. "I realize a lot has happened the past few days, but it's only been a week since we mentioned we might be making a move."

"To Faial?" I said. "The Azores?"

That's right." Amah nodded. "We've been giving it a lot of thought."

"What about Jack's work," I asked. "What's he going to write about if he's living on a volcanic island in the middle of the Atlantic Ocean?"

Jack laughed. "In forty-plus years, I've said about all there is to say about hunting deer and turkeys. I'm ready to write up some new adventures, and from what your daddy tells me, there's a lot of fishing and sailing to be done around those islands."

"But what about the llamas?"

Jack and Amah exchanged glances. "That would be up to the two of you," Jack said.

"Oh, I hadn't thought … you want us to take over the herd?"

"Let's say *watch over*," Amah said. "And only until we make a permanent decision."

"I think I understand. We're the only ones you trust to take care of the llamas, aren't we? Without our help, you'd have to either sell the herd or give up on making a second home in the Azores."

"Aimee, honey, take it easy. You look like you're going into shock," Amah said. "At this point we're only exploring the possibilities. We aren't rushing into anything. We'll be living in Gabe's condo, acclimating to island life, and spending some quality time with your mom and dad." She went quiet for a moment. "I miss them, sweetheart. I miss my son."

Okay, deep breath, I thought. "How soon do you want to leave?"

"As soon as we can, but that depends on the two of you,"

Jack said. "Have you talked this over? Decided how you feel about moving out of the barn and into the house?"

I didn't know what to say. I had been so tied up in solving the mystery of Dr. Mac's death and the crimes at Potterville Prison that I had nearly forgotten about Jack and Amah's plans.

Nick found his voice first. "One condition," he said. "We'd rather not keep up the turkey flock, if that's okay with you. With our jobs, neither of us will have the time or the expertise."

Jack squinted at Nick. "If that's what it takes, we'll make other arrangements for the birds." He turned to me. "What about you, Aimee Rose? Any conditions you need met?"

"The snake," I said. Do we have to keep feeding live mice to the snake?"

Amah laughed. "Told you, Jack. That's the deal breaker."

"Snake's going to the natural history museum," Jack said. "It'll be billed as the oldest living king snake in captivity."

"Then that just leaves Fanny," I said. "The cat and I get along. Or are you planning to take her to the islands with you?"

"Nope," Jack said. "She'll be happier here."

"Then it looks like our conditions are met," Nick said. "Except that Aimee and I have had almost no time to talk this over with each other." He reached out for my hand. "What do you say we sort this out tonight and give them our answer tomorrow?"

"Agreed," I said.

Chapter 47

A FTER WALKING THE DARK lane back to our apartment over the barn, neither of us was eager to confront the topic that had been dropped in our laps.

Nick pulled a beer bottle from the fridge. "Want one?"

"Yes, please."

"Deck?"

"Sure."

We pulled on jackets and settled in deck chairs with Ginger planted near Nick's feet.

"You okay?" Nick asked.

"Kinda chilly." The night was clear, with a full moon taking center stage in a star-studded sky. I took a long sip of beer just as a pair of bats flew over our heads. "They must know tomorrow's Halloween," I said.

"Probably making a practice run." Ginger stirred, and Nick stroked her head. "We're avoiding the subject, Aimee. The folks are going to need our answer."

"I know, but they're asking us to take a big step."

"The llamas will require more of our time with the folks gone, but I think we can handle it."

"Taking care of the llamas isn't what bothers me. It's Amah and Jack's expectations about us. Their assumptions about our relationship."

"You think they're hoping we'll get all settled in at the main house and decide it's time to take the big leap?"

"Don't you?"

Nick laughed. "They've been trying to shove us down the aisle ever since we got back together. Remember how happy they were when I moved into the barn with you?"

"Yes, but it didn't result in a wedding. I think they're getting desperate. Geez, moving to the Azores. You don't think they have ulterior motives?"

"Hey, It's not all about us. I'm sure they'd like to see us take the plunge, but in the meantime, who else would they leave in charge of the ranch? They want to explore a new way of life with the option of coming back, dividing their time between two homes. They'll want the llamas to be here. My guess is if we say no, they won't go. How would you feel about that?"

"Like a heel."

"So, what do you say? Do we have our answer?"

"I think so, but there's still one condition."

"Give it," Nick said.

"You and I agree that moving into the main house is about Amah and Jack's future and not about ours. No pressure?"

"Understood."

I reached out my hand. "Shake on it."

He pulled me up from my chair. "I have a better idea."

Photo by Harvey Spector

SHARON ST. GEORGE IS the author of the hospital-based Aimee Machado Mystery series set in rural Timbergate, a fictional town in Far Northern California. She is a member of Mystery Writers of America and Sisters in Crime and is program director of Writers Forum, a nonprofit organization for writers in Northern California. Her past writing credits include advertising copy, newspaper feature stories, three produced plays, and a book on NASA's Space Food Project. She holds degrees in English and Theatre Arts and enjoys acting and directing in local theatre productions in her Northern California hometown when her writing schedule permits.

Learn more at SharonStGeorge.com

www.ingramcontent.com/pod-product-compliance
Lightning Source LLC
Chambersburg PA
CBHW010440100726
47904CB00008B/2416